"*NORTH SAR*'S A GREAT READ. It really gave me the feeling of living on and flying from a carrier over Vietnam."

—Larry Bond, author of *Red Phoenix*

"A good war story—exciting, suspenseful and authentic . . . The reader is in the pilot's seat getting a 'having been there' insight into naval aviation and aerial combat."

—Colonel David H. Hackworth, USA (Ret.), author of *About Face: The Odyssey of an American Warrior*

". . . HEART-STOPPING . . . *NORTH SAR* CATCHES THE SPIRIT OF THE FRENETIC TEMPO OF OPERATIONS ON AN AIRCRAFT CARRIER. . . . *NORTH SAR* RINGS WITH AUTHENTICITY as Gerry Carroll drags the reader inside the cockpit of his machine to witness, from that unique perspective, all the horror, sadness, humor . . . excitement. . . . Suspense continues to build right up to the final page. . . . A fine story about helicopter pilots with the right stuff!"

—Rear Admiral Paul T. Gillcrist, USN (Ret.), author of *Feet Wet*

NORTH SAR

GERRY CARROLL

Introduction by
TOM CLANCY

POCKET STAR BOOKS

New York London Toronto Sydney Tokyo Singapore

A Pocket Star Book published by
POCKET BOOKS, a division of Simon & Schuster Inc.
1230 Avenue of the Americas, New York, NY 10020

Copyright © 1991 by Gerry Carroll

ISBN: 0-671-73183-1

First Pocket Books paperback printing November 1992

10 9 8 7 6 5 4 3 2 1

POCKET STAR BOOKS and colophon are registered trademarks of Simon & Schuster Inc.

Map designed by GDS/Jeffrey L. Ward

Printed in the U.S.A.

THIS BOOK IS FOR . . .

All those whose courage, constancy, and devotion have given the Wings of Gold their worth, especially:

My first hero, Aviation Ordnanceman 2c (CA) Merle L. Creel, USN.

My friend Lt. David M. Santille, USNR, Lost at Sea, December 1975.

And for my brother, Greg.

Acknowledgments

For an old retired naval aviator to complete a work such as this cannot be the result of individual effort. Just getting him to put down his coffee cup and quit talking about the days of the Old Navy is a major problem. The job took many people many days to accomplish but they appear to have succeeded.

My deepest thanks, first and foremost, to Paul McCarthy, senior editor at Pocket Books, without whom this novel would not exist; to my friend, Tom Clancy, for his encouragement; to Robert Gottlieb, Agent Extraordinaire, for his persistent faith.

To Capt. Roger P. Murray, USN, for teaching me what being a naval aviator really means; Capt. Russ Henry, Capt. Steve Kupka, Capt. Bill Walker, Capt. Virgil Jackson, Capt. Lew Dunton, Cmdr. Dave Finney, Lt. Cmdr. Tom Smith, Cmdr. Dave Kennedy, Lt. Cmdr. Brian Koenig, Lt. Cmdr. Beth Hubert, all of whom contributed time, energy, patience, and encouragement in teaching me how to make my landings equal to my takeoffs and how to make Santy and Boyle fly right.

Most especially to my family, whose support throughout twenty-one years of Navy flying never wavered. Not even once.

Introduction

Gerry and I go back almost thirty years—a daunting thought for two people who still think themselves young. We used to sit in the corner of 4-D at Loyola High School during Dick Prodey's English class and kibbitz. Gerry was my first critic, back when my literary efforts were confined to a student literary "magazine." Then in 1965 we parted company. I went to Loyola College in Baltimore. Gerry went to Boston College, and we didn't see each other again until 1985. Catching up took about five minutes and one beer. The twenty years didn't matter a bit. It's that sort of a friendship.

Gerry got his dream a lot sooner than I got mine. All he ever wanted to be was a naval aviator. He got those gold wings, and the remarkable thing about this big, tough—and rather loud—Irishman is that he is incomprehensibly modest about the things he did while he wore them. On being told by an Admiral who also happened to be Chief Test Pilot, U.S. Navy, that Gerry had been involved in "about the toughest helicopter rescue I ever saw," I yelled at him for not relating the story; Gerry observed, "Oh, yeah, I got the Navy

Com[mendation Medal] for that." End of story. He gets quite angry if you point out to him that he fits in his own rather thoughtful definition of "hero."

Like most professional warriors, Gerry's a romantic. People do not risk their lives often for things in which they do not believe. Warriors have their beliefs. To all of them, the world is a place whose primary battle is between order and chaos, good and evil, right and wrong, where conscience is both your best defense and your most ruthless driving force. But since they cultivate cynicism (at least on the surface), they proclaim that they are merely "doing my job" when they choose to undertake something dangerous. The giveaway, however, is that you can ask any of them what they are proudest of—in Gerry's case, it was getting a sick infant to the right hospital in Florida just in time. Or ask what frightens them the most— for Gerry it was being told there's a sick kid who needs a hot ride, because "sometimes you do dumb things when there's a kid involved." This from a guy who's been *shot down* three times, who has made a career of rescuing people under fire— and his "hobby" was making life miserable for submarine commanders who wanted to trifle with his carrier, a "hobby" at which he was one of the all-time champs. Along with a lot of others he freely chose a life which is statistically dangerous (he's helped to bury too many friends for his own good), both mentally and physically demanding, and not terribly remunerative, but when you ask people like this why they do foolish things, you get: "Hey, it's my job." Right. The truest mark of a warrior is that beneath the shell of adamantine steel hides a heart of pure mush—which embarrasses the hell out of them.

One thing Gerry and I share is a love of the written word. Dick Prodey was a superb English teacher, lo those many years ago, and his lessons took. Gerry and I both majored in literature. The best naval officer I know was an English major at a little place in Maine, and there's actually a study claiming that the best warriors are of an artistic bent—something I will leave to others for analysis. From the time we got together in April of 1985, I've been abusing my friend, demanding that he break down and write a book. I knew he had it in him. Well, he did. I figured it would be a pretty good book. I was right.

This novel concerns the Navy and the Vietnam War. Although our country has bad memories of that conflict, those memories result not from what our men did, but rather what was done to our men. Gerry and all the others did not choose to go there. They were sent. The Pentagon did not awake one morning and feel the need for the killing-rush. Three U.S. presidents got us in there, and then, having started a war, decided that the military did not know how to conduct it, and meddled a lot of young men into graves. And who got blamed for the way things turned out? That's right.

The warriors knew better, but the rules did not permit them to go public, and knowing that their country still needed them, knowing that they still had to follow their own self-imposed code of conduct, they kept faith with a country that deserted them. They watched a military structure collapse in public hatred, but they held it together, fixed what was broken, and never stopped doing their job because they knew the job was important even while most of us forgot. That is the measure of their romanticism—and their cynicism. They continued to wear their country's uniform, and served better than we had any right to expect until we rediscovered just what sort of people they are. It took us long enough.

As I write this, Americans are coming home from the Persian Gulf. Gerry wasn't there. After twenty years of service, he removed his wings and changed to a job that allows him to see his family on a more-or-less continuous basis. Part of him regretted that—there was a war and he felt the need to be there—but the kids he trained went there. People he'd rescued fought there. Like a generation of American warriors, in keeping the faith and passing on the experience, he helped prepare the next class of fighters in the hope that the next time the rules might be different—and they were. That's what keeping the faith means, I guess. It also invalidated his cynicism, but like all warriors he secretly hoped for that.

—TOM CLANCY

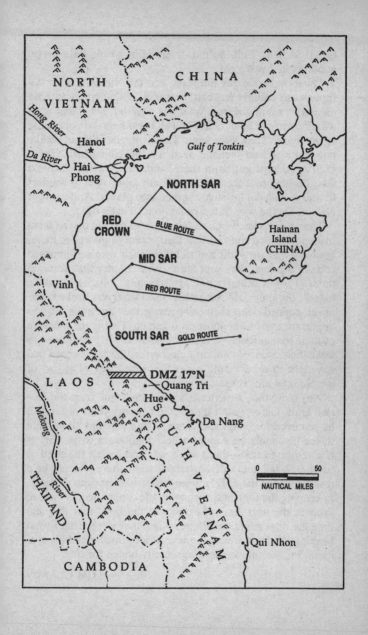

Transsderm-Nitro®

nitroglycerin

0.1 mg/hr; 0.2 mg/hr; 0.4 mg/hr; 0.6 mg/hr

Carbohydrate:
addicts Diet

629-12780-A

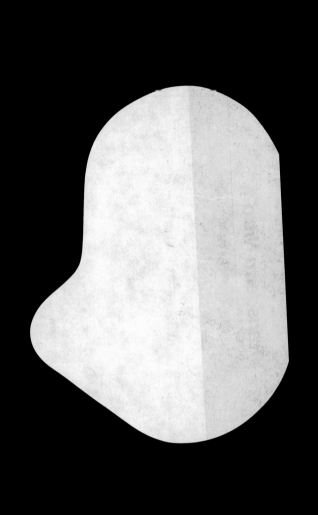

PART ONE

"One man in a thousand, Solomon says,
Will stick closer than a brother."

—Kipling

Chapter 1

July 11, 1972

Once the brake had been released, the rotor blades began spinning, slowly at first but accelerating rapidly and evenly until they reached the proper speed. As they did the entire helicopter rocked on its wheels with the centrifugal force, causing all five blades to fly at first slightly differently and finally all together in the same plane. Once the instruments on the panel in front of him showed that all was well, Lt. (J.G.) Tim Boyle, USNR, allowed himself to relax a little. He always paid a lot of attention to the rotor-engagement part of the checklist procedure.

Few of the many things that could happen during the preparation for flight could kill you or somebody else nearby but one of those few was the engagement, especially when it was performed on the small flight deck placed almost as an afterthought on the back of a U.S. Navy cruiser. The winds swirled around as the ship steamed through the water and the resulting turbulence on the flight deck sometimes tried to make the blades try to fly in attitudes and directions other than the ones intended by the designers. If the mechanical dampeners and restrainers built into the rotor system failed to do their jobs, the heavy blades could strike anything within their arc or even each other. The resulting mess of flying chunks and pieces caused by such collisions could go anywhere and through virtually anything. Boyle had never seen that happen but the rocking motion and the downward flexing of the blades toward the steel deck of the ship always kept his undivided attention.

Boyle, although he was the copilot of the crew, was strapped into the pilot's, or right-hand, seat of the large Navy HH-3A Sea King Combat Search and Rescue helicopter on the fantail of the USS *Galveston,* an old World War II–vintage cruiser which was called to serve in one more war before she was to be retired. In the left seat sat Lt. Bob Watkins, the HAC, or Helicopter Aircraft Commander. It was a rule in his crew that the pilots traded seats each mission. Watkins had all the experience he needed and believed that the younger guys ought to be taught as much as possible before they were given a crew of their own. Except for the wheel brakes on the right side and the fact that the guy in the right seat made most of the landings, there was little real difference in the two pilot positions. There was a subtler purpose there: the guy in the right seat always *felt* in charge even if he were not. That feeling went into the experience store, too.

Soon, the rest of the checklist was completed and the aircraft and crew were set to go flying. Watkins flipped the side position lights to "steady-bright" and gave the thumbs-up to the helmeted sailor standing on the ship's deck well clear of the rotor arc. He in turn signaled to two other sailors, who rushed doubled over toward the helicopter and removed the two wheel chocks and four tie-down chains which kept the helo from sliding around the deck with the movements of the ship.

When they had run past him carrying their clumsy burdens, the sailor took one last look to make sure everything was clear and, after rotating his hand over his head a couple of times, pointed up and out in the signal to launch aircraft. Having completed his part in all this, the young sailor dashed around

4

the corner of the after superstructure, getting behind some protective steel in case the pilot blew the takeoff and tried to fly through part of the ship.

Watkins hit the last three items on the last checklist and placed his right hand up on the throttles, telling Boyle over the intercom system that all was set.

Boyle drew a breath and smoothly lifted the aircraft into a hover over the deck, making one last check to see that everything was doing what it was supposed to and that there were no red lights or funny noises among all the normal clatter and vibrations. Since all was in order and he could think of no reason why not, Boyle dipped the nose and increased power, forcing the aircraft to move left, away from the deck, and into forward flight. He eased into a left climbing turn to 1,500 feet and steadied out on course for their holding position off the coast of North Vietnam.

Boyle keyed the radio switch on the stick with his index finger and checked the helicopter in with the E-2 radar control plane orbiting high over the Gulf.

"Keyboard, this is Angel 802. We are airborne and heading to station."

The reply came quickly telling Boyle that both his radio and the automatic radar identification transponder, or "Parrott" were operating normally.

"Roger, 802, Keyboard 600 has you loud and clear. Your Parrott is sweet all modes. You are cleared to proceed to station."

Boyle wiggled a little in his seat and headed the helo on the long trip to its station.

Once he felt the downwash from the helo diminish, the young sailor raised his head and watched the huge green aircraft fly away. He was proud of his job on the flight deck because it let him have a little extra responsibility and prestige among his peers and because it let him be around aircraft. He had decided that someday he, too, would be a Navy pilot. But he wouldn't fly helicopters. The goddamned things were too dangerous. None of them looked like they were supposed to actually fly and no amount of explaining by the crewmen was ever going to convince him that riding around in them was survivable in the long term.

Boyle and Watkins belonged to a very special Navy helicopter squadron called Helicopter Combat Support Squadron 17, or HC-17 for short. Early in the war the Navy and the Air Force had realized that there really was no effective way to get downed airmen out of either North Vietnam itself or the enemy-controlled areas of South Vietnam. The lesson cost the lives of many well-intentioned but ill-trained and ill-equipped helicopter crews. HC-17 was established in early 1966, with uniquely modified versions of standard fleet helicopters, given intensive training in Combat Search and Rescue (Combat SAR) tactics and operations, and sent over to the Gulf of Tonkin, to "Yankee Station." Their presence had improved the recovery rate for downed aircrewmen and the survival rate for the rescue crews. But the thickening and ever more sophisticated Russian antiaircraft systems used by the North Vietnamese meant that whatever advantage had been gained by the specialization of the helicopter crews was reduced drastically by the increased defensive capability of the North. The work was as extremely dangerous as ever but at least everyone had a better chance of survival than they had several years before.

Yankee Station was not really a place. It was actually three large areas of the Gulf off the coast of North Vietnam, called "routes," in which steamed one carrier and her escorts. At least two of these routes were usually occupied; which ones depended upon which areas of North Vietnam were being targeted at the time. The routes were named "Blue" (northern), "Red" (central), and "Gold" (southern). Each route contained a single-helo SAR station, North, Mid, and South, to cover missions into the corresponding areas of the North.

The carrier USS *Concord,* presently occupied the northern area, called the Blue Route, and was the flagship of the commander of Task Force 77, in charge of all the American naval ships in the Gulf of Tonkin. The other carrier, the *Independence,* was assigned to the central, or "Red" route. At the northernmost point in the Blue Route, just about seventy-five miles east of Hanoi and its port city, Haiphong, was the vastly smaller area in which the *Galveston* steamed. That area, or station, was called North SAR.

When a large mission against the Hanoi-Haiphong area of North Vietnam was scheduled from one of the aircraft carriers positioned out in the Gulf of Tonkin, a helicopter from the North SAR ship, presently the *Galveston,* would take up a holding point in a position close in to the coast of North Vietnam to be ready to go in and retrieve any airman who had a chance of rescue. This aircraft and crew were detached from a larger unit aboard the carrier *Concord* which was the mother unit to all the SAR detachments in the Gulf.

There was no need to hurry in getting to the holding point, so Watkins and Boyle kept it at about ninety knots, each lost in his own thoughts, communicating only what was necessary for the actual flying of the aircraft. The two pilots had been crewed together for nearly four months and had exhausted all the idle chatter about things back home and things over here. It would be at least another ten minutes before the jets which would be flying today's strike launched from the *Concord* and another twenty or so after that for the strike aircraft to form up and get in over the target and the shooting to start. So it would be a while before they could possibly be called into action.

Watkins always got the helicopter airborne earlier than was actually required. He felt that the pilots in the attacking jets should never be left uncovered as far as rescue was concerned and the early launch was designed to make sure that the helo was mission capable. If something were to go wrong with it, a replacement could be launched from the main detachment back aboard the carrier in time to cover the strike. Watkins's crew had been late only once, because of a balky starter, and even though no one had been jeopardized by his absence, Watkins never wanted to have to spend another hour worrying and sweating it out like he had that day.

Back aboard the carrier, simply because of the sheer complexity of flight operations involving up to forty aircraft, Watkins would have been restricted to the launch-and-recovery cycles dictated by the fixed-wing-aircraft schedule because the carrier could not alter its plan for just one helicopter. Aboard the cruiser, Watkins was the senior aviation officer and could make up the plan as he saw fit with little interference from an extremely tall pyramid of command such as that in place on the carrier. When the opportunity arose for him to take over the single-helicopter detachment aboard *Galveston,* he had jumped at it.

The other thing he liked about being in the forward-deployed detachment aboard *Galveston* was that it was closest to the heaviest defenses of the North, so he was at the point of the spear. Most other men would gladly see the war from the rear, participating in the overall effort and being (usually) justifiably proud of their contributions. Some, by far a smaller percentage, were doing the actual fighting and would more than gladly see one of the rear-echelon pogues come up and trade positions. A very few, like Watkins, were the true warriors. These men, like most, would rather not have a war at all but as long as there was one they would participate to the fullest extent of their talents. These men are the true heroes, those who day after day do their jobs quietly, professionally, and effectively with a minimum of complaint, all the while knowing the dangers and accepting them.

It is one thing to act in the passion of the moment especially when everyone is watching and applauding from the sidelines. Unless you are completely craven, you will swallow your fear and get on with it. It is quite a different thing in combat to do your job day after day, knowing that it is never finished, that tomorrow you will have to go out and do it again with the same risk and the same gnawing fear.

Watkins knew this well: this was his third tour as a rescue pilot in the war in Vietnam. He was not a war lover by any means but he knew that he flew these missions far better than most. He simply felt that he would be letting his side down if he took an easier way out. He was also sure that later in his life it would begin to eat deeply into his spirit if he ducked what he believed was his duty.

One of the chief reasons Watkins had quietly arranged to get Tim Boyle as his copilot was that he saw much of himself in the young man.

As soon as he felt the acceleration of the *Concord*'s catapult stroke end, Lt. (J.G.) Mike Santy raised his landing gear and waited for the speed to increase enough to raise the flaps. Once that was accomplished, he followed the standard departure route to climb up and join the rest of the bomb-laden aircraft in the strike. Santy was in an A-7 Corsair attack bomber, Condor 307, and now, in the third month of his first deployment to the Vietnam war, was finding it to be generally far less glamorous than it had seemed back in Pensacola or San Diego.

All the bombs slung under his wings made the Corsair handle like his mother's station wagon as opposed to his shiny new Corvette. He hoped that Tim Boyle's girlfriend, Meghan Collins, was taking care of it as she had promised. He smiled under his oxygen mask at the thought of his best friend falling for a woman who was so unshakably antiwar. Of course, her falling for a Navy pilot was a mite odd also. He was momentarily angry at himself for thinking extraneous thoughts. Don't get complacent, Sandman, that'll bite you in the ass, he told himself.

He soon spotted the other twenty-odd aircraft grouped in five divisions and slid easily into the number-four and last position in the division led by his squadron commanding officer, Cmdr. Jack Wilson. It would not be long before he was given the opportunity to lead somebody else and quit being Tail-end Charlie. Any day now, he thought.

Very shortly, the rest of the strike aircraft were assembled and the leader, Cmdr. Frank Greenwood, the Air Wing Commander, or CAG (Commander, Air Group) as this position had been called in the flying Navy nearly forever, turned the strike inbound toward the coast of North Vietnam eighty miles away, giving the signal for everyone to switch to the mission frequency.

Santy reached down and changed to the frequency by feel. He took his eyes off his leader momentarily to make sure that he had selected the right one. Now that he was headed west toward the target and getting nearer the coast and the anti-aircraft weapons, Santy began to feel the familiar dryness in the throat and the cold lump in the belly that always accompanied flight into combat. He knew well that all the others in the formation felt the same way even though it was never really discussed. But from the precision with which everyone flew, you couldn't tell that they were going anywhere special. Santy stole a glance to his front right and saw two other A-7s from his squadron, Matson in Condor 301 and Rizzo in Condor 306, which were assigned to go after the surface-to-air missiles, or SAMs, emplaced all around the target. He was momentarily glad he wasn't one of them.

Few things in aviation are as boring as is flying around on an airborne rescue station: you just have to stay close to a geographical point on the planet and wait for somebody to get in trouble. If that station also happens to be in a place like the Gulf of Tonkin, it can also be incredibly hot in the cockpit, especially if the front end of the aircraft is mostly glass, like a large greenhouse. The Nomex flight suit you have to wear to protect you from fire in the event you screw up and crash seems to be designed to itch only in places that can't be gotten at with normally jointed arms. Flights usually last about four hours unless "they" decide to bring you back to the ship for a fast refueling, which means that you get to sweat and scratch for four more hours. This is something that the recruiters fail to mention among the handshakes and promises.

Boyle sat in the worn seat wiggling his butt and body, trying to get less uncomfortable. He was fervently wishing that the "alpha strike" from the carrier would hurry the hell up and do their thing so he could get back to his ship and out of the goddamn seat.

"Their thing" today happened to be dropping lots of bombs on a petroleum-oil-lubricant (POL) depot twenty-five miles inland. Over one of the helo's two UHF aircraft radios, one of which was always tuned to the strike frequency, Boyle and Watkins were now waiting for the leader, Greenwood, in an A-6 Intruder, call sign Utah 1, to switch to the frequency and check in.

There were twenty-one aircraft in this strike: eleven A-7 Corsairs, six A-6 Intruders, and four F-4 Phantoms along as fighter escort. As alpha strikes went, this one was sort of half-alpha. Ever since Washington had resumed the bombing of the North after the latest three-week halt, the two Carrier Air Wings on Yankee Station here in the northern Gulf had been flying two strikes a day, sometimes three, over the North. Because the Vietnamese had been given time to re-supply and redeploy their SAM sites and other antiaircraft systems without harassment from air attack and because of the heightened pace of U.S. operations, this meant that air-craft attrition had increased markedly. *Attrition* was the cur-rent buzzword for aircraft that were lost to enemy defenses or in operational accidents. For the pilots of the aircraft lost over the North, attrition normally meant injury, death, or tortured imprisonment as a POW. If they were among the very fortunate few for whom absolutely everything broke their way when they were shot down, there was a chance of rescue.

For the Combat Rescue crews, like Boyle and Watkins and the two crewmen in the back, there were going to be more customers. The waiting for the shooting to start and the knowledge that they could soon be called upon to go get some aviator forced to eject overland was wearing beyond words. They fervently hoped that any damaged jet would hold to-gether long enough to get out over the water. If not, they would have to go into North Vietnam and get him.

Boyle and Watkins had been airborne for only forty-five minutes. It seemed like forty hours. As the time got closer for the strike to go in, the adrenaline began to build within the crew. Now they were as ready for this mentally as they could be; but nothing, in Boyle's mind, was as bad as the waiting.

The waiting made every little thing become twice as aggravating. No matter how much time had seemed to pass since the last time they looked at the clock on the instrument panel, it was always about two minutes in real time. The eyes always stung from the sweat that came down from the helmet in only one place no matter what was done to adjust things. In addition to the incessant itches, your ass started hurting within milliseconds of your first thought that it hadn't begun to yet. The cigarettes Boyle was smoking one after another tasted like stale goose crap.

But when Greenwood's voice finally broke the silence on the radios, all the discomforts suddenly went away.

"Echo Three Delta Control, Utah has all aboard. Heading in."

"Delta Control, Roger that, Utah. Good luck," the faceless voice back in the *Concord*'s Combat Information Center, or CIC, answered crisply.

On the other radio, Boyle heard Greenwood check his strike in with "Red Crown," the Navy's air control ship stationed off the coast which was tasked with keeping track of the entire picture of the air war over the North. Watkins, now taking his turn flying, eased the helicopter, Angel 802, into a smooth descending turn until they were headed west at 300 feet.

Boyle twisted around in his seat to look into the large passenger and cargo compartment behind the pilots. "All set in the back?" he asked the two enlisted crewmen in the rear.

"Yessir. We're ready. All secure," the first crewman, Petty Officer Denny Strand, replied, giving Boyle a grin and a thumbs-up.

Boyle automatically returned the gesture and turned to face front again. As his eyes roamed over the instrument panel and the lower console between the pilots' seats, he rechecked that his Browning 9mm pistol was loaded and securely hanging between his thighs, covering his crotch. Among the seeming thousands of things he had learned from Bob Watkins was

that the Navy-issue .38 caliber revolver was only good for
shooting yourself in the leg. On Watkins's advice, he'd bought
the Browning and a holster and belt for it before he left the
States. Its reassuring encumbrance always made him feel a
bit of a swashbuckler, a bit more confident. Maybe that was
what Watkins had had in mind.

He looked across the cockpit, saw Watkins checking his
pistol the same way, and stifled a smile. "Looks like we're
set, Bob. Everything's okay up here, too."

But I wonder if Mike's flying on this one, he thought. Mike
Santy was his best friend and had been ever since they had
met in Pensacola. The thought of something happening to
Santy bothered Boyle constantly on a level that was deep in
his spirit. Consciously, he knew that Mike could take care of
himself very well but when the shooting was about to start
Boyle always had a moment of fear for his friend. Knowing
Mike and being around him had given Boyle a different view
of the world and his place in it and had helped him eliminate
many of the doubts he had had about himself all through his
young life. Boyle forced himself to put these thoughts firmly
away for another time when they wouldn't be a distraction.

High above and now far ahead of the helicopter, the aircraft
of the strike spread out on Greenwood's signal. The plan was
to divide into two groups which would approach the target
from different directions, thus making it harder for the NVA
gunners to get a decent shot at the bombers. Santy, as the
number four in his division, moved out about seven hundred
feet behind and slightly above the number three. This was
the part he hated most, getting to the target. Once there, you
got real busy and forced your feelings down. You followed
the rules and tactics forged the hard way by those who came
before you and did your best. You dove on the target, concentrating solely on accuracy. Then, when your bombs were
gone, you used every ounce of skill you had to get your jet
and yourself the hell out of there. You climbed or dove,
yanked and banked, twisted and jinked, all the while keeping
your mind ahead of the situation. You had long ago been

taught by those far more experienced than you that if you merely kept pace with the situation and with what your aircraft was doing, it was only a matter of time, like maybe seconds, before you were dead. Another name in the book they keep in the Chapel at Pensacola and a picture on a mantel in somebody's living room.

The hell of it is, thought Santy, there is nothing on earth I'd rather be than a Navy attack pilot.

Santy watched as the four "Iron Hand" A-7s carrying Shrike antiradiation missiles in addition to some normal bombs accelerated down and ahead of the group. Their job was to get to the target area twenty to thirty seconds ahead of the main force and take out their assigned "high-threat" SAM sites in the immediate area of the target. In their seven-hundred-foot "combat spread," the Iron Hands quickly grew smaller and smaller. Santy didn't envy them except that their job would be over before his was.

The Iron Hand mission was arguably the most dangerous assignment for the aircraft flying this strike. They were chumming for SAMs. When the threat receivers sensed a SAM radar, they gave off a warbling tone in the pilot's helmet and gave him a general direction on a screen in the cockpit. All the pilot then had to do was turn to the threat and fire the missile which would home in on the radar emitter and blow it up. This would not always destroy all the SAM launchers that depended upon the radar but it would effectively wipe out the missileers' ability to accurately *guide* their missiles. Since there were often more radars around the target and along the route to it than there were Shrikes loaded on the aircraft, you did what you could, hauled ass out of there, and hoped you'd done it right.

Unfortunately, while you were trying to kill the radars, gunners at the Antiaircraft Artillery, or "Triple-A," sites in the area were trying to kill you. So was everyone else on the ground who could see you and who was armed. There were even stories of jets hit with arrows on low-level attack missions.

Lt. (J.G.) "Rat" Rizzo, flying Condor 306 from Santy's squadron, VA-19, was the Iron Hand wingman on this mission. Although this was his first deployment to the war, he was showing great promise as an attack pilot. He had received the specialized training back at NAS Lemoore, in California, to fly the Shrike mission. On his twenty-six previous Iron Hand missions, he had done very well and had earned enough of the skipper's confidence to be assigned as wingman to the less senior leaders. Now, on his twenty-seventh trip into North Vietnam, he was supremely confident not only in his own abilities but also in the inability of the North Vietnamese to do anything about his presence over their country.

The main difference between Rizzo and Santy was that, although they possessed nearly identical levels of experience and knew their jobs very well indeed, Santy was aware that he still had much to learn.

Listening to the early part of the action over the radio, both helo pilots could usually tell how the strike was going by the number and pace of "look out" calls the jet guys were making. The fewer there were, the better the chances that rescue services would not be needed. That wasn't necessarily true but it made the rescue pilots feel a little better.

Today, it sounded bad. Almost as soon as the strike crossed the coast, people started calling out SAM launches, apparently from far too many sites for the Iron Hands to deal with completely. Boyle and Watkins could pick out the warnings and Shrike launch calls from Rizzo and the other three Iron Hands. It was apparently getting real dangerous in there.

On top of all this chatter about SAMs, were the normal calls dealing with the Triple-A, or antiaircraft, fire from some of the millions of 37-, 57-, 85-, and 100-mm guns the North Vietnamese seemed to have parked anywhere they could find an open square yard of land. "A chicken in every pot and a flak gun in every garage," went the Communist campaign slogan, according to Watkins.

Boyle could not tell from the voices whether or not Santy

was involved. The oxygen system in modern jet aircraft provides oxygen at a constant rate of flow so that the effect is like breathing in a steady breeze funneled into your mouth and nose. The breeze goes in every time you open your mouth so that your voice when you speak into the mike located inside the mask sounds like your normal voice only in pitch. There is sort of a brassy, sharp flatness to your transmissions when heard through another radio. Unless the listener has heard your voice over the radio constantly for a while, he cannot readily pick you out from the others, though that ability will come in time. As close as they had been, Boyle still couldn't identify Mike's voice among the others. Adding this additional bit of uncertainty was only making Boyle feel worse.

"Sounds like they really hit it today," observed Watkins. "I guess we might as well do the checklists again, huh?"

Boyle pulled out his blue plastic book and began reading the items. As he did, each crew member responsible reported the step complete. When he was finished, Boyle reported, "All set. Checklist complete. Switches set. Power's up. Lock your harness, Bob." He reached down and pushed the lever on his own seat forward, grinning as he did because Watkins absolutely hated to have his shoulder harness locked. He swore that it constricted him in his flying. Watkins did it anyway, grudgingly.

"Angel 802, this is Keyboard 600."

This transmission from the E-2 radar plane orbiting high over the *Concord* wiped the smile off Boyle's face as he listened to Watkins acknowledge on the other radio. Since the helo was too low and too far away for the line-of-sight transmitters aboard the carrier to reach, the E-2 was used to pass on messages both ways.

"Keyboard, this is 802. Go ahead."

"Roger, Angel, be advised they want you to take a new station closer to the strike's coast-out point. Come left to 260 for 20 miles."

"Angel 802, roger. 260 for 20. Interrogative the change?" asked Watkins as he banked and settled out on the new heading. The change sounded like one of those ordered by "Delta

Control," the guys allegedly with the Big Picture, back aboard the *Concord.*

"Falcon 66, Angel, Falcon 66. Keyboard out," said the E-2 controller in an almost light-hearted tone.

Watkins sighed, resignedly. Another change in the plan after the show started. "Why do we bother briefing these missions anyway? Winging it would be easier," he said over the intercom.

"Yeah. Falcon 66. Which one is that, Bob?"

"I think it means, um, I'm not sure. Look it up."

Boyle took out his plastic book again and thumbed to the back and his mimeographed copy of the extremely unofficial and periodically proscribed Air Wing 33 Falcon Code sheet. The Falcon Code was used to convey messages which couldn't be put in the normal, permissible transmissions. Most of the reason that they had to be put into a code was that the language was deliberately and expressively obscene. The other reason was that the content usually conveyed a healthy and youthful disrespect for the higher-ups.

"Let's see. Falcon 66 is: 'How the fuck should I know? I'm only a junior officer.' That's nice."

Less than a minute later, as Boyle was lighting another cigarette, one transmission on the strike frequency jumped out from the pile.

"Angel, Angel, this is Condor 301. My wingman, 306, is hit." Even with the flat tones of the radio, the voice sounded very concerned. "Pilot seems okay. Unknown aircraft damage. We're headed out for the water. Switching to SAR frequency, Button 19."

Watkins answered immediately: "Roger, Condor. Angel's headed in now. Switching Channel 19."

He paused, then keyed the radio again. "Keyboard, Angel 802. Say pigeons to coast-out for the Condors." *Pigeons* was the word used for range and bearing from an aircraft's present position to somewhere else. The helo crew needed to know where in relation to themselves was the point where the stricken A-7's course would cross the coast, or "coast-out."

"802, Keyboard. Your pigeons are now 225 degrees at, um, 28 miles. Condor 301, you copy?"

"Angel 802, roger. 225 for 28. Estimating twelve minutes. Hold it together, Condor, we've got your taxi all set."

"Condor copies."

Chapter 2

July 11, 1972

Mike Santy had it relatively easy today. No SAMs came at him. It seemed that absolutely everyone else had seen the front end of one of those deadly "telephone poles" and had had to take the wild, twisting, rolling, diving evasive action that got them away from the threat. All he had to deal with was the flak.

Statistically, far more aircraft were shot down by Triple-A than were hit by the SAMs. But going against the guns and getting out again was really a matter of chance. The guns were aimed at a piece of sky through which the attacking jets had to fly to accomplish their objective. Most of the time the jets got through relatively unscathed. Sometimes they took some severe damage and sometimes, although less often, the damage was fatal. If a pilot flew smart and played by the rules that had cost other men's lives to learn, he could usually beat the guns and get back out safely. If he was going to be stupid about things then the C.O. certainly would soon have to write a condolence letter to the next of kin.

The SAMs, on the other hand, were aimed at a specific

aircraft. That made the fight intensely personal. The missileers would guide the SAM to the limits of its maneuverability to chase you and try to blow you up. They didn't even have to hit you to do it, either. The SAM put out a cloud of debris when it exploded. If you were close enough to the center of the cloud, within about three hundred feet or so, the detonation could cause fatal damage to the aircraft. The missiles would detonate in one of three ways: they could actually hit your aircraft, or their proximity fuses could explode their warhead close to you, or the guys on the ground could detonate them themselves. Whichever way it happened, the SAM had long before earned the respect of everyone flying over the North.

Most of the warning calls had come on the way in or just before the jets rolled in on the target. Santy had followed his leader down and then, when his bombs were gone, up and outbound. It was not until they were well clear of the area that he heard Rizzo's section leader, Jack Matson, call the SAR helicopter and tell them about Rizzo's problems. There was not a damn thing Santy or the rest of the pilots in the flight of four could do to help at this point. Commander Wilson, Santy's division leader and squadron C.O., called Red Crown and said that he and his three A-7s could fly cover for Rizzo and Matson at least until the designated rescue cover aircraft, or RESCAP, showed up.

Rizzo had made a dumb mistake. He had pulled out of his last Shrike launch run too low. Fascinated with his handiwork, he had watched the flight of his missile a bit too long. Thus, he'd gone below the "floor" of 3,000 feet and into the edge of the deadly barrage fire of the Triple-A batteries around the target, bottoming out his dive at about 2,000 feet. Before he could get the nose of his jet pointing above the horizon, he took two jarring hits from a light flak battery on a small hill to his left. One of them just chewed up the sheet metal on the wing. The other went into the belly and took out part of his hydraulic flight control system. It also damaged his engine, which was rumbling and surging in protest.

Afraid that any reduction of rpm would cause an engine seizure, he left the throttle up, and turned to a course of 120 degrees to get out over the American-owned water of the Gulf. From nearly anywhere in North Vietnam, a 120 heading would be the right direction.

When Rizzo had tried to call Matson and tell him of his situation, he'd gotten no answer. Being alone and in a sick airplane over enemy territory was as bad as it could get. He looked around in time to see Matson in Condor 301 rejoin in a loose formation. Rizzo used hand signals to show that he had major problems. He'd suddenly found that his radio could receive but not transmit. He signaled that to Matson who then dropped back to be free to watch for further enemy fire and shepherd his damaged wingman home.

Watkins called and asked Matson for the position of the wounded A-7 purely to calm Rizzo down a little and to give him the warm feeling that he was not all alone with his problem. Being the pilot of a single-seat attack jet is a neat feeling. But it gets excruciatingly lonely when something is dreadfully wrong with your aircraft. Your wingman hangs out there in space nearby giving you all the encouragement and advice he can but he can't actually *do* anything for you. If you make it back, that's great. If you don't, you go down alone. But simply knowing that the rescue guys were handy often made a big difference in a man's survival.

"Condors are estimating feet wet in one minute. We're at 8,000, headed 120." Matson just hoped that Rizzo could make it to the water, "feet wet," before something happened. The coastline now looked tantalizingly close out the windshield of his A-7 Corsair.

"Angel 802 from Keyboard. He's on your nose now at about five miles. Come left to 180. That'll cross him from your right to left high."

"802, roger."

Boyle looked high and to the right for the two approaching A-7s. He had to release his harness lock to do so. He heard a chuckle from Watkins, "See, I told you not to lock it."

He couldn't keep from smiling but just then caught a momentary glint high in the hazy blue sky. He keyed his transmitter, calling Matson.

"Condor 301, 802, tallyho. We're at your left ten o'clock low." He looked around the surface of the sea, checking the area once more.

"I don't see any fishing boats around down here so you should be in good shape if you have to get out." North Vietnamese fishermen received a cash bounty for captured Americans.

"Condor 301, roger. We're feet wet and we have you in sight down there, 802. Looks like—*oh shit!* Rat, you've got a large fire now coming from your wheel well! Eject, eject!"

The Corsair had finally given up the ghost. Since he had already done everything he could to prepare himself and the cockpit for a possible ejection and tried everything that he and his leader could think of to keep the jet flying, Rizzo didn't have to waste any time checking to see if there was anything left undone. He reached up over his head and pulled down the face curtain handles, which fired the ejection seat and blasted him up through the canopy, free of the burning aircraft.

Matson now made the proper transmission, giving the range and bearing from the Concord to the point where Rizzo ejected.

"Mayday. Mayday. Condor 306 is down on Echo Three Delta's 275 radial at 60 miles. Good chute."

Boyle saw the flash of the ejection seat's rocket and watched as the parachute deployed. The helo crew was too far away to see the man hanging below, but the clean dome of the nylon canopy was easily visible. Boyle transmitted over the radio that they had the chute in sight, then took over the controls since it is the pilot in the right seat who makes the approach and hover over the survivor. Watkins released the controls and leaned forward, peering up until he too had Rizzo in view.

"Wind's out of the west, Tim. Switches are set, power's up, ready for manual approach. In the back, okay, you guys, we have a single ejection, good chute, pilot's condition unknown."

Strand's laconic "Okay, sir" was enough.

Boyle glanced up and to the left to make sure that the abandoned A-7 was not going to come down on them. It wouldn't. The long smoking arc would intersect the water well to the east. But he kept an eye on it anyway, just in case. Looking back at Rizzo, it appeared that the pilot would come down about three miles off the beach. Since there were no Vietnamese fishing boats around and they were out of range of almost anything fired at them from the shore, they probably wouldn't need additional rescue cover aircraft and since Matson had enough fuel to stick around for a little while, he called the Keyboard E-2 and canceled any RESCAP.

Timing the approach so as to arrive over Rizzo's splashpoint after the parachute had come down in the water, eliminating the danger of the chute's being blown up into the helicopter's rotors, Boyle came down to ten feet over Rizzo's bobbing head. "Swimmer stand by. . . . Jump now, now, *now*."

On the third "now," the swimmer, Airman Dick Bangert, who was sitting in the cargo doorway, pushed himself out and away from the aircraft. He hit the water ten feet from Rizzo and swam over, careful to avoid entanglement with the parachute shroudlines floating just beneath the surface. Rizzo had not been able to release one of the Koch fittings on his torso harness and was still attached to the chute. He was thrashing around trying to free himself but, encumbered by all his flight gear and his inflated life preserver, was just making things worse for himself and more difficult for Bangert.

The swimmer came up to Rizzo and got him to calm down and remain passive. Slowly dragging the pilot away from the parachute, Bangert carefully removed each line and, when Rizzo was completely free, unfastened the Koch fitting. He signaled the first crewman and hoist operator, Strand, that they were ready for pickup.

Strand's voice over the intercom coached Boyle in moving the hovering helicopter over the two in the water. "Swimmer signals ready for pickup. Move easy right and easy forward.

23

Easy right. Easy right, easy forward. Stop forward, easy right. Easy right, fifteen more feet, easy right. Stop right, steady hover. Steady, steady. Hoist going down."

Boyle responded to Strand's commands and, thumbing the trim switch on the very top of the control stick, gently hovered the helicopter over to Bangert and Rizzo so smoothly that it didn't even feel as if the helicopter was moving at all.

"Gauges good, all in the green," reported Watkins since Boyle's attention was completely outside of the helo.

" 'Kay," was all the acknowledgment he got. It was all Boyle really had time for.

"Hoist is in the water. Swimmer and survivor hooking up . . . thumbs-up from the swimmer, hoist coming up. Stand by for weight on the aircraft . . . now."

Boyle compensated easily for the added weight of both Bangert and the sodden Rizzo, whose eyes, reported Strand, reminded him of an owl. Now, with the two out of the water and coming up on the hoist and the most difficult part over with, Watkins and Boyle allowed themselves a small laugh.

"Okay, sir, swimmer and survivor are at the cargo door." Strand reached out and pulled the two into the helo, unhooking the rescue slings and securing the hoist. "Swimmer and survivor are in the aircraft. Cargo door is closed. Cleared for forward flight. Looks like they're both okay back here. Survivor's name is Rizzo, Frank. One real wet and real scared jaygee." There was a pause as Strand asked Rizzo one more question. He continued, "Says he's from VA-19 on the *Concord*, Mr. Watkins. I suppose we can take him home, huh?"

"Yup. Looks that way. Nice job back there, guys. We could have done our part in our sleep the way you handled it."

Watkins never forgets the troops, thought Strand. That's why we fly with him. "Yes, sir, thank you," was all the crewman said.

Boyle eased the helo into forward flight and when they were passing through 300 feet, turned to a course of 090 degrees, generally heading for the *Concord*. He told Watkins to take over. After stretching his tightened muscles and wiggling his aching fingers, he pulled a crumpled Marlboro out

24

of his sleeve pocket and lit up. "I'll make the calls, Bob. It's good that we get to go over to the *Concord*. Been a while."

Watkins, lighting his own cigarette, just nodded so Boyle keyed his mike, "Condor 301, this is Angel 802, rescue complete. Your boy is fine. You're cleared to return to base."

"Keyboard, you copy? Condor is cleared RTB. We estimate our arrival in seven-zero minutes at Echo Three Delta." This was the *Concord*'s daily changing call sign.

"Roger, 802, Keyboard copies. Your pigeons to Echo Three Delta are 095 at 80. Say your state."

Boyle looked at the clock; he was surprised that it had only been an hour since Greenwood had led the strike across the beach. He glanced at the fuel gauges and did a little mental math, converting pounds of fuel into hours and minutes of further flying time, not including of course the normal reserve for each of the kids he might sire in the future. "802's state is one plus four-five. Copy 095 at 80. Request fuel and a shutdown on arrival."

Before Watkins could ask, Boyle explained. "We haven't been near the big boat for a week. We can get the mail for our ship and maybe mooch a decent meal off the attack guys. Maybe Strand can get a couple of cases of Cokes."

Watkins knew Boyle's real reason but let it pass. "Okay. I could use the time to talk to the boss anyway."

"Angel 802, Keyboard."

Now what? thought Boyle. "802, go ahead, Keyboard."

"Be advised all other Utah strike aircraft are feet wet. Echo Three Delta Control says to expect a shutdown on landing. And the Condors would like to buy you guys a dinner."

Boyle felt a quick flash of relief that if Mike had been going in today, he was now safely on his way home.

"Roger that. Tell them we accept. 802 switching tower."

Boyle reached down and changed radio frequencies. He looked over at Watkins placidly pulling on another cigarette, "See, Bob, I knew they were gonna offer. I just beat 'em to it."

Watkins laughed at Boyle's feigned innocence and shook his head. "All right, Tim, you win. Just don't kill us trying to land on that huge deck. Remember, you're not used to them."

Boyle brought Angel 802 up the wake of the *Concord* and landed on the angled deck as the Air Boss in the Tower directed him to. It had taken the helo nearly an hour and a quarter to reach *Concord* and she was about to begin the last recovery of the day. Boyle and Watkins just gave Rizzo over to the care of the ship's medical department, got a quick thousand pounds of fuel from the "Grapes" or flight-deck fuelers, so named for the purple color of their identifying jerseys, and took off again to clear the landing area. Boyle entered the D-shaped helicopter holding pattern on the right side of the massive carrier and waited for the deck to be clear for his final landing.

"Star-D," short for "Starboard Delta," was always fun for Boyle. For the helicopter detachment stationed aboard the carrier, it was pure boredom. Four hours of right-hand turns, waiting for somebody to need rescue, or, in between fixed-wing launch and recovery cycles, hauling whatever passengers and cargo the carrier wanted moved to or from the accompanying ships, wore down the morale of even the most eager pilot long before the six-month deployment was half over.

Boyle, since he did most of his flying from the *Galveston* driving around North SAR, only rarely got to fly around the carrier. He loved watching the jets catapult off the bow and slam back down on the stern. The magnificent and terrible beauty of the carrier under way on the great wide sea and the sheer power of her air wing were things of reverence for him. More than once while watching a launch or recovery, he had glanced down at the gold wings stamped on the leather name tag Velcroed to his flight suit, and had a momentary flash of unbelief that he was actually a naval aviator. That he really had done it, that he had become the only thing he had wanted to be since he had been a small boy.

Watkins, understanding, just let him fly and watch the airplanes. It was during moments such as these that Boyle's unconscious brilliance as a pilot became evident. He was not maneuvering the helicopter, he was maneuvering himself, his body. That a nine-and-a-half-ton flying machine happened to be strapped to his back didn't matter. Boyle was flying, doing the one thing in God's creation he was born to do. Watkins hoped that Boyle would continue to discover his abilities slowly as his experience grew. There were many men at the bottom of the sea whose confidence exceeded their experience. Overconfidence and professional arrogance has probably killed more pilots than warfare, Watkins thought.

Immediately after the Keyboard E-2 landed, or "trapped," aboard the ship, it was Angel 802's turn. They landed again on the angle, and shut down, leaving the rotors spread. They would be leaving in a couple of hours to get back to the cruiser before dark. Carrying the mail back would almost make the captain of the *Galveston* believe that there was a good reason for the length of the stopover. As they climbed down the steps from the helo, Watkins turned to Boyle and, deliberately looking up at the rotorhead, told Boyle to take off.

"You go ahead, Tim. I'll finish this up and meet you in the wardroom in an hour. Say hi to your friend for me."

Boyle realized that he hadn't fooled Watkins for a minute. He'd known all along that Boyle was looking for any excuse to get aboard the carrier so he could go see Mike Santy. Watkins somehow knew it. And let him go.

Boyle nodded and took off for the island structure and the ladders leading below. "Thanks, Bob. I'll see you in an hour," he said over his shoulder.

Watkins watched him run across the flight deck and turned back to the postflight inspection with a smile.

Chapter 3

July 11, 1972

L t. (J.G.) Mike Santy eased his A-7, Condor 307, back into the number-four position in the right echelon. Now that all the strike aircraft were again out over the water, he could allow himself the luxury of simply flying as opposed to the wildness of dodging SAMs and looking out for Triple-A fire and, somewhere in there, dropping a load of Mk-82 bombs. He was almost certain that he had hit the target: he felt pretty good about that. He had escaped with no damage to himself or his aircraft: he felt pretty good about that, too. The only dark cloud on his day was that he was going to have to take his turn in the barrel as the Squadron Duty Officer when he got back to the *Concord*. The job of SDO was, in the estimation of most J.O.'s, about as much fun as licking an open electric circuit, only with fewer rewards.

Santy reached up and unfastened the left side of his oxygen mask, letting it dangle in front of his face. He worked the muscles in his face, glad to be free of the constricting rubber at least for a few minutes. The sweat that had poured out of him before and during the strike, despite the air-conditioned cockpit, was drying, leaving an added coolness from his soaked flight suit. Now that he was beginning to experience postcombat letdown, he mentally reviewed the events of the past eighty minutes.

The opposition to the strike had been every bit as tough as the briefers predicted. Although there had been a lot of it, it was mostly inaccurate. The terrain was good enough so that the tactic of coming in from different directions had worked, in that the land did not dictate the approaches. Nor had there been any of the politically created buffer zones to contend with. In and out quickly; one run apiece and the strike aircraft hauled out of there.

Only two of the jets failed to make the rendezvous, the two Iron Hands from his squadron. Santy had heard the May-day calls from Matson but, when it became apparent that there was nothing he could do, had stuffed the concerns for his squadronmate to a little corner of his mind. Now that he was out of personal danger, he could allow himself to fret about Rizzo. They had been together in the Replacement Squadron (RAG) and had reported to VA-19 within a month of each other. Even though they were not particularly close, they had been through enough together for Santy to feel real worry.

Although he had overheard only the very last part of the radio transmissions from the rescue scene, he was certain that one of the voices from the helicopter had been Tim Boyle's. He chuckled softly.

For some reason, Santy had always had a mental image of the fighter and attack communities as the last of the breed that had begun with the knights of old and carried on through the cavalry and ended with the tactical guys on the carriers. The picture he had of the helicopter rescue types always seemed to be straight out of "Terry and the Pirates." They flew rickety-looking machines, low and slow, right into the worst of situations and emerged, sweaty, besmudged, and sort of unscathed from all the smoke and chaos at the other end, looking contemptuously over their shoulders at the bad guys as if to say, "I thought you were better than that." He knew that wasn't a true picture but that was the type of man Tim was and he fit right in with the rest of the SAR breed. All he needed was a glass of old bourbon, a cigar, and his arm around the Dragon Lady to make the image perfect.

Approaching the carrier, the strike broke up into its separate parts to enter "Marshal," the holding pattern aft of the ship, and, from there, the racetrack-shaped landing pattern itself. The F-4 Phantom fighters went into the break first. They were always low on gas. Their giant J-79 engines sucked fuel at a phenomenal rate. The A-7s were comparatively miserly so they had to await their turn.

The lead Condor, Cmdr. Jack Wilson, the squadron C.O., brought his four A-7 Corsairs up the right side of the ship's wake and, taking his interval on the last Phantom, broke sharply left to enter the downwind leg of the approach. The others followed in order so that they were all properly spaced, one behind the other, for landing.

Ideally, Navy aircraft come aboard the ship at exactly timed intervals and everybody catches one of the four arresting wires strung across the angled deck on the first try, the rear part of the flight deck being angled to the left 10 degrees to prevent a bad landing from ending up among the parked aircraft on the bow. If all works exactly right, the ship will have to spend minimum time steaming into the wind. Since the wind never seems to come from the direction that the ship needs to go, the captain hates to spend any more time launching and recovering aircraft than is absolutely required. Herein lies the major conflict between the ship's requirements and those of the air wing.

Landing on a carrier requires a tremendous amount of finesse. The ship which is the runway is moving away from the pilot at whatever speed is required to get a decent amount of wind over the deck in order to reduce the aircraft's speed relative to the ship at touchdown. Less speed equals less kinetic energy equals less strain placed on the arresting wires and the tail hook on the airplane. Since the angled deck is offset axially to the left, or port, the pilot cannot line up with the true axis of the ship, therefore he has to put in a slight right drift to compensate for the movement of his "runway."

In addition to all this, the "runway" is about 70 feet above the water, so it's as if the pilot has to land on the top of a seven-story building moving along an interstate in coastal Georgia. To help him, on the port side of the ship there is a visual landing aid system called the "Ball," or the "Lens," which through lining up a yellow light and a row of green ones allows the pilot to keep a steady rate of descent all the way to touchdown. It seems a simple and straightforward way to do things until you are sitting in 40,000 pounds of aluminum and fuel moving at around 150 mph trying to keep everything dry. Once you get the hang of doing all this during a nice sunny day, they let you do it at night in the rain when you can't see more than 150 feet in front of you.

If more than a couple of pilots miss the wires, or "bolter," or, if they are slow clearing the landing area once they land, and the next guy has to wave off, a very loud and very insistent telephone rings in the tower.

The man who has to answer this phone and say "Yessir" a lot is the "Air Boss," usually a commander who has recently finished his tour as a squadron C.O. Over the past few months, he has been driven certifiably insane by the incessant telephone calls and by the foibles of the idiots flying the aircraft and helicopters around the ship. Not too long ago, he was out there with the idiots but, of course, they are far stupider today than they were back when he was flying.

There is an intercom box at the Air Boss's left hand which has a very shiny and worn talk button. This box is connected to all the ready rooms below decks and the boss uses it to express his displeasure with the idiots directly to the offender's squadron. Having delivered his avuncular commentary, the Air Boss begins mumbling things to himself about settling someone's hash or shipping the dumb sonofabitch off to Tierra del Fuego or, even worse, to a patrol plane squadron.

Since the physical direction of the tirade is downhill, gravity helps to accelerate the fury. At the receiving end of this electronic snit, is the individual squadron duty officer. His intercom box never seems to have an operable volume knob and every time one of these blasts comes in to the ready room, the SDO has to gingerly tell his chain of command about the content and form of the message, leaving out all but selected bits of the threats and profanity. Thus, the C.O. of the particular squadron, who is responsible for the dumb bastard, ultimately has a one-way chat with whichever pilot made today's hit parade.

Wilson, Santy's C.O., was a bear on looking good around the ship. He felt that poor performance on the part of his pilots reflected directly upon his personal reputation, which, in fact, it probably did. He made this abundantly clear to every pilot who reported to the squadron, usually upon first meeting.

Today, things went well. Santy, as the last of the Condors to land, came onto final a tad high but compensated nicely and was on speed with a centered "ball" crossing the fantail. He caught the "optimum" number-three wire and folded his wings as he taxied clear of the landing area to the bow. While he was shutting down his Corsair, he noticed the extra helo in Starboard Delta. He also noted the side number, 802, when it flew past the ship on its upwind leg. Walking across the deck, Santy waved, hoping that Tim would see, and headed below to Ready Room Six for his debrief.

Cmdr. Wilson had been the first of the Condors to land and was waiting for Santy when he walked in. He motioned him to be seated with the other three VA-19, or Light Attack Squadron 19, pilots who had flown the strike. They were all there except Rizzo, who was down in sick bay getting looked over by the flight surgeons for ill effects from his ejection and swim. Santy grabbed a cup of coffee and sat.

What followed was an in-depth discussion of the entire mission from the briefing ninety minutes before launch time to landing on the ship. All the while the pilots were filling out the interminable paperwork that went along with flying Navy airplanes. These forms were broken down by the analysts into their separate parts and the data was carefully checked, rechecked, and laboriously fed into the Navy's computer system. Some months later, it would be discovered that a sailor had spilled a root beer into the computer and that the data had been lost forever. It would then be discovered that the data wasn't what the bean counters needed in the first place to support their preconceptions and was therefore irrelevant. A blue-ribbon steering committee would be carefully formed and chartered to create a new multi-page comprehensive form. A directive would also be issued proscribing the inclusion of root beer in the soda machines.

At about midpoint, the air wing landing signals officer, or "Paddles" as he was known, came in and graded everyone's approach and landing as is required after every flight. Santy's grade was the best of the five and it was difficult not to feel smug when he had bested the C.O. The one pilot whose grade was poorer than Wilson's received a cool and superior stare throughout the critique.

Finally, the debrief ended but not before Wilson had told the pilots about the invitation the squadron Executive Officer, the X.O., had extended to the helo crew and added a couple of comments about letting helo drivers sit at the same table as "real" pilots. The other pilots chuckled dutifully. Santy's eyes narrowed and the muscles in his jaw clenched. He tried to mask his expression but too late to avoid notice by the C.O.

"Something wrong, Mike?" he asked.

"No, sir," Santy said and turned and headed for the SDO's desk to assume the duty.

Wilson watched him walk away. I'd better keep an eye on that one, he thought. Something about Santy's attitude; there didn't seem to be the proper respect, the right touch of subservience that a J.O. ought to have. Wilson thought rather highly of Santy and believed that he had quite a future in the Navy. The young man had responded admirably to all the challenges that Wilson had thrown before him. But the slight touch of rebelliousness he had just seen would get young Mr. Santy in trouble someday if not dealt with soon. Wilson resolved to wait just a bit longer to see if Santy would get pissed off enough and ask to have a chat with him. If not, Wilson would have to initiate one to straighten him out. It would be for his own good, Wilson thought. The young pilot certainly had the talent. It just needed to be refined.

The present SDO was as glad to be relieved of the job as Santy was glum about taking over. Since it was now late afternoon, all the unpleasant duties, like getting the flight schedule to the pilots' staterooms and filling out the squadron's daily flight time and mission debrief forms would be concentrated in Santy's sixteen or so hours of duty. The only bright spot was that the night's ready-room movie would be shown in about five hours and he could hit the rack immediately after that.

While he was dejectedly going through the desk inventory, he heard a familiar voice at his shoulder and a horribly phony Irish brogue.

"Well, now, Mikey me lad. Aren't we all safe and everythin' with the famous Sandman at the helm of this here foitin' outfit?"

Santy laughed. "Jesus Christ! They'll let anybody aboard this goddamn ship." He turned to see Tim Boyle standing there with his ever-present grin.

"I thought that was you in the Angel. I guess I'm gonna miss chow with you unless you can wait until I can find somebody to take over for a while."

"Hell, send out for room service. They have to wait on the star of the show, don't they? You see, my son, royalty need not be troubled with anything as mundane as schedules." Boyle looked around the ready room slowly, taking in all the plaques and pictures of the A-7s hanging on the walls. "So this is how you guys live. Looks sorta official. Probably could use a few centerfolds hanging around."

Santy laughed again. "You know how we jet pukes are. We'd rather be dead than look bad."

Boyle asked brightly, "How've you been, Mike? Were you flying on that strike today? How'd it go?"

"One at a time. Yes, I was on the strike. It went fine. As

for me, not too bad, I guess. Although I could use about forty gallons of beer and a couple of Swedish stewardi."

Despite the smile, Santy looked tired. Deep lines marked the corners of his mouth and his eyes. They were not the kind of lines one got from laughing a lot. He didn't look like the blithe spirit half of the friendship that he had always been. This worried Boyle immediately and immensely.

"You wouldn't have a cup of coffee and a seat for a tired traveler around here, would you?" he asked.

"Sure. Let's go sit in the back. I can listen for the phone from there."

Santy led the way back to the huge coffee urn that seems to be a fixture in every ready room, probably installed before the deck. When they had each gotten a mug of the strong bitter brew preferred by sailors and airmen, Santy moved to a couple of chairs as far away from other occupants of the room as possible.

Before Santy could start speaking, Boyle said bluntly, "Mike, what the hell is wrong? No offense, but you look like shit."

Santy looked around to see if there were any authority figures within earshot and drew his hand down his face. "I don't know. Maybe it's just me. We get to fly a lot and the missions haven't been too bad so far. I'm even the number-one J.O. in the squadron in landing grades. I'm doing good in my ground job, according to my department head."

He sighed. "I just can't figure out the skipper, though. I can't seem to do anything completely right. No matter how hard I try or how long I work at something, he always finds something to criticize. It's always 'That's right but. . . .' " Santy stopped, realizing that he was talking to someone outside of his little tribe, his squadron. But then, Boyle always had a knack for getting him to open up.

Boyle looked around, spotting the C.O. instantly. "You mean that short little fucker over there? The one that has the 'I smell shit' look on his face?" When Santy nodded, he continued.

"Looks to me to be the kind of guy who ought to be standing

around with his hand stuck in his jacket, like Napoleon. Are you the only one he picks on?"

"Not really. Most of the other J.O.'s take their share too. It just seems that I'm the one who gets most of it. We all feel the same way: he's just got to back off. I can't keep redoing my work till all hours and then get up and fly the Dawn Patrol. This shit really sucks sometimes."

"Well, why don't you knock on his door and have a heart-to-heart? If you don't want to do that then try the X.O. It doesn't make any sense to get deeper and deeper in the hole without at least bringing it up. Maybe he doesn't realize what he's doing to you all."

"I've been a little afraid of asking him stuff like that. I don't want to get—ah, I don't know."

"Mike, there's something you're holding out on me. What is it?"

Santy sighed. "When I checked in, he gave me the usual welcome aboard bullshit but really seemed kind of cold as if I was intruding or something. Anyway, at the end of the interview, he asked me if I was Dave Santy's son. When I told him yes, he just kinda grunted and said, 'I thought so. You look a lot like him. That'll be all, Lieutenant.' I couldn't tell what he was thinking or anything. I don't know if my dad pissed him off or what. Wilson's never mentioned it since."

Boyle thought about Mike's father, Commander Dave Santy, who had been killed in a landing accident during the Cuban Missile Crisis in 1962. The elder Santy was still a legendary figure in Naval Aviation circles. He had been an ace in two wars, first in the Pacific in World War II, shooting down nine Japanese aircraft in the great air battles of 1944–45. After that war, he had stayed in the Navy and had been among the first to make the transition to the new jet fighters which were replacing his beloved Hellcats and Bearcats. When war came again in 1950, his squadron was one of the first sent to Korea. Although their main mission was ground attack, Santy and the others had found that the skills learned in the Pacific had not dimmed at all when the MiGs came south to challenge American supremacy in the air. Santy shot down seven more of the enemy in these high-speed encounters despite the fact that the aircraft he flew was not considered in any way superior to the MiGs he had to face day after day.

After that war he had come home to his wife and six-year-old son and taken them with him on a happy succession of progressively more responsible tours of duty, culminating in his receiving command of an A-4 light attack squadron, VA-188, flying from one of the new Forrestal-class carriers. He was a rising star in the Navy, always trying new things and pushing for ever more thorough training for the pilots and the sailors who maintained the jets. As a fighter pilot turned attack type, Santy had led his squadron with the same élan and go-to-hell attitude that had made him the brilliant flier that he was.

Despite his success as a fighter pilot, it was when he had transitioned to the Douglas A-4 Skyhawk that he left his peers in the dust. Mike had several times told Boyle that one of the best memories he had of his father was the day the elder Santy had taken his family to the hangar and, sitting in an A-4 cockpit with eleven-year-old Mike on his lap, had pointed out and explained all the switches and controls in the new jet. Mike still kept the picture that his mother had taken, ignoring the teasing from the two in the cockpit about her lousy photography.

Mike had that day decided to fly Navy airplanes and neither the later death of his father nor the firm opposition of his mother had kept him from his goal. Mike's only real regret was that the only time he had been able to fly the A-4 was in the Training Command. By the time he had gotten to the fleet, they were being replaced by the new A-7.

Boyle looked at his friend now staring into his coffee cup. "Mike, look. It's not doing you any good to sit there and wonder and brood about it. You have to find out what the deal is with the C.O. Otherwise, you're just going to feel progressively worse and more gunshy until you're completely worthless. I mean more worthless than you are normally."

Santy smiled. "Yeah, I guess you're right. I'll try seeing him later today. Be like pulling an aching tooth."

Boyle went on, "Look at it this way: the guy might have terminal hemorrhoids or he probably owed your dad money and worries about the interest that's piled up. Get it? Piled up? Hemorrhoids? Piled up?"

Santy groaned, then said, "Thanks, Timmy."

"No sweat, Mike. Sometimes you just forget to read the *Book*."

Mired in his own concern, Santy had failed to utilize Boyle's stroke of genius, the *Book of Cosmic Perspective*. Boyle used it exclusively to analyze problems. If it didn't always eliminate them, it did minimize their importance.

"So what would the *Book* say about my problem?"

"Bowing to small men only makes the blood rush to your head. You can't get low enough. Page four hundred ninety-six. See? Never forget the *Book*."

Santy smiled and nodded. Boyle was right again. He wished they could have been in the same squadron.

Santy slapped Boyle on the knee. "So, how are you, Tim? How's the rescue business? Oh, nice job picking up Rizzo. Thanks."

"Piece o' cake. Anyway, we couldn't just leave him floating around out there. That wouldn't have been right. He'd have been a hazard to navigation. Besides, on the hoof, he's worth a whole bottle of booze for each of us."

Santy laughed, merrily this time. "Glad to see you've still got your priorities in order. Speaking of them, how's Meghan?"

"As of her last letter she was fine. Can't wait for me to get home and away from the 'illegal war' but fine. I've been over here five months and I miss her more than I ever thought I would. That's a bad sign, methinks."

"Yup. You're doomed, pal. How you and Miss Activist ever hooked up in the first place I'll never know. You've even stayed that way despite my best efforts. You ought to marry that girl. Who knows, once the war is over you guys might find something that you could protest together. You could even raise a bunch of little Democrats. Your folks would love that."

Boyle laughed at the thought of his dad having a liberal in the family. "That would make Thanksgiving dinner interesting, all right."

Boyle snapped his fingers. "Oh, yeah, I almost forgot. She says that the head gasket on your 'Vette needed changing. She had it done and you owe her two hundred fifty dollars."

Santy's eyebrows flew up at that, not because of the amount but because he couldn't stand the thought of anything wrong with "Junior," as he called his beloved Corvette.

"What was she doing, racing it?"

"No, just what you told her to do, driving it around a couple of times a week."

"Okay, I'll send a check over next payday. You can send it to her. But tell her to be careful, no racing. Anyway, it doesn't sound like she's still mad at me for getting her little sister drunk."

"No, Mike, she never really was. She knew all along that your intentions were sort of honorable. She just knows which of your buttons to push. You're easy."

"Yeah, she's got us both figured. Look, let me try to dump this duty for a while and we can go up to chow together. I suspect that you're the day's hero and I want to watch you blush. You're so cute when your ears are red."

"Come on, I'm only the copilot. But I really want you to meet my HAC. This guy can really fly a helo. I can't believe how much I'm learning from him. He's cool, too, takes no shit from anybody."

Santy walked over to another young officer who was writing a letter in the corner of the room. Boyle couldn't hear what was said exactly but the disgusted expression told him that Santy had sold the duty for a little while.

Mike came back and led Boyle out the back door.

Chapter 4

July 11, 1972

As the two friends stepped out of Ready Room Six on their way up to Wardroom Two, Boyle ran smack into a stocky full lieutenant who was about to enter the ready room. It was like hitting a brick wall, Boyle thought. Backing up and excusing himself, Boyle looked down at the shorter man, who had the gold ropelike aiguillette of an admiral's aide on his left shoulder. Pinned above the left breast pocket of his khaki shirt was the "Budweiser label" insignia of the Navy's elite SEALs. These specialists in dirty tricks impressed Boyle to the soles of his flight boots. Rigorously trained to run around in enemy territory, they carried out all sorts of clandestine missions, gathering intelligence, kidnapping or killing enemy officials, and generally making the bad guys' lives more miserable than they already were. He admired them but in no way did he want to be one of them. They ate snakes.

It was their eyes that really gave Boyle the willies. Every SEAL he had ever met seemed to look at him as if trying to decide with which knife to cut Boyle's throat, the sharp one or the rusty one.

The SEAL looked at the leather name tag on Boyle's flight suit, then looked up at his face. Same eyes, thought Boyle.

"You're from that helo, right? The one that picked up the A-7 guy today? I'm Kevin Thompson." He turned and walked toward the hatch. "C'mon. Admiral wants to see you."

Santy, as would any good young naval aviator when a fellow is called to see the powers above, told Boyle that he'd wait for him in the wardroom and slipped away with a sad last look at the condemned.

Following Thompson, Boyle nervously wondered why the admiral wanted him. Was he in trouble? He couldn't recall anything he'd done that would be bad enough for him to be hauled before the task force commander. Climbing the ladders up to Flag Country, as the area where the admiral and his staff worked and lived (*lurked* would be a better word, Boyle thought), was torture. Finally, he couldn't stand it any longer.

"Hey, Lieutenant, what's the admiral want with me? Did he tell you?"

Thompson turned as he pulled open the thick armored door which led into Flag Bridge. "I don't know, but he was smiling when he sent me to find you. He doesn't do that if he's gonna shoot somebody. Just remember to say 'sir' a lot and you'll be okay." He winked as he stepped aside and allowed Boyle to precede him. The wink didn't ease Boyle's paranoia one whit.

Inside the bridge area among all the radar repeaters and banks of communications gear, stood the majority of the admiral's operations staff, holding sheaves of papers and clipboards and looking harried. Off in a corner, talking with two captains whom Boyle didn't recognize, stood Bob Watkins and Lt. Cmdr. Don Hickerson, the Officer in Charge of all the HC-17 Combat SAR detachments in the Gulf and thus the senior officer present from Boyle's mother squadron. When Boyle entered, they all looked toward him with friendly, smiling faces. It didn't look like a lynching but Boyle was now even more nervous. He had gotten himself ready to be one on one with the admiral but with all the other "heavies" gathered, he felt awfully out of place.

Rear Admiral Welch was sitting in his raised chair on the left side of the Flag Bridge reading a clipboard full of messages and initialing each one. He glanced up at the young pilot and smiled.

"Be right with you, son," he said, looking back at the papers.

There was no chance of being inconspicuous, nor of acting like he belonged up here, so Boyle looked pleadingly at Watkins, who grinned at him and came over to stand next to him. The others had all gone back to what they were doing when Boyle entered, so he just gawked around. He noticed suddenly that he was the only man there who didn't have a hat on, who wasn't "covered" on the bridge. He seemed to recall that this was a serious breach of some regulation and, with another major drop in his confidence, felt his chances of ever making full lieutenant evaporate.

He turned in response to a gentle nudge from behind. Thompson, standing just inside the small galley area, handed him a black baseball cap with "CTF-77" embroidered above the bill. Boyle took it and put it on, whispering his thanks to the straight-faced Thompson and silently vowing never to say another disparaging word about the Navy SEALs.

"You owe me five bucks for the hat, fly-boy. I'll collect it later," Thompson whispered, causing Boyle to modify his vow to include only the present environs.

Watkins leaned closer and said in a low tone, "Relax, Tim. The admiral is going to present you with a medal. You're getting your first Strike/Flight. You've got well over twenty missions and you're due. Welch has always tried to give as many awards personally to the younger troops as he can. He feels it gives him a chance to meet them and let them see the guy who gives the orders. Damn good idea, I think."

Boyle was immensely relieved. The Strike/Flight Air Medal was given in recognition of a given number, usually twenty, of combat missions. When you amassed that total, or multiples of it, you were entitled to wear the medal with a numeral signifying the number you had earned. Every time you reached another plateau, you were authorized to raise the number on the ribbon correspondingly. It was essentially an "I was there" award but the higher the number the greater your prestige with your peers. A gold star on the ribbon signified that the medal had been given for a single act of heroism, which placed the medal on an entirely different, and higher, plane.

The admiral handed the clipboard to a yeoman standing next to his chair and stood. As he did, Tim Boyle got his first good look at one of his heroes, the man who commanded all the American naval vessels in the Tonkin Gulf. Rear Admiral James J. Welch was of average height with broad shoulders and massive forearms. In his late forties, his sandy hair was now finally turning gray. His face, although deeply lined and tanned, still had a boyishness about it. Maybe that's because his eyes are so blue, thought Boyle. On the admiral's shirt, below the gold wings, were only three ribbons, the only three of his twenty or so that he chose to wear. There were the blue and orange of the Air Medal with two gold stars and the numeral *8*, the red, white, and blue of the Distinguished Flying Cross, and the blue and white of the Navy Cross. All of these had been earned in combat flying from the deck of a carrier in World War II and Korea. Here he was, back at war again, only this time he was the one who had to send the young men out to fight and die while he was forced to stay behind. And wait. And worry.

The young pilot stood rooted as Welch walked over and stuck out his hand, ignoring Boyle's failure to remember to salute.

"You must be Tim Boyle. First, I'd like to thank you for saving that young pilot, Rizzo. Your OIC and Lt. Watkins have a lot of good things to say about you. Mr. Watkins tells me you're an excellent pilot and should make aircraft commander soon."

"Yessir, Admiral. I've been studying for the exams and the board for a while now. I think . . ." He shut up, realizing that he was going to babble.

Welch grinned a little and turned to his chief of staff. "Harry, could I have the citation, please? All right, attention on the bridge."

He took a blue folder from the chief of staff and, opening it, turned back to face a now red-faced Tim Boyle and began reading the citation. "The President of the United States takes pleasure in presenting the Air Medal with Gold Numeral One for the first Strike/Flight award to Lieutenant (Junior Grade) Timothy J. Boyle, United States Naval Reserve, for service as set forth in the following Citation: For heroic achievement in aerial flight as a pilot in Detachment Alpha, Helicopter Combat Support Squadron Seventeen (HC-17), embarked in USS *Concord* (CVA-58), during missions in support of combat operations in North Vietnam . . ."

The rest was lost to Boyle as he thought back on all the missions he had flown over the past few months. It didn't seem like any big deal to him since he had not done anything really spectacular. Even today's rescue was sort of a routine SAR in that everything clicked nicely and there was no threat from the enemy. The few times he and Watkins had gone over the beach into North Vietnam had been pretty tame, none of the survivors had been down in areas that had been heavily defended. They had been quick rush-and-snatch jobs. The thought struck him that his perspective had changed greatly since his days in the RAG. Back then, Combat SAR seemed as mysterious and romantic as the Foreign Legion.

Hearing his name, he forced his mind back to the present.

". . . Lieutenant (Junior Grade) Boyle's skill, courage, and devotion to duty in the face of hazardous flying conditions were in keeping with the highest traditions of the United States Naval Service. For the President, Robert D. Reynolds, Vice Admiral, U.S. Navy, Deputy Commander in Chief, U.S. Pacific Fleet."

Welch closed the folder and took the small blue box from the Chief of Staff. He removed the medal and pinned it to Boyle's flight suit. Tim, in turn, saluted and thanked him.

Boyle, feeling embarrassed and out of place, accepted the congratulations of the others present. Watkins was last in line and quietly reminded him that they still had to get back to their own ship by sunset. Boyle nodded and told him about Santy waiting in the wardroom. Watkins moved away to make the necessary excuses to Hickerson.

Admiral Welch buttonholed Boyle and led him into a quiet corner.

"Tim, I meant what I said before. You are establishing a good reputation over here. I know that medal is a little late and you probably will earn a few more before your tour is up but I wanted to meet you and an award presentation is as good an excuse as any. Lt. Watkins told me that you had your choice of aircraft and communities and chose helos and Combat SAR. I'm curious. Would you mind telling me why?"

"Admiral, I'm not exactly sure. I love flying helicopters and I kind of like being down in the weeds and seeing what's around me. I didn't want jets too much because I don't really care about high and fast. Multiengine seemed real boring. I'm glad I got my pick because we are doing some good here and I feel like this is where I belong. Like this is where I *ought* to be. I don't really understand it too well myself," he finished lamely.

"Does all the razzing you take from the jet guys about being a 'rotorhead' bother you?"

"Not really. It doesn't matter what you fly as long as it's off a ship. Besides I just tell 'em that they're on my No Pickup List and they get real respectful, real quick."

Welch nodded slowly and indicated that it was time for him to get back to work. Watkins moved over and he and Boyle excused themselves and left for the wardroom. Once outside Flag Bridge, Watkins asked if Boyle was going to wear the medal to bed. Tim hurriedly unpinned it, put it back in the case, and stuffed it in the leg pocket of his flight suit. He sighed, feeling a little stupid, and followed Watkins down the ladder.

As the hatch closed behind the two helo pilots, Welch motioned the captain of the *Concord,* Capt. Sam Andrews, over to the far corner of the bridge. The two of them had been friends for over twenty years. Andrews always seemed to be about a year behind Welch as they went from duty station to duty station. He had joined Welch's first fighter squadron just in time to go off to Korea. Assigned as Welch's wingman, he had learned most of what he knew about staying alive in a Navy airplane from him. In the years since, he had learned everything he knew about being a naval officer from him, too. The friendship had grown to the point that each was the godfather to the other's children; in fact, there were strong indications that their two oldest children, Welch's son and Andrews's daughter, were about to get engaged. It was a topic that filled the daily letter each got from his wife. And a situation that quietly thrilled each man.

"Y'know, Sam, I like that kid. He doesn't seem impressed with either being up here and talking to me or even about that Air Medal. I'll bet inside he was scared shitless about getting called up here, though. Reminds me of a wingman I had once."

Andrews chuckled. "Yeah, I know what you mean. When he makes aircraft commander, he'll be assigned back here and a new copilot will be assigned to Watkins up on North SAR. We'll get a better look at him then."

He paused for a moment. "You know, I really like that whole HC-17 bunch we've got out here. I hope they are all that good."

Their conversation went on about ship's operations for a few more minutes and then Andrews saluted and left. Welch looked out over the huge flight deck and watched as the sailors, *his* sailors, their shirts removed in the late afternoon sun, worked on the now almost quiet flight deck. They were moving the jets around and towing them to their proper places, respotting the deck for tomorrow's first launch. He thought of Boyle's words: "This is where I ought to be." The admiral knew exactly what the young pilot had meant.

There are two wardrooms on aircraft carriers and the officers can choose which they wish to use. The lower one, Wardroom One, is below the hangar deck, and it is here that the officers have to wear regular uniforms to eat. Each evening at 1730 or 1800, they have a sit-down meal complete with napkin rings. The ship's executive officer or the next most senior department head, presides. At all other times, the meal is served cafeteria-style but you still have to get dressed up. It is also an excellent place to get face time in the hopes of improving your fitness report, if that is your need. Some officers have to be dragged kicking and screaming to eat there because it is normally very boring.

Wardroom Two, the "Dirtyshirt," on the other hand, is often a lot of fun. Located just below the flight deck, there is no dress code. You can wear your flight suit, your khakis, or your greasy flight-deck jersey. The food is always cafeteria-style and, although the menu is the same as the other wardroom, it just seems better. There is always a large amount of banter among pilots and among squadrons, sometimes obscene, occasionally barbed, and usually funny. The difference is roughly the same as that between eating in your grandmother's formal dining room on Christmas and a crab feast in your backyard on the Fourth of July with all your crazy, half-bombed uncles around.

Boyle and Watkins stepped into Wardroom Two and found their seats at the table where Mike Santy and his squadronmates were busily speculating about the next port call, allegedly Hong Kong. Today's cuisine consisted of trail markers, sometimes called elephant turds, large lumps of blandly seasoned ground beef covered with a gray, tasteless gravy good only for making the things less dry. The best thing about trail markers is that they do not interfere in any way with the flavor of the ketchup liberally poured on them.

With introductions and handshakes all around, the pilots at the table greeted the two rotorheads warmly, as most fixed-wing guys do after one of their own has been pulled out of the water. Since he had been the HAC on the rescue, Watkins was quickly drawn into conversation with the more senior men of VA-19. Boyle and Santy were free to drift into the background and resume their earlier talk. They came up with a plan to get Meghan to meet Tim in Hong Kong when the *Concord* finished this line period and pulled in there for some

R&R next month. That was the easy part. The hard part was to get Boyle assigned to the "home base" HC-17 detachment aboard *Concord* in time to ride the ship into port.

The conversation naturally moved into easy discussion of the wonderful and exuberant times they'd had in San Diego and how it would be again when they got home from the war. Never in either of their lives had they had such pure fun. Boyle and Meghan, during the five months before he had been sent to Vietnam, had slipped naturally from the dating stage to the gentle comfort of a relationship with an as-yet-unaddressed long-term future. Santy, as the third member of the trio, was the brash and wild brother to each of them in every sense but the biological. With luck, they would all pick up the threads when they got home and Meghan would once again happily resume her quixotic attempts to find the right girl for Mike.

Soon, too soon, it was time for the two helo drivers to get back to their ship. They stood and made their farewells to the A-7 pilots and with Santy in trail headed up to the flight deck and their aircraft.

Strand and Bangert were waiting in the helicopter and greeted their pilots with an air of complete innocence. Something was up. As Boyle moved away to show off his aircraft to Santy, Watkins looked at the crewmen suspiciously and asked how the aircraft had looked on their preflight inspection.

"Fine, Mr. Watkins. All preflighted and ready to go. We even cumshawed six cases of Cokes for the det." Strand said.

"Yeah, and we got the mail for the whole ship. Only weighs eight hundred pounds. What with the Cokes our gross weight is fine. We're all set, sir," added Bangert.

"Uh-huh. That's great, guys. Anything special I should know?"

"No, sir. Everything's fine. Just, um, I guess maybe you shouldn't turn on the doppler is all. It's kind of weak and, well, we ought to have the ATs check it when we get back home," Strand said.

"Okay, then we won't use it if you say so," Watkins said with a tiny smile.

Once, two months ago, Strand forgot to caution Watkins about another "doppler problem" and the heat generated by the perfectly operating system caused a bottle of Jack Daniels hidden in the doppler well to explode. The resultant flood of booze not only fried the doppler transmitter but was also an absolute bitch trying to clean up before anyone from the cruiser's crew, or "ship's company," smelled it. Strand had thought that Watkins was going to throw him overboard on the spot. He'd never seen his HAC so pissed. Watkins couldn't get out a coherent sentence. Even his legendary cursing had failed him.

"Hey, Tim," Watkins called. "Time to go."

"Yeah, be right with you." Boyle turned to Santy and stuck out his hand.

"See ya, Mike. Keep your ass out of trouble will you, please."

Santy grasped the hand. "No problem. Take care and give my love to Meghan. Tell her the check is in the mail and I'll see her in Hong Kong. That'll definitely get her over here. No way will she be able to stand the thought of you loose in Hong Kong with me."

"Will do. 'Bye." Boyle hustled over and climbed up into the helo.

Santy stepped back across the foul line and watched his friend, sitting in the right seat, go through the checklists.

Taking a step back from the downwash, he smiled and waved as Angel 802 lifted off and flew out of sight, headed home to North SAR.

He walked up to the bow of the carrier and stood there, feeling the clean sea air as he and the ship passed through. He thought again of his friend Tim, the best friend he had ever had. With just a little bit of surprise, he realized that he really couldn't remember what it was like before they had met, way back in Pensacola.

Chapter 5

July 13, 1970

TWO YEARS EARLIER

Nope.

It just didn't make any sense.

There was no rational explanation for the goddamn bubbles. They appeared from nowhere on the side of the glass and drifted up, ever so regally, to meet the weak and dying head on the beer.

No matter how he twisted the glass, they kept coming. His examination of the wonders of carbon dioxide or monoxide or one of those oxides was making him feel worse. It was making him acutely aware of his academic shortcomings.

No way, he thought, no way am I going to understand all the technical things. I can't do long division, so how the hell am I going to learn how to navigate and all that other stuff you need to know to fly? I even failed Geology. Boyle, you've really put your foot in it this time.

Timothy J. Boyle, formerly of Boston College, formerly an All-Conference lacrosse player, formerly a holder of the magic 2-S deferment, held his chin on the back of his left hand, which rested upon the bar in the San Carlos Hotel in

Pensacola, Florida. This was the place where generations of future naval aviators had been sent by the recruiters to spend their last night of civilian life.

The San Carlos Hotel was an anachronism, with all the dowager dignity of the best places the Old South could offer. She stood on a corner on Palofox Street, holding her aging head high, kind of tawny, kind of sandy, kind of tattered. She had a pride to her. She dominated the corner.

Across the room from Boyle stood a slightly discomfited Mike Santy. He had just been shot down by a gorgeous but somewhat dim blonde. He had tried the old "We who are about to . . ." line and failed. The blonde had been around P'cola too long and had heard that bullshit too often.

Santy scanned the room and, seeing no other likely targets, figured that the best plan at this point was probably to have another glass of Perspective. He saw a space at the bar next to a big guy hunched over his drink.

Boyle was dimly aware of a presence arriving at his immediate right. The bubble mystery was now becoming the consuming question in his mind. Over his shoulder, he heard a soft West Florida drawl.

"Want another beer, Ace?"

Boyle looked gloomily around at the voice.

"Yeah, I guess so. But I might have had enough already. I gotta report in to INDOC tomorrow."

"Me too. It can't make any difference if we're hung over or not. Besides, we don't have to show up until noon anyway. The drill instructors are going to be assholes no matter what. We may as well relax tonight because we won't be able to for a while."

Boyle looked closely at his new companion. He was built like a running back: wide shoulders, slim waist, hands that hung slightly forward of his hips open and ready. Black straight hair, dark brown, intense eyes which were moving about the room, not giving the impression of disinterest in Boyle, but just naturally not missing anything.

Santy waved the lady bartender over and ordered two more. He looked at Boyle, taking stock. Boyle was six feet three inches and Irish as hell. Curly, dirty-blond hair, broad shoulders, green eyes which had a smile in them despite the obviously morose mood.

"Mike Santy."

"Tim Boyle," he said, sticking out a paw.

Grasping hands, each matched the other's pressure, taking yet another unconscious measure of the man.

As they released their grip, a soft-hard female voice broke their stares, "Here's your beer, y'all. That'll be an even dollar."

Boyle pushed aside the nearly flat beer he had just been contemplating and ruffled through his cash, finally forking over two ones, grandiosely telling her to keep the change.

The bartender, in the fading days of her beauty, picked up the bills and moved away, but not so far that she couldn't hear the conversation, which she had heard hundreds of times before and probably would hear hundreds more. Always between young, eager, bright-eyed men. Many never made the grade, some didn't survive, most she never saw again. The very few she saw who came back to the old barroom, remembering their "Last Night," had grown, aged somewhat beyond normal time, but fuller, more confident men. They were, every one, a whole lot wiser, a lot wilder, and, usually, just a bit sad.

"You said we don't have to report until noon, but don't we get brownie points or something for showing up early?" asked Boyle.

"Nope. A guy from my team came here last year. He's now in Texas flying jets. He said that he only made three mistakes. Checking in early, checking in during the summer and checking in. He said all you can do is get a good night's sleep because it'll be your last for a while. I'm going over at eleven-thirty."

Boyle thought that over. He was beginning to believe that his recruiter might not have been completely honest. He might possibly have left out a couple of salient points about flight training. It did nothing for his already diminished self-confidence.

"A couple of guys from my school were supposed to get in last night. They're not in here so I guess they've checked in already. I wonder how they're doing." Boyle sighed. "I guess we'll find out soon enough."

With nothing else really to say, Boyle asked Santy where he had gone to college.

"Florida State. I graduated last Friday. I had to go to summer school since I managed to party my way to an F in one of my courses."

Boyle laughed. He saw the question on Santy's face and explained.

"Me, too. Being a jock was a lot more fun than studying. I figured since I was carrying an A at midterm I was a lock for at least a C in my last philosophy course. Problem was, I had a girl write my research paper on Kierkegaard to get the A and I didn't have any idea what he really said. The final was eighty percent Kierkegaard. I didn't even spell his goddamn name right, which probably was a real good indicator to the prof that I was full of shit."

"Philosophy? What the hell was your major?"

"English. I've always loved reading. I was lousy in anything but Liberal Arts. My high school pinned a note to my shirt when I went away to B.C. that said: 'If you let this man within one hundred yards of your Math and Science building, he'll set your program back fifty years.' "

"Well, that friend of mine said that there was some math but it wasn't too bad. I did pretty well in it so if you need any help . . ."

"Thanks, Mike. I guess I'm kind of worried about that. The rest of it doesn't scare me near as much as washing out over something like a math test."

Boyle's feelings of aloneness had begun to evaporate with Santy's arrival at the bar. For his part, Santy felt that he had found a kindred spirit in Boyle. Their conversation continued into those subjects which young men are naturally easy with—sports, women, and the relative merits of their hometowns. As it did, a bond, threadlike at first, but ever-strengthening, grew until it lay just beneath consciousness, firmly and irrevocably rooted.

The time passed easily for the two. As the locals paid up and left the bar, the only patrons remaining were the dozen or so soon-to-be aviation officer candidates, most of whom were now abjectly glancing between their watches, the wet rings left on the bar by their sweating drinks, and their slightly distorted images in the large mirror behind the rows of bottles on the other side of the bar. Several wistful glances passed over the two large men laughing softly at the almost true tales bouncing between them. Soon, only Boyle and Santy were left, bantering with the bartender who laughed gently with them and who contributed stories of other young men she had served, of the wild things done, of days now passed, and, once, an unembellished, adjectiveless description of one young man's fiery end.

July 11, 1972

Mike Santy looked out over the ocean and thought of all the other moments he and Tim had shared, of the many times one had cajoled and pushed the other through flight training and through the tough times since. He chuckled softly at the new page from the *Book* that Boyle had come up with, as usual, with perfect timing.

The harsh clang of a metal chock being dropped on the flight deck behind him brought Santy back to the ship. He remembered that he had the duty in the ready room and headed for the ladder, his stride much easier than it had been only two hours earlier.

Chapter 6

August 26, 1972

Santy pulled up the left leg of his flight suit and inspected his shin. He was listening to the enlisted weather briefer's description of the present and predicted conditions in the target area but since it had been summarized in the first sentence as generally good, the specifics didn't really matter. He'd get a last best guess from the ready room TV right before he manned his airplane for launch. With no major weather movers coming in, it should be just like yesterday: light clouds, isolated thunderstorms, winds out of the west at about ten to fifteen knots.

He had to gingerly pull the Nomex away from the damaged spot on his shin where he'd barked it on the sharp edge of a "kneeknocker." These are the holes cut through the main structural frames of the upper levels of the carrier to allow the passageways to proceed fore and aft. They are cut smaller than the passageway itself and flanged so that one has to simultaneously duck and step over to pass through. One can pass through these a thousand times and never notice that they are even there but every once in a while the trailing shin comes in contact with the edge. This causes immediate eye-watering pain, fluent if unoriginal cursing, and ultimately, a dime-sized brown scar.

Since the bottom part of the flange is unpainted and must be kept shined by the sailors responsible for the cleanliness of the immediate area, or "zone" as it is properly called, stepping on the flange is considered bad form. So, the only thing to do is take it like a man, knowing that someday you'll get to explain the scars to your sons who will undoubtedly be impressed by their father's ability to withstand the hazards of life on a warship.

Today's duty briefer was the intelligence officer from VF-117, one of the two fighter squadrons aboard the *Concord*. Lt. Jack Morgan, a tall, bespectacled officer nicknamed "Secret Squirrel" mostly because of his bizarre sense of humor and his complete inability to be awed by any superior officer, began his description of the various SAM and Triple-A sites both on the route to the target and in the area surrounding it. Santy listened intently, forgetting all about his shin.

The mission for this afternoon was a power plant which had been hit periodically throughout the past two years but never hard enough to put it completely out of action. The Vietnamese knew that the Americans would revisit it sooner or later and had strengthened the antiaircraft defenses accordingly. Reconnaissance photographs taken the day before by an RA-5C Vigilante from the *Concord*'s air wing showed heavy Triple-A guns and an unusually large concentration of SAM sites in the vicinity. The pilots and mission planners knew that there were probably more antiaircraft sites which the Viggie crew had not spotted, so instead of the normal two pairs of Iron Hands there would be six.

The six teams of Iron Hand A-7 Corsairs would carry two standard Antiradiation Missiles (ARMs) each while their F-4 Phantom escorts would be carrying Mk-82s and Rockeye cluster bombs for flak suppression. The tactics were for the F-4s to drop on the gun sites while the A-7 Corsairs took out high-threat SAM radars. If the fire from the ground was deemed to have been sufficiently reduced early on, the strike would be directed to hit the power plant. That decision would be made just prior to the main force's reaching the target area by CAG Greenwood, who would be in the lead A-6 Intruder, based on the recommendation of the Iron Hand leader. If the flak was still too heavy, the strike would go after as many of the sites as possible. This called for a quick and accurate assessment by the Iron Hands, since the strike could not safely switch targets after they had committed.

Santy, who was to fly his first mission as section leader today, suddenly became nervous listening to the plan. He had thought that all he would have to do this time was play follow the leader and hit the assigned target. He worried now that he might miss a target switch order and lead his wingman into serious trouble. He hadn't figured on the feeling of responsibility that came with being in charge of even the smallest element in the strike. Section leader had been just another step, albeit the first, in his development as a combat pilot.

Soon, all the briefers were finished and it was CAG's turn to address the crews. He stressed flight integrity and reviewed tactics, including the detachment sequence for the Iron Hands, reminding everybody about the dangers of multiple runs over the target—one pass only, and of the sheer stupidity of trying to duel with the flak sites. After the bombs were dropped, they were to "egress" by sections, using maximum evasive maneuvering since the safest route back to the ship was never a straight line. He finished on a hopeful note with the "safe areas" for rescue and the frequencies and call signs of the rescue assets which would be orbiting off the coast. On that sobering idea, the briefing broke up and the crews headed for their separate ready rooms to put on their flight gear and to get any last-minute details straight among the smaller parts of the strike.

The carrier steadied out on its launch and recovery course and ceased her heel to port. Santy always hated being parked close to the deck edge because the heel of the ship made him feel as if he and his jet were about to fall over the side, especially at night when sensations were magnified. The H-3 immediately to his left flicked on its anticollision lights and lifted ponderously into a fifteen-foot hover. The nose dipped and the green helicopter eased forward into flight. As soon as it crossed the deck edge, the wheels retracted and it began an easy turn to the left to arc around the stern into Star-D.

Santy's attention turned to the yellow-shirted taxi director positioned to the left of the nose of his Corsair. From up ahead on the bow, he could feel the roar from Catapult 1 as the first of the Phantoms came up on the power prior to launch. Above the huge retractable jet blast deflector (JBD) raised behind the Phantom, the thundering exhaust plume turned from greasy black to shimmering clear as the afterburners cut in, blasting pure heat from the tailpipes. The catapult officer touched the deck and the F-4 was hurled down the track and into the air. Before the first fighter had its wheels up, the second was at full power and about to go from Cat 2.

Aircraft after aircraft was blasted into the air from the controlled frenzy of the flight deck, the entire ship shuddering each time a catapult piston slammed into the waterbrake at the end of a stroke. Soon it was Santy's turn. He followed the director's hand signals, taxiing his A-7 to Cat 4, the port outboard catapult on the angled deck. Since this was the shortest of the four, the acceleration had to be stronger to get the jet up to the proper "end speed" so that it would safely remain airborne. More than one Navy aircraft had been lost because there had not been enough poop in the launch stroke.

He lowered the nose tow bar and eased the Corsair into position. The final checkers gave his aircraft a quick onceover, making sure all was well. When the "holdback," which kept the catapult from firing before everything was ready, was in place the director gave him the "in tension" sign and he went to full power. Gripping both the rigid "T-handle" pulled up from the left console and the throttle itself with his left hand to prevent the sudden acceleration from pulling his hand and the throttle, and therefore engine power, back. He gave the gauges one more look, ran the stick around the limits of its travel to make sure the controls responded properly, saluted the catapult officer, and placed his head back in the headrest.

The cat officer returned the salute and touched the deck with his hand. When he raised it, the greenshirt in the catwalk fired the cat. All Santy saw for about three seconds was the blur as the ship went by. At the end of those three seconds he was traveling at 160 knots.

Slapping the gear handle up, Santy made a quick clearing turn to the left to get away from the ship's course and to avoid being run over if something happened to the aircraft and he had to ditch or eject immediately after launch. It had once been carefully explained to him that the purpose of the turn was to avoid an "82,000-ton enema."

The climb-out and join-up went perfectly this afternoon. There had not been a single word spoken on the radios. There hadn't even been a peep from the fighters as they hit the airborne KA-6 and A-7 tankers to top off before going in over the beach. The silence was comforting because it meant that everybody was in good shape but it really didn't fool anyone since the ever-present Russian "trawler" which followed the carrier around had already transmitted the strike's takeoff time and the number and types of the aircraft to the Vietnamese defenders.

When CAG steadied out on course for the beach and began to climb to the coast-in altitude of 22,000 feet, the aircraft spread out wide enough to avoid two of them being shot down by the same SAM, and the pilots flipped the switches and pushed the buttons that armed the weapons systems, turning the strike into a deadly force rather than just a gaggle of airplanes. Santy checked his twice and then again. He had a fear of fighting his way in and finding out that he had missed a switch or something and was unable to do what he had come for.

Behind and slightly above the formation, the F-4 Phantom fighter escorts weaved back and forth trying to keep pace with the more heavily laden and slower attack jets. The escorts were assigned to the TARCAP, or target combat air patrol, whose job was to engage any of the North Vietnamese

Russian-built MiGs that might decide to come up and play. Out to the sides were two more sections of Phantoms carrying Mk-82s which would add their weight to the flak suppression effort. The whole formation was spread out over several square miles of sky.

As the coastline passed under the nose of CAG's A-6, he transmitted the "feet dry" message to the radar cruiser holding station fifty or so miles off the coast.

"Red Crown, Utah. Feet dry."

"Utah, this is Red Crown. Roger feet dry. Good luck." Expecting no further transmissions from the strike leader, the chief petty officer on the radar screen leaned forward in his chair and stared intently at the scope. His job now was to spot any MiGs taking off from the airfields around the area and warn Utah of the threat and then vector the TARCAP fighters to intercept. If somebody went down, he would steer the rescue assets to the scene. He fervently hoped that his next transmission would be simply to acknowledge the strike's "Feet wet" call.

CAG now began a gradual descent which would bring the strike to their roll-in points at 12,000 feet. This descent also allowed the aircraft to build up the speed and dynamic energy which would give them more maneuverability when the SAMs were launched at them. Without a word the Iron Hands broke away, accelerating ahead to take out their assigned sites before the main force arrived.

Santy realized with a start that he was concentrating more on keeping station in the formation than he was with looking out for the threat from the ground. He took deep even breaths of oxygen from his mask to keep himself calm and scanned the ground far below for the telltale dust cloud that would mark a SAM launch. So far, there hadn't been any of the frightening high-pitched tones in his earphones which would alert him that the SAM guidance radars were emitting. But the NVA missileers had become cagey lately. They knew that prolonged emissions from their radars on the guidance frequencies would invite a visit from the Iron Hands, so they would track the aircraft and only take little peeks with the guidance systems. Given the warning they had of the Americans' approach, and the predictability of the incoming attacks, a quick look was usually all that was needed to get a good lock-on.

"Utah 1, Live Oak 212, recommend primary target." The Iron Hands felt that the antiaircraft defenses didn't warrant the full weight of the strike.

"Utah 1, roger. Utah flight, this is lead. Go for the power plant."

As the strike split up to come in from the three assigned headings, thus splitting up the defenses, the threat receivers suddenly began to give off their warnings. The radios immediately came alive with chatter as the pilots spotted the SAMs coming up. The Vietnamese had waited just long enough to throw off the reasonably delicate timing of the strike before they let fly with everything they had.

"500, SAM at your two o'clock. Break! Break!"

"Okay, Hog, I got it."

"Utah lead's in. Watch the Triple-A on the ridge north."

"103's got the Triple-A, CAG. I'm in on it."

Santy followed his division lead in an arc around the target, spacing himself so as to follow his run by about ten seconds. The flak was heavier to the north and he hadn't seen any missiles yet so it wasn't too bad where he was but the white, light gray, and black puffs of smoke all over the sky were still plenty dangerous. When he reached the roll-in point he pulled the stick into the left rear corner, rolling 120 degrees and pushing the nose down, holding it until his Corsair was pointed at the target in a 45-degree dive then rolling the wings level. His "310's in" was buried among the dozens of other transmissions.

When the green symbology on his heads-up-display, or HUD, was right and he was passing through 4,500 feet, he released his bombs. As soon as they were gone, he hauled back on the stick and slammed the throttle forward, reaching nearly five "G's" before his nose was pointed back up into the clear blue sky and he was through the barrage fire from the light-caliber antiaircraft guns. Climbing at a 60-degree angle, he jinked a bit and, passing through 15,000 feet, he glanced over his shoulder to see how the target looked.

The black smoke from the bombs was mixing nicely with escaping steam from something in the power plant. Momentarily distracted, he was brought back to reality by a call from his wingman climbing out below and behind him.

"Sandman, SAM at your three o'clock! Watch out!"

Santy rolled his A-7 and looked down and right. The SAM was still in the first five-second boost phase of its flight which meant that he could pick out the bright white flame of the motor. His wingman, Lt. (J.G.) "Snake" Mitchell, must have seen it leave the launcher. His quickness and sharp eyesight probably saved Santy's life.

As in most things in life, timing is everything. Santy had to wait until the proper moment to make his move. Too soon and the missile would be able to follow his maneuver; too late and he wouldn't be able to escape the kill zone of the missile's warhead. The maneuver had to be done in two planes, the horizontal and the vertical. Santy timed it perfectly. He would trade his altitude for safety.

He hauled hard back and right on the stick, bringing his Corsair into a right barrel roll and ending up in a screaming dive as the SAM roared by, going ballistic, unguided and unpowered, when it found no target, finally exploding high above. He frantically scanned for the second SAM which they usually fired in the hopes that a pilot would fail to spot it while dueling with the first. He couldn't find one and continued his dive to get as low as he could, heading for the water. His wingman joined him and together they hauled ass for the coast. Behind them the radio calls gradually diminished as almost everybody else got away from the target.

The two jets were within sight of the coast when they heard a Mayday from one of the Phantoms which had been assigned flak supression.

"Mayday, Mayday! This is Starfighter 106. 103 is down 36 miles bearing 126 from the target. One good chute."

That position was slightly south of where the two escaping

Corsairs were. Looking right, Santy saw a large fireball just off the coast as the abandoned F-4 went in. He checked his fuel and, seeing that he had a reasonable amount left, called the remaining Phantom, which he could see orbiting high above the area where Starfighter 103 had gone in.

"Starfighter, Condor 310. Have you in sight. Switch Button 19."

Reaching down and rocking the switch six clicks, Santy got on the frequency just as the Phantom was calling him.

"Condor, Starfighter. It looks like only the backseater got out. I didn't see another chute. The front looked pretty badly damaged. Maybe the pilot passed out or something. The chute came down in that little harbor over there."

"Roger, Condor copies. Say your state, Starfighter."

"I got, umm, 4.2. Can you provide RESCAP? I have to go find a tanker now. I'll get Red Crown on it."

"Okay, Starfighter, we're RESCAP. I have the raft in sight. Making a pass now. Snake, you stay high."

"Roger, Mike. I'll orbit out over the water."

Santy examined the small harbor. It was really just a deep indentation on the coast with two low breakwaters extending out from the land on either side, north and south, and angling together to form the shelter. There was a gap of about seventy-five yards between the two tips forming the harbor entrance. It looked like a sleepy little place with nothing nearby but a couple of villages and the river mouth just to the north.

Santy rolled in, adjusting his flight path to pass just to the ocean side of the aviator floating in his raft. No sooner had he leveled out, low and relatively slow, concentrating on the survivor, who was waving both arms madly over his head, than several streams of tracer fire reached for him from the shoreline. Santy didn't know which had gotten his attention first, the tracer or Mitchell's radio warning.

"Shit! Mike, watch out! They're hosing you!"

Santy slammed the stick hard left and the throttle forward. Headed out to sea, he climbed up to an orbit where he could keep an eye on the guy in the raft and still be out of range of the guns on the ground. None of the stuff that came up at him was heavy caliber and there didn't seem to be anything down there worth defending but, on the other hand, the Vietnamese had weapons everywhere and seemed to love to shoot at anybody flying over. He called Snake and told him to set up an orbit on the opposite side of the circle so one of them would always be in a position to roll in and strafe any boat that came after the Phantom crewman. That was twice today that Mitchell had saved his ass. He owed the lad some serious booze.

"Snake, say your state. How are you fixed for ammo?"

"I've got about twenty minutes to stay here with and I've got a full load for the gun."

"Roger, me too. Be sure to select Gun Low." Santy was telling him to remember to select the slower rate of fire for the 20mm gun the A-7 had aboard. The higher rate of fire was for air-to-air fighting where filling a block of sky with "max BBs" was the way to go. Strafing or air-to-ground shooting usually required fewer rounds to do the job. It also meant that the supply they carried would be depleted more slowly.

"Red Crown, this is Condor 310. We have a survivor down in a small harbor just south of where the river empties out. He appears to be in good shape. There's a lot of small Triple-A along the shore but nothing big yet. We can stay on station for another twenty minutes, more if there is a tanker handy. All we have is 20-millimeter. Request relief."

The chief aboard the cruiser who had been monitoring the strike-and-rescue frequencies and was frantically making calls on other frequencies, was pretty much doing as the Condor pilot had requested. Deep within him lurked a feeling that this was going to be a bad one. He had never been able to put that feeling into words but he couldn't remember its being wrong. He reached for a cigarette with one hand, and the buzzer to summon the watch officer with the other.

"Condor 310, this is Red Crown. Copy your situation. Stand by."

Chapter 7

August 26, 1972

Angel 801, from the home detachment aboard *Concord,* was orbiting off the coast when the call came from Red Crown. The pilots, Lt. Bill Lenehan and Lt. Ted Martinez, and the crewmen, Petty Officers Jesse Ball and Tom Peterson, immediately left their station and headed at top speed for the scene. The forty miles would take them twenty-five minutes. As they prepared the helo for rescue, Martinez requested Red Crown to launch the backup helicopter, Angel 802, standing by on fifteen-minute alert back aboard the *Galveston,* steaming on North SAR. Another SAR situation might develop and it would be good to have a second helo handy.

Back aboard the *Galveston,* the pilots of Angel 802, Watkins and Boyle, were watching the mission over the shoulders of the radar operators down in CIC, the ship's Combat Information Center. They were also listening in on the mission frequency, using a couple of spare headsets. Whenever they were not actually flying the airborne SAR, Watkins would take Boyle down there and have him watch the action. As it took place, the HAC would explain the little things that attended the strike. Boyle thus came to be as familiar with as many facets of tactical jet aviation as was possible without actually flying it. Watkins also insisted that Boyle study the manuals for every aircraft flying missions from the carriers, manuals which had inexplicably turned up missing from Ready Rooms all over the various carriers. He was not expected to memorize any of it but he had to at least know the varying degrees of seriousness for the different emergencies the jets could suffer. Complete and unhesitating knowledge of the H-3 and its mission was a given. Watkins's theory, repeated over and over to Boyle was: "What you know will never hurt you; what you don't know will kill you or kill somebody else." It was a theory which Watkins, at thirty-three, had seen proven over and over.

When the call came from Red Crown, the two dropped their headsets on the console and headed aft to man their aircraft. The crew hustled up from the mess decks where they'd been in the midst of an excellent poker game, using the coins on the table only to keep score, of course.

Within ten minutes, the ship had turned to get the proper winds over the tiny deck and the helo crew were airborne, being vectored to their station by the same controllers they had just been watching.

From the *Concord,* two A-7 Corsairs from VA-187, loaded with all sorts of weapons for close air support, roared off to relieve the two Condor A-7s as RESCAP. Flown by the C.O. and the squadron operations officer, they had been waiting on five minute alert status for just such a call.

As they climbed, passing 10,000 feet, they checked in with Red Crown.

"Red Crown, this is Cobra 404, flight of two. Wingman is 409. Airborne to you for RESCAP. We'll have one plus four-five on station. That's one hour forty-five minutes."

"Roger, Cobras, your pigeons 235 at 124 miles. Switch button nineteen contact on-scene commander, Condor 310, for sitrep. How copy, over?"

"Cobras copy all. Switching."

Commander Nick Finney, in Cobra 404, eased into a gentle left turn and steadied out on a heading of 235 degrees, figuring that he ought to be arriving in about fifteen minutes. He looked at his wingman and gave him the hand signal to switch frequencies.

"Two," was all 409 said when he came up on the new frequency.

Finney listened for a second to make sure he wouldn't be breaking into somebody's transmission and called Santy: "Condor 310, Cobra 404. Inbound to you for RESCAP. Request sitrep."

"Stand by."

Santy and Mitchell were completing their third orbit when the Starfighter RIO finally came up on the rescue frequency using his hand-held survival radio. The fact that no one had heard his emergency locater beeper nor heard him call on the survival radio had become a concern. Hearing his voice at least let everyone know that he was in possession of some of his faculties.

"A-7 orbiting Song Kiem. This is Starfighter 103. How do you read? Over."

"103, this is Condor 310. We're on top. The Angel is inbound. Say your name and condition."

"I'm okay, Condor. My name's Hurst, Donald J. I don't think my pilot got out. They hosed us right when we came off the target. He said he was hurt but I didn't know how bad. Maybe his seat didn't work. I had the handle in the right position. Did you see anything?"

Santy realized from the increasingly shrill tone that Hurst was justifiably scared and had the adrenaline pumps going full bore. Santy had to calm him down if this rescue was going to work.

"Okay, Starfighter. Take it easy, pal. Understand only one for pickup. Suggest you stay off your radio as much as possible to conserve power on the battery. We've got some more Corsairs coming to cover you. The gomers can't get to you without exposing themselves so if you stay right there you'll be okay. If you see anything let us know."

"Roger that, Condor. I can see what look like boats and piers over to the south under the trees but that's all." He paused and continued in lower tones. "Thanks, three-ten. I was a little shook, I guess. My seat pack radio didn't work and I had to use my backup. Worried me some."

Santy answered in the pilot's universal acknowledgment by clicking the radio transmit switch twice: "Click-click."

While all this was going on, Mitchell thought he saw a couple of small boats leave a pier near a group of low buildings on the north shore. On the next orbit, he was sure of it.

"Sandman, I've got a couple of boat loads coming out into the harbor. I'm in on 'em."

Mitchell rolled his Corsair over and dove at the lead boat. Passing through 4,500 feet he lined the pipper on his HUD up with the bow and fired a short burst. The splashes began just short of the boat and within a millisecond the entire craft disappeared among fifteen-foot geysers of white water. When the water fell back, all that was left was little bits of boat, some briefly flaming, and a small red stain that quickly faded into the foam. The other boat turned tail and headed back for shore as fast as its one-lung motor would take it. A couple of streams of tracer followed Mitchell back up, falling far behind and ending as soon as the gunners realized that there was no chance of harming the jet.

"That ought to hold the little fuckers a while, Snake. Nice shooting," said Santy.

From Hurst's vantage, the show was sobering. When Mitchell announced the commencement of his strafing run, Hurst had whipped around in his raft and spotted the boats about seven hundred yards away. The crews in them were small and pretty distant but still they were distinctly people.

He had never seen anyone actually killed before. Warfare from a jet aviator's point of view is mostly inanimate. You fight it out with another machine or drop bombs on something that looks like the model train layout you had as a kid. Unless you are shot down, you never get to see what your weapons do. A bridge may collapse, a bunch of trucks may explode all over the road, or the secondary explosions from an ammo dump may wipe out the village next door, but those are just *things*. Your heart can be in your throat from time to time when the missiles and gunfire seem to be directed at your aircraft but the guys on the ground are shooting at a bunch of aircraft, not yours particularly. If you get nailed it is just bad luck or, in a few cases, your own stupidity. It's really a very clean and neat way to fight a war. No less deadly than any of the others, but neat and clean.

Santy was trying to figure out exactly how this operation was going to have to work when he got the call from the Cobra.

"Condor 310, Cobra 404. Inbound to you for RESCAP. Request sitrep."

"Stand by."

Santy finished what he was doing and called the Cobra back.

"Cobra 404, this is Condor 310. Sitrep follows. We have a single survivor down in the harbor on the west bank of the Song Kiem where the river hooks south about one mile from where it enters the gulf. The harbor is about a mile and a half square. How copy so far?"

"404, copy all."

"Continuing. There are some light Triple-A sites along the shoreline. Looks like 23-millimeter. We haven't seen anything heavier. No SAMs so far and no tones on the threat receivers. There are some boats along the shore but we can't tell if they are military or just fishermen out for the reward. We chased a couple away, sinking one. How copy?"

"404 copies."

"Okay. We can't get the helo in there until we take out the guns. The survivor is in the middle of the harbor so he's pretty safe for now. All we have is twenty-millimeter so when you get here we'll make a couple of runs and draw some fire. You can take out the sites. We're anchored at angels seven at the river mouth."

"Roger, 310. We're at angels sixteen, estimating four minutes." Finney looked over at his wingman. "Arm 'em up, Two."

Lt. Cmdr. "Jackie" Robinson, in 409, hit all the arming switches and spread out to about 200 yards from his leader's wing. Looking ahead, he could see the coastline becoming more distinct. The little river called Song Kiem trailed off to the west toward the higher terrain. He spotted the two Condor A-7s in their wagonwheel just out of range of the Vietnamese gunners.

Finney spotted them at the same time. His assessment of the area was that it should be reasonably benign. There were two large roads leading to the harbor and not much else other than a small village about a half-mile south of the harbor and another about a mile to the north.

"Okay, 310, Cobras have you in sight. We'll join the circle. Go ahead and start your run."

"Roger, 310's in."

Santy rolled in and aimed at the area where two of the streams of gunfire had come from. He lined up the pipper and fired a burst into the trees. It was as if he had lit a match in a fireworks store. His airplane was slammed from side to side as every kind of gun he had ever seen opened up on him. Black, gray, and white bursts of smoke were everywhere intermixed with at least eight streams of tracer.

"Sonofabitch! Condor, get outa there!" shouted Finney over the radio.

Santy broke hard right and down and hauled ass as fast as he could get his airplane to fly. As he did he flew directly over Hurst, floating easily in his raft, missing him by what seemed to Hurst to be mere inches.

Mitchell had been just about to roll in when he saw the "shit storm" Santy had flown into. He yanked his Corsair back up and took off to check Santy out.

"Mike, you okay?"

"Yeah, I think so. Stand by." Santy took a few seconds to scan his gauges, hoping that his hands would quit shaking soon. Jesus Christ, that was close, he thought. Several deep gulps of oxygen later, he convinced himself that he was indeed still alive and flying an intact A-7.

Mitchell joined to port and checked him over then slid gently under to the right side. "Looks like you're okay, Mike, no damage that I can see. You want to tell me again how much you like flying RESCAP?"

Santy almost smiled at Mitchell's question. Instead, he called Finney.

"404, Condor. This is going to take more firepower than we've got. That's nothing but a flak trap down there. How long can you stay on station?"

Finney did a quick calculation. If he didn't have to do a lot of hard flying he could stretch it to an hour and thirty minutes. Just the presence of the two A-7s should keep the Vietnamese from trying to get at Hurst. With sunset at about eight o'clock, there were still about six hours of daylight left so if they got some help they ought to be able to pull this off.

"We've got about one plus three zero left on station. Head on back. We'll coordinate with Red Crown to get some help."

Santy turned out to sea and after checking out with Red Crown, switched off the frequency.

Back aboard the *Concord,* Admiral Welch had been listening in to the transmissions from the scene. The original strike was now landing back aboard and the jets were taxiing forward and being parked on the bow. There were not a lot of them that could be turned around, fueled and rearmed quickly enough to arrive at the SAR scene in time to keep continuous coverage over Hurst. Several had battle damage which would take time to repair. Several more had had systems problems, which would be simpler to fix but still would take time. On the plus side, only one aircraft, Starfighter 103, would not return. The problem was that the situation required a lot of aircraft in the air over the scene continuously but the aircraft had only limited time before they had to be brought back for more fuel and ordnance.

There were rules and procedures which had long been proven effective in dealing with most of the situations which cropped up in fighting an air war. Unfortunately, those rules and procedures could become a hindrance when the situation was not one covered by the book.

Welch ran his hand over his face, feeling the oiliness left after the heat of the day had broken through the air conditioning of Flag Bridge. He looked out over the flight deck and watched the crew directing the jets to the bow after they landed. You have a choice, James my boy, he thought. You can play it safe and by the rules or you can do what *needs* to be done.

He sighed as he made his decision. You're getting too old for this shit.

Welch turned to his aide. "Kevin, have CAG report to me as soon as he shuts down. No detours. We have a problem."

Thompson hustled out, throwing a "Yessir" over his shoulder. He had seen that look on his boss's face a few times before. He was planning something and it looked like one of his I-don't-give-a-shit-about-why-you-can't-just-get-it-done! plans. Thompson loved it when things went that way. That's how his beloved SEALs operated and he missed that attitude.

Welch called down to the ship's bridge, using the "bitch box," the intercom system that connected important parts of the ship with each other.

One deck straight down, Andrews heard the intercom and answered, "Bridge Captain Andrews speaking."

"Sam, this is Welch. Come up here, please. We are going to have to get creative about this SAR effort."

"On the way, Admiral." Andrews released the switch and, turning control of the ship over to the officer of the deck, walked out. He didn't even hear the traditional "Captain's off the Bridge" announcement.

When Andrews entered Flag Bridge, he found Welch bent over a chart of the area that Hurst was down in. Next to him were several of his staff officers and, judging from the hubbub, there was not a lot of agreement about something. They were all consulting clipboards or pointing at the chart with pencils. Welch himself seemed to be ignoring the noise and concentrating on his own thoughts. From long experience, Andrews knew that Welch had made a decision and was allowing the staff to feel involved in it.

"You sent for me, sir," Andrews said quietly, standing just behind Welch.

"Yeah. Hello, Sam," the admiral said, turning away from the table. "We are going to have to send some more RESCAP out to help those two A-7s we have on top. I've told Red Crown to pass to them that they are not to take any action for now unless the Vietnamese try to do something to our boy in the water. Last we heard, he was okay except he was pissed at the A-7 that flew over him getting away from the guns. Made him dive out of his raft. He really had some unkind things to say about attack pilots. You probably heard all that but I'm just getting my mind going telling you about it."

"Yes, sir."

"Okay. The way the deck looks it will be at least forty-five minutes before we can get a lot of aircraft back in the air loaded and ready to go. We do have the two Condor A-7s headed back here so I suggest that we rearm and refuel them immediately and send them straight back out. We can do that right back there on the angle behind the catapults. Meanwhile, tell the squadrons to load up everything that will fly. Get 'em ready to go. Oh, and I've also told the *Galveston* to steam in closer to the scene at best speed in case the helos run low on fuel. What do you think?"

Andrews let out a long breath before answering. "I guess we don't have any choice. What does the Cobra lead have to say?"

"He feels that they may be able to get a helo in there for a real quick pickup if he gets a couple more airplanes to suppress the flak. He's the on-scene commander so I told him to use his best judgment but not to try anything until we got some help out there. The amount of fire they've run into has me worried. If there is that much flak around, the bastards are up to something. I just hope we're not sending those boys into something that's over their heads."

Andrews nodded. He hadn't thought of the situation in

terms that large. What had been a relatively straightforward problem was beginning to look like it might get out of hand.

"All right, Admiral. We'll get it done. May I suggest, though, that we not launch everybody on the first go. If we stagger the aircraft, we can constantly keep cover over the scene and not risk it all on a one-shot try."

The admiral nodded, grateful that Andrews had once again put a small brake on his enthusiasm. Welch knew that he sometimes got caught up in the moment and tended to act without looking at all the little things. Andrews had often almost jokingly told him that he should have been born in time to have ridden with Stuart's cavalry.

He started to thank Andrews but spotted CAG entering the bridge, still loosening his sweaty flight gear. Welch gestured for him to come over to the chart table. The staff officers stepped back and made room for him.

"CAG, you're aware of the problem we have getting more RESCAP out to the scene what with the strike just coming back aboard." At CAG's nod he continued, outlining the whole plan for him.

When the admiral was finished, CAG had only one question, dealing with the Condor A-7s. "Sir, do you mean that we are going to rearm and refuel those two with the engines running? That's prohibited since the fires on *Enterprise* and *Forrestal*. Besides, we can get a couple of more experienced pilots in there if we shut 'em down."

"CAG, I know it's against the rules but this is one of those 'operational necessity' times. I'm authorizing you and Captain Andrews to do it that way. Just make sure that they are well grounded. We don't need any stray electrons screwing it up. You said 'more experienced' pilots. Who's flying those A-7s?"

"Santy and Mitchell, Admiral. They're both first-tour jaygees."

CAG misunderstood the admiral's expression. "I'll get a couple of other pilots. It shouldn't take that long. . . ."

"No, you will not. Those two are familiar with the area and have seen the Triple-A firsthand. We'd have to get them to brief the new guys, which would take time that we don't have. When they land, load them up and launch them. Questions? Anyone?"

CAG moved away to a telephone and began issuing the orders which would put the plan into action. He hung up and left. The others on the Flag Bridge moved away, attending to their chores.

Welch looked at Andrews and, beaming, said, "A couple of nugget jaygees! How about that, Sam? I would have figured them for some old hands the way they are handling that problem. I wouldn't take this mission away from them if it was Nixon's own ass down in that harbor."

He pounded on the chart table in punctuation. "And you make goddamn sure, Sam, that their skipper hears about what I think. You tell him that you are proud of them, too. Okay? Man! That's great. Nuggets!"

Chapter 8

August 26, 1972

Boyle and Watkins arrived offshore from Song Kiem less than five minutes after Santy and Mitchell departed. Since they were only the backup, they didn't confuse the issue by asking for a full briefing over the main rescue frequency. Once they had joined the orbit with Angel 801, they both switched to their squadron common frequency to discuss the situation. Angel 801, as the primary helo, gave 802 a brief account of what had happened so far and what RESCAP aircraft were on the way to help. The 801 pilots had decided to make their approach down the coast rather than directly from seaward. They felt that that might give them a small edge, as opposed to being in full view of the gunners on the ground throughout the entire approach, as they would be if they flew straight in.

Watkins agreed and offered to be a decoy, coming straight in and keeping the Vietnamese's attention. If they both timed it right, Watkins and Boyle would break off just out of range at the same time 801 arrived at the harbor mouth. All this would happen while the RESCAPs were keeping the gunners as busy as possible.

The problem with taking a helicopter into a situation like this is that the advantages all lie with the other side. You have neither altitude, nor speed, nor armor worth a damn. You have to hover, at least briefly, in one very predictable spot at low altitude. The gunners know exactly where the helo has to be to accomplish its mission. All they have to do is train their guns and wait and when the helo comes chugging over the horizon, pull the trigger. The ocean offers very little cover.

Lenehan and Martinez, in 801, knew all this very well. Both of them were on their second tour in Vietnam. They had begun flying rescue missions in the single-engine H-2 helicopter which had the reputation, deserved or not, of killing more airmen than it saved. This meant that they were survivors.

Perhaps because this was happening near the sea, where naval aviators are most comfortable, or perhaps because the two pilots were more confident of their own abilities than they were respectful of those of the Vietnamese, their plan set them up for disaster.

To keep himself busy, Boyle had double-checked that the checklists were complete and then consulted the charts which Watkins insisted that he update daily with the latest intelligence reports sent over from the carrier. Looking carefully at them, Boyle could find absolutely no reason for there to be as much antiaircraft weaponry around that pissant little harbor as the A-7s had run into. The two of them had overheard much of the radio chatter on the way in and were completely surprised by the sudden change in everyone's tone when Santy had attempted his second run.

Boyle was certain that he had recognized Mike's voice in there and the few moments before he said that he was okay had seemed like hours. He was more than glad that Santy was on the way home and out of this one.

The two Condors came up the wake at 600 feet and broke off at the bow, circling to land over the fantail. Since there were no other aircraft in the landing pattern, they both came in and trapped without problems. Just before Santy turned final, the Air Boss came up on the radio and told him not to shut down on landing, but to taxi clear and stand by.

Once out of the wires and clear of the landing area, Santy watched Mitchell catch the number-three wire and come to a roaring halt. Mitchell raised his tail hook and, looking over at his lead, lifted his hands in a what's-going-on? gesture. Santy shook his head and, with Mitchell trailing close behind, followed his taxi director's signals back down the deck to an area just behind the waist catapults.

Sailors wearing all sorts of colored jerseys swarmed around the two Corsairs. Purple shirts dragged out fuel hoses, green shirts opened the inspection panels, brown shirts attached tie-down chains to the aircraft. Off to the right several ordnance-men in red pushed loaded bomb dollies under the wings and hauled over heavy ammunition cannisters for the guns. While he was looking around for the squadron's flight-deck maintenance chief for an indication of what he was supposed to be doing, a voice crackled in Santy's earphones, using the admiral's personal call sign. Looking up at Flag Bridge, the young pilot could see a group of faces peering down at him from behind the armored glass.

"Three-ten, this is Buccaneer. Don't transmit with all that ordnance around you. Give me a thumbs-up to acknowledge."

Santy craned around to see if Mitchell was hearing this also. He was answered by a huge grin and a quick nod. He raised his hand outside the open canopy and gave the sign to the admiral. The voice began again instantly.

"Roger. We're sending you two back out there. Cobra 404 thinks that the four of you can keep the gomers' heads down long enough for the helo to run in and make a quick snatch. We're loading you up with Rockeyes and giving you a full bag of gas. We will be sending some more aircraft out as soon as we can turn them around in case the first try doesn't work."

Santy was pleased that somebody on the ship was thinking. The Rockeye cluster bomb units (CBUs) that he was getting were the perfect weapon for taking out "soft" targets like flak sites. They burst over the ground sending out large numbers of baseball-sized bomblets which explode on contact. They have the effect of hitting an area with a gigantic shotgun.

The admiral continued, "Excellent work out there, 310. Keep it up. Good luck. Buccaneer out."

Looking around the flight deck, Santy could see that it was an even bigger madhouse than normal. Everything and everybody was in motion. He thought of Boyle and was damned glad that it wasn't his helo out there waiting to go in. Angel 801 was from the detachment aboard *Concord*.

While all this was happening up on the flight deck, Cmdr. Wilson, C.O. of Santy's squadron, stormed into CAG's office and demanded to know why the two nuggets were being sent right back out.

"CAG, those two kids up there are first-tour types. This probably is going to require pilots a lot more experienced than they are. We can swap them out with other guys really quick and we can do it without slowing things down much at all."

Greenwood looked up at the diminutive C.O. "Jack, who do you have ready to go?"

"The X.O. and Ted Bowles, the Ops officer, are next in the barrel and there are several others getting briefed right now. The others can go as soon as we get some jets turned around and ready."

Greenwood was surprised and relieved by Wilson's answer. Since he had taken command of Air Wing 33 three months ago, Greenwood and Wilson had not exactly become bosom buddies. Wilson's leadership style seemed far too autocratic for Greenwood's tastes and the younger man had sometimes seemed resistant to CAG's policies. Greenwood had never been able to put Wilson in the proper pigeonhole: his responses to things were not predictable, as were those of the other squadron C.O.'s in the air wing. Greenwood hated confusion and uncertainty; they upset his easy, calm, and laidback, albeit remarkably effective, approach to his job and life in general.

He had expected Wilson to tell him that the next pilot to

be ready was Wilson himself, which would indicate a glory-hunting attitude which, in turn, would finally tell CAG all he needed to know about Wilson as a commander of men. The fact that Wilson was planning to send the men from his squadron out fairly, according to some policy of rotation, threw one of his preconceptions out the window.

Greenwood looked at Wilson, who was doing his best, at five feet six inches, to loom over his seated CAG.

"Jack, the admiral himself is driving this one and I agree totally with his decisions. Your two young tigers have performed beautifully so far today. It is quicker and more effective to have guys familiar with the situation and the area out there first. Finney believes it can all be over if he can get some firepower on the area before the gomers can really get organized. If that doesn't work, we will have a major fight on our hands and we might lose some people retrieving Hurst, if we can do it at all. What I need from you and your men is the fastest and most effective flight-deck work you've ever done. Okay?"

"Yes, sir. It's just that I think those two might be overmatched in this one. I have a bad feeling about that place. It shouldn't be as heavily defended as it is."

Greenwood was surprised again by Wilson's answer. He hadn't before shown himself to be the type who would be that concerned for his men and this last answer now made Greenwood certain that he had been a tad hasty in his judgment of the man.

"Sit down, Jack. I have a couple of things that are bothering me and now is as good a time as any to clear them up."

Wilson sat down in the leather chair opposite the desk and pulled out a cigarette. Greenwood waited until he had lit up, and then leaned back and put his feet on the desk. This was his "put 'em at ease" pose. He wanted honesty from Wilson, not the party line.

"I'm curious about some things you've been doing with your squadron, Jack. Do you mind if I ask you a question or two?"

"No, sir." Wilson had no idea what was with CAG, discussing his squadron in the middle of the present situation. But he was the boss. "Go ahead."

"Okay. You are really hard on the people in your squadron. You drive your J.O.'s as hard as you can and you seem to demand that they always give just a little more. You are notorious for riding them about their landing grades and their paperwork. You come on like Hitler in khakis. Yet you walk in here and act like you're trying to protect them from something that it's their job to face. I don't understand. Explain it to me. What's with you?"

Wilson looked Greenwood right in the eye, his expression hard. There was no hint of a smile to match CAG's open look. He began to speak in an even but firm voice.

"CAG, it is not my job to be the fucking Sun King. I don't give a rat's ass whether they want to run me for president or throw me overboard. What I do care about is that I take as many of them home alive as I can. But that's not completely up to me. We have a whole country full of people over there whose job it is to make sure that I take as *few* home as possible. And we have the help of our own beloved government, which seems to think sometimes that public opinion is more important than the lives of its citizens."

Wilson stood and began slowly pacing the room.

"Now, for me to get those people home I have to teach them as much as I can as fast as I can. They have to learn a whole lot of things which aren't in the book or the syllabus or the goddamned programmed text.

"The Navy decided that they wanted me to be a C.O. but never bothered to lay out any leadership style that I have to use. Okay, fine. In that case, I'll use whatever style I see fit. Whatever style is most comfortable for me and which I think is the most effective.

"I don't want to be their best pal or nice old uncle. I have a responsibility to my men and *how* I perform that responsibility is *my* business until *I* fuck it up. Then, as my immediate superior in command, it will become *your* business and you can relieve my ass and get somebody else. But until that day, I will push those men and give them as much experience and knowledge as I can about how to be the best naval aviators and officers using whatever method I think most effective.

"Now, the reason I am concerned about those two young guys is that I do not want the system or the Navy to get them killed because they happened to be in a situation that they were not ready for. This time, it looks like circumstance wins. They're out there and they'll have to hack it. They're good enough. I just hope they're lucky enough."

Greenwood, nodding, was silent a moment. Wilson was absolutely right in everything he said. He realized that he really liked and admired the little C.O. all of a sudden. Even though he disagreed with Wilson's style, he had to admit that it was working. The performance of his squadron not only today but every day since Greenwood had taken over the air wing was one of the two best he had seen. Wilson was also right in that it was not CAG's job to meddle in the squadron until Wilson fucked it up.

"Have you explained this to your J.O.'s, Jack? They might go along easier if you did."

"When they come to me individually and bitch about it, I do explain but not until then. That's another lesson. So far, only Santy has come forward. He didn't agree with me but he understands and our relationship is better for it. He'll be the best J.O. in the squadron if he'll settle down and keep his temper. But then, he's Dave Santy's son."

Greenwood made the connection. He'd never met the elder Santy but certainly had heard of him.

"Did you know Dave Santy, Jack?"

Wilson raised his chin proudly, almost defiantly. "Damned right I did. He was my first C.O. I can honestly say that he taught me most of what I know about flying and about leadership. He was the best."

Wilson turned and walked out of CAG Office and headed back to the ready room to organize the squadron for the rest of this rescue effort.

Before Santy passed 5,000 feet, Mitchell joined him in a loose cruise formation to starboard. His Corsair looked like pure menace hanging out there with its nose cocked up and all the bombs hanging from the wings. Santy knew that his own Corsair looked exactly the same and that gave him a strange feeling of pride. After watching the frantic pace of the hundreds of men and dozens of aircraft rushing around on the flight deck of the *Concord,* it felt good to be the first to go into this battle, however small its significance in the grand scheme. In a way, it was *his* battle. He had been there when it started and now, if things went as it appeared they were going to, he would be there at the finish.

There was also a feeling of nobility about this one, instead of just dropping a load of bombs on a target that, like as not, would be repaired and back in operation before the week was out. Here, there was a purpose, a finite, attainable goal: getting one man out, saving him from imprisonment and, possibly, torture and death. He smiled a little at the realization that his thoughts sounded a lot like Tim Boyle's explanation of his reasons for flying SAR, given quietly and passionately one night long ago, on a beach in San Diego when Meghan was trying to understand why anyone would want to fly in a war when his draft number was 326.

Getting back to the business at hand, Santy gave Mitchell the hand signal to switch frequencies back to the rescue mission.

"Cobra 404, this is Condor 310. We're back with you for RESCAP. We've got full loads of CBUs and fuel for two hours on station. We're up for your control."

Finney answered immediately. "Ah, roger, Condors, welcome back. Request you join the circle and space yourselves at ninety-degree positions."

Finney and Robinson had been flying on opposite sides of the circle offset to seaward from Hurst. Now, with the addition of two more aircraft, there would always be two sets of eyes on the scene and an aircraft in a position to roll in immediately on anyone venturing out into the harbor.

It was obvious to the Americans that the Vietnamese figured that they could capture Hurst as soon as it got dark and that they simply had to keep the helicopter away from him and he would be theirs for the taking. That they also stood an excellent chance of shooting down another two or three airplanes was a bonus. Since it cost about one million dollars to put a pilot in each of these aircraft, over and above the cost of the aircraft itself, it could be an expensive afternoon for the Americans.

The Vietnamese were well aware that they themselves were going to pay a rather heavy price for their victory. But gunners were easy to come by; all they had to do was put a levy on the nearby population for a few dozen more Heroes of the Revolution. Replacement weapons were more expensive, in that they actually had to be paid for. But they were still readily available from their Russian and Chinese pals. After all, the ports of North Vietnam were full of Communist Bloc shipping waiting for pierside space to unload.

Taking one more orbit and looking at the scene from all angles, Finney thought over the plan again. He couldn't think of anything to add to it. Now was as good a time to start as any.

"Angel 801, 404, when you are in position, we will begin flak suppression. Wait for our call then start your run. Starfighter, do you copy?"

After the excitement of his ejection, the initial stages of his rescue operation, and his hasty dive overboard when Santy had blown by directly overhead getting away from the Triple-A, Hurst's confidence was rapidly diminishing. He was occasionally shivering in a postadrenaline reaction. He knew that the guys from his air wing were doing all they could to get him out as fast as possible. He had been allowing himself to get into the "Yeah-but-what-if-they-can't?" hole mentally. Any sort of action was welcome instead of the waiting, worrying about the worst. He double-checked that all his gear was ready and that his pistol was loaded with tracer ammunition to show the helo exactly where he was. He picked up his little survival radio and told the guys upstairs that he was as ready as he was going to get.

"Condor 404, this is Angel 801. We're in position to the

south. Angel 802 is going to be the decoy. He'll be approaching from the east. We'll come up the coast right on the deck. We'll commence on your call. And, Starfighter, don't abandon your raft until we tell you to."

Finney heard Hurst acknowledge the helo's direction and said, "404's commencing. RESCAP follow as briefed."

Santy watched as 404 rolled in on an area Finney had picked out when the flak had come up and surprised everybody earlier. As 404 passed through 8,000 feet, seemingly millions of bursts of smoke appeared all over the place. Finney continued his run, releasing two cluster bombs and yanking his Corsair back up toward the relative safety of the sky. The bombs burst, scattering their smaller bomblets all over several of the camouflaged sites, killing exposed gunners and setting off secondary explosions among the ready ammunition stored near the guns. The other three aircraft picked their targets, performing a sort of mental prioritization.

Each aircraft dove, scattering explosives all over the guns, pulling four or five "Gs" as they screamed back up to start another run. They varied the angles from which they attacked, trying to be as unpredictable as possible, not giving the gunners a chance to load up any particular sector of the sky with chunks of metal from the exploding flak in the hope that an A-7 would fly through it. There was a gradual lessening of the flak as several sites were damaged or wiped out completely and others ran out of ready ammunition and had to be resupplied from the below-ground bunkers situated some distance from the guns.

Finney soon judged that the helo had a good chance of making the pickup since he and the other three pilots were more than keeping the gunners occupied. He called in the Angel.

"Eight-oh-one, the ground fire is not too bad now. Commence your run."

"Roger, Cobra. 801's inbound."

Boyle and Watkins turned their helo inbound to the harbor, staying high enough for the Vietnamese to see them clearly. From the left, they could see the dark-green shape of Angel

801 as it flew right down on the water as fast as the pilots could make it go. High above, the A-7s continued their dives on the guns, pulling out and coming in again. The radios were strangely muted in that the voices were much calmer and more curt than they had been during the strike earlier in the day, despite the fact that the fire from the ground still looked pretty heavy to the helo pilots.

Boyle had heard the Condor flight check in when they returned from being rearmed back aboard the *Concord*. He had thought he recognized Santy's voice way back when this whole mess started and he and Watkins were listening in back aboard *Galveston*. Now, hearing the same voice again, he was certain of it. It was bad enough that he had to be here but worse that Mike was now actively being shot at.

Just as Angel 801 was calling that they were one minute out, one of the A-7s disappeared in a large black smoke cloud from a heavy-caliber flak burst. It reappeared still heading down but at a shallower angle, turning seaward with a long thin plume of white vapor trailing behind it. Boyle's heart was in his throat until he heard the pilot on the radio. It was not Mike's voice.

"Lead, 409's hit," Robinson called. "I think she took something in the belly. Heading feet wet. Keep at it until the helo's out. I'll orbit out past the second helo." His jet didn't seem to be hurt that badly but it would be foolish to press on with his attack without knowing the full extent of the damage. They were so close to effecting the rescue that having somebody come out and look him over would jeopardize success.

Watkins looked up making sure he knew where 409 was in case something else happened to the wounded Corsair. He made a mental note where the A-7's orbit was centered. He keyed his radio and let the pilot know he was in sight.

"409, Angel 802 has a tally on you."

"Click-click."

In Angel 801, Lenehan and Martinez saw Robinson pull away from the fight. The southern arm of the little breakwater was coming up quickly now and they began a shallow climb to clear it. As the scene beyond revealed itself, they spotted one round of tracer going up from the center of the harbor. Low in his raft, Hurst had been waiting for the first appearance of the H-3 and fired a round to give them a quick location to aim for. They turned ever so slightly and headed straight for him. Setting up to do a quick stop into a 40-foot hover over Hurst, they warned Ball and Patterson to get ready to drop the hoist cable. So far, it looked like their plan had worked. Everyone on the ground was either watching the other helo or shooting at the A-7s attacking from above.

Everyone except one humble sergeant and the two privates assigned to man one small 12.7mm machine gun hidden near the water's edge about one quarter mile from Hurst. The sergeant had been expressly ordered to shoot only at the helicopter coming in from the sea and to pay no attention to anything else. He had found it rather easy to ignore his own fears when the bombs and bullets started flying all around his position but both of his men had soiled themselves and tried to run deeper into the vegetation concealing their weapon. The sergeant had tackled them and bullied them back to the position. He'd kicked one of the privates squarely in his rear end and now the sergeant had shit all over his foot, which pissed him off even more.

Angel 801's approach had been a complete surprise to them. They had been training their weapon on the helicopter to seaward and it was only when the other helicopter entered one of the privates' peripheral vision from the right that they realized that the Americans were using a decoy. The sergeant aimed his gun at the nose of the second helicopter and waited for it to slow down over the man in the raft. When its nose came up and its speed began to drop off, he squeezed the trigger and used the stream of tracers to help him adjust his aim.

Lenehan and Martinez found out that they were in deep trouble when a row of splashes erupted from the water between them and Hurst. They were in the worst possible position to maneuver—nose high, slow, decelerating, and at extremely low altitude. Almost before they could recognize their plight, the gunner adjusted his aim up and slightly right, stitching the helicopter from nose to tail.

Some of the rounds hit Lenehan, sitting in the left seat, in the upper body and head, killing him instantly. Martinez was hit just above the left knee but somehow kept control of the aircraft. Shoving the nose down and hauling up on the collective, he got back down as close to the water as he dared and headed out to sea, chased by the now wild bursts of fire from the hidden machine gun. His cursing over the intercom drowned out the pleas for help from the crewmen in the back.

Santy was partway through his turn lining himself up for another run when he saw the tracer come out of the trees and into the helo. He rolled hard over and down, releasing a CBU at the gun and pulling out to the right over the harbor. The sergeant and his men, intent on their target and with ears numbed by the sudden series of reports from their weapon, never heard Santy's Corsair overhead or the sound of the CBU bursting. Santy had released the bomb far lower and at a steeper dive angle than he normally would have had he not been so enraged. The bomblets were thus far more concentrated than they would have been had they been dispersed at a higher altitude.

The sergeant, his two smelly privates, and the entire emplacement ceased to exist amid the fifty-odd explosions that went off within twenty yards of them. It would have taken an expert police forensics team to find anything remotely human when the smoke cleared.

Once safely out of range, Martinez reached up and chopped the throttle on number-one engine and pulled the "T" handle which closed the firewall fuel valve and armed the engine compartment fire extinguisher. The fuel control had been shot away and the pumps were pouring fuel out the severed lines and into the engine compartment. The last thing he needed now was a fire. When he had transmitted his situation, Boyle and Watkins in Angel 802 had rushed over and joined in formation to starboard, escorting him out to sea. Patterson had come up from the back of 801 and reported that Ball was dead, killed by the same burst that got Lenehan. After cutting away Martinez's flight suit to expose and treat the wound in his leg, Patterson had removed Lenehan's body from his seat as gently as possible and laid him out on the deck. He was now occupying the copilot's seat ready to help Martinez fly the thing back to the *Concord,* or "Mother," as she was called in the pilot's brevity code.

"Angel 801, this is Cobra 404. How are you making out?"

"We're still flying and I think we'll make it back to Mother. We have two dead, the copilot and the first crewman. Pilot's wounded but it's not too bad so far. Suggest you call Red Crown and have them send the plane guard helo to take over escort from 802."

"Roger that, 801. We'll take care of it."

Martinez looked back over his shoulder at the still form of his old friend, the face covered by a blanket from the rescue equipment bag, the blood streaming across the gray painted deck. He cleared his throat and called the A-7 leader back.

"Cobra, this is 801. Please get that guy out. I'd hate for this to be for nothing."

Before he switched frequencies he heard Finney's acknowledgment.

"Click-click."

Chapter 9

August 26, 1972

In the Combat Information Center aboard Red Crown, the chief controlling the support assets realized that his premonition had been correct again. This SAR effort, which had been going on for two hours now, was turning into a mess. He had gone over the intelligence reports, as had his lieutenant who was in overall charge of the cruiser's CIC efforts. There wasn't a goddamn reason on earth for the gooks to have as much Triple-A around that harbor as the pilots had run into. No reason at all. It really wasn't his problem, though; it belonged to people far higher in the chain than he. He shrugged the question off and went back to work finding a tanker for the shot-up A-7 and getting the plane guard helo from the carrier to come and escort Angel 801 back to the *Concord*.

Fifty miles southwest of Red Crown, Robinson was now well aware that his Corsair was losing fuel at a frightening rate. He didn't have enough to make it back to the ship, nor could he make it south to Danang, the primary divert field for all the aircraft operating off the coast of North Vietnam.

Most of the damage was to the belly of the aircraft, where most of his fuel was. Pilots try to burn it out of the wing tanks first since they have a larger surface area and take a correspondingly larger percentage of the hits from ground fire. Unfortunately, while Robinson's wings with their nearly empty tanks were undamaged, his fuselage tanks with most of his fuel were not. With Cobra 404 along as escort, he was headed east as fast as he could go. Robinson could not control the rate at which he was *losing* his fuel but he could control the rate at which he was *using* it. He was gaining distance to the east, toward the tanker A-6, which the carrier had launched in advance of the next wave of aircraft assigned to the RESCAP effort.

When he finally had the tanker in sight, he figured he was about twelve minutes from flameout. The tanker would stream a hose and basket into which Robinson would stick his refueling probe and begin receiving fuel. This would keep his engine running long enough to make it back to the carrier. Leading him to the ship in a flameout profile approach, the tanker would break off just far enough behind the ship to allow Robinson to safely transition and trap aboard. The only drawback to this was that the tanker became unavailable to the other aircraft which might need its help.

Looking across the hundred feet of sky at 801, Boyle could see very little obvious damage aside from a few bullet holes. He knew that the damage was far greater inside the aircraft. Looking at Watkins, who was intently flying formation on the stricken helo, he knew the damage was pretty bad inside him, too. Lenehan had been Watkins's first HAC when he'd come over to Vietnam. Most of the lessons Boyle was learning had been passed down from Lenehan. In silence, except for the necessary cockpit talk, they flew on waiting for the plane guard helo to meet them.

When the airborne E-2 called and gave them the final update for the intercept, it came as a relief to Boyle in that they could soon get on with what was now their responsibility. He dreaded going back to that goddamn pissant harbor and the vicious little battle that was surrounding Hurst.

Boyle was more afraid now than he ever had been before in his time over here. To be sure, he had been scared every time he and Watkins had had to venture over the beach to try to get somebody out. Usually, it was a cold-lump-in-the-gut kind of fear which you could stuff down with activity like rechecking things or concentrating on flying. This was vastly different because they had seen the volume of fire coming up at the A-7s and had to take this extra time to think about what awaited them. Two men whom they knew well and who were alive only thirty minutes ago were now dead, killed because they were willing to go to the aid of a complete stranger. But the stranger was an American aviator, and it was their job. Despite his fear, Boyle wished the plane guard helicopter from the *Concord* would hurry up so that they could get back and get this rescue over with.

The plane guard was from a different detachment stationed aboard the carrier. They were not trained or equipped to do the Combat SAR stuff so they did everything else, from hauling passengers and cargo around the ships to staying airborne to rescue anyone in trouble outside the range of the enemy guns and missiles. It was not glamorous; in fact, it was usually a downright boring job—but a necessary one nevertheless.

"Angel 801, this is Dipper 706. I have you in sight. I'll be joining starboard. 802, you're relieved."

No sooner had the plane guard called than Watkins wordlessly banked steeply away and increased speed heading back for the harbor.

After a few minutes of silence, Watkins spoke in his normal professional tones.

"Okay, Tim, we're next up. We won't go in there until the jet guys knock down some more of that flak. We'll come in from the harbor mouth so we can see the area. We'll stay low so they have to really be good or lucky to get us since we won't be profiled. They know we're coming and 801 used up the surprise bit. Sound all right?"

When Boyle agreed, Watkins addressed the crewmen.

"You guys in the back. We'll be going in nose on so your door guns won't do us any good. Both of you get back by the cargo door and let out about forty feet of slack in the cable. We'll throw it to him, hook him on, and haul ass; then we'll stop a couple of miles away and reel him in. I'll come to a lower hover so you can throw it better. We won't drop you in unless he's hurt too bad to hook himself up. Lie down on the deck so you won't get hit if they open up on us. Any questions?"

Bangert looked over his shoulder at Strand, who grinned and gave him a thumbs-up, as he left the forward left gun position at the passenger door and moved aft. "No, sir. We're ready in the back. Just make sure you guys don't get cute up there. No air shows, okay?"

This broke the tension as everyone chuckled. Watkins was always ending his pilot's brief with that caution. He wanted to ingrain in Boyle an attitude which would keep him from doing something stupid when he became a HAC. His philosophy was that "the only spectacular thing you can do with a helo is crash."

"No problem, Strand, I'll be good."

Admiral Welch looked down on the flight deck and noted with satisfaction that the rearming and refueling were still going smoothly after two and a half hours. He had never seen the sailors and pilots work this quickly or this well. As soon as an aircraft was loaded and fueled, it was launched to wait for a wingman. When two were joined up, off they flew to join the gaggle holding off the coast. The recovery of the two Cobra A-7s hadn't even slowed operations down, let alone screw up the deck.

Robinson had been dropped off by the tanker two miles behind the carrier and had continued to a near-perfect landing. No sooner had his Corsair stopped at the end of the cable run-out than twenty-odd men surrounded it. They freed the tail hook, attached the tow tractor, pulled him out of the way, and had the cable back "in battery," ready for the next arriving aircraft, in less than ninety seconds. Less than ten seconds later, Finney had trapped. Most of the men working around the deck never even looked up as the two jets landed.

A runner had met the pilots as they climbed down from their Corsairs and given them the word to report to Flag Bridge. Both pilots were now on their way up to give the admiral and the staff firsthand impressions of the SAR effort so far.

When Finney and Robinson entered Flag Bridge, they found it a maelstrom of voices, ringing phones, and officers moving all over the place. Welch spotted the two sweaty aviators and came over.

"I hate CIC and the situation room. Makes me feel like I'm running a war game with little cardboard pieces representing people." He gestured toward the flight deck. "Up here I can see that they are not cardboard. Besides a pilot needs to see the sky to think straight. Okay, tell me what happened in there."

Welch listened intently while the two described what had gone on around the harbor. They alternated giving their perspectives and held nothing back. The only adjectives they used were merely descriptive in that there was no excusing or ducking responsibility. Finally, Welch looked Finney in the eye and asked about the helo.

"Well, Admiral, I felt that we had done the job and suppressed them well enough for the Angel to make the attempt. I didn't see the gun that got him. It was my call. If I had it to do again, given the same circumstances, I'd probably make the same decision. I do believe now that we need to put a whole hell of a lot more ordnance on the sonsabitches before we try again."

Robinson chimed in. "Skipper's right, sir. We had it quieted down a lot. I didn't see the gun either and I had made a drop about a hundred yards away. They were waiting just for the helo."

"All right. Get yourselves ready to go back. Find yourself another airplane, Robinson. We're going to shuttle airplanes and bombs in there. As soon as somebody has dropped everything he has, he comes home for another load. No waiting and no fucking around with squadron or group integrity. Launch, drop your bombs, and return. Got it? Go." Welch turned away and left them staring.

They looked at each other and broke into huge grins. This was how it ought to be. With one decision, Welch had blithely cut several miles of red tape and political restrictions. Neither could remember this area being on the latest list of Washington-approved targets but Welch had made it approved. That he was willing to take the political risk for just one man would soon be all over the ship and all over the fleet. Nothing he could have done would have inspired more loyalty among all his sailors and aviators than this one decision would.

This would be known in later years as "The Day the Pentagon Lost Control of the War," a day that would become legend. Many men who were not present would later claim that they had been, like some would about the day Maris broke Ruth's record. Countless more men would deeply wish that they could have been a part of it.

Chapter 10

Santy called Hurst to see how he was doing. In all his excitement and concern for the crews of the two damaged aircraft, he had momentarily forgotten the man that all this was about in the first place. When the Cobras departed, he had once again been left as on-scene commander of the rescue effort.

"Starfighter, this is Condor 310. How're you doing down there?"

"Lonely as hell. But otherwise okay. Now that the shrapnel has stopped falling all over the place, I'm back in my raft. I sadly fear that it won't hold air much longer what with the holes it's got in it. It's getting kinda late in the day. We got a new plan yet, Condor?"

Santy looked at the eight-day clock on the instrument panel. It was getting close to four-thirty. "We're waiting on some more help from Mother. Should be here anytime. The helo made it and should be landing aboard about now. Stay cool, Starfighter. We're going to get you out."

Watkins broke in. "Condor, this is 802. We've got about

two hours' fuel left but I'd be more comfortable with a full bag. While there's a break here we'd like to run out and get some gas from our home plate. We can be back in about twenty minutes."

Santy thought that over. It would take at least that long for the other aircraft from the *Concord* to arrive and begin pounding the area around the harbor. It would be better to have the helo with four hours' fuel than to risk having him have to leave right when the chance came for a quick pickup.

"Roger, 802. Go HIFR. We have the time now. Monitor this freq in case something changes."

Watkins acknowledged and turned to the northeast. The *Galveston* had closed at best speed to within thirty miles of the coast and was standing by at Flight Quarters. So it wouldn't take long to get the fuel. HIFR was the generic term for ship-to-helicopter refueling. Normally, if the ship had a deck capable of taking a helicopter landing, the helo could land aboard and be refueled with the rotors turning.

If the ship was not large enough to accommodate a landing, the helo would come over the fantail and pick up the fuel hose with its hoist. The crewmen in the back plugged this into the receptacle on the helo and the ship pumped away with the helicopter flying a slow formation alongside. When enough fuel had been transferred, the hose was lowered back to the deck and the helo flew away, ready for another four hours on station. This technique is known as "Helicopter In-Flight Refueling" or, HIFR, pronounced "High-fur." This one would go the easy way, landing aboard.

Looking down at the scene around the harbor, Santy became aware of the change in the past couple of hours. It had earlier been almost idyllic, like one of those little lagoons in the movies. All it needed was a British man-o'-war in the middle and the scene would have been perfect. Now, there was bomb damage everywhere. The treetops were mostly blasted away and small pillars of smoke rose from several fires started by the bombing. Santy shook his head with regret that in a very little while, once the rest of the jets from the carrier

Concord got through with it, the place would look like a state park in Hell. He wondered if the little harbor would ever again be as pretty as it had been. How long would it take for the scars to be covered by nature? He wondered if anyone now alive would be around long enough to see that happen. Probably not, he thought.

Another thing that kept creeping into the back of his mind was the fact that, as on-scene commander, he might have to be the one to make the decision to send his friend, Boyle, in Angel 802 down there, into the same cauldron that had already cost the lives of two would-be rescuers. That was a responsibility that he wanted no part of but, at the same time, he knew that he would give that order if it came to it. He also knew full well that Tim would never forgive him if he did not give it when the time came.

These thoughts were suddenly broken by Hurst's tinny voice in his ears.

"Condor, Condor, the fuckers are shooting at me now from the beach! I've bailed out of my raft. I'm okay and there's just been random shots so far."

"Roger, Starfighter. We're doing everything we can. We'll have some more help here in a few minutes." Santy was amazed at how calm Hurst sounded now. If the positions were reversed, he wasn't sure that he could handle it that well. Especially now that the Vietnamese had apparently decided to raise the stakes a bit. Maybe they figured the Americans would get totally pissed off and make mistakes or maybe they were just assholes. Probably both. He was tempted to just roll in and pickle off the few CBUs he had left but that wouldn't help anything but his morale. He decided to stay professional and wait. His turn would come.

Boyle heard the first of the newly rearmed aircraft from the *Concord* check in with Santy. There were four of them, all A-6s loaded with twenty-four bombs apiece, and Santy had wisely decided not to try to be a hero and attempt to suppress the guns with just his two remaining A-7s. It would be at least fifteen more minutes until he and Watkins were back on station ready to attempt the pickup anyway.

Once the fuel had been taken aboard and the helo was airborne, Boyle took over the controls and headed back to their holding station off the coast. He called Santy with his report.

"Condor 310, Angel 802 is inbound to station, HIFR complete. State is four hours to splash."

"Roger that, Angel."

Santy gratefully turned over the responsibility as on-scene commander to the A-6 flight leader. The two men in the Intruder, sitting side by side, a pilot and a bombardier-navigator, or B/N, were much better equipped to handle it than he, both from the standpoint of probable experience and because there was an extra man aboard who was not engaged in actually flying the aircraft and who could devote 100 percent to the tactical problem. Now Santy could get back to being just a regular old attack pilot.

The A-6 leader, Lt. Cmdr. Tom Bennett, in Gypsy 506, was an old hand at this sort of thing. He was on his fourth Vietnam deployment and, as a young jaygee, had been in the first squadron to fly the A-6 into combat. His reputation throughout the fleet was as a superb combat pilot and leader. He was the type of warrior whom juniors revere, peers respect, and superiors fear. The movers and shakers would quietly see to it that he remained at his present rank and was never admitted as an acolyte to the halls of power, for they were not certain that he could be forced to accept their hierophantic approach to their profession. Bennett, for his part, couldn't care less about what they thought of him. He just wanted to be the best A-6 pilot and the best officer he could be. He had already completely succeeded in those goals and, years later, he would take great satisfaction in that success into his retirement.

As he looked over the area inland from the harbor, his experienced eye picked out something that the others there before him had apparently missed. There were two roads leading to the harbor passing through villages which stood about three miles to the northwest and southwest. In an area of relative flatland, this was not at all unusual. They were too far from the water to be fishing villages, so their economy would probably depend upon agriculture for survival. What struck Bennett was that there was no evidence of any sort of farming anywhere near them. He rolled the aircraft slightly so that his B/N could take a look.

"Hey, Mort, take a look at those villages. Do they strike you as odd?"

"No, they look like normal Gookburgs to me. Why?"

"I don't know. They just don't look like they fit somehow. Like maybe they're sort of painted on for effect. Doesn't look like there's any farming going on and the roads that lead through them are a little big for villages like that."

"Yeah, that is funny. Maybe the roads are bigger because they were built to carry truck traffic to and from the harbor and the villages just grew up along the way. But I don't see any areas for truck parks, though. And there aren't any facilities in the harbor for unloading a lot of cargo. Oh, well, let's tell the Secret Squirrel about them when we get back."

Bennett agreed but couldn't put away the funny feeling he had about the villages. He resolved to make a bombing run later that would allow him to fly over them on his pullout from the dive. Maybe he'd find an answer that way. Missions like this carried a prohibition against collateral attacks. You were only allowed to attack sites directly shooting at you or to prevent the capture of the guy on the ground. Bennett was one of those men like Watkins who devoutly believed that it was always easier to get forgiveness than it was to get permission.

With that decision sorted out and firmly placed in the back of his mind, Bennett turned his attention to the task at hand. The two A-7s were down to about a third of their original bomb loads and would be heading back to the ship for more. On the way were four more A-6s and at least nine A-7s. Several F-4 Phantoms were due shortly to add to the weight of metal landing on the gunners. Might as well get started, he thought.

"Condor 310, this is Gypsy 506. Request you make a run on the area you consider the biggest threat. Drop everything you have and head back for more. We have enough help coming that it may get crowded around here."

"310 concurs. Give us a minute to get set up."

"Roger. Angel 802, Gypsy, we'll call you when we're ready. Stay close."

"Angel, roger."

Santy looked at his wingman, Mitchell, and signaled that he was breaking off to set up for his run. He set the switches to release his weapons at the proper interval when he hit the button.

"One pass, Snake. Join east," was all he had to say.

"Roger."

Waiting until the target he had picked out was just ahead of his right wing, Santy pulled the nose up and rolled right. When the nose came through the horizon and was pointed at the little cluster of huts next to the shoreline, he rolled out and, making small corrections, held it the few seconds until the symbology on the HUD was right. At the proper instant, he released the CBUs and pulled into a hard four "G" pullout.

No antiaircraft fire had come up at him until he was headed back up and away. Mitchell did not have so unopposed a run but he too got away with no hits. As they headed east, they flew directly over Angel 802 lumbering around in its orbit. Looking down at the green helicopter, Santy was very glad that he had at least the relative advantage of speed. He looked back at Mitchell and smoothly turned to the course back to the ship.

Behind the two A-7s, Bennett's A-6s noted where the Triple-A sites were and began pounding them. One of the problems with a catch-as-catch-can mission like this is that the benefit of concerted intelligence and targeting is lost. No standing toe-to-toe with a reasoned assessment of the other side. It is like a brawl at the pitcher's mound as opposed to a football play. No one knows going in what to expect. You dive in, throw a few heavy punches, and beat feet for another try before you get hurt.

The Triple-A at first was as heavy as it had been when the original rescue attempt had been made. The gunners had used the pause to good effect. They had dashed back to the ammo bunkers and loaded their little carts with as much as they would hold and then pushed them hurriedly back to the guns, dumping the shells in piles that would never pass a military inspection. They had run back for another load again and again until either the bunkers were empty or the carts broke, then the rounds were carried on shoulders. Empty shell casings and dead gunners were unceremoniously dragged away from the guns and thrown anywhere out of the way. Crews from damaged guns were combined with serviceable weapons. Anyone without a specific job to do was handed an AK-47 and told to shoot at anything in the sky above. Several men from the small infantry contingent assigned as guards for the area moved to the water's edge and began to crawl half in and half out of the water along the small breakwater in order to get closer to Hurst and have an easier shot at him. No longer were the Vietnamese willing to wait to capture him. They were determined that he not escape. If he were not to be captured, he would be killed. Enough bullets fired at him would eventually do the job.

Hurst watched the A-6s make run after run at the guns. Very quickly the entire shoreline became wreathed in smoke both from the guns and from the bursting bombs. From his vantage point, about six inches from the surface of the water, the volume of fire from the Triple-A wasn't diminishing at all. All around him, pieces of shrapnel from the explosions rained down. Several had bounced off his helmet and shoulders hard enough to make him wish he were an amphibian. When the jets had resumed the bombing, the rifle fire directed at him had ceased, for a while anyway. He had thought at first that somebody up there got lucky and blew the bastards away but several of the recent splashes nearby had seemed different from the ones made by the falling chunks of metal. They were shooting at him again but he couldn't see enough to be able to tell where the riflemen were.

"Gypsy lead, Starfighter. I'm getting some more small-arms fire around me but I can't tell where the bastards are. I just thought I'd mention it."

Bennett heard and looked around the harbor quickly but couldn't see them either. There wasn't a damn thing he could do about it anyway. He and the others just had to press on and attack the guns. Hurst would have to take his chances.

"Roger, Starfighter. We're looking."

"Gypsy 506, this is 500. Joining from the east with four Intruders." The call from Bennett's squadronmate came at the right time since he was almost out of bombs to drop. The other three in his flight ought to be about there too. It was time to set up for the run to check out one of those villages.

"Roger, 500. We'll be off target after these runs. Request you take it as soon as we're off. The Triple-A is still pretty heavy and seems to be mostly from the area just back from the shoreline. We've been hitting them as hard as we could but they can take it down there. The survivor is taking small-arms but we can't find the shooters."

"Okay, 506. Expect a fast turnaround when you get back aboard Mother."

"Click-click."

Bennett rolled in from the southeast and dropped his remaining bombs on what seemed to be a 57mm site but his concentration was on the northern village in the distance beyond the gun. He pulled out deliberately low and, jinking all the way, roared past the guns toward the open country to the west. He set up for as low a pass as he dared and steered the Intruder so as to give each of them a good look down at as much of the place as possible.

"All right, Mort. Take a good look at that village. Something's not right, damnit. See if you can tell anything."

"Okay."

Bennett was half-expecting a horde of natives to leap out of the scrub bushes and begin blazing away at him but there was absolutely nothing. Once past the village, he yanked the A-6 into a hard bank and, slamming the throttles forward, headed northeast for the water.

With the beach behind and clear, smokeless sky ahead, Mort exhaled for the first time in what seemed to him like six or seven hours. He looked at his pilot and saw a look of puzzled concentration. "Well, what did we find out?" he asked.

"There was nothing there. The hooches were all new-looking. But there were no people or even signs of them."

"Maybe they were all in the bunkers. Hell, I don't know. It looked normal enough to me."

"Yeah, but there should have been pigs or something in the pens; they looked like they were all overgrown with weeds. No bicycles, no clothes hanging out, no well either. Don't tell me they carry their water two miles from the river every time they want to cook dinner. There weren't even any paths leading anywhere. Just the road in and out. I think that place is a dummy. There's something there that they don't want us to find. And they put all that Triple-A around that harbor."

He sighed. "Nothing we can do about it now, though. Make sure we tell the Squirrel about it like you said before."

With that Bennett put the place out of his mind for the present. He checked to see that the three other jets in his flight had joined up and gave them the signal to switch frequencies for their return to the ship.

Boyle watched the second set of A-6s begin their attacks on the Vietnamese guns. This whole effort was foreign to him. Usually, when he had had to go overland into North Vietnam, they just ran in, picked up the guy, and hauled ass. There had been no waiting around. Once in a while they had been too late to prevent the downed aviator's capture, in which case they just hauled ass.

Watkins was quietly pulling on one of his incessant Marlboros, looking at the land around the harbor and occasionally following one of the jets from the time it began its dive until it had climbed out of sight. Boyle knew that he was deeply hurt by what had happened to Angel 801. He could only imagine what he would feel like if something like that happened to Mike Santy. Boyle wished he knew what he could say to Watkins that would let him know that he felt for him, that even though he hadn't known Lenehan well, he still felt lousy about it all. He wisely chose to say nothing and just fly the helicopter.

Listening to the radio calls from the Intruders gave him a sense of how it was going. The Triple-A, although heavy, was much less accurate than it had been. The unpredictability of the angles and the altitudes from which the attacks were coming were causing the gunners to swing their weapons around hastily and making the fusing sequences haphazard. The Vietnamese had probably lost many of their better gun captains and best-trained crews. They were definitely taking a beating but unless the Americans could get Hurst out, the day would belong to whatever gunners survived.

It seemed to Gypsy 500 that a few more runs ought to do it. Nobody in his flight had been hit yet nor had anyone from the previous A-6 flight. The A-7 Corsair gaggle with Cobra 412 in the lead was about five minutes out and they would pick it up as soon as he and his flight were done. It was time to get the helo ready.

"Angel 802, this is Gypsy 500. The Triple-A ought to be pretty much suppressed in a few minutes. The Corsairs will take over and make the call for you. Just hang loose out there, okay? Starfighter, you copy?"

"802, roger."

Hurst looked around the harbor. "Starfighter copies."

Watkins sat up in his seat and took over the controls. "I've got it, Tim. All set?"

"I guess so. Checklist complete, switches set, power's up."

The next six minutes seemed to the helo crew to take an eternity. The A-6s made their last runs and departed. Without a pause, the newly arrived Corsairs took over pounding the shore. Nobody saw the guys with the rifles who had crawled around almost to the center of the small breakwater.

Finally, the call came. "Angel, this is Cobra 412. Start your run."

Watkins steepened his bank and dove closer to the water. He aimed straight for the spot from which Hurst's tracer round had come on the previous attempt. No more than five feet from the water, he was so low that he would have had to climb a few feet to bank the H-3 anything more than slightly. Boyle stole a glance at him and was shocked by the intensity in his eyes.

When the Angel was less than one hundred yards from Hurst and within extreme range of the men on the breakwater, they rose as one and opened fire with their AK-47s on full automatic.

Chapter 11

August 26, 1972

In a way, Boyle and Watkins had benefited from the disaster that had befallen their friends in Angel 801. They knew that there was no chance of deception and no way that they were going to get to Hurst unnoticed by a preoccupied enemy. They *expected* to take fire from the shore. Their approach was such that they could see nearly the entire harbor and thus would have just a tiny bit of warning that they were in trouble, and would be able to make moves that would keep things under control. That little bit was going to be just enough.

Behind the helicopter was a wake of spray on the surface of the sea. Watkins at the controls couldn't divert his attention from flying for even the split second it would take to glance inside at the airspeed indicator. That sort of thing is the co-pilot's job. Each pilot must trust the other guy totally.

The pilot at the controls must take in an uncountable number of bits of information from most of his senses each second. In order not to make that one tiny little mistake which will send the helicopter cartwheeling across the surface of the water, exploding into small pieces of metal and flesh, he must sort them all out and react properly before his conscious mind can realize that he has to.

At the same time, very few things are as exhilarating as that mad dash at low level. One hundred and eighty miles an hour with the water only five feet away, water that is as hard as concrete at that speed. It is very like what the cavalrymen of old must have felt as they charged across the open fields toward the enemy. The air rushes and rumbles past the open side windows. The whole machine jolts and bounces as it flies through the air currents which become almost solid walls at high speed. Above the pilots, the engines wail at full power and the transmission whines metallically as it takes every bit of the 2,700 horsepower the engines ram into it, turning it into shuddering, roaring, pounding speed.

Your senses are heightened to a degree almost beyond belief. Each small wavetop stands sharply frozen ahead of you until it suddenly blurs as it passes beneath or beside. Every tree and every other feature on the shoreline stands out with a clarity that no photograph could ever duplicate. The gauges on the panel vibrate madly and your helmet and survival gear bounce and jostle and dig whatever sharp edges they have into you but you don't feel that at all. Whenever you hit a particularly sharp gust of wind, you are thrown hard into your shoulder harness. It is a wild, terrifying, visceral experience but, by God, it is something that you will carry with you for the rest of your days. And you will carry it fondly.

The Vietnamese troops on the northern arm of the breakwater, in their eagerness to get the American helicopter, had opened fire too soon. Even if they had waited until 802 was hovering over Hurst, it would have been tough to hit it effectively with the initial bursts. The AK-47 is actually a pretty lousy antiaircraft weapon unless there are a whole lot of them and you fly directly over a concentration of people firing them straight up. Beyond about a hundred yards, they are not terribly accurate and these soldiers were not among Hanoi's finest, so the rounds that flew around the helicopter were mostly misses, splashing water all over the place. Just the same, there were a hell of a lot of them. Two dozen or so of the rounds hit the helicopter and, although they did little damage, they were a solid demonstration to the two pilots that more work needed to be done in pounding the area around the harbor.

Watkins was just about to raise the nose into the "quick stop" maneuver over Hurst when Boyle's small side window disappeared in a shower of Plexiglas fragments that rattled off both men's helmets and visors. Another round knocked off the free air temperature probe at the top of the windshield before lodging itself in the circuit breaker panel above Watkins's head. Several more plunked into the aircraft behind and below the pilots, chewing up electronic boxes but hitting nothing really vital. One round, almost spent, carried away the pad of paper on Boyle's kneeboard.

"Sonofabitch!" yelled Watkins, as he yanked the aircraft up slightly and around to get it out of there.

Once headed out, Watkins asked if the crew were all okay. Two less-than-assertive "Yessirs" came from Strand and Bangert in the back and a funny-sounding "Yeah" from Boyle. He was holding up the wreckage of his kneeboard, deeply gouged where the bullet had torn across the top of it and smashed through the little light on the top that never worked anyway. The HAC had to laugh at the look of surprised anger on Tim's face as he inspected his kneeboard.

"Look at this shit! Those fuckers are trying to kill us, Bob. You didn't say anything nasty about their mothers on the radio, did you?"

Watkins shook his head as he keyed the radio. "Cobra lead. Angel 802. We had to bail out of there. We took a bunch of hits but they were all small arms. I didn't see where it came from but I don't think we can get in if we're gonna be bore-sighted like that."

The A-7 leader replied, "Roger that, Angel. I didn't see anything either. We'll just have to keep at it a while longer.

We have some more aircraft inbound just launched from Mother. Stay loose out there."

"802, roger."

Hurst watched as the helicopter banked away, its rotor blades coming within inches of the water. He looked over his shoulder and saw something that could have been men ducking down behind the breakwater. They were pretty damned close. Most of the rounds they fired had cracked over his head on their way toward Angel 802. A few had splashed into the water around him.

At the very first, his reaction was one of deep fury at fate that his salvation had again been so tantalizingly near at hand and then had been cruelly snatched away. As soon as he spotted the movement on the breakwater, the rage turned against the enemy. He fished around for the lanyard that held his radio.

"Cobra, this is the Starfighter. I think I saw the guys that shot at the helo. They just ducked on the far side of the breakwater from me. There's at least four of them."

"Okay, Starfighter. We're fresh out of CBUs but the next flight will have some. They'll take those guys out. Angel, you copy?"

"Angel copies. We're standing by."

Back aboard the *Concord*, Admiral Welch watched two of the Gypsy A-6s catapult off the bow and dip their wings into the clearing turn. The Condor A-7s, Santy and Mitchell, had launched about five minutes ago, inbound with another load of CBUs. He smiled at the thought of what the two jaygees must be feeling right now. They were on their third attack mission of the day. They had done well and he wished for a moment that he could have gone with them.

The A-6s had gone off with loads of Mk-82 "iron bombs" since the rescue effort had depleted the store of ready CBUs. More were coming up the elevators from the magazines below, but the air wing ordnance officer, or CAG Gunner, as he was known, had decreed that it was better to keep aircraft over the scene than it was to wait around for the exactly proper loads. The iron bombs made very large holes in the ground and whatever happened to be sitting there when they hit. Welch made a mental note to commend the gunner to CAG himself when this was over.

Behind Welch, in an out-of-the-way corner of Flag Bridge, Master Chief Aviation Metalsmith Rick Hayes stood chewing the end of his luxuriant mustache. He held a sheaf of messages from the High Muckymucks back at Fleet Headquarters in Pearl Harbor and from the Pentagon. The messages had been coming in with increasing frequency and stridency over the past few hours. Stripped of their official structure and vocabulary, they all asked the same question: "What the fuck are you doing over there?" At first, they were polite inquiries, then came the gentle reminders of established policy. Most of these were drafted by underlings.

Finally, the heavy guns began to come out and the "personals" arrived. Hayes had figured that the admiral was busy enough trying to get one of his boys out of a major jam and didn't need his elbow jogged by the "chair-bound political assholes" he hated. Since Hayes already had twenty-nine years in the Navy, he figured that he could take the fall for the lack of response to the messages. The admiral could honestly say that he hadn't seen the damn things and that one of his staff had been lax in performing his job. He knew full well that Welch would have ignored the messages anyway until the rescue had been concluded. This way Hayes felt he was covering his boss's "six-o'clock position."

Hayes was another man who went back a long way with Welch. He had once been Welch's plane captain when Welch was a jaygee and he had been an airman reduced in rate from petty officer third class for some transgression manufactured by the Shore Patrol in the bar at the Royal Hawaiian Hotel during the tail end of World War II. To this day, he still swore that the lady had voluntarily given him her panties and that the husband, a patrol plane pilot, had simply misunderstood her patriotic fervor. The husband had to have been a real good buddy of the Shore Patrol officer since they were so adamant about taking him in for questioning. Hayes had been perfectly willing to answer anything they asked as long as he could stay in the bar. They insisted and, after vehemently protesting, Hayes was finally persuaded to come along to headquarters. The three shore patrolmen that wound up in sick bay must have tripped or walked into doors or something.

Welch had made sure that he stayed out of further trouble and when Hayes had made master chief, had brought him along as senior enlisted man in every unit he had commanded since. Hayes had remained in the Navy long after he could have retired only because he figured that Welch, being just an officer, would be helpless without a chief to keep him straight. When Welch retired, so would he.

"Um, Admiral, excuse me, but these messages have come in. You should maybe look at them, sir." He handed them to Welch and took a very military-looking step back.

Welch looked at the first and noted the date-time group, which gives the date and hour to the minute that it was transmitted. When he read the content, he looked at Hayes with a mixture of surprise and confusion. Looking back down, he read each one with increasing speed. The redness crept up his neck and over his face until his hand was shaking with anger. When he finished scanning the last one, he stared furiously straight at Hayes's face.

Before the explosion could happen, Hayes held up a hand and kept a look of pure innocence on his weathered face.

"Admiral, you said that you didn't want to be bothered with chicken shit. All they want to do is make sure that they don't look bad and have to explain something to their boss that they can't take credit for. If you had seen these earlier, you'd only have told me to lose them for a while anyway. I've got it covered with the Comm guys. We've sent off for some retransmissions since our system is having problems kind of suddenly."

Since he hadn't been beheaded yet, Hayes pressed on. "I did send an acknowledgment of the second one there saying we had a SAR going on which we expected to conclude shortly and that we would send them a complete report most skosh when we were done. I guess they didn't quite buy it so they sent that last one there on the bottom."

Welch took a deep breath. "And just exactly whose name did you put on the acknowledgment?"

"Commander Strickland's, sir. You know how he's always trying to get himself noticed. I assumed that he would be eager to help. He was real busy being important though, so I didn't bother him with something so trivial."

That did it for Welch's anger. Strickland was a holdover from the previous admiral's staff. He was a mealy-mouthed, ambitious little weasel as far as Hayes was concerned. Welch had kept his opinion to himself but didn't trust the fat, pig-eyed sonofabitch either. He had a momentary flash of what Strickland's reaction would be when he found out. He laughed abruptly when he thought of the affronted dignity and the barely suppressed rage that would erupt when he learned what had been done. He only hoped he could be present to see it.

"Goddamnit, Master Chief. One of these days I'm gonna have to hammer you for something you've done. I swear I'll do it too. Now, send the chief of staff over here so we can figure out how to keep Pearl and Washington off our backs until we get that kid out. Once you've done that, go below before you cause any more trouble and stay in the Chief's Mess." He paused and lowered his voice. "Thanks, Rick. Good work."

Hayes nodded gently and turned away, hoping fervently that they could pull this off without getting Welch in too much more trouble. If they lost another aircraft or if they failed to pull off the rescue there would be hell to pay for everybody involved. Not to mention what awaited Hurst if the Vietnamese bagged him.

Mike Santy arrived back over the harbor only minutes after Angel 802 had escaped from the hail of bullets thrown at it from the breakwater. He checked himself and Mitchell in with the lead Cobra A-7 and was told to wait until the five other aircraft were off target. On the way in, he had checked with Red Crown, who told him of the many aircraft from all over the Gulf of Tonkin which had called up wanting to know if they could help out. Several tanker aircraft had been positioned in strategic areas in case somebody needed them. Four fighters from the other carrier, the U.S.S. *Independence,* had volunteered to fly spare MiG-Combat Air Patrol (MiGCAP) missions. They would soon be relieved by four more and four after that. A dozen or so *Independence* attack aircraft were hanging around near the tankers to fill in any gaps in the coverage if the *Concord*'s jets needed them.

Red Crown's last question and a stranger's reply had stuck with Santy.

"Looks like you Airedale guys aren't gonna take no for an answer today, are you?"

"No fucking chance, Red Crown," came the answer from some other pilot up here in the sky over the Gulf. Santy felt that this summed up the mood pretty well.

Looking down at the harbor, Santy saw that his earlier impressions had been correct. It really was blasted to hell and gone. None of the trees or buildings were still standing. The small piers were just a collection of little chunks of wood washing against the shore. The small boats that before had been tied up to the piers no longer existed. The very shape of the harbor was different. It was as if the land had suddenly been given the world's worst case of acne.

The Triple-A that was coming up was far less intense than it had been only an hour ago but it could still bite. Not a time to get cocky, thought Santy.

"Condor 310, Cobra Lead. We're off target. There are some troops with small arms on the far side of the breakwater. They're the ones who hit the helo. Use your CBUs on them and that ought to get the helo in and out. Use the Starfighter as your spotter. He's standing by. Cobras departing and switching."

"Starfighter, Condor 310. You still okay down there?"

"Roger that, Condor. But I really have had enough survival practice. I'd like to go home now. Those guys are about seventy-five yards from the seaward end of the northern breakwater. They are on the far side and occasionally pop off a few rounds at me. The only fire that hit the helo came from there as far as I could see. Somebody must have gotten the ones who were shooting at me earlier."

"Roger, Starfighter. Condors will be commencing in one minute."

"310, Gypsy 506. Flight of two Intruders about two minutes out."

"Roger, Gypsy. You take the Triple-A again. We're going for the breakwater. Snake, I'll take the shoreward end, you get the water end."

"506, wilco."

Santy elongated his orbit slightly and then rolled over and down, adjusting his dive to line up with the long axis of the breakwater. Passing through 5,000 feet, he punched off two bombs and pulled hard up and left. Mitchell followed his run almost exactly except that his dive was a tad steeper so he could adjust his bombs to cover the nearer half of the breakwater. Once his bombs were gone he pulled left to follow Santy.

All four weapons hit exactly where the two young pilots had intended. The bomblets spread out and burst all along the length of the breakwater. The Vietnamese saw the jets coming down at them and dived under the water which was their only protection. When the water kicked up by the explosions subsided, there was nothing left to see but some bloody foam and bits of khaki cloth bobbing in the little waves.

Watkins watched the jets start their first run. As soon as they pulled up, he turned the helo toward the harbor and accelerated.

Boyle keyed the radio and warned Hurst to stand by for another try. He rechecked everything in the cockpit for about the eighty-seventh time that day and sat back against his seat to back up Watkins. As they passed the mouth of the harbor, Boyle could see the second set of CBUs explode over the breakwater and, farther ahead and to the left, the larger balls of black smoke and fire from the iron bombs from the two Gypsy Intruders.

This time there was absolutely no fire coming at the helo. The approach to Hurst went just as rapidly as before but this time thcy got there. Watkins raised the nose steeply and climbed into the hover over him. The crewmen in the back dropped the rescue sling, or "horse collar," to thc survivor and watched as he put it around his back. The calm drone of Strand's voice began.

"Sling's in the water. Survivor has a hold of it and is putting it on. Steady hover. Easy right, easy right, stop right. Steady. Stand by for weight on the aircraft. Steady. Survivor is clear of the water, coming up. Survivor is at the cargo door. Survivor is in the aircraft. *Go!*"

Bangert pulled Hurst down on the deck and threw himself on top of him. Strand dropped to the deck and wrapped an arm around a support leg of the troop seat.

Watkins yanked the collective up, shoved the nose down, and stomped on the right rudder pedal. The helo spun right and slid toward the water as it accelerated out of the harbor. Once clear, Watkins asked if everyone was okay as he gave the control of the helicopter to Boyle. He reached up and pulled a semicrushed Marlboro out of his sleeve pocket. As he lit it, Boyle could see a slight tremor in Watkins's hands and when Boyle reached down to switch the radio transmitter at his side, he could see one in his own hand.

"Condor 310, this is Angel 802. Pickup is complete. We've got him. He appears to be okay." Boyle found that his voice too had a slight tremor.

"Roger, that, Timmy. Good job. I'll pass that to Red Crown."

Before Santy could pass the word on, the airwaves erupted with radio calls from everybody congratulating everybody else. When things quieted down, the chief aboard Red Crown tried to sound professional in sorting out the aircraft and giving them their vectors home but with all the background yelling and cheering that was going on in his ship's CIC, he failed.

Santy decided to dump his remaining ordnance on what was left of the installations around the harbor. As he and

Mitchell rolled in, it was as if the Vietnamese had just quit and dived for cover. No fire came up at him and, at the last instant, he turned the Corsair slightly and pickled his bombs into the water of the harbor. Mitchell, correctly guessing what his leader was thinking, dropped his harmlessly in the water nearby. The two suddenly older pilots headed their jets up and out to sea and toward home.

Bennett, who had again arrived on scene about five minutes after Santy and Mitchell got back, had only dropped four of the bombs he had brought along. He watched the two A-7s blow up the harbor and decided that this was his chance to find out what was with those two villages. He told his wingman to stay high and rolled in from the north.

"Okay, Mort. We'll drop everything on this pass. Get a good spread so we can hit whatever's there." The B/N, deducing that his pilot had finally lost his mind, just nodded and did his thing.

The A-6 became ripplingly lighter as the 500-pound bombs fell away. When the last one was gone, Bennett slammed the throttles to make sure he was getting everything the airplane had and hauled it around to the east. He resisted the temptation to look back at his handiwork (looking back is a very bad habit for a pilot in the jet age to get into, what with the speed with which things happen in front of you). He got safely away from his target but he missed seeing about a square half-mile of North Vietnam abruptly disappear.

His bombing had been perfect. The first Mk-82 hit the northernmost of twelve large underground fuel tanks hidden beneath the dummy village northwest of the harbor. The rest of the bombs struck the others. The tanks exploded almost simultaneously, throwing a fireball nearly a mile across into the sky. The orange and black ball climbed almost as high as the orbit of Bennett's wingman who had a front-row seat. Both crewmen looked open-mouthed at each other, then back at the explosion.

"Jesus Christ, Tom. Look what you did," was all the pilot could say.

Bennett, now safely out over the sea, turned his Intruder to look and was stunned by the size of the pillar of smoke and flame. He then realized with no little satisfaction that he had been right to trust his instincts. His next thought was that there still was another village that looked like a dummy, at least from a distance. He could tell his wingman to drop what he had left on that one but he hadn't flown over it and hadn't seen what exactly was down there. It would take one more run to check it out and one by his wingie to bomb it. That was twice more into the lion's den with all the other aircraft headed back to their ships. There was also the chance that this one was a real village. Maybe it was even where the families of the men who had so courageously defended the little harbor lived.

For now, enough was enough. Bennett was certain that Admiral Welch would have it checked out by a reconnaissance bird and if it was still suspicious, the *Concord*'s attack jets would be back.

Bennett told his wingman to jettison his bombs over the water. When he had done so and rejoined on Gypsy 500's wing, Bennett turned east and headed home, away from the setting sun.

Chapter 12

August 26, 1972

The chief aboard Red Crown leaned back in his chair and watched the last of the little lighted slashes move steadily toward the right edge of his radar screen. There were two of them. One represented the two Gypsy A-6s which were the final jets to depart the little harbor. The other, moving at about one-fourth the speed of the first, was the helicopter. Angel 802 was now flying eastward, all alone over the sea, no longer the lead tenor in the opera.

All the jets, the chief knew, were now busy with their own concerns as they came back and landed aboard the *Concord*. They had switched off the rescue frequency with curt-sounding farewells to the Angel, each one of which had been acknowledged by a very tired "Roger, thank you." Somehow, it didn't seem fair to the chief that the helicopter should be left alone like that. There ought to be bugles and drums and flags and a huge escort. After what they had done, there ought to be more.

It seemed that it was the helo that took the greater risks. The jets were in bunches and getting hit was largely a matter of chance. There was only one helo going in at a time and everybody knew that sooner or later, it would have to fly into the fire as long as there was the slightest opportunity to rescue the downed airman. The jets had spccd and maneuverability and could shoot back, while the helicopter guys had only the hope that they didn't get shot up too badly. All they had for armament was two crummy machine guns in the doors and a limited field of fire.

And a large set of brass balls, he thought.

He watched the helo's little slash touch the edge of the screen, and reluctantly keyed his mike.

"Angel 802, this is Red Crown. You are departing my area. Contact Keyboard six hundred on Button Six for radar following to Mother. Good job in there, Angel. Red Crown out."

Before he removed his headset, he heard the answer: "Roger, switching. And thank you."

The chief smiled a little as he stood up, gently placing his headset down on the console. He had only two thoughts as he stepped through the curtain which was supposed to keep stray light away from the radar screen. One was that he was bone-weary and the other was that he was damned glad to serve in a Navy that had men like those in Angel 802 and the other aircraft who had risked so much in the battle for just one man.

The helo flight back to the ship had been quiet after the near euphoria of the successful rescue had worn off. As soon as they were well out over the water, Hurst came forward and patted each of the pilots on the shoulder in gratitude and then went back aft and sat down on the troop seat. After twenty minutes of staring unseeing out the open half of the cargo door at the monotonous blue of the passing ocean, his head slowly fell and rested on his arms crossed on top of his knees. He had never been so spent both emotionally and physically.

The two crewmen had lain down on the deck with their heads on the seven-man rafts and gone to sleep. A few moments later, the conversation between the two pilots petered out altogether and they flew on in silence, each lost in his own thoughts.

Boyle was reasonably pleased with his own performance. He had been more fearful going in this time than ever before but he'd handled it. He'd known what to do and had done it without hesitation or error. He'd held up his end. That was all that could be asked of him. He was beginning to think that he might be a pretty fair Navy pilot.

Watkins had decided before this mission that it was time for Boyle to have his own crew and his performance today had further confirmed that decision. There was little else that the young man could learn as a copilot. He needed to go out and get the experience that only comes with being the guy with the responsibility. Watkins looked at Boyle and for the first time could *see* him as a HAC. There was no doubt about it. Tim Boyle was ready now.

Watkins would miss flying with him. For the past four months, they had been one hell of a team.

September 20, 1971

ELEVEN MONTHS BEFORE

It was anything but beautiful. It seemed more like a green Winnebago than a flying machine. Slab-sided, sort of chiseled-looking. The few curves it had only served to connect more angles. It had a face only a mother could love.

Lt. (J.G.) Timothy J. Boyle, U.S. Naval Reserve, stood looking at the Sikorsky HH-3A helicopter, loftily named the Sea King, and sighed almost ruefully. He was thinking that maybe he should have chosen a different career path. Flying Huey gunships with the Navy's helicopter attack squadron, HAL-3, in South Vietnam looked a whole lot more glamorous than driving one of these monsters around the fleet. Combat Search and Rescue had sounded very noble back in Pensacola.

When the time had come back in flight training to choose

the type of aircraft he had wanted to fly in the fleet, Boyle had had good enough grades to get his choice and had selected helicopters. Mike Santy had tried to convince him to select jets but Boyle had remained adamant. There was just something about flying around low and slow that had appealed to him. In primary helicopter training, after his first flight in the tiny TH-57, the Navy's variant of the Bell Jet Ranger helo, he had been convinced that his choice had been the right one. But he had never had to fly anything as big as this goddamn H-3.

Boyle had been caught up in all sorts of heroic fantasies as his instructor at Ellyson Field had told hair-raising tales of his experiences off the coast of North Vietnam. Like those of almost all the veterans, his stories had become more magical and gripping as the level of beer decreased in the pitchers and increased in Boyle and the other student naval aviators. It had become a major concern to the Training Command pooh-bahs that Combat SAR had become the assignment for which the students competed since the "career-enhancing" billets in ASW (antisubmarine warfare) were normally the way to go. Boyle, at twenty-two, was too young to be able to plan for the ethereal future so he chose what he felt was right for him, Combat SAR. He was doing what he had always dreamed of since he had been a small boy in southern Maryland. He was learning to be a naval aviator. Career worries would come later.

He'd loved flying the TH-IL Huey that the Navy used for advanced "Helo" training, which was nearly identical to the Hueys the gunship squadron used, but even that experience couldn't sway him from his choice. His academic and flight grades had easily been good enough to get him his first pick and he'd stuck to it despite the avuncular attempts by the career counselors to get him to choose ASW. He wanted to get in the war.

To do that, he could have chosen only between the gunship squadron or Combat SAR. Not ASW. Now, six weeks after he'd received his wings, he was not so sure.

Yesterday, when Boyle had followed another, more advanced, student around on his preflight walkaround inspection, he had not really felt the sheer size of the H-3. He had not had a single moment of doubt about his flying ability since his "Six-check," a routine progress check flight on his sixth training flight all the way back in primary training. He'd gotten the only failing grade of his entire time in Flight School on that one. Even though he was one of the handful who had gotten through with only one "down," the memory still rankled.

Now, standing on the flightline at the West Coast Fleet Replacement Squadron (or "RAG" as it was widely known), he had a serious doubt. The goddamn helicopter was huge—counting the rotor blades, over seventy feet long and over sixty wide. It weighed over nine and a half tons.

All naval aviators are inherently cocky. Seagoing types are even more so. That is part of the personality which allows a man to fly from the deck of a ship, at night, in the rain, over and over again; to complete the mission, then find the ship on the great wide sea, and land his aircraft on the moving deck. What is not obvious to an observer is that once in a while the confident appearance belies a large cold lump in the belly. This was one of Boyle's "once-in-a-whiles."

"Big sonofabitch, isn't it, Tim? Don't worry. It flies just like any other. Just not as nimble as some."

Boyle turned to see his instructor, Lt. Bob Watkins, standing just behind him. His expression was one of understanding and confidence. After all, he'd been there once himself.

The instructor led Boyle up the steps into the aircraft, beginning the flood of information about this business that would never abate as long as Boyle kept flying. Big things and little things. Each had caused somebody a problem somewhere. A few had killed some crews. Starting with where to hang the helmet bag ("The copilot can hang his on the seat post but the pilot has to hang his on the map case, since one jammed somebody's collective control a while back") and ending with the tail rotor ("Make sure the blades all face the same way because I knew a guy who had one put on backward and it tore out the whole gearbox"), the lesson covered the entire helicopter, inside and out.

Once they had settled into their seats and had connected and adjusted the straps, belts, cords, pedals, and levers, they began the checklists which would turn the helicopter into a living beast. All the while Watkins kept up the patter of things to remember and all the little things to look for "in case." Boyle's apprehension gradually diminished as they got further along in the procedures. Very soon he was doing things and asking questions as if he had been sitting in these aircraft for weeks instead of for the first time. In a sense, he had.

Boyle had spent many extra hours beyond the requirements in the procedures trainer, or OFT, a working mock-up of an H-3 cockpit which could be programmed to simulate seemingly millions of failures, fires, and other nasties that awaited him in the real aircraft. He loved spending the extra time simply because he loved anything that flew or was even remotely connected with aviation.

He had spent many additional hours asking questions of the mechanics and the instructor pilots. His extra effort in learning would save his life several times in the future. Others, who sought only the result but not the process, would not be as prepared and thus, not as fortunate.

Boyle's dedication occasionally caused raised eyebrows, for some thought that he might be just another brownnoser but his earnestness and ingenuousness soon won them over. The answers he got were gradually more complete and usually illustrated with lessons the instructors had learned in their "Fleet" tours. He never tried to impress with his growing store of knowledge but he naturally became the one to whom the other student pilots in his class gravitated.

His instructor on this, his first H-3 familiarization flight, his FAM 1, was an alumnus of HC-17, the Combat SAR squadron to which Boyle was headed when he completed the RAG. Watkins had asked to take this one to see if Boyle was for real. He knew well that a phony and a brownnoser was nothing but trouble in a squadron composed largely of small detachments farmed out to ships scattered all over the Gulf of

Tonkin. He still had a lot of good friends in those detachments and wasn't about to let some wiseass skate through and get one of them killed. So this was sort of an evaluation flight, both to see what Boyle could do and to start his education.

For his part, Boyle was unsuspecting. As he always had, he'd prepared for this flight and the next. Taxiing out, he gradually relaxed. He was simply enjoying himself. He knew his stuff and the aircraft was doing exactly what he wanted it to. The only difference he felt was that the H-3 seemed to shove its way around as opposed to the easy glide of the Huey.

Watkins patiently and precisely demonstrated each maneuver and then had Boyle repeat it. They went through the entire syllabus reasonably quickly; Boyle showed a respectable ability and no unsafe habits. He answered all the systems knowledge questions accurately and completely, displaying none of the "I'm gonna show you how much I know" tendency of the young pilot to over-answer. Usually, a nervous student will give a knowledge dump in the hope that the right answer will be in there somewhere. Boyle just gave simple, unembellished, and unfailingly correct replies. No matter what the instructor asked, Boyle was ready, often asking a follow-up question of his own. It soon became more of a Socratic discussion than a quiz. All the while Boyle guided the helicopter around the pattern with sure and smooth control inputs.

When Watkins, now fairly impressed with Boyle, had gone over everything required on the syllabus card, there was still about thirty minutes left before the scheduled landing time. He took the controls and began to show Boyle some of the little tricks.

In the beginning of the flight, they'd departed the pattern and gone out over the Pacific, where Boyle had gotten the feel of the H-3 both in normal flight and with one or the other of the hydraulic flight control systems off. Now, back at Ream Field, the instructor had Boyle making approaches and landings with them off. Each of the five landing pads marked out on the tarmac mandated a different approach, either a tighter turn to final or a shorter downwind leg. Boyle handled them all beautifully. Only once, when Boyle had underestimated the effects of the ridiculously thin San Diego air, did the instructor touch the controls.

Finally, Watkins had him land and attempt a running takeoff.

Since everything in the Navy has to be introduced properly, first came the canned description; "A running takeoff is a maneuver used when the power available to the pilot is insufficient to effect a normal vertical takeoff and achieve a stable hover in ground effect. This lack of power available is caused in conditions of high gross weight and high-density altitude. This maneuver should never be attempted over rough terrain or from a ship."

Watkins continued the spiel as he began demonstrating the takeoff: "We simulate this by limiting the torque used to that required for hovering in ground effect. The takeoff is accomplished by increasing lift through forward motion until the helicopter flies itself off the ground. Smoothly increase collective pitch and ease the cyclic stick forward until the aircraft begins to roll forward. As it accelerates and the helicopter becomes light on the landing gear, the nose tends to tuck under and can damage the ARA-25 antenna on the runway if you're not careful. The aircraft will fly itself off. Smoothly allow it to accelerate to 70 knots and climb out normally. Don't raise the nose too soon or you'll lose it and settle back onto the deck. Got it?"

When Boyle nodded, Watkins said, "Okay, Tim. You have the aircraft. Land it and give it a try."

With a deep breath, Boyle took the controls. "I have the aircraft. Takeoff checklist, please."

Watkins hit the necessary buttons and switches, reported the checklist complete, put his hand on the throttles, and sat back to watch Boyle. This was one of those "feel" maneuvers which established the differences among pilots. The first try was always a little rough but, with practice, they usually got better. Watkins, throughout his time as an instructor, had used this maneuver to make his judgments about a new replacement pilot, a little harsh according to some, but rarely was the judgment proven wrong. This "kid" had already shown a lot of talent but now for the discriminator.

Boyle eased up on the collective and trimmed the cyclic forward. The helicopter moved forward ponderously at first but gradually accelerated. Looking across the cockpit, Watkins saw that Boyle was a study in relaxed concentration, his hands gentle and loose on the controls, his eyes moving rapidly from the instruments to the runway ahead, his jaw flexing as if he were chewing gum. No apprehension, no look of confusion, absolutely no indication that this was not his hundredth running takeoff. As the helo approached lift-off speed, Watkins moved his hands nearer the controls to be ready in case Boyle screwed it up.

"I've got it," said Boyle quietly but leaving no doubt.

Watkins was so surprised at his tone that he glanced back over at Boyle just as the helo lifted off. He suddenly became aware that they were airborne only because the sounds of the wheels running along the uneven runway had ceased.

He looked forward just as they were passing through 50 feet and beginning the turn to the downwind leg. His own best efforts had rarely been that smooth. There had been absolutely no nose tuck, no bouncing of the tail. The only indication of the lift-off had been aural. It had to have been a fluke.

"Not bad, Tim, but you had a little right drift. Try it again."

Boyle knew damn well that there had been no drift but instructors were instructors and, if you were smart, you never got in a pissing contest with them. They'd invariably get angry at your impertinence. They'd push and push until you did something wrong or forgot something and then they'd write paragraphs of extrapolated "tendencies" about you on the flight grade sheet. All he wanted to do was to learn to fly this monster of a helicopter, graduate from the RAG with no major hassles, and get on to the fleet. He allowed none of these thoughts to show in his expression.

"Yes, sir. I guess I'll need a little better rudder control after we break ground, huh?"

"Exactly. What you need to do is try to feel it. Try to *think* it off the ground. Compensate for the winds with just a touch of wing down trim, too."

They came around and landed. Boyle's next attempt was equally flawless. He broke ground within feet of his first take-off point and flew straight down the painted centerline of the runway to prove that there was no drift. Bitch about that one, asshole, thought Boyle.

"Better, Tim. Now, let's take it in. We can get the debrief done and still make it to Happy Hour early."

August 26, 1972

Watkins thought of the three other flights he and Boyle had had in the RAG. After Watkins had transferred back to HC-17, Boyle had completed his training and been sent over about three months later. Watkins had watched Boyle develop and when the time came for him to take over the North SAR detachment he had been able to select a copilot to go out with him. He was very glad that Hickerson had granted his request and assigned Tim as his copilot, but, as soon as the paperwork came through, that time would be past. Pride and sadness had a small tug-of-war inside him at the thought.

Sadness won.

Chapter 13

August 26, 1972

Santy rolled his A-7 out on final approach course. The "ball" was perfectly centered and the small yellow "doughnut" on his Angle-of-Attack indicator glowed, both of which taken together showed that his jet was right on the glide path. He was outwardly calm and semirelaxed but inside he was ecstatic. They had gotten Hurst out and he had had a major part in it.

The statistics on the whole were terrible. Throughout the war only about 16.5 percent of Naval pilots and aircrewmen who were known to be down and alive in North Vietnam were rescued from capture. Early in the war, before the Navy got wise, about the end of 1965, Combat SAR was a hit-or-miss proposition. Untrained aircrews, the unarmed and unarmored helicopters that they had to use, and nearly nonexistent tactical doctrine caused the losses to the crews to be nearly prohibitive. It never ceased to amaze the Vietnamese that the Americans would expend so much of their available assets in trying to save just one man from a stay in their humane and friendly guest quarters.

For many of the pilots on Yankee Station, SAR missions at least had a tangible goal and rescued aviators were a finite measure of success. Thus it was for Mike Santy. Today was a victory, sharp and clear. There were losses to total up, to be sure: it was definitely not "cost effective" to expend what they had. But the men who flew could go in knowing that the Navy would keep the faith and do everything that was possible, risk whatever it took as long as there was hope. This was not a particularly great advantage but it did make loyalty a two-way street. It also made the American fliers feel that their country really cared about them and that they were not merely tools, cheaply purchased, to be replaced without thought or regret when broken or lost. And that sometimes could be enough.

Santy's approach continued with no comments from Paddles out on the LSO platform and the A-7 rolled out to a rocking halt. Raising his tail hook and taxiing clear of the landing area, he followed the directions of the yellow-shirt directors. He gave the thumbs-up to the flight-deck chief from his squadron indicating that the Corsair was okay and didn't need maintenance other than normal servicing to be ready for the next scheduled launch. The chief grinned hugely and, throwing a fist in the air, ran over to Mitchell's aircraft and received the same answer. This time he applauded.

Mitchell and Santy looked across at each other in amazement. The chief was one of those men who seemed to be constitutionally unable to see the bright side of anything. He earned his nickname, "Dr. Doom" when, sighing loudly, he once told the C.O. that although it was okay that the previous deployment was over, they were still going to have to go out again next year. To the young pilots, actually seeing a smile on his face for more than a microsecond was like seeing it rain *up*.

The two climbed down from their jets and, walking stiffly, met by the nose of Mitchell's Corsair. They stood for a few seconds looking at each other wordlessly, each very glad that the other had gotten out of this mission in one piece. Santy let out a deep sigh and broke the silence.

"Jesus Christ, my ass hurts."

"Mine does too, probably more, since you're the one who's got more natural padding."

"Yeah. Sometimes being a scrawny bastard has its disadvantages, doesn't it?"

Mitchell's reply was drowned out by the roar of Bennett's A-6 running out to the end of the arresting wire. The two watched as Bennett taxied by, and turned back to watch his wingman come aboard and run out the wire. The two stood just looking around at the activity on the flight deck, in no real hurry to go below for their debrief. Tom Bennett came over trailed by his B/N, Mort Stevens, both still loosening the straps and zippers on their flight gear.

"Hiya, Snake, Mike. Nice and quiet around here, isn't it? How'd you guys make out?"

"Not bad. But I don't want any more five-hour hops. I'm getting too old for that shit," said Santy.

Bennett looked around at the sky. "Well, at least you don't have to put up with whining B/Ns. All I heard all day was him complaining about how much his ass hurt and bitching at Grumman for putting bricks in the seat cushions. It's enough to drive a guy to drink, I swear. Worse than listening to my mother-in-law tell me I should get a real job."

Stevens assumed a put-upon expression. "Yeah, sure. At least I can figure out where we're going. Without me to navigate for you, you'd get lost in your stateroom. You couldn't find your zipper without both hands and a five-man working party. Speaking of zippers, have you guys heard whether they've decided yet when we go to Hong Kong?"

The other three shook their heads and the conversation descended into speculation about what delights awaited them on liberty in the famed British protectorate. Bennett, as the only one of the four to have been there before, began an almost true soliloquy about one of his visits there. The others listened respectfully and skeptically like kids do when their uncle tells them about the ten miles he had to walk through thigh-deep snow just to get to school every day in Florida.

They were interrupted by the 5MC, the flight-deck loudspeaker system used by the Air Boss to blow in the eardrums of anyone standing too close to the speakers.

"On the flight deck, LSE to Spot Four on the angle. Heads up on the angle. Landing a helo on Spot Four. Landing Angel 802."

The four watched as a green-shirted sailor hustled out of the catwalk onto the flight deck and stood facing aft with his arms spread straight out. He was the LSE, or Landing Signalman, Enlisted, whose job it was to stand up there and direct the helicopter to a precise landing, usually with the wheels straddling a catapult track. It is extremely embarrassing to the helo pilots to have to lift and reposition their machine after landing in the wrong place. You will usually hear about it from someone, often the Air Boss, always with a sneer.

Santy watched the helo land in its normal rocking way. As soon as the brown-shirted chain-runners had put the chocks and chains in place, the helo's side position lights changed from steady bright to flashing bright and the 5MC blared again.

"Heads up on the angle and around the Angel. Disengaging rotors on Angel 802. Heads up." This announcement warned the gathering crowd of flight-deck personnel, who took a few steps back, suddenly reminded that the flailing blades had been known to behead sailors who were too close when something broke.

Santy, intent on the helicopter's approach and landing, didn't notice until just then that nearly everyone on the flight deck had stopped his work and was moving over to watch the helo land. Normally, other than to check their own clearance and safety, most men on the flight deck pretty much ignored the comings and goings of the helicopters. Looking around at the throng, Santy thought that 802 couldn't have drawn a bigger crowd if they'd promised that six *Playboy* centerfolds would step out of the H-3 completely nude. Well, anyway, it would be close, he thought.

When Watkins chopped the throttle on the number-one engine and the whine rapidly diminished, the flight-deck medics moved forward to assist Hurst out of the helo. He shook off the helping hands and jumped down from the cargo door. A huge cheer went up from the gathered men as he forcefully declined to lie down in the wire stretcher and be carried below. The flight surgeon, who had enough experience to know that the aviator's pride would cause a fistfight if the medics insisted, walked over and led him toward the hatch in the side of the island structure on the starboard side of the flightdeck. As he crossed the deck, Hurst turned and threw a sharp salute at the cockpit of the helicopter. Watkins, unstrapping himself from the seat, grinned and returned it carefully.

Santy walked through the smiling gaggle of sailors and stood at the foot of the steps leading down from the front of the helicopter. He greeted Watkins as he came down and looked up, waiting for Tim Boyle to appear.

Boyle, stuffing his helmet in its bag, ducked under the top of the hatch and stopped on the top step when he saw his friend standing anxiously on the deck below. He grinned, receiving an equally large smile in return. He continued down until the two pilots were standing face to face. They shook hands firmly and began to speak at the same time. Boyle stopped chuckling first.

"Thanks for covering our ass in there, Mikey. You guys did good."

Santy gave an airy wave of dismissal. "Think nothing of it. We needed the practice. Besides your mom told me that you're too dumb to look out for yourself."

His tone changed slightly. "You looked awfully low going in there judging from the roostertail you left behind on the water. Seems that you brought back most of your airplane anyway," he said, inspecting several of the bullet holes in the fuselage directly under Boyle's seat. "I like your window, too."

Boyle looked at the outside of the H-3 for the first time. There were at least seven holes just at the level of the floor-boards. The rounds had apparently deflected down: had they gone upward they would have hit him in the feet and lower legs. Two more had hit the window frame at the top, level with where the important parts of his head usually were. The fifteen or so others had missed killing him by feet instead of mere inches. He suddenly felt like a man who has had the wall of a building topple over on him only to discover that he had been standing where an open window happened to land. The hand which he ran down his face to wipe off the sudden sweat was trembling more than it had just after they picked Hurst up out of the water.

Santy had seen how Boyle's smile faded when he saw the bullet holes, and watched him slowly grow ashen as he realized how close he had come to getting killed. He threw one of Boyle's favorite quotes from Winston Churchill back at him, "Remember, Tim, 'Nothing in life is so exhilarating as to be shot at without result.' So how come you're not being exhilarated, Timmy?"

Boyle chuckled. "Sir Winston was right as usual. I am exhilarated. In fact, I'm positively overcome with the stuff. If you don't believe me take a look at the brown exhilaration stains in my flight suit." He paused for a second and continued more brightly. "Looks like my kneeboard is overcome too," he said, holding it up for examination.

Santy carefully hid the sinking feeling in his gut when he saw the damaged kneeboard. Now he was scared, thinking of what could have happened to his best friend. He continued the light chatter until Watkins strode up and expressionlessly signaled Boyle that it was time to go below to the Ready Room to talk to the maintenance people.

As they walked away, the flight-deck guys arrived to hook up the low tractor that would tow the helo to the elevator so that the troops could patch it up down below in the hangar bay. Fixing 802 would be a snap compared to what had to be done for 801.

Rear Admiral Welch looked down from the Flag Bridge catwalk which overlooked the flight deck at the dissipating mob of men around the helicopter. He watched the two young pilots inspecting the damage to the left front and felt that he could give an almost exact quote of their conversation. He had been there a few times himself. He was just very glad that after the first disaster with 801, everyone else was back safely. In the letdown that always struck him immediately after the action was over, he was dreading the message conversation he was going to have to have with his superiors.

The incumbent Commander-In-Chief, Pacific, Admiral Frank Glover, back in Pearl Harbor, was a man who brooked no originality from those who served him. He was a man who, once crossed, never forgave or forgot. His ruthlessness in his career was legendary and many were the subordinates who long regretted their angering of the Slasher, as he was called. One didn't even need to be wrong to wind up collecting camel turds in Pakistan. All one need do was to fail to be Right According to Glover. It was said that he'd fired his mother when he found out that the Tooth Fairy wasn't real.

Welch disputed that story. From his long acquaintance with the man, beginning at the Naval Academy, he knew that Glover had her and all her kin executed.

The problem with the prick, in Welch's view, was that he was not, and never had been, a warrior. He'd carved out a career as a sycophant to the powerful. Each successive promotion had given him a stronger base of operations from which to seek the next. In the entire sixteen months that Welch had been CTF 77, Glover had personally sent no communication to him or anyone else out here that was not negative. Even his goddamn Christmas greeting had been signed for him by the deputy.

Welch knew that he probably wouldn't be fired for what he'd done today. His reputation and record of performance were far too strong for Glover to risk himself by publicly relieving him. But there were many other avenues of vengeance that could be taken. Welch's covering himself in every way would have made him a man just like Glover. Welch would rather be dead.

He heard a gentle cough and turned to find Hayes and the *Concord*'s captain, Sam Andrews, standing discreetly behind him. Hayes held a clipboard with a single sheet of paper on it. Welch arched his eyebrow questioningly and held out his hand for the clipboard. It was a personal message from Glover, just as he'd expected.

Without even the normal but abbreviated military courtesies, Glover got to the meat of it. "Hereafter, you are directed to make no extraordinary efforts in pursuit of Search and Rescue efforts. All aircraft launches to extraordinarily reinforce Search and Rescue assets will be cleared with this Headquarters. No, repeat, no valuable assets will be placed in jeopardy unless a clear and strong probability of success exists. No, repeat, no targets other than those directly, repeat, directly threatening success of these missions will be attacked without express concurrence of this Headquarters. You are further directed to acknowledge receipt of this order by immediate message followed by signed Naval Letter posted within twenty-four hours. Glover."

"Sounds like he's pissed about something," said Welch, initialing the message and handing the clipboard back to Hayes. "I guess I have to draft an answer."

"You already did, Admiral. Or at least the chief of staff did," said Hayes, handing him another clipboard.

Welch looked at the drafts of replies his COS had come up with. As usual there were two for each form of reply demanded by Glover. The chief of staff had learned early in his association with Welch that he liked to have options presented because, as had been said on their first meeting, Welch was well aware that he had never really shed his fighter pilot's go-to-hell attitude and was prone to take whatever positive action first came into his mind. Almost without fail, these actions were the right ones but a good pilot always has a fallback position. Welch's motto, "Do something. Lead, follow, or get the hell out of the way, but do something," was the philosophy that permeated the entire staff, with only one exception, Commander Strickland, who would be transferred soon anyway.

The first drafts of each type of reply were reasonably bland but compliant nonetheless. The second drafts were what Welch really thought the situation called for. After the formatted beginnings, both said the same thing with no acknowledgment that the policy was correct or that Welch had been wrong to use as much effort as he had in saving Hurst. As the staff all knew he would, those were the ones Welch selected. They said simply, "Receipt of Reference (a) is acknowledged. Welch."

"Send 'em," was all he said, dismissing the grinning Hayes with a nod of thanks. Master Chief Hayes went below, smugly anticipating collecting the five dollars Welch had just won him in a bet with the ship's communications chief.

Welch waved Andrews to follow him forward to the corner where his chair stood and, sitting down tiredly, resumed looking out over the huge expanse of the flightdeck. He asked Andrews about the mission's cost.

"On the whole, we came out pretty well on the machinery side of things. Counting the original strike and the SAR, five A-6s have some degree of battle damage but only two will be down longer than a day or so. We lost that one Phantom but no damage to the others. The A-7s got off pretty easy too except for the one Condor that got shot up during the rescue, but then we were really lucky that Robinson got it back here. CAG maintenance says that it won't be airworthy for at least a couple of weeks but the good news is that there are enough good parts in it so we can cannibalize them and put them into those two hangar queens, so we'll actually gain one A-7 in a couple of days. The damage to the other Corsairs is all superficial. The big problem we have is with the helos. 801 will be down for at least two weeks because there was some major structural damage in addition to the systems problems. Martinez did an incredible job flying that thing back despite all the blood he was losing. I suggest that we make sure he gets something for it."

Welch nodded firmly. "Yeah, and everyone else that you and CAG feel deserves it. Don't forget the troops who busted ass to keep the jets over the scene either."

Andrews continued. "802 should be back up by day after tomorrow but our problem will be pilots. We lost both guys in 801, even though Martinez will be out of surgery shortly. He'll be a hundred percent again but his war is over for at least a year. Both of them were aircraft commanders so that leaves the SAR guys short. The helo boss, Hickerson, says that Boyle is about due. He was the copilot in 802. Did a damn good job, too. I suggest that we draft a few of the pilots from the HS squadron to fill in for a couple of weeks. Hickerson says there's a couple who've been around and know how to fly the HH-3 and he feels comfortable with them. That will let us take the two pilots from North SAR with us to Hong Kong. They've been out a relatively long time and could use a break, Watkins especially, since both of the pilots in 801 were close friends of his. Hickerson says that the commitments can be covered while we're gone especially since there'll only be one carrier operating out here."

Welch agreed with the suggestions as presented. He felt drained and profoundly sad suddenly. Someone had told him long ago of the two rules of warfare. Rule 1 was that young men die. Rule 2 was that nobody could change Rule 1. It was true but that didn't make it any less shitty.

He looked at Andrews and told him that he would like to address the crew of the ship that night before the evening prayer over the 1MC, as the ship-wide loudspeaker system was called. He'd like to tell them all exactly how magnificently they had done today. And he wanted messages of commendation sent to the *Independence,* the *Galveston,* and to Red Crown for their help. They, too, had all performed flawlessly, making up the plan and filling in the gaps as they went along.

It had been as if the whole force had decided in unison that they would draw a line in the dust. In all his years, Welch had never seen anything like it. The men of the force had given the finger to the rules and their authors and done what was right. Nothing could ever take the shine from what they had done for themselves and their honor. No human intervention could ever stain their accomplishment or their courage. No cold historical assessment of today's triumphant success could ever detract from the pure nobility they had displayed, every one.

Jim Welch looked down at the helicopter being towed to the elevator. He remembered other machines which carried that red, white, and blue roundel and star from other ships in other days.

"And you make goddamn sure that Pearl and Washington get info copies of those messages, Sam," he said.

"Okay, Admiral. You know that Glover is gonna be pissed when he sees them. You have to watch that sonofabitch. He's a bad enemy. He'll get back at you somehow."

Welch scratched his chin. "Yup. But actually there's nothing official he can do. I know he'll think of something but I'll be damned if I'll run my task force based on fear of Glover." He winked as he turned and walked out.

When Boyle found him, Watkins was sitting asleep in a chair outside the recovery room in sick bay, waiting for Martinez to come out from under the anesthesia. Boyle stood looking at him, thinking about how much he owed the rumpled pilot. There were deep lines on his face which were caused by years of squinting into the sun from the cockpits of Navy helicopters and by the natural smile that was a normal part of his demeanor. Even though he was only thirty-three, to Boyle he had always seemed to be the Master at whose feet he sat, endlessly receiving patient answers to his questions. Hickerson had just told him that the paperwork to make him a HAC had gone in. He'd come to find Watkins to thank him for that.

Boyle realized that this was not the time. Watkins didn't need any of that now while he waited for his friend. It would be better if he came back later when the rest of the helo detachment was allowed in to visit. Watkins would undoubtedly still be there.

He'd buy Watkins a couple of beers when they got to Hong Kong. Meghan would even get to meet the guy whom all the letters had been about. Tim Boyle smiled a little at the man in the chair and walked away to find Santy and tell him the news.

PART TWO

"His wrong's your wrong, and his right's your right,
In season or out of season."

—Kipling

Chapter 14

September 13, 1972

The small gray-and-white officer's boat pitched easily in the swell as it headed for Fleet Landing on the seawall in Hong Kong. The early morning mist had hung on long after dawn and the steady rain had beaten down the sea, wearing out the small choppy wind waves by its sheer persistence. Now, at 8:30 A.M., the raw damp was losing its battle with the sun, which was breaking through the low cloud in ever greater intervals.

In the boat's forward cabin, among twenty or so other assorted junior officers, sat Mike Santy and Tim Boyle, talking eagerly about what awaited ashore. Gibes, brags, barbs, and general youthful bullshit flew around the cabin at the speed of light, which most of the young pilots seemed to feel was the speed at which the ladies on the beach were going to succumb to their charms. Across from Boyle, Bob Watkins sat with his head back on the blue plastic cushions, eyes closed, smiling at the chatter.

In the rear cabin, the more senior officers sat and quietly discussed the events of the past six weeks on the line on

143

Yankee Station and what awaited on the next line period. The *Concord*'s navigator, a portly captain, long out of the cockpit, pontificated about the coming end to the war, an event which was just as solemnly discussed and predicted today as it had been on a thousand other boat rides from a dozen other carriers in a score of other ports. Two or three officers whose promotions had only recently entitled them by tradition to ride in the after cabin listened raptly to the conversation; a couple more kept their eyes on the speakers and their ears and hearts on the raucousness bubbling back from the J.O.'s up forward.

Once inside the protection of the land and out of the freshness of the sea air, the conversations suddenly turned to the strange smell of Hong Kong. Every port has its own aroma and old sailors always swore that they could tell what part of the world they were approaching simply by taking a whiff from the nearest porthole. That trick was more difficult today with the amount of carbon monoxide in every port city but there was still distinction enough.

Few of the junior pilots in the boat directed their conversation toward either Boyle or Watkins. The others were mostly jet drivers and felt little in common with the rotary wing community. The squadrons in the air wing had all been assigned to the *Concord* for several years and thus had formed a tight bond with each other.

The helo pilots from HC-17, on the other hand, were nomads. They would be aboard one carrier for a while and then "cross-deck" to her replacement, beginning the laborious process of integrating themselves and their requirements into another nearly closed society.

Boyle didn't mind being left out. He didn't even mind when Mike was drawn into the banter and left him to sit, alone in the crowd, thinking of Meghan and her arrival the next day. He had gotten leave and did not have to be anywhere near the Navy or responsibilities for the next ten days. Tonight, he and Watkins were going to cut loose a little. They both had reserved rooms in the Hyatt and were going to make an hour-long shower, beer in hand, the first order of business.

Then, the biggest steaks they could find, followed by more beer.

After a few moments, Santy let himself out of the conversation with the other air wing pilots. He looked down at Boyle, who was now staring out the small window at the land. When Meghan arrived tomorrow, Hong Kong might even seem like home with the three of them together again. Maybe they'd even be able to find a quiet beach.

January 20, 1972

EIGHT MONTHS BEFORE

On a cool Friday evening, the three of them sat around the small fire they had built from driftwood, mostly, on the beach just down from Boyle's apartment. Tim and Meghan were huddled under one blanket and Santy sat across from them under another. They were passing one of several bottles of Boone's Farm Apple Wine back and forth as they talked.

Boyle had finished his RAG training that day and was due to report to his new squadron, HC-17, on Monday for duty. He already knew that he was scheduled to be assigned to the detachments off the coast of North Vietnam but the actual date of his departure was still up in the air. It had been only a month since Bob Watkins, one of his earliest H-3 instructors and now a friend, had been detached from the RAG and sent back to the detachments for his second tour.

Now, Meghan leaned close as if she could somehow hold him here a little longer. It had been pretty much unspoken but neither one could conceive of a future that did not include the other. They had slipped quickly into an easy familiarity wherein each could sense and fill the needs of the other. Meghan, who worked as a secretary in an accounting firm, was working toward a degree in marketing and spent many evenings studying in Boyle's apartment with Boyle sitting in a chair at the opposite end of the room reading or catching up on his studies for his RAG training. Just the presence of the other was enough.

Meghan spent most of her nights at Boyle's apartment but was still keeping her own in a sort of attempt to avoid the cloud of guilt that she would probably feel if they were actually "living together."

Santy usually arrived Friday evenings after Tim and Meghan had returned from the ritual Happy Hours at the Imperial Beach Officer's Club. The rest of the weekend was a study in youthful indolence. The three would drive Boyle's treasured Mustang down to Tijuana for a bullfight or do a little surfing or crew on an old cabin cruiser that several helicopter pilots had refurbished and passed on to others, when they were sent overseas, so many times that no one had any idea of how many owners the boat had had.

From the first day they had met, when Boyle dropped a jar of pickles on her foot at the supermarket, Meghan had been enchanted with Tim's humor and exuberance. She stood in the checkout line and watched nearly hysterical with laughter as Boyle wiped up the pickle juice with his T-shirt and Santy gave a running commentary to the checkout girl. Meghan had accepted Boyle's invitation to dinner at his apartment in spite of Santy's volunteering to chaperone and protect her from the clutches of this complete oaf of a helicopter pilot.

At dinner that evening, she had found both of them to be intelligent and charming. The conversation had drifted easily from college to where everybody was from and finally to their jobs. Meghan was new to the area and had never met a Navy pilot before.

Throughout her time in college near Chicago, she had followed the normal campus routine of protesting American involvement in the Vietnam war but it had always been a distant protest in that she was largely marching and mailing and chanting against what she saw in the local newspaper and on the six-o'clock news. Now, after dinner, as they sat on the small balcony overlooking the moonlit Pacific, she wanted to know what had made these two men decide to volunteer to fly airplanes against a country they had never seen for a nation of people whom they had never met.

Boyle was silent for a long moment as he tried to frame his answer so that it wouldn't drive Meghan away. She had expressed her opposition to the war logically and forcefully. Boyle normally had no time for those who called him and men like him "baby-killers" or "murderers" or "slaves of the government" but Meghan had kept her statements on a plane far above the personal.

Boyle realized as he thought about it that he wanted desperately to see Meghan again and again. He looked down at her lovely face and big eyes and hoped that she would simply understand, not agree, just understand. He looked out over the moonlit waves and spoke as gently and carefully as he could.

"Meghan, I have an uncle, Buddy, who was a turret gunner in a Navy bomber in World War II. He has always been one of my biggest heroes and I've always thought that what he and the other men like him did was kind of noble, like the Confederate cavalry in the Civil War. Ever since I was about eight, all I've wanted to be is a Navy pilot and a part of something like that. I've never had a moment's doubt about the goal, only about whether I would be good enough to get there. I volunteered for it; I wasn't drafted." He chuckled, "My draft number was three hundred twenty-six so I wouldn't have been either.

"I've never been to war and, frankly, the thought of it scares me, but I think that if I let that keep me from doing what I have always dreamed of I would regret it for the rest of my life. I worked real hard to get my first choice, Combat Rescue, because it seemed to me that it would be something worthwhile."

He looked down again at her but couldn't read her expression. He had never explained any of this to anyone and he suddenly realized that he wanted this woman, above all others, to understand. He sighed and turned back to face the ocean.

"When I played sports I always wanted to play defense. I

147

never wanted to be the quarterback or the halfback or the pass receiver. I just felt most comfortable in the back of the team picture. That's kind of how I feel about Combat Rescue. There won't be any headlines but there is a purpose to it that I like very much. I like the idea of saving lives. Of being on the defense."

He laughed a little shyly. "I've never even told Mike that."

Meghan looked at his profile and suddenly realized that despite all the craziness of the day there was a lot more to this man than to anyone she had ever met—certainly more than the pampered boys she had known in college. She wondered if their differences would drive them apart. Reaching over and placing her hand on his, she hoped fervently that they would not.

"Okay, fly-boy. What do you say that we make a pact to discuss this only in broad daylight and not waste a moon like this again?"

Boyle didn't know what to say. He just nodded and held her hand.

Meghan stood and dragged him to his feet. "Let's take a walk on the beach."

She pulled him to the steps that led down to the sand.

Santy, in a rare moment of tact, had slipped into the apartment, leaving them alone, because he really hadn't wanted to talk about that stuff. He smiled as he watched them walk down the beach. Don't blow this one, Tim. She's quite a prize, he thought as he cracked a beer and flipped on the TV to catch "The Midnight Special."

Now, sitting across the fire from them, Santy was very glad that they were still together. He was even more glad that Meghan had understood how close he and Tim were. She had joined the pair and simply made it a trio.

September 13, 1972

The boat pulled alongside the pier with a great gunning of the diesels. After the rear cabin had been emptied, the J.O.'s in the forward part climbed the three steep steps to the center deck and then jumped onto the concrete. After more than two months at sea, even on a ship as stable as an aircraft carrier, it felt strange at first to be on solid ground. The pilots, in little groups of threes and fours, set off to find the Hyatt and their Admins.

Each squadron's officers had pooled some of their money and rented a suite, known as an "Admin." In times past, officers were required to return to the ship every morning to demonstrate that they were alive and had not been kidnapped by pirates or fallen prey to some nefarious plot by foreign agents. This was a complete pain; many burgeoning international relationships had been cut short by the requirement to catch the early boat back to the ship.

Someone, almost certainly a J.O., got the bright idea to set up a place ashore where the reporting could be done with only minimal impact on the officers' playtime. Since no regulation strictly and specifically forbidding it could be found, despite a brief and superficial search of the books, the idea stuck and spread throughout the fleet. Later, by the time the rigid morning muster died from pure neglect, Admins had become a system unto themselves since they were a great way to have a place to keep your clothes and purchases without the long boat ride back to the ship, where you might inadvertently be caught up in something, like your job, which could drastically reduce the time available for cultural exchange.

There were only two drawbacks to the Admin system. One was the fact that there were usually witnesses around to see how less-than-ravishing the girls you hooked up with really were, thus reducing the credibility of the stories you could later tell in the wardroom. The other was that the C.O. and the X.O. usually hogged the beds, forcing everybody else to sleep on the floor. But, since most of the time everyone was suitably anesthetized, sleeping on the floor was not all that bad. Except for getting tripped over by later arrivals.

Santy hung back from the group of other pilots from VA-19 and fell in step with Boyle and Watkins. They gawked at the new and strange sights of the city. Other than brief stops in the Philippines and Danang, only long enough to change planes, neither Boyle nor Santy had ever set foot in a foreign country. After a few hundred yards, Watkins began a quiet travelog of the many things that they could see in Hong Kong and some dire warnings about places to avoid.

"What's your plan, Mike?" asked Boyle.

"Well, I thought I'd drop my stuff in the Admin and get a couple of beers while I wait for my turn in the shower. Maybe I'll make a call home to my mom. How about you?"

"Tell you what. Meg doesn't arrive until around eleven or so tomorrow. Why don't you stay in my room tonight? That way you don't have to fight for a bed and you get the second shower. While I go first, you go find the beer. We can hit the pool and then go to dinner. How's that sound?"

Santy nodded. He didn't really want to spend his first free evening in months with the same people he had spent every waking hour of those months with.

"Okay, but I've got to make that call before the pool."

Boyle turned to Watkins. "That okay with you, Bob? You can give us both Hong Kong lessons at least until you leave for Australia tomorrow."

In the face of Boyle's enthusiasm, Watkins grinned and agreed.

"Sure, Tim. I'll meet you guys by the pool at about noon. Don't forget to bring your towels from the room. And, Mike, you're not going to find a package store near the hotel so just order some up from room service."

Forty-five minutes later, Boyle was leaning his head on his arms which were crossed on the back wall of the shower. The water was as hot as he could stand it and was hitting him on

150

the neck and upper back. His height made the stream nearly horizontal and one of the tiny jets was squirting over the curtain onto the tile floor, creating a small pond.

Boyle was deep in a reverie about the last night he had had with Meghan when the curtain disappeared, and he heard a series of thumps, several loud curses, and the crash of a breaking bottle.

He looked down as Santy struggled to untangle himself from the curtain and sit up. He turned off the shower, reached for a towel and began drying himself, all the while watching as Mike finally propped himself up against the vanity.

"So where's my beer?" he asked during a lull in the cursing.

"Over there, you asshole," Santy said pointing to a foamy pile of brown glass in the corner and taking a swig from the one that survived. "This one's mine."

Boyle wrapped the towel around himself and stepped gingerly over both the rim of the tub and Santy. At the doorway, he looked back down at his friend and said, "My, my, such nasty language. Do you kiss your mother with that mouth?" He ducked around the corner, his shaving kit missing his head by a foot on its trip across the bedroom.

Boyle walked over to the small refrigerator and took out a beer. By the time he had put on a pair of shorts and sat down on the balcony overlooking the pool, Santy had joined him, plopping down in another chair.

"You can have the shower now. I'm done," Boyle said, looking off into the distance.

"Fine. As soon as you fix the shower curtain, I'll use it."

"Ain't my curtain."

"Yeah, but it's your room and you have to pay for it. Besides, it got broken while I was on an errand of mercy."

The two finished their beers in silence. They got up and together repaired the damage to the bathroom. Boyle placed a call to his parents back in Maryland and went back to the balcony until the hotel operator rang back with the call.

The conversation went well except for his mother's repeated requests for assurance that he was fine and safe. He told her that he was and promised to write more often. It was one of those talks on the phone that cover only the essentials, both sides aware that there is much more to tell but aware also of the fact that the subjects can never adequately be discussed except face to face, on the back porch in the cool of the evening, when time and distance disappear.

Boyle hung up after promising to call again in a couple of days, after Meghan arrived. Many minutes later, as he sat looking at the telephone, he heard Santy's voice behind him.

"I felt the same way, Tim, when I talked to my mom. There's no way to tell them about it all. That's a whole different world back there."

"Nope. I guess it's just as well that they don't know." Boyle sighed and stood abruptly. "C'mon, let's go down to the pool. The rest of the guys ought to have taken over down there by now. Maybe I can help you find yourself that stewardess you've been dreaming about. Of course, with your moves you'll probably get picked up by a queer flight engineer."

Things didn't work out exactly that way.

By the time the two young pilots got down to the pool, things were beginning to look like spring break in Daytona. Teams made up of several F-4 guys from each of the fighter squadrons were having piggyback wrestling matches, or "horsefights," in the shallow end of the pool. There was a biggest splash contest going on in the deep end among a bunch of A-7 types. Most of the normal patrons were sitting on the chaises longues smiling at the horseplay. A few, middle-aged women with rhinestone sunglasses and big straw hats, were not particularly thrilled to see the concrete ambiance of the hotel disturbed. It was just as well that they got up and left before the boys really got rolling. As they moved off, their husbands looked wistfully back over their shoulders and then followed their marching wives into the hotel.

Santy and Boyle picked out a couple of recently vacated chairs near the bar. They dumped their towels and small gym bags containing wallets, towels, and Coppertone and bought a couple of large, expensive, green drinks which seemed to have rum in them. As they sat down, Watkins came over and pulled up a chair. He dropped his bag and looked at the drinks in the huge glasses. He bent down and fished his wallet from his bag.

"What are those?"

Boyle answered, "Green."

Santy studied the glass in his hand. "I don't know but they're right tasty."

"I think I'll try one. It got awful dusty walking all the way over here. The throat, don't ya know." He turned and walked toward the bar.

Boyle looked carefully at the level in his glass and then at Santy's. He checked the distance to the bar, all of thirty feet, and the crowd around ordering drinks, perhaps five people. "Hey, Bob, as long as you're going all the way over there, bring back a couple more of these. We'll be ready when you get back. And shitcan the little umbrellas. We don't want to look like Air Force pilots. Bad for the reputation."

The rest of the afternoon passed predictably and routinely, as least as far as the pilots were concerned. The usual group of ladies showed up, invited by a fast-talking pair of J.O.'s. The horsefights soon included girls on the shoulders of the fighter types. The bartender wisely switched to plastic cups on Watkins's advice, then narrowly avoided a dip in the pool when it was immediately discovered that the plastic cups held less than the glasses did at the same price. A conference was held and the bartender eagerly agreed to get some bigger cups and keep them handy as long as the Americans were in residence. He did a land-office business selling the green drinks since it was discovered that the girls sensibly wouldn't drink anything that they thought dangerous and the green ones looked and tasted pretty safe. They were safe as long as you drank them slowly, say at the rate of one every month.

The chaise longue races started at about three and went on for an hour or so. The girls were the drivers at first but then a handicap system was devised, putting at first one and finally three pilots in the chaise with one female driver. The only drawback was that the girls would not give their correct weights so handicapping became a subject of great debate, usually winding up with the arguers being thrown in the pool for using bogus logic. Somebody swiped the scale from the luggage room, which helped speed things up until the hotel's chief porter and two of his minions tracked it down behind a row of potted plants. Several of the husbands returned and bought rounds of drinks, braving both bankruptcy and their wives' wrath. Since they were mostly businessmen who had been in somebody's military a long time ago, they brought a couple of new ideas for games which quickly caught on.

Around six, it became obvious that rum and beer were not particularly nourishing and the crowd of players began to shrink as the young men went back to the rooms to change for dinner. The girls figured that this had been as much fun as they had had in a long time and planned to bring as many of their friends as they could find to the pool tomorrow when it opened. Some dashed back to their rooms to change for the dates they had made with the Americans.

It had been a nice, if unconventional, afternoon. Everyone behaved reasonably well and the hotel manager could find no damage anywhere except for a dozen or so blobs of sticky green stuff on the pool deck and some unusual wear on the wheels of several chaises longues. That was a small price to pay for the money that had been made in the middle of the slow season.

Boyle, Santy, and Watkins met the rest of the crowd in the bar off the lobby. It was now well after midnight. Rather than brave getting lost on one of the ferries which ran around the harbor, most of the pilots decided to eat in one of the restaurants nearby, which all suffered severe damage to their steak supplies. Nearly everyone was yawning mightily after the impromptu party of the afternoon and a huge dinner as their mental springs wound down, so the carrying on in the bar consisted mostly of loud talk and cheers as the dice cup passed back and forth along the bar. The loudest cheers were saved for when one of the squadrons' C.O.'s or X.O.'s lost a roll and had to buy the round. At one point, Boyle, Santy, and Watkins had three extra vodka tonics lined up in front of them. They moved away from the bar and found a little table in the corner. It was quite an impressive juggling act getting four drinks apiece over there through the crowd without spilling a drop, but then, they landed aircraft on ships for a living so their reflexes were above average.

After Watkins had made his excuses and left for bed, Boyle looked around at the crowd of happy, playful men and remembered a night long ago in another bar, an evening that was a bit more subdued. He wondered what ever happened to the bartender in the San Carlos Hotel in Pensacola.

"Hey, Tim, remember that night we met? Doesn't seem possible, does it?"

Boyle was not surprised at all that Mike had been thinking the same thing as he. He shook his head and laughed a little.

"No, it doesn't. I was just thinking how glad I am to be here with these maniacs. Awful lot of guys never made it this far."

"Yeah, but an awful lot did. Enough of that, Timmy me boy. Here's to us, none better!" Santy said, raising his glass.

There was a long silence, each lost in his own thoughts until Santy leaned over and asked, "What time does Meghan get in?"

"Her flight arrives at eleven-ten. Pan Am. I really can't wait to see her, man. Nothing against all you guys, but I'd like to talk to somebody who doesn't have a mustache and doesn't smell like jet fuel. That's not asking too much, is it?"

"Not really, but don't let it get out that I agree with that or Skipper Wilson will give me another lecture on my attitude."

They continued talking of small things for a while until Santy finished his last drink. "Looks like we're empty. Let's get back in while the heavies are still losing. I love having commanders pay for my drinks."

"Okay, but I'm not touching any more of those green bastards tonight. I have a feeling that they can give you terminal diabetes."

"Not true. The latest medical evidence shows that only the guys get diabetes. Girls, for some reason, suffer only a paralysis of the No reflex after two of them. More research needs to be done on this phenomenon for the good of all humanity."

"Let me guess. You're going to sacrifice yourself and take the lead in the research. What a guy!" said Boyle.

"Yep, it'll have to be me. No one else is that brave and unselfish. But first, I've gotta get that recipe. Imagine the possibilities in a place like California, all those frustrated and unsuspecting American girls. They probably don't even know that the No reflex is a birth defect. I could be the next Jonas Salk. You can handle the manufacturing and office stuff and I'll take care of the sales end of it. We'll make millions with the patent on those things."

As they walked back into the dice game next to the bar, Boyle had a momentary mental picture of Santy selling the green stuff from the back of a covered wagon in the middle of the UCLA campus. He'd probably recruit several cheerleaders to dress things out. The funny thing about the picture was that there was nothing strange about it. Santy was the only man he knew who could pull something like that off with a straight face, or who would dare try. Just for the sheer hell of it.

Chapter 15

At eight-thirty the next morning, Watkins was standing at the newsstand in the airport looking over the stacks of papers from all over the Far East when Boyle stepped out of the elevator and spotted him. As Boyle approached, Watkins picked out two day-old papers from Brisbane, Australia. He was paying the clerk when Boyle spoke up.

"Getting yourself up on the local politics, Bob?"

Watkins laughed. "Hi, Tim. Nope. I have to make sure I know who's where in all the sports leagues. My Aussie friends don't talk politics unless they really get sloshed and I've never been able to keep up with them long enough to see that happen."

"So when does your plane leave? Do we have time for me to buy you a drink?"

Watkins accepted his change. "I've got about an hour. A large Bloody Mary sounds real good right now. I gotta quit trying to stay out with you young guys."

Boyle groaned as they headed for the bar near the Pan Am gates. "I've gotta quit trying to keep up with Mike. The man

157

is unstoppable except I'm up and sort of at 'em and he's still asleep." Boyle looked at his watch and almost giggled. Santy still had almost two hours before his morning would start with a bang.

Watkins moved to two empty stools in the darker interior of the bar. He dropped his bag at his feet and waited while Boyle placed the order.

When the drinks arrived, they raised them silently at each other and sipped. Boyle spoke while looking down at the wet stains his glass was leaving on the veneer of the bar.

"Bob, since I got the designation, I haven't had a chance to thank you for recommending me for HAC. I know it's been longer than it should have been but, um, well, thanks."

Watkins had wanted to talk to Boyle about this but the two hadn't had the chance on the way to Hong Kong; there always seemed to be some commitment or meeting or flight which kept them going in different directions. When they got back to Yankee Station, they would be aboard different ships; since Boyle was a junior HAC, he would be aboard the *Concord* with the main detachment and Watkins would take a new copilot out to North SAR. Watkins was suddenly very glad that they had this opportunity to talk, away from the demands and hustle of shipboard life, during the unconcerned and care-free time on liberty.

"I didn't do you any favor, Tim. One, you earned it. And two, you are not going to find it as terrific as you think now."

Boyle began to say that he knew about that but Watkins raised his hand.

"I always give my 'New HAC' speech to every one of my copilots. I realize that you've probably thought about it all but it's traditional. Bear with me.

"While you are working for it, a HAC designation seems like the end of the quest. It's not. What it is is the start of another one. All you have done is reach one plane and you now have to learn how to operate there. You are a junior HAC and now you will have to learn a whole new set of responsibilities. You won't have somebody sitting next to you to pull you out when your ass is in a crack. When something bad happens, you will be the guy who has to answer for it no matter who in the crew screwed up. With the trust and respect you earn getting to be a HAC comes the responsibility and the added danger. Those're the rules. Do you see what I'm saying?"

Boyle nodded, listening to Watkins put many of the thoughts Boyle had had since he'd made HAC into words. Watkins continued on a different tack.

"How did you look upon being a lieutenant when you were still a jaygee?"

Boyle had been promoted to full lieutenant two days after the *Concord* left Yankee Station for Hong Kong. He had had the requisite time of service and hadn't blundered seriously enough to earn a substandard fitness report, so he had been promoted when the lieutenant's list came in. Santy, since he had been originally commissioned on the same day as Boyle, was now a lieutenant, too. Santy said that this was a "Fog the Mirror" promotion because that was about all one had to do to earn it.

Boyle answered, "Well, I thought it was a big deal until I was given the three collateral jobs that the boss said went with my new station in life. They don't waste any time laying it on you."

"Exactly. It's the same with the flying. You get what the position calls for. Except that the flying has a bonus. You can get yourself and your crew killed. Nobody ever died from a paper cut. What I mean is that you have to understand that your ability to complete the mission grows with your experience and your responsibility for successfully completing it grows, too."

"I understand, Bob. I've seen you pull off things that I can't do yet."

"Right. But there's more to it than that. There will come times when people will try to put you in a situation that's over your head. Your aviator's pride will con you into giving it a shot. That's what will get you killed. Don't let yourself get cocky or let the situation carry you along. Stay cool and in control. When you get all emotional and your blood is boiling, back the hell off. There are going to be times and situations where there is nothing at all you can do to change anything. You have to be smart enough to recognize them and brave enough to leave them alone. That's something which you are going to have to work on because nobody can give you that knowledge or make those decisions for you. Okay?"

Boyle nodded. The little twinges of worry about how he'd do as a HAC shrank further as he realized that he was not unique in having them. He was really glad that he had decided to come to the airport early today and wait for Meghan there as opposed to pacing the hotel room.

"Thanks again, Bob. I'll try and remember that."

"Trying won't cut it, Tim. Remember it." Watkins looked at the counter where the line waiting to check in for his flight was now almost gone.

"Well, I've gotta go. I'll see you back on the ship. Enjoy your leave and thanks for the drink." Watkins shook hands with Boyle and walked to the counter.

Boyle watched him hand his ticket to the agent and walk toward the gate. Watkins glanced once at Boyle and waved a little, then he was gone.

An hour later, Boyle was feeling the full effects of last night's partying. The chairs in the air terminal were designed for dwarfs. No matter which way he twisted his frame the circulation to something got cut off. Part of his problem, Boyle thought, was that the blood being pumped around in his body probably had the consistency of maple syrup. The second Bloody Mary that he had picked up in the bar on the way to the gate wasn't having any effect so he walked over to a snack bar and bought two large Cokes.

Returning to his seat, he thought over the events of last night. He and Santy had been unable to escape from the party in the hotel bar until well after three. When they got back to the room, they found that the alcohol had not made either one as sleepy or as drunk as they thought it had in the dark and close confines of the bar. They sat out on the balcony talking about all those things, big, small or irrelevant, that they had missed talking to each other about amid the demands and lack of private times at sea. They hadn't had any real time to just sit back and relax since they were last together in the apartment in San Diego. Meghan occupied the apartment now because it had been sort of the headquarters for all three of them and both Boyle and Santy had left all their possessions and cars there. All their bills went to the apartment and Meghan paid them from money that they sent her by allotment each month. Since both of them were fiscal morons and usually had to change banks in order to unsnarl their checking accounts, Meghan's stability and common sense had probably saved both of them from debtor's prison.

They weren't long on the balcony before the events of the day caught up to them and they went in and collapsed on the beds. They were asleep within seconds.

When the telephone rang with Boyle's wake-up call, Santy didn't even stir. Boyle took a shower, shaved and put on some industrial-strength after-shave that he had picked up on the ship. He went back in and shook Santy nearly awake.

"Mike, c'mon. You gotta get out of here. The maids need to make up the room so it looks okay for when Meg gets here."

"All right, all right. Don't worry. I'll be long gone. Now go away and let me go back to sleep." Santy turned back over with a contented sigh and quickly began to snore softly.

Boyle debated throwing an ice bucket of water on him but that would leave the bed wet. Rolling him onto the floor or setting fire to the sheets was out, too. In the end, he set the telephone volume up as high as it would go, put the phone down on the floor on the far side of the other bed, and placed a sheet over it. He called the front desk and arranged for six wake-up calls, spaced five minutes apart, beginning at ten-fifteen.

That ought to do it, he thought, imagining Santy's wrath when the third one came. As he stepped into the hall and closed the door gently behind himself, he knew that the payback from Mike would be interesting. They always were.

Boyle was just finishing the second Coke when the PA

announced the arrival of Meghan's flight. The English one was the second of the announcements in several languages which all had "Pan Am" in them. He got up and walked over to the exit from the customs area and waited. Now that she was almost here, his hangover was forgotten.

Meghan appeared in the first part of the herd approaching the customs lines. She was at least half a head taller than most of the people in front of her and, from what Boyle could see of her face, she was furious. Once through the narrow passageway and into the larger area short of customs, she turned and shook her finger under the nose of another passenger, a tall, aristocratic-looking man in his mid-thirties who had been following close behind her. The passenger simply kept a small insouciant smile on his face and looked back at her. Boyle didn't like the look.

Meghan turned and made sure that the shoulder bag she was carrying accidentally hit the passenger between the legs as she swung around. The passenger was fast enough to avoid most of the impact and watched her walk away through the crowd with that same look on his face except for a flash of cold anger. Boyle was ready to punch the sonofabitch just for that look.

Meghan had reached the head of one of the lines by the time Boyle got her attention. The look of cold fury on her face was instantly replaced by the broadest smile Tim had ever seen her have. She began to bounce and fidget as the customs inspectors took their time going through her luggage. It only took about five minutes but, for Boyle, the process lasted a week.

Then he was holding her. He didn't swing her around like they do in the movies, he just held her. Neither spoke and they didn't lean back to look into each other's eyes. They just embraced.

Finally, Meghan sighed and said, "If we don't move, they'll have to sweep the floor around us. I love you, sailor."

Boyle chuckled and, blinking a little rapidly, looked down into her eyes. "Yeah, but you're easy," he said.

The old joke between them broke the logjam and they both began to speak at once then stopped.

"You first. How was your trip?"

"Fine, except for this weasel who wouldn't leave me alone. Let's get the hell out of here before he comes after me again."

Boyle picked up her bags and they started to walk away toward the front entrance. "You mean the guy you tried to turn into a soprano?" He looked around and didn't see the man. "It's okay, babe, he's gone. Anyway, besides me, we've got a whole damn air wing to protect you with over here."

Meghan had never in her life felt safer than she did at that moment. She now knew the answer to the question she had been asking herself all through the long trip across the Pacific. Not trusting herself to speak, she simply grasped Tim's left arm with both hands and pressed it to her chest. She looked up at his strong face and the smiling green eyes that never stopped taking in everything around them and was very, very glad that she had come.

The trip to the hotel seemed to take no time at all. They skimmed the surface of several dozen subjects between moments when they took in the mystique and beauty of Hong Kong. They held hands and talked but neither would remember what they talked about nor would they care. They just looked and felt like they were sixteen and on the big pre-summer date.

By the time they were standing outside the door to the hotel room Meghan was running out of steam. With the time change and the long trip, she was badly in need of a couple of hours' rest. She said nothing of this to Boyle, who had dropped the bags and was fishing in his pocket for the room key.

"Where's Mike?" she asked. "I figured he'd find some way to horn in on you meeting me. Don't tell me he's tripped over some discretion in his travels."

"Not a chance. When I left him, he was tits-up in your bed. I hope he's cleared out and gone off in pursuit of some sweet thing. We'll see him later."

The door swung open and Meghan peeked in, ready to be grabbed in one of Santy's loud and enthusiastic bear hugs. The room was clean and neat, which it wouldn't have been if Santy were still in residence.

"You sure you have the right room, Tim? This looks like something out of a travel brochure."

Meghan walked over to the dresser. There were a dozen red roses in a vase and a bottle of champagne in an ice bucket. She removed the card and read it.

" 'These are compliments of Lieutenant Michael T. Santy, Jr., United States Naval Reserve. They have been carefully and laboriously chosen and purchased at incredible expense to fit the grand and glorious occasion of your arrival in the Far East, which is referred to in Hong Kong as This Neck of the Woods. Enjoy and I'll see you later.' "

Meghan laughed and shook her head. As she was passing the card to Boyle she noticed the word "over" written in small letters in the corner of the card. She turned it over and read the handwritten words, "I put this on your room tab, Tim. Love and kisses, Mike."

That did it. She collapsed giggling on the bed watching Boyle shake his head in resignation. He turned and looked down at her with the overgrown puppy expression she always drew from him.

"You want to open the champagne now or wait a while? You really look like you could use some sleep, Meg. Come to think of it, so could I. Mike kept me up most of the night keeping an eye on him. He's a terrible influence."

Meghan looked at Boyle, standing shyly at the foot of her bed. She knew very well that what he really wanted to do was spend the afternoon making love, as did she. One of the things she loved about the big dope was his nobility. "I know what you're thinking, Tim, but we've got ten days here. Let's not try everything in the first half hour. Besides, I'd be worthless without a nap. Trust me."

Boyle couldn't imagine her being worthless with or without a nap. But she was usually right, so he just watched as she got up and pulled a football jersey out of her suitcase and walked into the bathroom. He turned down her bed and, stripping down to his skivvies, climbed into his own.

When Meghan came out of the bathroom, she stood over him for a moment, then bent down and kissed him gently on the forehead. "You're gonna be in deep *kimchi* when I wake up, sonny. So get some rest now." She climbed into her bed with a deep sigh.

As Boyle switched off the light, she said, "You better get us another room tomorrow, Tim, one with a king-sized bed. If you think I came all this way to sleep like June Cleaver you're out of your mind. This separation crap is just as hard on us girls as it is you guys."

Chapter 16

September 14, 1972

Boyle rolled over and aimed his watch at the curtains across the sliding glass door. It was just before three and he had been asleep for nearly two hours. He looked across the gap between the beds and spent a few minutes watching Meghan sleep. As usual, she had pulled the covers up until all that he could see was the top of her head and her face with her brown hair across most of it. She was, he thought, just about the most beautiful thing he had ever seen.

Boyle quietly slid out of his bed and moved across the room. He pulled back the curtain and eased his way through the door and onto the balcony. He pulled a less-than-cold beer out of the ice bucket he and Santy had left out there the night before. Opening it, he took a long pull and leaned back in a chair, staring out over the buildings at the highlands in the distance but his thoughts were on Meghan, only twenty feet away after all those many days apart.

He knew that he was hopelessly in love with her. When he first saw her at the airport, there was none of the letdown one often experiences after seeing someone whom separation has buffed and polished into something greater and finer than the real thing. If anything, the separation had failed to do her justice.

When a man is at sea for a long period, he learns to sublimate thoughts of home and those whom he has left behind. They are placed in a little gold box in the mind which is only opened when the demands of flying or routine paperwork have been dealt with for the day. If a man carries his heart on his sleeve and moons about what he is missing at home, he only makes himself and everyone around him miserable. Worse, he becomes far less efficient and effective than he must be. In the case of a man on a warship, he or someone else can suddenly and horribly die because of that inefficiency, that one little mistake when he is distracted by the thought that "this sucks and I wish I was home." He must learn to allow that sort of thing to surface only when he has the time to deal with it. It's cold and difficult but it works.

Now, sitting here in the sun on a balcony overlooking a city filled with people totally unconcerned with Tim Boyle, was the time and place for him to allow those thoughts to run their course. His mind was running free, not stopping at any one point but circling one central theme: there was no way he could imagine the rest of his life without Meghan Collins in the middle of it.

He was reaching for his second beer when he heard the glass door behind him open. Meghan came up behind him and placed her arms around his chest. She pressed herself against his back and sighed. It was obvious that she was no longer wearing the jersey she'd had on when she went to sleep.

"Hey, fly-boy," she said, "want to take advantage of a weary traveler?"

Boyle turned and, with his arm around her, led her back into the room. He thought briefly about the people of the city below. Ten million people around here and right now I'm the luckiest one of them all.

* * *

167

Shortly after four, Santy was hanging on the edge of the pool, trying to regain his breath, when he spotted Meghan and Tim weaving their way through the maze of chairs and groups of people around the pool. The crowd was at least twice as large today as it had been the day before. Many more of the officers from the air wing had finished up last-minute paperwork and other odds and ends and made it in. Most who had been to sea before waited for the second day before they went ashore. This accomplished two things: first, they could get a feel for where to go and what to miss from the crowd that returned from the first day; second, the dust had normally settled on the first day's craziness and they could spend the remainder of the port visit having a good time without too many hassles from the Shore Patrol. Today's activities at the pool had leveled off about where a really good and fun singles bar would be if it had a pool.

There was also an amazing number of single and allegedly single women around. The odds were good for both sides. Santy had even met a couple of stewardesses whose responses were promising, to say the least. It was one of these who had gotten him out of breath. She turned out to be a fierce horse-fight contestant who beat all comers until her horse, Santy, collapsed from exhaustion. She was also a tall, gorgeous Brit who flew for some airline based in Hong Kong.

Santy hopped out of the pool and ran up behind Meghan. He grabbed her up with a roar and, ignoring her shrieks, carried her to the edge of the pool and dove in with her. She returned to the surface and swung at him wildly, missing only because her long brown hair was over her eyes. When she could see again, she found Santy sitting on the edge of the pool looking at her innocently.

"Hi, Meg. Have a nice trip?"

"Santy, you sonofabitch, you're dead. Paybacks, bucko. You just wait." She dove and retrieved her sunglasses from the bottom of the pool.

Santy stood up and reached down for her hand. "Here, let me help you out."

"No, thanks. I don't trust you." She climbed out and stood looking at him, hands on hips. "Oh, hell. Hi, Mike," she said and grabbed him and gave him a huge kiss on the lips.

"C'mon. Cut it out." He turned to the crowd looking on and said loudly, "I've never seen her before in my life. She means nothing to me. Honest. Officer! Arrest this woman." The tall Brit looked back at him coolly.

The two turned and walked over to where Boyle was now sitting. They plopped down in two chaises longues next to him, Meghan in the middle.

"Did you guys get the champagne and flowers?"

"Yeah, nice touch, Mike. Meg was totally whelmed," said Boyle.

"Aw, shucks, think nothin' of it, ma'am. You two want a drink? I'll be right back." Santy scurried off toward the bar.

Boyle lay back on the chaise. "Meg, if he brings you a green drink, be careful with it. We haven't completed the tests so we aren't sure what dosage is lethal. We can't use Mike as a reliable test subject because he has a hollow leg and no perceptible brain."

Meghan looked at Santy's broad back for a minute and then at Boyle. She sighed as she leaned back in her chaise. "You know, I can't imagine my life without both of you, but I sure am glad it's you that I'm in love with."

Boyle had one of those flashes of perfect timing that only come to a man about twice in his lifetime. "Well, we could always make the arrangement permanent, you know. Except for that asshole, Mike, of course. We'd probably have to make him live in the basement."

There was a long silence. Meghan sat up slowly and turned so that she was looking him straight in the face. "Take off those sunglasses."

Boyle did so and stared straight back at her.

"Tim Boyle, are you asking me to marry you? Here? At the goddamn pool on the other side of the world? Without even a moon?"

"Yup, I believe I am, Meg. What do you say?"

"Yes." She nodded once with her chin out as if defying something or someone. Boyle had always loved the little-girl look that one expression gave her. He sighed deeply in pure relief, which was followed instantly by pure joy, which was followed instantly by pure worry. The cycle repeated itself as he reached for her hand. They sat there wordlessly just feeling the moment and when he saw what was in her eyes, the cycle stuck on joy.

"Ahem. Are you two holding a seance or something? While you're at it see if you can get ahold of my Uncle Nick. The old bastard died owing me twenty bucks." Santy stood over them with the drinks, all green. As they took them and turned back to each other, he plopped down on the foot of Meghan's chaise. He watched them raise their glasses to each other and suddenly understood.

"Well, I'll be damned. You did it. You said yes, Meg, didn't you? About damn time."

They both turned to him in amazement.

"It was easy. I set you up with the champagne and the flowers. I sprayed the pillows with essence of 'green.' See? I told you this stuff works." He suddenly got very serious. He stood up and raised his glass.

"Here's to you guys. I don't think that anything in the world could make me happier. This is just fuckin' wonderful!" He turned around but before he could open his mouth Meghan pulled him down.

"Shut up, you jerk. Give us a chance to get used to the idea before you tell the world."

Santy sat. Meghan noticed an expression she had never seen on his face before. She moved over and hugged him. She leaned back again and ruffled his hair as one would a little brother. "Maybe I'll give you another chance with my sister. She needs a project."

Mike began to complain about being a guinea pig for Meghan's cooking. He said that love made a man immune to poison so he'd probably have to increase his life insurance if he were going to hang around the apartment any more.

Meghan looked at him and said, softly, "You'd better hang around, Mike. You just better."

It was five days later that Tim and Meghan visited the ship and reality. All had been peaceful and quiet, almost idyllic for the two of them. They had found a jeweler who was recommended by a couple of the older hands in Santy's squadron. Since there were no opportunities to spend his money at sea, the engagement ring that Tim and Meghan picked out was much larger than she would ever have expected to get. Tim, for his part, thought that the joy in her eyes was worth twice the price of the ring.

The two wandered around the city and took in all the sights, several two and three times. They found a couple of floating restaurants and ate leisurely, trying a selection of items. Almost all were excellent. After a while, they both felt the need for a jolt of American food, so Tim took her on the long ride out to the ship. Putting aside her feelings, Meghan steeled herself to visit the ship but once aboard soon found herself in awe of the thing. Tim's barely suppressed enthusiasm and pride in the ship were infectious and she soon found herself wanting to know everything about the world he lived in.

After they had eaten in the formal wardroom (they were fortunate; the meal was real meat in the form of "sliders and rollers," cheeseburgers and hot dogs), they visited Tim's tiny stateroom. Meghan could not believe that two men could simultaneously use this tiny space for living and working. It was about the size of the bathroom in Boyle's apartment back in San Diego. The visit to the ship was becoming a depressing intrusion on the beautiful time they were having together and, without mentioning the feeling, they both decided that it was time to go back ashore. Tim led her down the ladders to the hangar deck, taking a great deal of pride in the appreciative looks Meghan got from the crew members they passed.

They were standing on the quarterdeck, waiting for the officer's boat to be called away, when Admiral Welch and his chief-of-staff appeared through the hatch leading down from

Flag Country, his area of living and working quarters three decks above.

Welch turned at Boyle's "Good evening, Admiral." He seemed genuinely pleased to see Boyle and positively beamed when Boyle introduced Meghan as his fiancée. He invited them to go ashore with him in his special boat, or "Admiral's Barge," and when Boyle hesitated, Welch said, "Miss Collins, you are coming with me. If he wants to take the longer way in, that's fine. It's probably what he deserves for dragging you all the way out here when you two should be sitting in a quiet corner somewhere."

Everyone laughed, even Boyle, who was not sure if J.O.'s could be shot for even thinking of refusing the admiral.

The ride back in was a pleasure for Tim. The admiral showed a great paternal interest in Meghan and pointed out for her all the sights from the deck of the barge. Meghan, for her part, quickly fell in love with the gruff older man with the laughing eyes. She dearly hoped her Tim would be just like him when he reached that age. She also felt strangely glad that this man was the one who made the decisions for Tim and all the men out there.

The conversation inevitably got around to the war and Boyle waited for the fireworks to start. He was stunned when the admiral agreed with Meghan.

Welch fixed his eyes on Boyle and said, "I know that what I say will not be repeated to anyone. Isn't that correct, Mr. Boyle?" Boyle mumbled a "Yessir" and the admiral sat down and gestured the two of them down on the bench across from him.

"Meghan, you are absolutely correct that we should no longer be involved in this war. I think you are wrong, however, about whether we should have gotten involved in the first place." Meghan opened her mouth to speak but shut it again.

"When I was first over here in nineteen sixty-five, there was a purpose and we believed that it was a noble one: to keep the people of South Vietnam out of the Communist sphere. We could have ended the war easily and relatively inexpensively. We had the will and the power to do so. But we also had, unfortunately, President Johnson, who was overmatched by the demands of overseeing a military solution to the problem. Are you with me so far?"

Meghan nodded and leaned forward with her elbows on her knees, eyes narrowed in concentration on what the admiral was saying. She realized down deep somewhere that Welch didn't get to open up much and she was somehow glad that he was doing so now, to her.

Welch continued. "Our plan was to hurt them without really hurting them. We tried to cut their supply system and damage their war-making capability without damaging their society or killing anyone we didn't have to. We've learned that the North Vietnamese could not care less about the casualties they suffer or how long they will have to suffer them. Their view of the war is a long one. They have been fighting it for hundreds of years and expect it to continue for a while yet. They have outlasted all of the others with whom they've fought and will beat us the same way.

"We believed that North Vietnam would see that we had the ability to destroy their whole country if we wanted but were restraining ourselves in the name of humanity and that they could never hope to match our strength and power. What we failed to note is that the enemy had no intention of matching us; all they had to do was adjust and we'd eventually add up the cost and decide it wasn't worth losing an entire generation of Americans for a bunch of people whose lives won't change no matter who wins. We're at that point now. The Vietnamese are at the table in Paris using the same basic tactics there that they've used for centuries at home on the battlefields. They're dragging their feet and trying to outwait us."

Meghan sat back and looked at him questioningly. "But if that's what has happened, that proves my point about being here in the first place. We should never have come."

Welch smiled and shook his head. "No, Meghan, what that proves is that we ought to get out now, before we lose the society we have built at home. We are being torn apart by this and I'm afraid that the scars will take some time to heal.

"What I meant is that we should have gone in immediately and completely destroyed the ability of North Vietnam to sustain the war, including stopping all shipments from other countries. We could have closed them down in a month by mining the harbors, blockading them by sea, and by destroying the railroads and the road system. We could have prevented the deaths of thousands of people on both sides had we done it that way. Now that it's almost too late we're doing all those things."

"But why didn't we just do it? Why didn't the military make them see that in Washington?"

Welch smiled wanly. "For two reasons. As I see it, the politicians underestimated the courage of the people who elected them and those who were supposed to be running the war didn't understand the nature of war itself. By the time we got men in there who did, it was too late. As for the military, I suspect they tried to tell them but I doubt that their opinion was even listened to. I'm not sure how hard they tried either, but that's a question for the historians—not for us sailors, I'm afraid."

"What are the questions for you now, Admiral?"

Welch, looking out over the harbor, waited so long to answer that Boyle began to think that he wasn't going to. Finally, he fixed them with a look of pure determination.

"Whether we can get as many men out of this as possible, alive, intact, with their honor. And that includes most especially our POWs. The nation is going to need those men and their example badly someday. They can't just be stuck off in a corner somewhere, out of sight and out of mind, and be expected to stand out there for us all when the next time comes. And believe me it will come. I'm not going to quote it to you but someday look up the poem 'Tommy' by Rudyard Kipling. That'll explain what I mean better than I can."

He smiled, a little embarrassed by his speech to the two young people. "I'm sorry. They shouldn't let old admirals loose around pretty girls on beautiful evenings. Makes them lose their fierceness."

The boat was by now approaching Fleet Landing and the admiral helped Meghan up the steps to the small area known as the "Coxswain Flat" where the coxswain ran the boat from and where passengers boarded and stepped ashore. He looked at Boyle and Meghan and asked if they were going to the party which the British Naval officers were going to throw for the American Navy types the next night. When Boyle looked surprised, the admiral said, "I forgot. You've been ashore on leave. You're also not attached to any squadron aboard, so it's no wonder you hadn't heard. Anyway, please come and bring Meghan. It's semiformal so you don't have to buy a whole new wardrobe. You, Mr. Boyle, can wear your blues. I'll see you then."

He bowed slightly to Meghan. "I truly enjoyed meeting you, Meghan. I hope you'll save me a dance at the party. Good night."

Boyle and Meghan watched the admiral and his chief of staff walk away down the quay. She looked up at Tim and asked, "Are they all like that?"

Tim was still watching the two men recede into the distance. He shook his head.

"No, Meg, they're not. I wish they were. It would make things a whole lot better for a whole lot of people if they were."

He looked at her almost innocently and grinned. "Where do you want to go?"

Meghan reached for his hand and pulled him along the other way. Soon, they were walking along gaily in step, laughing, teasing, oblivious to the whole world.

Twenty minutes later, as they were waiting for the elevator in the hotel, Meghan looked up at him and said, "You know, the showers in this hotel are supposed to be dangerous. I don't suppose there are any lifeguards around."

Boyle grinned. Dinner was going to wait a while. "Funny you should mention that. Not only do I happen to be a famous lifeguard, but I have invented several new resuscitation techniques which will someday revolutionize the whole Red Cross. Perhaps you would allow me to demonstrate."

"Certainly. I'm always up for new techniques."

As the elevator door closed behind them, Boyle was beginning a ridiculous description of the all-new "Stepover Liplock" to Meghan's delighted giggles.

Chapter 17

September 20, 1972

Meghan stood by the door and watched as Boyle gave his tie one final adjustment. He inspected his uniform and let his eyes rest for a moment on the gold wings which rested exactly one quarter inch above the five ribbons he had earned in his five months over here. He gave his reflection a quick nod of approval. He picked up his hat and walked over to Meghan.

She smiled up at him. "Aren't you going to inspect me, too?"

Boyle grinned and then gave a short laugh. "You don't need inspection, babe, but all the other ladies there will spend half their evening wishing they looked as good as you and the other half telling themselves that you must have had surgery. In fact, I think I'll check you over for scars when we get back."

Meghan stepped through the door when Boyle held it open for her. As she passed him, she pinched his rear end.

"If you haven't found any scars on me by now, fly-boy, you won't."

Santy was waiting in the hallway, idly fiddling with the fire extinguisher hanging on the wall.

"Timmy, I was wondering if I ought to bring this along in case you and Meg get all steamy in a dark corner. I hear the Brits are having some World War II swing band that their admiral likes so they'll probably play lots of slow songs with trombones in them. You know what trombones do to Meg. She starts licking her lips and breathing heavy and stuff. I'd hate for you two to disgrace the flag and embarrass me in front of my date."

The thought of Santy standing fireguard on them broke both of them up.

"Great idea, Mike. When your date walks out on you, you can talk to it. It's probably got more personality than she does anyway. Come on, you two, I want to show off my new ring."

The three marched down the hall to the elevators, with Meghan in the middle linking her arms with both men. Santy began a lecture about the normal British reserve being mistaken for a lack of personality which lasted until the elevator discharged them on the ground floor. As the three strode through the lobby and out the front door, the sight of the two large men in uniform and the shorter, laughing woman in the middle reminded the night manager of Dorothy and two of her companions on the road to Oz.

Standing at the bar in the British Officers' Club was Lt. Cmdr. Andy Fisher. One of the earliest arrivals at the party, he had been in the club for about thirty minutes and was deep into his third vodka tonic. He was alone amid the growing crowd of officers and their dates from all over the Crown Colony and the visiting American ships. For Fisher, being alone was nothing new. He had become so used to his personal isolation that he almost didn't notice it anymore except for occasions like this when everyone else had companions.

After his flight to Hong Kong had arrived from the States, Fisher had immediately checked in with the air wing duty officer aboard *Concord*. It was inconceivable that he would do it any other way, for example by spending a night at the hotel where the air wing officers had set up their Admins just to get a feel for the men with whom he would work and live for the next year or so. Fisher knew that most other officers would have done it that way but to him it was militarily improper not to make himself available to his superiors at the earliest opportunity. The Navy had given him the stability and order that he had never been able to find in his entire silent and lonely life.

He had gotten an appointment to Annapolis through hard work in the three high schools that the various foster homes had sent him to and because the other young men who received the appointments declined them for opportunities at schools which did not have a military obligation. When he had left the small Iowa town and his foster home, he did so without regret, much as one would walk away from a motel room in the middle of a cross-country trip. In a week, you wouldn't even remember the name of the town.

At Annapolis, he had found himself comfortable with the rules and structure, graduating near the top of his class. After graduation, he had married the daughter of the academy commandant, the same man who was now Commander in Chief, Pacific, Admiral Glover. Dubbed the Ice Princess by Fisher's classmates, she and her father selected all his assignments: each perfectly safe, each career-enhancing, each high-visibility. Whenever Fisher had expressed a desire for something that he might like to do, his wife and Glover explained the advantages of their desires until he finally gave in.

Now, with the war winding down, it was decided that it was time for him to get some combat decorations on his chest and in his record, and some green ink, signifying combat flight time, in his logbook. He had been assigned as the new Detachment OIC for the Combat SAR helos and naturally that assignment was aboard the flagship. The only problem with this assignment was that the thought of actual combat absolutely terrified Fisher. It was one thing to discuss warfare drily, theoretically, and comfortably in San Diego, but quite another thing to be about to fly into a place where people are seriously trying to kill you and all your hopes and desires. For the first time in his life, as he got closer and closer to North Vietnam, Andy Fisher was discovering that he was, in fact, like other men. That the truth about life lay somewhere between the tattered and practical rooms he had had in the foster homes and the prim fragility of the drawing room of which his wife was so proud.

Here in the club, Fisher was having his first good look at the other officers in the air wing. As he ordered another drink, he was wondering what it would be like to be as carefree as they all seemed to be.

The drink came from the increasingly harried bartender. Fisher pushed across the bills and declined the change. He turned and leaned his back on the edge of the bar and began to watch the door for the new arrivals. He had been watching for only a few minutes when he was jolted fully erect. Just walking in through the portal was the woman from the flight over. She was on the arms of two young lieutenants and was laughing merrily at something the darker one was saying. Both were large men but seeing the sheer beauty of the woman, with her low-cut dress, made him begin to plan how he could separate her from them and continue the advances he had begun on the airplane.

He watched as another equally stunning woman walked up and greeted them, grasping the darker lieutenant's arm possessively.

Fisher was a man who spared himself nothing. His loveless marriage gave him the excuse he needed to pursue women whenever the opportunity arose. It mattered little what he said or promised for he would never see them again after the next morning anyway. He succeeded more often than not and only rarely accepted a first brush-off as final. He leaned back and put down his half-full drink. He watched her and the others move to a table and her date head for the bar.

Santy was correct about the style of the band. He had feared that this would be one of those "Command Performances" where the officers were required to show up and endure an evening of abject boredom while the senior types danced the goddamn Lindy until they got hot flashes or something. He had never had any experience with the Royal Navy and so could be forgiven his ignorance.

By the time the three arrived, the party was beginning to pick up steam. Virtually every Royal Navy officer available in Hong Kong and most of the Americans from the *Concord* were present. The small groups of friends were beginning to break from their defensive knots and mix with everyone else, and the laughter was beginning to sound natural and not merely polite.

Santy's date, Barbara Gibson, was the stewardess from the hotel pool and had turned out to be the daughter of one of the British captains. Although they had all spent time together, Boyle had not appreciated just how take-off-your-hat-beautiful Barbara really was until he saw her standing in the foyer of the club, dressed to kill.

She greeted them at the door and led them to a table she had staked out in the middle of the large mahogany-paneled room. Boyle went off to fight his way to the bar for the drinks and Meghan looked around at all the military officers and their ladies in the room. I'd better get used to this, she thought. I'm in it for the long haul.

Meghan had been to several military social events in San Diego with Tim and, after she got over her preconceptions about the people who were directly involved in the war she hated so much, found them to be far less rabid about it than she had supposed. She found their realism refreshing and their sense of fun catching. Meghan was one of the minuscule fraction of people who are able to separate individuals from their beliefs and accept them for who they are and allow them to wear, unchallenged, the intellectual overcoats that they affect.

She wondered what it would be like when Tim became a senior officer. She dearly hoped that they would be able to keep the fun and laughter with which their youth blessed them.

She suddenly had the feeling that she was being watched. She turned her head and saw an average-sized man standing across the room appraising her. It was the guy, somebody

Fisher, from the airplane, only now he wore the uniform of a lieutenant commander with the wings of an aviator pinned over the single row of ribbons above his left breast pocket.

She looked toward the bar but Tim had been swallowed up in the mob trying to get the bartender's attention. Santy and Barbara were in a world of their own, heads together discussing something that was making their eyes shine.

Fisher placed his drink on a table as he walked over and stood looking down at Meghan. He put one hand on the back of her chair and the other on the table and smiled. The look reminded her of a tarantula.

"Well, we meet again. Are you enjoying your visit to Hong Kong, Miss Collins? You left the airport before I could offer you a ride to your hotel. I was quite disappointed."

Meghan turned to face him squarely, her voice a little louder than she intended. "I've asked you several times to go away and stay away. I don't like you and I have nothing further to say to you. Please leave me alone."

Fisher's smile hardened just a little. "Your young boyfriend isn't here just now so I'll avail myself of the opportunity to invite you to have a drink later and we can discuss then what will come next. You'll find that I can be very persistent and I think you'll also find that it will be well worth your time."

Throughout this, Fisher's expression hadn't changed. Meghan had a cold feeling in her middle and discovered that it was a twinge of real fear. Before she could recover her composure, she heard a familiar drawl over her shoulder.

"Everything okay, Meg?"

Fisher looked up into the hard eyes of Mike Santy who placed his left hand protectively on Meghan's shoulder. Meghan nearly smiled as she saw anger flash across Fisher's face. He stood erect and faced Santy, looking him up and down appraisingly.

"Everything's fine, here, um, Lieutenant. We were just renewing an acquaintance made some time ago. We've traveled together quite a distance actually. So if you'll excuse us . . ." Fisher deliberately resumed his position looming over

Meghan. When Santy made no move to leave, Fisher stood again and looked at him, coldly this time.

"Perhaps you didn't understand me. I said that everything was fine. Now, run along and play with your date, Lieutenant." The last word was delivered with deliberate emphasis.

To Meghan's surprise, Santy smiled and looked down at her. The slight tremor he felt in her bare shoulder was enough for Mike. He looked back up at Fisher and, moving closer, placed his right arm around the man's shoulders and clutched his collarbone. Fisher winced with pain.

"C'mon, Commander, sir. We'll have a little chat." Santy took a step forward and Fisher had no choice but to follow, to go where the huge paw moved him.

Maintaining the pressure, Santy steered Fisher away from the table toward the quieter rear of the room. Whenever Fisher tried to squirm away, he found that Santy's fingers dug in just a little bit more. Once they were clear of the other guests Santy turned Fisher to face him and released his grip. Fisher instantly took the offensive.

"How dare you touch a superior officer? This is an assault!"

"No, it isn't, sir. I was merely protecting you from harm. If you had been there when her fiancé, repeat, fiancé, returned and he saw the expression on her face when you were talking to her, I'm certain that it would have taken major surgery to remove your head from your ass. Think of this as an act of mercy."

"That's bullshit. No one will take your word over mine."

Santy grinned pleasantly at him and said, "Come to think of it, you may well be right, Commander. If I'm in this far, I might as well go all the way."

Mike's expression darkened greatly. "Here's the plan. If you come within ten feet of that woman again and I see you, you slimy little shit, I will pull your lungs out through your nose, slowly, one at a time."

Santy's eyes bored into his and Fisher felt his gut begin to turn to water. He tried to take the offensive.

"You may be sure, Lieutenant, that your C.O. will hear

about this and that your career is over. He'll have your balls."
It came out less forcefully than he had hoped.

"Don't need 'em. I've got a set of my own and they're genuine solid brass, too."

Both turned at the new voice to find Cmdr. Wilson, Santy's C.O., standing there watching the two of them. He introduced himself to Fisher and stood looking up at him with a mixture of amusement and anger in his eyes.

"Did you hear that entire conversation, sir?" Fisher asked, and when Wilson nodded, he continued. "He threatened me and assaulted me. You saw it and certainly you can't ignore it!"

Wilson grinned. "What I saw was Mr. Santy straightening the collar on your uniform jacket. I'd consider that a very nice gesture. As to his alleged threats, he was merely explaining, in theory of course, the certain and very painful consequences to you of an extremely hazardous course of action. There's nothing wrong with that. Oh, and I assure you that my word will definitely be taken over yours." He clapped his hands together and asked pleasantly, "Okay, guys, do we all understand each other?"

Fisher glared at the two pilots and turned to go, muttering that this would not be the last they heard of it. Wilson's voice, now edged with steel, stopped him.

"Fisher! Come back here. Now."

As Fisher approached, with much of his "attitude" suddenly gone, Wilson asked Santy to go get him a beer but it was not a request.

When the young pilot was out of earshot, Wilson addressed Fisher. "I gave you a chance to back off, slick, and you didn't take it. So now, we'll take it from the top. The lady you were going after obviously didn't want you around. You heard what Mr. Santy said, that she is engaged to Santy's friend who was temporarily absent. Santy was doing exactly what he should have. The fact that you are still standing is a testament to Mike's restraint. You are out of line and I would suggest that you apologize to the lady except that you would have to get within ten feet to do it and that would cause a scene with you and your lungs lying on the floor separately. Not a pleasant sight at a nice party like this. So you will get your hat and leave. Or, you may remain if you stay clear of all the other principals in this little drama. Furthermore, we have, in fact, heard the last of this unless you are masochistic enough to bring it up later on. Do you understand?"

Fisher nodded. He had lost this one but he would get his at-bats. He was already composing the letter to his father-in-law, who commanded the whole Navy here in the Pacific.

As if reading Fisher's mind, Wilson began again. "Fisher, there are several of us over here aboard the *Concord* who know who you are, what you are, who your father-in-law is, and why you showed up here this late in the war. Do not be foolish enough to assume that you can behave here as you have in the past at your previous commands. You are now just another unproven and inexperienced helicopter pilot. The celebrities here are the men who do their job as professionals. This is the fleet, not the staff back home. If you screw up over here, or try to take the easy road and somebody gets hurt as a result, there will be no one you can hide behind. Remember that. Good night."

Wilson spun on his heel and strode over to Santy, who was standing well out of earshot holding two beers. Wilson took the proffered beer and nodded his thanks. He saw that Santy was about to say something and raised a hand.

"It's okay. Go have a good time, Mike, and don't worry about him. He just didn't understand that nobody fucks with my guys but me. Especially not some snot-nose prick like him. See ya later. Oh, and I like your style, Sandman."

Santy watched Wilson walk away and shook his head. Not bad, he thought. Ever since Boyle had convinced him to talk to Wilson, the C.O. had constantly surprised him. He discovered that he really liked the banty little bastard now.

He walked back to the table, trying to figure out how to explain this to Boyle without him going on a Fisher safari right here at the party. Maybe he could get Meghan to sit on him while he explained. Now there's an idea, he thought.

* * *

Except for a slight narrowing of his eyes, Boyle accepted the reports of the incident with Fisher with surprising calm. Both Meghan and Santy took this as an extremely bad sign. It took several minutes for the two to convince him that all was well and that no further action was required. By the time Meghan dragged him to the dance floor, he was willing to forget or at least ignore the whole thing.

When Meghan and Tim finally returned from the dance floor, the party was really beginning to roll. By now, all the shyness and xenophobia had disappeared. British and American officers were well intermixed, pleasantly, if not particularly quietly, debating the relative merits of whatever topic came up, from the differences in their different models of F-4s to the real truth about who invented radar to who would be stupid enough to try to outdrink the few Australian officers in attendance.

Someone got the bright idea to have the First Annual Colonial/British Steinway Piano Stakes. Teams were quickly formed and a course laid out through the building with several curves and wicked switchbacks. Each team pressed a "volunteer" lady jockey into service and placed her and a pitcher of beer on the piano. The object was to have five men carry the piano and negotiate the course in minimum time. Penalties were assessed for allowing the piano to touch the floor but spilling either the jockey or the pitcher was given far greater weight. Losing the beer meant disqualification.

One of the jockeys was Santy's date, Barbara. Kicking off her shoes, she climbed aboard and gleefully flogged the international group of officers carrying the piano with the cloth belt from her dress. Her team completed the course without penalty. Meghan was invited to participate but declined: she had been the center of enough attention for one night. All she wanted to do now was stay a polite length of time and slip out with Tim. Their time together was running out in the way that it always does when you desperately wish it would not.

At one point, when Tim had again gone to the bar for another round, she found Fisher's eyes on her again. He was across the room staring at her with no trace of a smile. It was an expression of raw, evil emotion. This time, however, she had had time to put him in perspective. She carefully mustered her number-one expression of smug and grandly raised the middle finger of her right hand to him. He strode from the room without a backward glance.

That gesture somehow deflated her. She felt drained and caged at the same time. When Boyle got back he sensed her changed mood and asked if she wanted to leave. She just nodded almost girlishly. Boyle took her hand. They headed for the other room to find Santy to tell him they were going.

When they did find him, he was at the bottom of a pile of bodies, both male and female. The new game which had been proposed by the Americans to make up for their defeat in the piano races was "Buck-Buck" in which groups try to see who can support the weight of more of the other team as they run across the room and jump on the pile one by one. The group on the bottom get together in a rugby-style huddle for mutual support. Most of the fun of this game is found in taunting the other team. Coed Buck-Buck can really get going: women are usually the best taunters.

"Hey, Mike, we're leaving."

Santy pushed a stockinged leg from his chest and sat up. "Aw, come on and stay. We're losing here and we need a couple more people, especially some big ones. Just play a little at least until we beat these goddamn Limeys once."

" 'Goddamn Limeys,' eh? You Yanks couldn't beat eggs," announced Barbara with an elbow to Santy's ribs. She stood and marched back to the British side of the room, wiggling her rear end at the three Americans.

"See what I mean? Those people are insufferable. We can't let the Redcoats beat us at our own game. That would be worse than Pearl Harbor. How could we live with ourselves?" He stuck out his tongue at Barbara who was standing across the room, hands on hips, grinning at him.

Meghan laughed heartily for the first time in over two hours. "Come on, Tim, let's play a while. We can't let this idiot down, can we?"

"Not a chance." Boyle followed Meg over to the wall where she dropped her shoes and waited for him to dispose of his shoes along with his uniform jacket and tie. When Boyle looked back at her he saw all the playfulness and fun in the world right there in her eyes.

She pulled him by the hand and they joined the group of Americans preparing to assault the British formation.

The remaining time in Hong Kong passed all too swiftly for Boyle and Meghan. After she had gone home, Boyle was faced with one aimless day before the *Concord* was to get under way to return to the war. He had a choice of going back to the hotel and participating in the last-day-in-port craziness or going back to the ship alone. He chose to go back to the ship.

Looking up at the *Concord* from the deck of the liberty boat, he realized that her grayness matched his mood perfectly.

Chapter 18

September 21, 1972

The next day, when the ship was about one hundred miles from Hong Kong, Boyle walked into maintenance control to get a cup of coffee and to see if there were any flights today which needed another pilot. There were only two of the squadron's aircraft aboard, the rest having been transferred to the other carrier, the *Independence,* when *Concord* departed for Hong Kong. When *Concord* returned to Yankee Station, those aircraft, their crews, and all the maintenance troops would have to pack up all their gear and move everything back aboard. The two helos left aboard *Concord* were both "hangar queens" which had been in need of major maintenance. A special group of technicians had been flown to Hong Kong from the Philippines to take care of several of the major problems which could not be fixed by the troops assigned to the squadrons. Both projects were nearing completion and Boyle figured he could get back in the air soonest if he made himself a big enough but not too obnoxious pest to the maintenance chief. So far it seemed to be working. He hadn't even opened his mouth when the chief told him that it would be at least another day until one was ready for a test flight but that he would let Boyle know as soon as it was ready. The other piece of news was that Boyle was wanted in the ready room as soon as possible.

"But Lt. Watkins was by a few minutes ago and he told me to tell you that you'd better go see him first before you go to the ready room. I think that might be a good idea, too," said the chief.

Boyle had no idea what was going on but if Watkins and the chief both felt that he ought not go in unprepared, it probably wasn't good. He nodded his thanks to the chief and went aft to Watkins's stateroom.

Watkins answered Boyle's knock on the metal door and ushered him into the room.

Boyle sat down on the chair and looked up at Watkins, who began to pace the cramped cabin. The two hadn't seen each other since the second day in Hong Kong at the airport. When he flew back in from Brisbane, Watkins had gone back to the ship straight from the airport, long before Boyle had come back aboard on the last liberty boat.

"What's up, Bob? How was your leave?"

"Leave was pretty fair. I had a good time and managed to stay out of trouble. I'll tell you all about it later. What I need to talk to you about is Lt. Cmdr. Fisher. What did you do to piss him off so much?"

"I don't know what you're talking about. I've never met a Fisher over here. The only guy I know of by that name is some asshole who was hitting on my fiancée and being a pain in the ass about it. I didn't even talk to him. Mike scared him off at the party with the Brits. What's going on?"

"Tell me the story, Tim."

Boyle did, starting with the scene at the airport where Meghan nearly deballed him and continuing with the little show at the party. He finished with an aside about Wilson's part at the end.

"I never said a word to the guy. In fact, I never even saw him at the party. I think he was gone when I got back to the table. Mike can be a little emphatic sometimes so I didn't even think about going looking for him."

Watkins took a deep breath and blew it out slowly. "Did you know that he is our new Officer in Charge and will relieve Don Hickerson when we get back on station?"

Boyle experienced a sudden sinking feeling. "No, I didn't know that. But I didn't do anything. Am I in trouble already?"

Watkins looked at Boyle and saw that the younger man had no idea what was going on in the endless game of personality and power. Oh, well, he thought, time for another lesson in Life 101.

"Tim, Fisher is an ambitious asshole. He always was. I'm afraid that you have managed to wind up on his shitlist. He sees you as somebody who is handy and can be blamed for his being embarrassed. Fisher is a man who gets what he wants and will step on anyone to get it. He even married an admiral's daughter to get himself some political drag. That admiral, by the way, is Glover, presently the biggest kahuna in the Pacific. Fisher expects to be here only long enough to get himself a couple of combat medals and a fitness report which will reflect leading men in a combat situation. As soon as he gets them, Daddy will pull him out and give him another staff job, which will punch a few more tickets. He has never been to war before despite being in the Navy since sixty-three. There was always someplace that his special talents were needed more than just being wasted in combat where any ol' slug can do the job."

Boyle had never come in contact with this sort of thing before and had no idea what he should do. He told Watkins that.

"I know, Tim. What you have to do is salute and give him a cheery 'aye-aye.' Don't give him any reason to jump on you. You're going to have to work extra hard and keep your nose clean. You are the junior aircraft commander out here but you have combat experience and Fisher doesn't. He will give you and the rest of the detachment some dumb orders and come up with some dumb ideas because he hasn't done any flying like we do over here. You'll have to go along to a point but do not allow him to put you in a position where you have no out. We talked about this stuff in the airport. Remember?"

Boyle nodded and Watkins continued. "Okay. Don't fly any mission or go in anywhere when you believe that you don't have a good chance of getting out successfully. You know what this is all about over here and you have a pretty good handle on your strengths and weaknesses. Don't let yourself get shoved in over your head. We don't need any more dead heroes. Do you understand?"

Boyle just nodded. Watkins paused, and looked at his hands. "Tim, I'm gonna be stationed back on North SAR so I won't be able to help you much. If you have any problems, you can always go to Jack Crawford. He'll still be the next senior HC-17 guy aboard *Concord* and knows the score. We go back a long way, Jack and I, and he's a damn good man. He may not always be able to do anything but he'll steer you straight. Okay? Now, go and see Fisher. Lay low and give him your best 'dumb J.O.' act and you'll be all right."

Boyle stood and walked to the door. As he pulled it open, he had a sudden thought. He turned back to Watkins. "You knew him before someplace, didn't you, Bob? I mean you worked around him, not just heard about him."

"Yeah, I did, Tim. I saw him in action and I didn't like what I saw. Just be careful. Come back and tell me what happened." Watkins closed the door, leaving Boyle to worry and wonder all the way to the ready room.

Boyle walked into the ready room and looked around for Fisher. He had only seen him once, in civilian clothes. He was saved the embarrassment of looking right past his future boss by a sharp and nasal summons from one of the chairs in the far corner of the room.

"Mr. Boyle, over here, please."

Boyle walked over and stood in front of Fisher. "You wanted to see me, sir?"

"Yes, I did. Sit down, please."

When Boyle complied, he continued. "You took your own

sweet time getting here, Lieutenant. I expect you to be in the ready room promptly at 0700 every morning. I like to know that my officers are not slacking off. Bear that in mind in the future."

Boyle nodded and mumbled a "yessir" at him.

"Now, you are the junior aircraft commander out here. As such, I'm sure you realize that it will be some time before you are 'proven,' as they say. I was not a party to your development and I intend to keep a close eye on your progress. If your performance is up to snuff, as I'm sure it will be, you may become a detachment OIC before you rotate home, which will look quite good on your record."

Fisher paused and waited for some response. There was none, not even the glint in the eye that he would have expected when he mentioned a promotion or favorable comments in the record. Strange, he thought.

"The only other requirement is loyalty, both to me and to the command. Do you have any questions so far?"

"No, sir."

"Good. Now for another matter." Fisher's voice took on a hard edge. "I'm sure that you are aware of the little misunderstanding at the British Officers' Club the other night. My intent was completely honorable and both your fiancée and your friend overreacted. Your friend is a hothead and exercises poor judgment. I suggest that you steer clear of him. You wouldn't want to be tarred with the same brush as he. I intend to make certain that he learns the proper respect for his superiors when the time is right."

Fisher made a gesture of dismissal as if, Boyle thought, Santy no longer existed.

He continued. "Your fiancée later that evening made an obscene gesture directed at me. That indicates that she is not yet familiar with the customs and proprieties of the military profession and her responsibilities as an officer's spouse. You should ensure that she does become familiar so that she does not embarrass you again in the future. I will not require an apology from either of you this time, given her ignorance of her station, but make sure that she learns her place. It will

be to your benefit when she does. All right? That will be all."
Fisher turned his attention to the sheaf of paper in his lap.

Boyle was stunned. Fisher had just hit him on every point
but his shoe size and he hadn't even officially taken charge
yet. Tim was willing to put up with nearly anything the Navy
could throw at him but cutting Mike or Meghan was not on
the list. He stood up and looked down at Fisher. You moth-
erfucker, he thought.

Except for a small whitening of his lips no one would have
been able to tell how much restraint he was using.

"Commander, Mike Santy has never made an idle threat
and he has never, in all the time I've known him, laid his
hands on another man without a lot of provocation. You may
have been innocent but you apparently didn't come across
that way to either him or my fiancée. And Meghan would
never make such a gesture at anyone who was not completely
out of line."

Boyle drew a breath as he leaned closer to Fisher. He
continued in a very level and very dangerous voice. "What
she says and does is up to her and I'll be damned if I would
try to change anything about her. As to my flying, Admiral
Welch himself presented me with my HAC designation letter
just before we got to Hong Kong. He seems to think that I'm
'proven.' That should certainly be more than good enough
for you. Sir."

Boyle deliberately emphasized the last word and strode
from the room, leaving Fisher staring after him with a strange
light in his eyes.

Watkins answered Boyle's knock and let him into his stateroom. He listened as Boyle repeated the entire conversation,
interrupting only to get Boyle back on track when his anger
got the best of him and he began to curse Fisher manfully. It
took nearly twenty minutes before he was able to calm the
young man and convince him that his best tack would be to
shut up and do his job and that throwing Fisher over the side
might not be received well up the chain. He finally had Boyle
laughing a little and with that sent him on his way.

After Boyle had gone Watkins sat on his bunk thinking about the last time he and Fisher had been together. It had been about four years before, when they both were assigned to another squadron, Watkins as the squadron schedules officer and Fisher as the maintenance officer. Fisher had been driving his men hard in an effort to surpass some record for sortie completion percentage and had been keeping them working long after their normal shifts.

There had been a crash, nearly costing the lives of all four of the men aboard. After the investigation, the cause had been laid to maintenance error. Rather than back off the pressure on his men a bit to ensure that the error didn't happen again, Fisher had had the men scheduled for extra training at the end of their workday. Soon, the sortie rate began to fall and no amount of threats from Fisher could make it rise again. It was not until the C.O. gingerly stepped in that the maintenance department got back to any sort of effective work.

Rather than accept the failure of his leadership methods, Fisher launched a whispering campaign to bolster his reputation, which ended only when he was transferred to the Wing to serve as the administrative officer. It took the next maintenance officer nearly four months to bring the department back to a level anywhere near their pre-Fisher performance.

Watkins had watched it all happen and had vowed that he would never treat his men like that. Now that Fisher was here, Watkins hoped fervently that the man had learned something in the past four years.

Boyle finally tracked Santy down on "Steel Beach." This was a changing area on the flight deck that was wherever there were no aircraft parked. There, off-duty crew members could lie around and work on their tans. Santy was lying face down, propped on his elbows, leafing through his NATOPS manual. The NATOPS, or Naval Aviation Training and Operating Procedures, program was created because of the horrendous accident rate that the Navy had had among its various flying communities. Someone decided, quite correctly, that there would be huge savings in men and matériel if operational procedures and indeed every other facet of naval aviation were standardized. Each aircraft type had its own manual, called the NATOPS, which was the definitive text on not only everything that a pilot needed to know about his trusty steed but also on about a ton and a half of irrelevant crap.

On the annual open- and closed-book exams and check flights that the pilots were required to endure, there was rarely any distinction made about whether a fact really mattered or not. Most examiners tried hard to make their mark on the program by revising the exams their predecessors had already revised until the program began to lose the original direction of its creators. Some commanding officers went so far as to fire an unlucky NATOPS officer if the command's pilots failed to surpass the grades of some other command's pilots.

The manuals were all written in eye-wateringly bad style, one which proscribed adjectives and adverbs and was the only style in the English language which actually droned when read silently. The books themselves seemed to be organized by simply throwing a pile of pages down a flight of stairs and putting them back in the book in order of retrieval.

The index for each manual always seemed to list only topics and sections which were not actually included in the book so that in searching to find the answer to one of the more obscure questions one usually stumbled across some tidbit that he could really use. Since many of the aviators considered the NATOPS as either the world's most effective nonprescription sleeping aid or merely a crutch for weak pilots, it was studied only under great duress such as an imminent annual requalification exam.

Boyle opened his lawn chair and sat down next to Santy's chaise lounge. He peered over Santy's shoulder at the page he was studying. It was a full page of text with a pull-out diagram of one of the A-7 hydraulic systems.

"Find any good dirty parts, yet?"

"Yeah, I found one place where the flap actuators are coupling with the check valves in the lines from the pump. Not much emotion in it, though. They seem to do their thing sort of mechanically. Must be boring as hell to get actuated without even small talk or a cigarette afterward.''

"Wait until you get to the landing gear accumulator section. Those blow-down bottles are really kinky.''

Santy chuckled and closed the manual. "Well, I guess that's enough learning for one day. I'll give my brain some time to settle. How are you doing? Did Meg get off all right?''

Boyle thought back on the scene at the airport yesterday. Both he and Meghan had struggled bravely to keep the departure light and their emotions under tight rein. They had succeeded by talking over the fun they had had and discussing the plans for the wedding. Both pretended that they would be separated for only a short while, as opposed to the four months or so that remained on Boyle's tour. Even though each had met the other's parents back in San Diego and had spoken on the phone from Hong Kong to them to announce the engagement, they were just a little nervous about the parents' reactions.

When Meghan's flight was called, they walked hand in hand to the gate. Meghan looked up at him and told him to stick close to Santy and take care of him. She then had to stifle a little sob as she threw her arms around his neck.

"Be careful, Boiler. Don't do anything stupid or anything heroic. I need you.''

"I won't, Meg. We still have to raise a future president, don't we? Don't worry. I'll be okay.''

"I love you, Tim Boyle.''

"I love you, too, babe.''

Meghan kissed him and turned to go, eyes brimming. As she did Boyle smacked her on the rear end. Meghan let out a yelp and turned around grinning through her tears.

Boyle held up his right hand. "Sorry. I couldn't resist. I promise not to wash this hand for a week.''

Meghan laughed and walked down the gateway to her plane.

* * *

"Yeah, she got off okay. She told me I have to take care of you, which should leave me no time to put up with my new OIC." He paused for a beat or two. "It seems you've met him."

Santy instantly looked guilty. "Sorry about that. I just figured him for a normal asshole. I didn't realize that he was *your* asshole until Skipper Wilson told me about it when I got back aboard last night. I hope I didn't get you in too much trouble."

"No, at least no more than Meg did flipping him the bird or trying to deball him with a shoulder bag at the airport when she arrived. Anyway, he says I've gotta stay away from you since you're a bad influence and have already pissed away any chance of making admiral. He doesn't want lowlifes like you in his Navy. He also said I've gotta shape Meghan up and try to make a lady out of her. Dumb bastard. If she was one of those white-glove bitches I sure as hell wouldn't be marrying her. I hear you can't get their panties off without a set of bolt cutters and a couple of prybars. It probably wouldn't be worth the effort by the time you had broken out all your tools."

Santy laughed. "Can you imagine somebody trying to square Meghan away if she didn't want to go along willingly? I'd pay big money to watch that. Be like sticking your face in a blender—loud, messy, and painful."

"Yeah, that wouldn't be pretty. Anyway, Fisher told me that I'm still suspect since I'm so junior. I got the impression that he is going to lock down on us real tight and basically try to make us all march in step. I haven't been around all that long but even I can see that that will really screw up the operations of the helos. I wish to hell I could go back out with Bob Watkins."

"Tim, do you remember when I was bitching about my skipper and you told me to go talk to him? I was thinking that maybe that might work with Fisher. I mean you talk to him, not me. He and I have already had our little chat."

Boyle scratched his nose in thought. "I thought about that but he's just a good old U.S. Navy prick and I can't see him changing much. Sure is gonna be a hell of a change from Hickerson."

Santy sighed. "Well, it doesn't appear that there's much you personally can do about him. Just keep your nose clean and do your job. You'll be going home in a few months and you'll be rid of him."

Boyle just nodded and changed the subject. "How did you and Barbara wind up?"

"Well, she had to take that flight back to England so I didn't see her the last day. Good thing, too. That woman about wore me out after I got past her standoffishness. Once her burner got lit, I could barely keep up. I managed, though, through sheer courage and stamina. I told her she ought to bring out an updated edition of the *Kama Sutra*. I do believe that I'll always look at former gymnasts in a different light. You know, in a way, I feel sorry for the poor guy she marries. She'll kill him but that would be the way to go I guess."

"Didn't need to use the green stuff on her, then?"

"Hell, no. You don't throw gas on a fire."

Boyle laughed merrily at the image of a bedraggled Santy being hauled back into a hotel room by his feet, pleading for mercy. He couldn't wait to write Meg and tell her that Mike had finally met his match. She wouldn't believe it.

There was another discussion going on one deck down from where Boyle and Santy were catching rays and remaining steadfastly unconcerned with any great matters.

This discussion was concerned with matters of great importance for every man aboard *Concord*. Admiral Welch and his staff, along with the captain, executive officer, and all the department heads from the ship's company were planning their actions and requirements for the upcoming line period. The plans that they had gone into Hong Kong with were now "OBE," or overcome by events, because now, at the beginning of the fall of '72, President Nixon had finally decided that enough was enough. He refused to accept any more foot-dragging or general bullshit from the North Vietnamese "negotiators" at the Paris Peace Conference.

For quite a long time, the Vietnamese had been throwing obstacle after objection after demand in the path of the negotiations. They believed that the American people would finally force the president to take what they were willing to give, and quit. They could see the demonstrations on their own televisions and firmly believed that the demonstrators represented the majority opinion in the United States. They did not realize that while the majority of Americans wanted peace, soon, they were not willing to throw in the towel and walk away with their tails between their legs. America had never lost a war and was not about to pull out in shame from this one. The North Vietnamese also did not reckon on Nixon's strength nor on his grim determination to end the war on terms he considered honorable.

The president had decided to show the Vietnamese that there would be an even greater cost to their country than they had already paid if they did not shut up, sit down, and quit screwing around, so he had removed the last restrictions on targeting. Nixon may have had many flaws but endless patience was not among them.

The discussion now going on in the Flag Operations room was concerned with the latest dictum from the commander in chief. The U.S. forces in Southeast Asia were now cleared for unrestricted bombing of military targets both within North Vietnam and without. There were no more exclusion zones and none of the old restrictions emplaced for fear of antagonizing third-party nations or perhaps causing one of those nations to intervene and thus widening the war.

Most of the discussion had to do with planning for the increased tempo: taking into account everything from schedules for the resupply ships to the amount of service life left on the engines in some of the jets to changing the times the ship's store would be open during flight ops.

Admiral Welch did little to meddle in these minor details and was listening with only a small portion of his mind. The larger part was drifting on a gentle tide of memory. He thought back on all the missions he had flown as a squadron C.O. and as a CAG early on in the war and on all the men he had known, in this war and others, who were no longer flying from the decks of carriers. Most had moved on to civilian life either through retirement or just getting out after their service obligation had expired. Many were dead from aircraft accidents; a few from enemy action. A smaller few were prisoners in the various hellholes in North Vietnam.

The admiral knew that this long-awaited policy change would bring about an end to the war in which so many of his friends had given so much toward a goal which always had had less form and substance than did a dream. He wished with all his heart, for just a moment, that those men could be here to see it end. He wished that, wherever they were, they would know that their part in things had been of value and that they had made a difference.

The admiral looked around at the officers gathered in the room. As he stood with a sigh, they all fell silent, expecting a pronouncement of some sort. He smiled at them and told them that they had a good handle on things and should just let him know what the final plans were. He turned and walked through the door and up to the flight deck. He passed the rows of aircraft, resting in the sun with their red "Remove Before Flight" flags flapping gently in the breeze. His hands unconsciously touched their fiberglass noses as he passed by.

Standing at the bow with the clean sea air rushing past him, and hearing only the gentle sound of the bow slicing through the waves as the ship headed west, Welch raised his eyes and whispered his thanks that he would be allowed to be there at the end.

Wherever his old friends were now, he hoped that they would know that he would carry part of them with him when, in time, the fleet at last sailed for home.

PART THREE

"For the Thousandth Man will sink or swim
With you in any water."

—KIPLING

Chapter 19

September 25, 1972

By the time the *Concord* had completed the three-day transit and gotten back on station off North Vietnam, the pilots and crew had shaken off the rust that normally builds up during a long period of inactivity. The pilots had all gotten their skills back up to speed; even their night landings had been remarkably good.

Beginning the first day out of Hong Kong, every pilot had flown a day hop followed by a twilight "pinkie" where they got to practice landing in the nearly dark. The pinkie was followed by the night landing refamiliarization which, as always, was a completely different psychological event.

There is a legend in naval aviation concerning a study done in the dim past. Scientists of unspecified persuasion had wired up several attack and fighter pilots from a carrier. The scientists discovered that the pilots' heart rates were demonstrably higher when they were flying the landing pattern at night around the carrier than when they were over targets in North Vietnam with all the SAMs and Triple-A coming up at them in the full light of day.

Immediately upon gathering their evidence, the scientists put their pens back in the white plastic shirt pocket protectors, folded their soup-stained lab coats, packed up their reams of EKG paper, and departed the ship for home and their Nobel Prize application questionnaires.

The pilots, left to continue their mundane task of fighting an air war, soon discovered that the scientists had come up with tentative findings: that night landings on carriers scared pilots because they were afraid of the dark. The negative publicity from this could be damaging.

Another study, informal but infinitely more accurate, was therefore done by the pilots themselves in several officers' club bars. They proved conclusively, albeit with absolutely no confusing physical evidence, that aircraft carrier decks actually grow and shrink in direct proportion to the amount of sunlight available. The darker the night, the smaller the deck.

Mike Santy was thinking about this as he flew his A-7 around the tanker pattern on the fourth night out of Hong Kong. He chuckled to himself when he recalled Tim Boyle's conclusive bit of evidence in support of the pilots' theory. There were always more people falling overboard at night so it had to be because the ship shrank, causing crew members to miscount their steps as they walked around in the dark.

Santy had launched about an hour after dark and had spent the last fifty minutes flying around waiting for somebody to need fuel. There was no A-6 tanker scheduled for this launch-and-recovery cycle so an A-7 with a "buddy store" or removable air-to-air refueling system had been tasked to fly. Santy was launched and had checked out his refueling system with the departing A-6 tanker from the previous launch. Everything was copacetic so he sat back and flew around just enjoying the hop.

He knew that things could get exciting very quickly if the deck got fouled or if one of the other pilots was having a bad night attempting to land aboard the *Concord*. So far things had gone smoothly.

The air wing was practicing operating tonight under what

was known as "blue water ops." This meant that there were no divert airfields ashore available in case somebody had a problem. Otherwise, a pilot could make a few attempts at landing and if he didn't make it aboard and was showing no signs of improvement he would be directed to "Bingo," or fly to the beach, normally to Danang in South Vietnam where he would spend the rest of the night trying to sleep among the bugs, heat, and noise in a crummy visiting pilots' shack. The next morning, he would fly back out to the ship and land during the day. While this was all fairly embarrassing, it was not fatal and by no means was it uncommon.

There was only one customer for Santy's fuel tonight, an F-4 who'd had to wave off because the guy ahead of him had been slow clearing the landing area. The Phantom was notorious for its fuel consumption, so bad in fact that a tanker version had been considered but dropped when it was realized that it would most likely take fuel rather than give it.

The F-4 plugged and received 2,000 pounds and then broke away for the landing pattern. Santy checked out the A-6 which relieved him and followed the radar vectors of the controller, back aboard the ship, to the final approach course. He picked up the lens at a mile and followed it down to a successful trap, catching the number-three wire.

All things considered, it had been an excellent way to spend an evening at sea. He was even complimented for his approach and landing by Cmdr. Wilson, who had observed the entire cycle from a chair in the Carrier Air Traffic Control Center, or CATCC, pronounced "cat-see." When he had finished filling out the paperwork and shoved the thick binder into its slot in Maintenance Control, he went off to find Boyle and see if he was up for a couple of gut bombs in the wardroom.

At Santy's knock, Boyle dropped the book he was reading, reached over, and opened the door. Santy stepped in and plopped down on the lower of the small bunk beds. He glanced at the book on the desk.

"*The Drifters,* huh? Isn't that about a bunch of hippies?"

"Yup. I'm reading about what we've been missing. I could go for that free love stuff."

"Meg would put your balls in the blender if you tried it. You went to school in Boston, for Christ's sake. Next to Berkeley and San Francisco, that was the hotbed of free love. Get it? Hotbed. Free love." Boyle shook his head as Santy went on. "What'd you do in school? You didn't study or anything unproductive like that, so how'd you spend your time?"

"Partying at the Tam O'Shanter or playing lacrosse. I always wound up with nice girls from Newton or Cardinal Cushing or Simmons. I would have killed for a date with a girl in ripped jeans and no bra. Very frustrating, I might add. I really got to hate Rod McKuen. Anyway, how'd your hop go?"

"Great. Flew around for an hour and a half burning up a prehistoric forest. Tomorrow, we've got an alpha strike on another power plant on the first launch. I'm a manned spare but maybe they'll launch me anyway." He stood up and kicked the back legs of Boyle's chair. "C'mon. Let's go get something to eat. We can catch the second movie."

"Why didn't I think of that?" Boyle dropped his feet to the floor and followed Santy forward to the wardroom.

At a little after one the next afternoon, Santy sat in the spare aircraft back on the port side of the fantail, sort of hoping that somebody else's aircraft would fail to make the launch. He had done his systems checks and gotten his navigation gear aligned. The Corsair was working perfectly, so he wiggled his butt on the seat a little, placed his forearms on the rails below the open canopy, and waited to see if he was going flying.

He looked across the deck, beyond the jets parked on the starboard side, and watched the plane-guard helo out in Starboard Delta make another of the endless passes up the side in its four-hour mission. He couldn't imagine himself stuck out there for that long with that little to do; at least the tanker got to talk to somebody once in a while. The plane-guard helo just drove around and around, 150 feet from the water, and waited for somebody to eject or fall overboard. Tim always said that he'd rather orbit for four hours somewhere else because then he'd at least be going somewhere else to be bored as opposed to being bored right next to the ship.

The target for today, the power plant at Quanh Dinh, had been hit several times before and was only now showing signs of rebirth after the last American visit in late May. Nearly every worthwhile target had been bombed over the past few months and the North Vietnamese were showing signs of breaking. The attacks had been so heavy that there were really no more big targets left. Even the famed Tranh Hoa bridge had finally been blown into the river after years of trying and countless bombs dropped against it.

There were fewer and fewer SAMs coming up anymore because the shipping routes into the North from the sea and south from China were mostly choked off and resupply was difficult and slow. There was still a lot of Triple-A around which could blow your tail off if you weren't careful but it was becoming clear that the war was well into its final stage. Kissinger was meeting in Paris with Le Duc Tho and trying to hammer out the last of the stumbling blocks to "peace with honor."

Santy considered himself fortunate to be here now. There had been several years of half-assed air war but now they could do the job as they had been trained. Even though there was an underlying mood of caution in many of the pilots and squadrons flying against the North, most were eager to get in there and get the war over with and go home. For Santy, there was a feeling that he was really helping to accomplish something. He hoped that he and the other Americans would be allowed to continue pressing the bastards until they gave it up.

Even if he didn't get to go on this mission, he still had one scheduled for later in the day. He was on for a road recce which entailed pairs of Corsairs flying around in a specific sector of the country and shooting up anything of military value. They were essentially free-lance missions, still fairly hazardous but not as bad as an attack on Hanoi. Daylight road recces were a lot better to fly than the night ones where you had to bomb under the light of parachute flares dropped by one of the Corsairs. The light from the flares was just good enough to make a pilot think he had a good idea of what was going on but not good enough to give a true and well-defined picture of the target or terrain. Many a pilot had flown into the ground trying to bomb under the flares.

Santy's attention was drawn back to the yellow-shirted director standing on the deck immediately to his right front. He was giving Santy the signal that he was going to be launched. He pointed down the deck at one of the other Corsairs from VA-19 and gave a thumbs down.

Santy closed his canopy and, after the chocks and chains were removed from his aircraft, followed the director's signals forward to the bow and the catapult.

The twenty-six aircraft were spread out over what seemed a huge expanse of sky. Santy, flying in the rear of the formation, looked to his left front and saw several of the other attack jets out there, weaving around in their spread formation. Beyond them and slightly higher, flew two of the six two-plane sections of F-4 fighters which made up the TAR-CAP, or target combat air patrol, protection for the strike. In each of the fighters were two pairs of eyes searching the sky for the enemy MiGs which they secretly hoped would come up and try to pick off an American.

Santy looked back in at his instruments, noting that all was well and that all his weapons were armed and ready. The strike had crossed the coast about ten minutes ago just north of Vinh and were still heading generally west. Very soon now, the leader would turn the whole gaggle northeast and come in on the targeted power plant almost from behind. Ever since they had crossed the coast, everyone had been hearing the sounds of their threat receivers telling them that the search radars were locked on to them. So far, there had been none of the scarier tones which would indicate that the radars which would guide the SAMs at their aircraft had found them. There had been no SAM launches, meaning that either the Vietnamese were biding their time or they were so short on SAMs that they were keeping them farther north to protect Hanoi. Santy fervently hoped that the latter was the case.

Without a word spoken on the radio, the entire formation turned right and began to descend, picking up the speed which would be translated into maneuverability when it hit the fan in another twenty miles, or about four minutes. Santy re-checked his gauges and wiggled his shoulders, making sure for the fifteenth time that his harness was snug and locked. He wiggled his fingers on the stick and throttle, willing himself to relax and fly smoothly. He reached up with his left hand and tugged on his oxygen mask, moving it into a more comfortable position and feeling it slide a little on his face. He was sweating despite the coolness of the air-conditioned cockpit.

"Lead's in."

Up ahead, Santy caught a flash of light reflecting off the canopy of the leader rolling in on the target. A few seconds later several black/brown geysers erupted from the ground where his bombs had detonated. As if it signaled the beginning of a train wreck, these few explosions were followed by complete chaos on the radio. Everybody was calling out everything and aircraft were diving and climbing and twisting through the sky over the target. The white wings of the Corsairs with streamers of vapor coming from their tips showed themselves in planform as the jets released their loads, pulled off, and headed east for the safety of the gulf.

The two fighters from the right side of the formation, their afterburners roaring, tore past just over Santy's A-7 as they hustled off to the northwest after something. Santy hadn't heard any calls about MiGs in the area among all the transmissions on the radio and he twinged when he wondered what else he might have missed. He banked left and right, craning over his shoulder to see if there were any MiGs back there lining him up. When he again looked at the target, he could see that it was wreathed in smoke with huge blue and white sparks flying from the tops of the two remaining towers. Several more planeloads of bombs were bursting among the smoke and flying debris.

Santy saw a string of green tracer reaching after one of the Corsairs which was just pulling off target. He hadn't noticed the Triple-A but now he glanced around at the puffs of smoke all over the sky. He decided to put his bombs on the flak site rather than add them to the dust and smoke where the power plant used to be.

Rolling the jet nearly onto its back, he pulled the stick back and held it until he was generally aimed at the circular flak site. He released back pressure on the stick, simultaneously rolling the wings back level. He made small stick corrections, moving the target to the center of the display. When the target was just about there, Santy relaxed the pressures on the controls, ensuring that the aircraft was in balanced flight, and aimed straight for the flak guns. He released his bombs and broke sharply to the right, continuing but shallowing his dive.

Two streams of tracer were chasing him, as the gunners below traversed their weapons, when a string of bombs erupted across the edge of the emplacement. Santy glanced up and saw another A-7 hauling ass away from the site at right angles to his course. He looked back and saw his own bombs explode across the exact center of the circle. Apparently, he and the other pilot had gotten the same idea simultaneously and carried out a completely inadvertent but perfectly timed coordinated attack. There won't be any more shit from those guys, Santy thought.

When he looked back out front, the sky was completely empty of aircraft. He could hear the first ones making their "feet wet" reports as they crossed the beach but he couldn't find anyone around. Feeling much like a kid walking past a graveyard, he slammed the throttle full forward and held the nose down, getting as much speed out of his airplane as he could to get away and catch up with the other kids.

He didn't want to climb any higher than the three hundred feet he was now maintaining because it would slow him down and give anybody on the ground who cared to try a better shot at him. At one point, about four miles from the water, he saw a small village on the nose. For some reason, he decided to fly over it rather than turn away.

At the incredible speed he had built up, he was past the village before the people in it knew he was there. Santy could picture the peaceful center of the village filled with bodies flattened by the sudden breathtaking sound of his passage. It wouldn't really hurt anyone but he knew that there would be an increase in pairs of black trousers in the afternoon's wash and some peasants who would curse him for however long it would take them to round up all their animals.

As the ribbon of beach flashed beneath him, Santy stayed low and headed out just over the water. When he was far out to sea, he pulled the nose back and the Corsair climbed into the cloudless blue. He did an aileron roll in each direction just from the sheer joy of survival and the indescribable fun of flying a machine like this.

"Red Crown, Condor 300 is feet wet."

"Roger, 300. You're the last one out and your tail is clear." This last told Santy that none of the MiGs had decided to follow him out and take a shot at him when he would least expect it. "Your pigeons are 076 at, uh, 95 miles. Contact the E-2 on Button 8."

"Roger, switching Button 8. Good day." Santy rocked channel selector until he had it on the preset frequency and glanced at his altimeter. "Keyboard, Condor 300's with you passing twelve thousand for sixteen."

"Roger, 300. Radar contact. You're bringing up the rear. You can head direct to the break. Switch Button 6 at 20 miles."

"300, roger."

Santy slid up his dark visor and looked lazily around the empty sky. Sitting in the cockpit over the wide sea made it seem as if he were suspended motionless in space. From sixteen thousand feet, the water looked like a blue washboard. The waves below were regular undulations which stretched as far as the eye could see on either side. It was only when he stared at a particular spot that he could detect motion but from this altitude there was no sense of speed. He looked in at his TACAN indicator and saw that the needle was pointing straight ahead at the transmitter on the *Concord,* and the little DME, or Distance Measuring Equipment, window in the indicator was unwinding nicely. He was now only about fifty miles from the ship.

Boyle had always told him that there were two things about flying jets that he didn't like. One was that jets never felt like flying. In a helicopter, you could never take your hands off the controls; the balance of forces was so delicate that constant attention and correction were required to keep the things from falling over the edge into disaster.

The other thing that Boyle didn't like was that in most fixed-wing flying you were too far away from the earth and thus couldn't really sense speed or see what was going on down there. Boyle loved tearing around down low, looking at whatever new and interesting thing presented itself, like a tourist completely unhindered by roads. Flying helos fitted Boyle: sleeves rolled up, windows wide open, cigarette dangling, eyes squinting into the sun, free of all the artificial life-support gear required in jets. If anyone could just hang out while flying a multimillion-dollar aircraft, Santy thought, it would be Boyle in his H-3.

He chuckled, remembering another line from Tim's *Book of Cosmic Perspective,* "Never fly higher than you're willing to fall."

With the wind out of the west, the *Concord* was steaming on a base recovery course, or BRC, of 270, directly opposite the course the strike aircraft had to take to get back to her. Santy descended to 2,500 feet and arced far around to the right, staying clear of the traffic pattern. He continued the arc until he was dead astern of the ship and then turned west to enter the pattern. He descended to 600 feet and lined himself up with the starboard side of the carrier. He lowered the tail hook and completed the landing checklist except for the gear and the flaps.

Up ahead he could see the last of the other strike aircraft, an A-6, turning across the bow and entering the downwind leg of the landing pattern. Santy screamed up the starboard side of the *Concord* and waited until the A-6 on the downwind leg was well behind his left wing, headed the opposite way. He shoved the stick left and banked sharply, pulling hard on the stick to increase the g-forces and dissipate his speed. He dropped the gear and then the flaps and rolled wings level on the downwind leg about fifteen seconds directly behind the A-6.

As he passed abeam the ship, he rolled into a left turn, easing off the power to start the descent. When he was nearly through the last part of the approach, he picked up the orange lighted lens and keyed his mike.

"300, Corsair, ball, 1.4." The last told the LSO his fuel state, fourteen hundred pounds.

"Roger, ball, Corsair."

Santy continued the last part of the approach, correcting for a slight settling tendency close to the end, and slammed down on the deck. He was reassuringly thrown forward in his straps as the hook engaged the arresting wire. At the end of his run-out, the wire pulled him back a few feet, and he raised his hook on the signal from the sailor to his right. The sailor pointed to a director ahead and Santy followed his directions clear of the landing area, folding his wings as he taxied forward to his parking spot on the bow.

Once the A-7 was chocked and chained and with the engine winding down, he climbed down and walked around the jet. He stood for a minute watching the bow of the ship swing ponderously to starboard as she reversed course. Looking back up at the nose of the Corsair, he grinned and shook his head. And the dumb bastards actually pay me for this, he thought.

Chapter 20

October 6, 1972

This is not going to be my day, thought Boyle.

For about the sixteenth time in the last two minutes, he looked at the small tachometer gauge which read out the speed of his starboard engine's compressor, willing it to hold still. It was fluctuating regularly above and below the proper reading. It was not supposed to be doing that and, despite the best efforts of two of the detachment's jet engine mechanics it showed no signs of suddenly getting well and acting properly.

None of the related instruments were acting in synchronization with it, which according to the manuals meant that it was most probably a faulty gauge. If this had happened in flight, Boyle would have continued the mission and "downed" the H-3 upon landing, which would have restricted the helicopter from further flight until the problem was fixed.

There is an old saying in naval aviation that something wrong on the ground will never get better in the air and now, sitting here on the deck of the carrier, USS *Concord*, before flight, there was no question. There were only about ten minutes to go before the carrier launched her jets for another strike into North Vietnam and there was no chance that repairs could be done in that time. So the aircraft was down, and the helicopter orbiting out in Starboard Delta would have to be refueled and sent back out to cover the mission that Boyle could not now perform. There would not be enough time to switch crews during the refueling, so the crew out in Star-D would have to take the mission too.

Boyle had been assigned to be the backup helicopter for the North SAR helo and to be ready to take over in case something went wrong with it or another SAR developed while the primary was busy rescuing somebody else.

"Okay, Ted. We're down. Get out the shutdown checklist," said Boyle as he gave the signal to the LSE, who immediately pressed the transmit switch on his flight-deck helmet notifying the Air Boss up in the tower of the problem. Within seconds, a flight-deck tractor drove up, followed by several men dragging a towbar.

Since Boyle had not waited until the very last second to tell the Air Boss that the helo was down, there was no accompanying blast over the aircraft radio. There are a million or so available ways of pissing off the Air Boss. Right at the top of the list is downing your helo and screwing up the timing of the jet launch. Downing the helo is okay; just don't screw up the launch of the "real" aircraft.

Boyle's copilot, Lt. (J.G.) Ted Kruger, began following through on the checklist as Boyle performed the steps. Normally, the checklist was done in a challenge-and-reply method in which Kruger would read the step and Boyle would do it; but since they had to get this thing shut down and towed away in a hurry, they did the checklist the fastest way.

Once the rotor blades had been hydraulically folded, Boyle reached up and chopped the throttle on the number-one, or left, engine. He told the rest of the crew to get out and head for the ready room; he would stay with it and act as brake rider while the flight-deck troops towed the helicopter tail-first back aft and stowed it in the parking area.

Boyle decided to stay in the helo and watch the launch-

and-recovery cycle from the cockpit. It was not a particularly safe vantage point, like "Vulture's Row," the small catwalk area up on the island structure, but it had a better, more immediate view. Unless somebody came by and ordered him out of his cockpit and to a safer vantage, he would not only get to see the cycle but would get to actually feel the roar from the engines as they were launched and recovered. Besides, Boyle didn't feel like going to the ready room and explaining five times what was wrong with the helo to everyone from the maintenance chief to the duty officer. Kruger could handle that. As one of the more senior copilots, Ted had been around long enough and was due to make HAC himself pretty soon. At least that was one thing that Lt. Cmdr. Fisher hadn't screwed around with, thought Boyle.

There is an unwritten policy of long standing in naval aviation that teams new aircraft commanders with the most experienced copilots and the least experienced copilots with the more experienced HACs. This policy gave the newer HAC an added margin of knowledge to support him in the critical and somewhat dangerous first couple of months. For the copilot, it provided a bridge between the womblike time when he was flying with an old hand and the time when he would become the guy with the full responsibility. The senior copilot also knew enough to put somewhat of a brake on the new HAC's feelings of power and overconfidence. The policy was having exactly the desired effect on both Boyle and Kruger.

Now, in the middle of his first month as Office in Charge of the HC-17 detachment in the Gulf of Tonkin, Lt. Cmdr. Fisher had left his mark on the structure of the organization. At least in Boyle's mind, morale was beginning to slip. Very few traces of Hickerson's policies or established procedures had survived. It seemed to Boyle that change had been made simply for change's sake. One of the things that Boyle worried about most was that Fisher had not pressed particularly hard to complete the twelve required familiarization flights which would then qualify him to fly actual combat missions as a HAC.

On several occasions, other pilots, Boyle included, had had

to go back out with a short turnaround time to cover a mission for which Fisher had been scheduled but was not able to fly because of his "administrative work load." Lt. Cmdr. Hickerson, the previous OIC, had never seemed to miss a flight. He would schedule his work so it wouldn't interfere with what he considered his primary job, flying.

Fisher was in the aircraft which was now waiting to come in and land and was about to find out that he was stuck with another four hours as the airborne backup for this afternoon's strikes. Boyle had no sympathy at all for Fisher but he did feel a little sorry for the other pilot with him, Jack Crawford, who was going to be strapped in the helo's seat for an extra four hours. Even though Fisher was not yet qualified to fly combat as a HAC, he could go as a copilot as long as the other pilot was qualified.

Sudden movements on the angled deck brought Boyle's attention back to the present. He reached up and turned on the battery switch and then the main aircraft radio so he could listen to what was being said as well as watch what was happening.

Fisher and Crawford in Angel 801 came up the port side of the ship and slid over to a landing in front of the jets waiting to be hooked up to the waist catapults. The "grapes," the purple-shirted members of a refueling crew, hauled out a heavy hose from the catwalk alongside the flight deck, dragged it under the tail close to the spinning tail rotor, and plugged it into the receptacle in the right rear of the helicopter. One of the maintenance troops from the detachment ran up to the pilot's side of 801 and handed several sheets of paper through the window to him and then ran hunched over across the deck to the island and the hatch which led below.

Over the radio, Boyle heard the Air Boss in the tower calling the helo.

"Angel 801, Tower. Your playmate 804 went down on deck. You're to assume his mission. After takeoff, steer 235 and contact Red Crown. Button 18."

"Uh, Tower, request you get the crew from 804 to switch with us." Fisher definitely sounded pissed.

"Negative, 801. No time. Tower out."

Boyle watched the fueling progress. Even though there were still four minutes to go before the launch was scheduled, the catapult officer for the waist cats was getting impatient, judging from the number of times he was checking his watch and looking up at the "time to go" lights on the tower.

For some reason, when a jet needs a little extra time nobody minds but when a helo is the holdup everyone on the flight deck mentally curses the "goddamn rotorheads." The reason, thought Boyle, was probably that the helo was the first aircraft off the deck and when it was slow in getting away or had to be brought in for fuel, as 801 had, it took up so much room that the deck became paralyzed: nothing could move around or through the area. Watkins had long ago taught Boyle that the best way to impress the people on the carrier was to tell them early, with no bullshit, what your requirements were and give them lots of time to plan for you. That way you didn't impede the rest of the operations. If you or your unit got the reputation of holding things up, you soon found yourself fighting for everything you needed rather than getting the help quickly and with a smile. That's why Boyle had downed his helo early enough to get the replacement in and out rapidly without hindering anything or anybody else.

Suddenly, people began hustling around 801 again. The grapes pulled their fuel hose free, dragged it back to the catwalk, and jumped down after it. Two brown-shirted sailors pulled the chains and wheel chocks free of the helo and followed the grapes into the catwalk. The LSE gave the raised-fist hold signal to the pilots in 801 and squatted, looking to see if there were any chains missed by the two sailors. He stood and, checking over each shoulder that the deck was clear, circled his hand over his head a couple of times, pointed outboard, giving the pilots the takeoff signal, and hustled clear of the deck.

801 bounced gently on its wheels a couple of times and lifted into a hover, the catapult crew behind it squatting and leaning into the heavy downwash from the rotor blades. After five seconds or so, giving the pilots a chance for a quick scan

of the gauges, the nose of the helo dipped slightly and it slowly accelerated up and away from the carrier, finally turning left and heading out for its assigned station.

Almost immediately the catapults began shooting the jets into the air. As each came up, the cat crews swarmed around it, attaching it to the catapult and running to clear the deck, all the while watching the other aircraft to avoid being run over or sucked into the howling intakes as they taxied by. In the maelstrom of noise that is a carrier flight deck, a man cannot distinguish the sound of a jet engine next to him from any other. Your eyes are the only things that keep you alive and what you don't see will kill you quickly and horribly. Unless he sees it happen, the first signs that the pilot who sucks you into his intake will have will be a sudden decrease in engine performance and horrified looks from your fellow deck workers.

Boyle watched the rest of the launch. When the last of the A-7s had taxied by on its way to the bow cats, he looked to his left and watched the first formation of four Phantoms come up overhead the *Concord* just off the starboard side as they entered the landing pattern. Much of their approach was going to be hidden from him because of the other aircraft parked around him out of the way, so he gathered his gear, climbed down from the H-3, and closed both halves of the passenger door behind him. Stepping nimbly over the nest of tie-down chains and ducking under and around the folded wings, droppable fuel tanks, and the various other aircraft projections and attachments, he made his way through the "Bomb Farm," the area where the weapons readied for loading were kept handy, and around to the hatch in the starboard side of the island structure which led below.

As he pulled the hatch closed behind him and dogged it, he had a momentary thought that Fisher was probably going to have a whole bunch of questions for him when he returned from what was now his mission. Screw him, Boyle thought. It's about time the sonofabitch pulled his own weight.

* * *

In the cockpit of Angel 801, it was becoming obvious to Lt. Jack Crawford that this was not going to be a pleasant flight. Fisher had been livid when he was told that there was no time to change crews and that he was going to have to spend the rest of the flying day in the air, backing up for the North SAR helo.

If he'd said it once, Fisher had said it ten times in the thirty minutes since they'd taken off that he was going to have to change the procedures so that there was always a crew standing by to jump in whenever the planned schedule went to worms as it had today. Crawford wisely kept his mouth shut and answered only in noncommittal monosyllables. As the operations officer for the HC-17 detachments, it was he who was going to have to argue Fisher out of trying to kill a flea with a shotgun. That would wait until after the flight when Fisher cooled off a bit. For now, they had a mission to carry out and pissing and moaning about the why of it wasn't helping them get it done.

In the back of his mind, there was another thought which was beginning to nag at Crawford. Fisher was ranting far more than he usually did and far more than this inconvenience warranted. The closer they were getting to their holding point, the faster Fisher was talking. A man heading out on his first mission that had a real possibility of combat should be asking questions and growing gradually quieter, as opposed to delivering a lecture on the proper structure of an organization. For the past half-hour, Crawford had been trying as hard as he could to keep his cool and not get into an intra-cockpit pissing contest but he was about ready to tell Fisher to shut the fuck up and do his job. Crawford was also aware that that would do no good despite being personally satisfying.

Crawford became aware suddenly that there was an odd pause and that something had been asked of him. He looked at Fisher and saw that he was waiting for some sort of an answer.

"I said I think that perhaps there was nothing really wrong with 804 and that we ought to check up on it when we get back to the ship. What do you think?" Fisher was apparently repeating his question.

Crawford wasn't sure what Fisher was implying so he played it straight. "If there was nothing wrong with 804, they'd be here now and we wouldn't. These helos have been driven pretty hard and things breaking on them is to be expected. There are only about a dozen or so H-3s modified for Combat SAR in the whole damn Navy and just thirty-two pilots to fly them day in and day out, so you have to expect wear and tear to take its toll.

"Hell, this one we're in has been shot up at least twice since I've been over here. Last time, it took us two weeks to fix it and that was mostly waiting for parts. You have to expect them to go down for maintenance once in a while."

Fisher had suddenly paled when Crawford mentioned that 801 had been shot up before. Crawford wondered what Fisher would have looked like if he had been told that two good men, Lenehan and Ball, had died in it the last time, back in August. It suddenly struck him that Fisher was scared to death and the endless talking probably was an effort to distract himself. Christ, if he sweats a backup mission like this so much, Crawford thought, what is he gonna be like when he has to take the primary?

Crawford reached down and switched his radio to the frequency for Red Crown. "Well, it's time to check in and see where they want us," he said lightly.

Fisher kept his eyes looking straight ahead. You can do this, he was telling himself, you've got to.

Chapter 21

October 6, 1972

Red Crown, this is Angel 801 with you, replacing Angel 804. We're on Mother's 290 radial at 46 miles. Our state is three hours to splash and we're up for your control."

"Roger, 801, loud and clear. Red Crown has you on radar. You're about twenty miles southeast of your station. Steer 320 for 20 miles. Current altimeter is 29.97."

"801 copies. 29.97."

Crawford reached forward and turned the knob on his altimeter, setting the current barometric pressure reading in this area, 29.97 inches of mercury, in the little window. An incorrect altimeter setting will cause erroneous altimeter readings, which, in turn, are among the thousand little fatal traps that a pilot must avoid every day. Since Fisher was still on the flight controls, Crawford reached over and set his altimeter for him.

"Thanks, Jack," said Fisher quietly.

"Yep. Okay, you guys back there. If you would be so kind, please rig the aircraft for rescue. You may also test your weapons." Crawford's sarcastic tone came through the intercom clearly and was met with grins from the two crewmen. There was little that a sailor/flight crewman likes to do more than fire the door-mounted machine guns. The hoist operator, Petty Officer Second Class Sam Satterwhite, came forward and cocked the gun mounted in the passenger door on the left side right behind Crawford in the copilot's seat. As he prepared to fire, he glanced forward.

"Better put your collar up, Mr. Crawford."

"Yeah, thanks." Crawford looked at Fisher and explained as he adjusted his flightsuit.

"Sometimes spent casings from the gun go down the back of the copilot's flight suit. They're hotter than hell so you put your collar up and fasten the Velcro to keep 'em out. They've tried about twenty different ways of fixing the problem and none work every time, so up goes the collar."

Fisher waited until Satterwhite had fired his trial bursts.

"Did you ever have that casing business happen to you?"

Crawford was about to deny it when Satterwhite broke in. "Sure did. Right after he got here, one I fired on a SAR went down his neck and he started hollering that he'd been hit. We couldn't do anything about it right then since the gooks were really pissed and were shooting the crap out of us so we had to wait until we got out over the water. By then the casing had cooled down enough that the pain was easing up so he figured he was either gonna live or had about a minute before he croaked. That was funny as shit, Mr. Crawford."

They could hear the swimmer laughing in the back as he test fired his gun.

Crawford laughed with them. "That thing felt like it burned the skin right off one of my shoulderblades. Every time I put on my flight gear for the next week it hurt like hell, too."

Fisher laughed dutifully at the story. Inside, he was thinking about the easy familiarity Crawford had with the enlisted crewmen. Fisher had always been convinced that there was a vast gulf between the officer and the enlisted which was there for a reason and should be preserved. He believed that circumstance should not be allowed to modify the principle. The concept of fighting men all being in the same boat, so to speak, had been foreign to him. But since he had taken over the detachment he was finding many of his preconceptions hard to support. In an environment like this, the principle did not apply to every circumstance.

In spite of his original rancor against Boyle, he'd found the young pilot to be an extremely competent J.O. Rather than settle his hash immediately, Fisher had decided to hold off until Boyle was transferred out of the detachment. That would be the time to put a subtle but damaging comment in his fitness report if it was still warranted.

As to Boyle's friend Santy, Wilson had made it clear that he was off limits to Fisher's retaliation. But Fisher was certain that there would come a time for it somewhere down the road.

Another thought crept in right on the heels of these. He was beginning to realize that his seniority and years of flying the H-3 were not going to be enough. To take the helo and crew into a combat environment called for qualities which he was not sure he had been granted.

Once they had reached their station and reported in to Red Crown again, they took up their wide orbit and waited. The crew moved around some of the gear in the rear of the aircraft to make things more comfortable and lay down to doze. If there were a call, it would take them less than a minute to put everything back where it belonged and man their stations.

The pilots, on the other hand, did not have the freedom of movement and so tried several times to make themselves more comfortable. Any change they made was only temporary in that the discomfort went away for about thirty seconds but reappeared in another part of their anatomy with a vengeance. For Crawford, the backs of his legs hurt the worst and even when he pulled out the simulated foam seat cushion to change the angle of the seat slightly, it only made his butt numb. Fisher changed nothing about his seat. He was more worried about what might be coming later in the flight than what his body was bitching about.

Several times, Fisher had surreptitiously glanced at Crawford to see how he was dealing with the possibility of getting shot at. Crawford had his left foot up on the aluminum rib that separated the upper and lower halves of his front side window and his right up on the navigation panel on the center console. He was quietly smoking a cigarette and was staring straight ahead through half-closed eyes, only occasionally and reflexively glancing down at the gauges on the instrument panel. He seemed miles away mentally from what Fisher considered imminent and probable death.

Fisher could not believe that a man could be so cool. Crawford was either a complete idiot for not realizing what lay ahead or so fed up with life he didn't care that he could be killed at any time.

Crawford, on the other hand, was doing what all good pilots do who plan to survive. He called it "thinking it through." At times during each flight, when there was nothing really taxing his intellect, Crawford would go over, step by step, every eventuality he could think of that he might have to face in the rest of the flight. He knew that he would never be able to anticipate everything that could happen but his experience told him that those parts he had thought through early did not become problems later on. He would not have to decide what to do about them because he had already drawn them through a decision matrix of sorts. Having thus reduced the amount of thinking he was required to do when things went to shit, he would have more available to deal with the surprises. He was not sure that his little mental process really had any tangible effect on his success but he had been using it since early on in his first tour and now, after fifteen hundred flying hours in the combat zone, he was not only still alive but completely unscathed.

Once Crawford came to grips with the fact that, as on every single flight which included the possibility of his getting shot at, he would rather be somewhere else but couldn't be, he placed the flight into his mental blender and did his best to make a daiquiri out of it.

Fisher had just taken over the controls again from Crawford and was checking the fuel gauges when he heard their call sign from Red Crown, telling them to switch to the primary rescue frequency for the day.

"Angel 801, Red Crown. Switch Button 19."

"801, roger," Crawford answered. "Switching 19."

He reached down and rotated the channel selector and looked over at Fisher. In the few seconds it took for the radio to channelize itself, Fisher grew pale and his hand tightened on the stick.

When Fisher showed no sign of making the transmission, Crawford keyed his transmitter. "Red Crown, Angel 801 is with you. Button 19."

"801, Red Crown. Loud and clear. Be advised that Angel 802 is engaged on a SAR for a damaged F-105 which is trying to make it out to the water. You are now primary SAR bird for the Navy strikes."

"801, roger. We're primary. We have two hours thirty to splash."

"Okay, Andy," Crawford said over the intercom, "I guess one of the Air Force birds out of Thailand can't make it back home and is trying for Danang or somewhere. We get them sometimes. You got the brief on the targeting changes, right?"

Fisher looked at Crawford and nodded. Crawford could see that his mind was at least temporarily diverted from thinking about what might lie ahead so he decided to keep up the chatter. "It's a long flight to and from Takhli or Korat or wherever, especially now that the honchos have removed the restrictions and expanded the targetable areas. The 105s have to refuel going both ways. Sometimes when they're hit bad it is easier and smarter to stay low, burn the extra gas it costs, and head for someplace in South Vietnam. When they do we provide SAR coverage for them like the Air Force does for our guys if they wind up over Laos or the western part of North Vietnam. They've saved a bunch of our guys and we've gotten some of theirs back. When this guy gets out over the water, 802 will cover for him until he moves farther south and into the next area down but, until 802 can get back here, we'll have to cover his area."

Fisher was warming to this; he loved organizational things. "Okay, who decides that 802 goes? Why not us, for instance?"

"Red Crown decides by whoever is closest or has the most fuel onboard. The way a chief on Red Crown explained it to me is that they look at it like a board game: moving pieces to fit the threat. That's oversimplified but I got the idea. They assume that when you check in for a mission you're completely prepared to carry it out, whatever it takes. That's why we have to be one hundred percent sure of ourselves and our aircraft before we ever launch. There ain't no time-outs allowed. You've gotta bring everything with you the first time."

Fisher thought about that last comment. Perhaps he had been premature in judging the crew which he and Crawford had had to replace. But then again, perhaps not, he thought; better not set a precedent and let the men think I'll let things slide.

Since Crawford appeared to be in an explanatory mood, Fisher began to ask his opinion of little matters that concerned the detachment, anything to keep his mind from dwelling on today's possibilities. Crawford answered apparently candidly until they were interrupted by Red Crown again.

"Angel 801, Red Crown. We have an A-7 going down south-southeast of Nam Dinh. Steer 245 for 20 miles and await RESCAP. How copy, over?"

Crawford keyed the radio. "801 copies. 245 for 20. Standing by."

"Okay, you guys in the back, we have a possible SAR overland. Rig for rescue. If we go in over the beach, keep your heads on a swivel and call out what you see." This was Crawford's regular crew and, although they had flown together as a team for quite a while, he never failed to give them exactly the same admonition each time they were alerted for a SAR. The sense of routine helped everyone.

"Nam Dinh, Andy, is a town about thirty miles down the

Red River from Hanoi. There is a major road system passing through the place and we bomb their bridge all the time but the little bastards keep building it back. The country around there is pretty heavily populated so we can expect some opposition. The A-7s flying RESCAP cover for us will help us out."

Fisher banked the helicopter to the new course. It took every ounce of will that he had to accelerate it up to red-line airspeed and thus approach danger as fast as the helo would fly. He was now certain that this was going to be his last day on earth. He looked at Crawford and saw no change in him at all. Crawford was calmly pulling out his chart of the area which had all the known antiaircraft and SAM sites marked in dark green ink. As he folded the chart to have just one page represent the entire route in and the area south of Nam Dinh, Fisher had the irrelevant thought that the chart and its markings had been sloppily done.

"What if your chart is wrong, Jack?" asked Fisher.

"Then it's wrong. I updated it this morning from the intelligence maps on the ship. If we don't find things satisfactory, we can always slap the spooks around when we get back."

"Do you update it every day?"

"Yep. If it's a habit you don't forget to do it. Doing things the same way every time keeps you alive." Crawford knew instantly that he had said the wrong thing. Fisher had not yet learned all the little tricks of the game over here and was now going to realize that there were large gaps in his knowledge which he would assume were going to get him killed. When Crawford looked at him, he could see that Fisher was sweating like a fat lady in July.

"Actually, Andy," he said reasonably, "that's why we match up the crews like we do. We only need one chart and by the time you get a nugget copilot you'll be the guy with all the experience. No sweat. We're okay."

Fisher didn't reply. Crawford was going to have to wait and see what happened if they got the call to go overland. He hoped they would get that call but a lot of things could still happen. The A-7 pilot might not have survived the ejection and RESCAPs might not be able to find him if he had. With the population around the area, the chances of a downed aviator evading capture for long were not very good at all, about one in six. The RESCAPs would not bring in the helo unless they were certain that they knew where the guy was and that there was a chance.

If the call came, Crawford would take the helo in and Fisher would have to take his chances with everybody else.

Crawford tuned the other radio to the frequency he had been told was the one for this strike. Nam Dinh was not one of the places that the jets from the *Concord* were supposed to be going today. The A-7 that was down had probably come from the other carrier steaming around the central part of Yankee Station, the USS *Independence*. Most of the *Indy*'s normal targets were in the southern part of North Vietnam and so the resultant SAR work had come under the HC-17 detachment down on South SAR. With the sudden easing of restrictions and the resultant increase in approved targets, the responsibilities had become mixed and now everybody was bombing everything available.

As soon as the channelizing tone in their earphones stopped, the helo pilots heard the chaos over the downed pilot.

". . . had a good chute. It looked like he came down near that little clump of trees south of the village. Got a strong beeper, too." The "beeper" was a wailing sort of tone sent out on a special frequency that all airplanes monitored constantly in addition to the selected one for whatever mission they were on. The beeper, a small hand-held radio, was activated automatically when somebody ejected, and had to be manually turned off. It could also be used to send and receive voice transmissions. Since Angel 801 was too far away to receive the line-of-sight transmissions from the pilot on the ground they had to surmise half of the conversation.

"Yeah, I saw an empty chute on the last pass so he must be able to move around. There's a bunch of people heading his way from the village. Do you want me to discourage 'em?"

"Negative for now. We gotta find him first. Is there a helo available?"

Crawford keyed his radio, interrupting the chatter over the site. "This is Angel 801. We're presently two miles out over the water about twenty miles down the coast from the mouth of the Red. We'll stay feet wet until you call us in. Standing by."

"Angel 801, this is Salty Dog 405. We have a single ejection, Salty Dog 412. He's down 235 for 16 miles from Nam Dinh. We're trying to pinpoint and authenticate now. We'll call when we're ready for you."

"Click-click."

Crawford asked the crew if they were all set for this. The crewmen in the rear chorused two "Yessirs" and there was a silent nod from Fisher.

"Okay. They need to find this guy and authenticate him before they call us. Since there is a village nearby we can expect small arms for sure and possibly bigger stuff. The jets will tell us if they see any when they escort us in." He held the chart so Fisher could see it, his finger pointing to a sharp ridge. "412 is down about here near the edge of this large karst. Looks like it's about twenty-one miles inland. There are no Triple-A sites near there and if we fly this route we can avoid those here and here," he said indicating two green circles on the chart close to the route he had picked. "We oughta be okay."

Fisher asked about the authentication procedures. "If they have to authenticate the guy, won't it take a while for them to get his card from the ship out here?" He was referring to the card on file in the Intelligence Center on the ship, which each pilot filled out with unique answers to several questions, answers only the correct individual would know. This was done to ensure that the voice on the ground end of the survival radio was not an English-speaking imposter sitting in a Triple-A battery.

"Normally, yes," Crawford answered, "but, being close to an enemy village, this one is going to be time-limited. The pilot overhead is from the same ship and squadron so they can ask for the C.O.'s wife's name or the star of the last movie they all saw in their ready room. That will do it just as well. The cards on the ship come in in a longer-term effort. Sometimes they can see the guy the whole time so there is no need to authenticate."

Fisher nodded. He began to go over as much of his training as he could remember, and everything he had been told about these missions. He would be the pilot at the controls when they went in and Crawford would do the navigating and talking. He was momentarily surprised that his thoughts were of "when" they went in, not "if." His trapped feeling of terror was growing stronger by the minute.

"Angel 801, Salty Dog 405. We've authenticated the pilot. He's on a small hilltop and appears to be surrounded by the locals. We're going to try and hold them off until you get here but you can expect some ground fire. Your escorts should be over you about now. Over."

"405, Angel 801. Roger. Standing by and thanks for the head's up." The pilot in 405 could have lied and made it seem less dangerous so that the helo crew would be more willing to go in but that was not how the game was played.

To Fisher, the situation seemed certain to get the helo shot down. The guy was surrounded deep in enemy-infested territory and the jets could only "try" to keep the enemy away. He told himself that he would be more willing if the odds of success were better but this was just plain foolhardy. Didn't Crawford know what the gooks did to helo crews that fell into their hands?

As if reading his mind, Crawford addressed the crew. "Okay. This one doesn't look too good but we're gonna give it the best we've got. You guys in the back call out anything you see. Andy, you concentrate on driving the bus; keep us as low as you can and as fast as you can get it to go. If the hilltop is clear, we'll land and grab him. If it's not, we'll hoist him up unless there's too much ground fire. If there is, we'll hook him up and get out of there to a safer area and reel him in then. Any questions?"

There were none, which was just as well because the escorts called as soon as he had finished speaking.

"Angcl 801, this is Salty Dog 411. We're over you now. Steer 275 for about 23 miles."

"801. Roger. 275."

Fisher banked the helo to the new heading and increased speed to the red line and a little beyond. Down at 100 feet above the surface, it was going to be a real bumpy ride. He backed the speed down to 135 knots to give them a little cushion against turbulence. When he had the heading, altitude, and airspeed squared away, he looked out through the windshield at the beach as it whipped beneath them. He was now flying over North Vietnam. He felt a huge urge to urinate which he found almost impossible to suppress. He reached down and rechecked that his shoulder harness was locked, and tried to concentrate on his flying, anything to stop the terror.

Overhead, Salty Dog 411 and his wingman, 410, flew on opposite sides of a protective circle, called the wagonwheel. That way, one set of eyes would always be looking out for the ground fire that the helo couldn't see and one 20mm cannon would always be ready to deal with it.

801 had gotten about halfway to the area and was in radio range of the downed pilot when they heard a transmission that was like a kick in the stomach.

"405, they're coming out of the brush at me! They're about fifty yards off! Ah, Jesus, I got nowhere left to run. Where's the fucking helo? I can't . . . ." Then there was silence on the radio. Then another voice.

"405's in." More silence.

If it is possible to hold your breath in a helo slamming into air currents at 100 feet, Crawford and Fisher accomplished it.

"Angel 801, 405. Get out of here. They've captured him and they're leading him downhill. I guess he really didn't have much of a chance but thanks for trying. 411, escort the helo out then go on home."

"411, roger."

Fisher banked the helo hard left and headed out the way they had come in. Now that the pilot was captured, the sense of urgency went away and he unconsciously began to slow the helo down and climb a little.

"Andy, damnit, we're still in Indian Country. I have the aircraft." Crawford took the controls, accelerating back to 135 knots and diving for the deck. "We still have ten more miles of bad guys to fly over. They can bag us just as easy now as on the way in."

The rebuke brought Fisher back to where he was. He had been thinking about the A-7 pilot who now had to face the agonies of interrogation and imprisonment in the miserable places in and around Hanoi. He was thinking that it could have been him, if he had survived capture at all. The thought had loosed the last restraint on his bladder but with all the perspiring he had done so far that day, the stain on his flight-suit would not be noticeable at all, except to him.

Except to speak to the escorting A-7s, no one said another word until the helo was again out over the water and reestablished in its orbit.

They were only required to stay on station for another forty minutes. The F-105 pilot had made it to safety at Danang, and the North SAR helo, Angel 802, had returned after refueling en route. The day's attacks were over and both helos were sent back to their ships, one pleased with the successful landing of the 105, the other crushed that they'd been unable to do anything for the A-7 pilot. It was a lousy feeling.

Despite Crawford's compliments on how he had performed today, all Fisher could do after they landed back aboard *Concord* was make a vague excuse asking Crawford to handle all the paperwork, and then go below to his stateroom where he could be alone with his failure.

Chapter 22

October 6, 1972

When Boyle walked into the ready room, Crawford was halfway through the postflight paperwork. He looked tired and his skin had the oily sheen that comes from too much sweat and jet exhaust. Boyle hung back until Crawford closed the binder which held all the forms and charts having to do with Angel 801.

Crawford walked over to the duty officer's desk and placed the binder in its slot. The operations and maintenance troops would soon pick it up and extract the information they needed, be it flight time for the daily summary or the list of "gripes" to be fixed by the maintainers.

Boyle came up and apologized for causing Crawford to fly the extra mission. Even though there was no way that Tim could have changed it, he still felt, as nearly all good aviators do, a little guilty that he had not been able to perform his assigned mission.

"I'm sorry about that, Jack. The damn Ng tach went tits up. They couldn't swap it out in time to make the launch."

"No problem except my ass hurts. Fisher was really pissed

about it, though. He wanted to change the whole flight schedule so that it won't happen again. I'll have to talk to him about that later."

"Good. Do you think he learned anything out there today?"

"Yeah, he did. When we had to go over the beach he really did well. He was just like the rest of us the first time, scared and a little behind the airplane. The only mistake he made was forgetting where he was when they called us off. I had to remind him that it was Indian Country down there. I did the same thing myself way back when. He gutted it out and did the job. I'm signing him off as completing the syllabus. He'll do just fine."

Crawford turned away in response to a summons to report to the maintenance chief, leaving Boyle to sit in one of the ready room chairs and pick up a worn copy of *The Stars and Stripes*. His mind really wasn't on it. He was thinking about what Crawford had told him of Fisher's performance.

There had been a sort of armed truce between him and Fisher ever since their first conversation after Hong Kong. Fisher had worked everyone hard and was never reluctant to criticize their efforts in what he obviously felt was a professional way. He seemed oblivious to the fact that his superior tone and his inflexible manner really pissed everyone off. The only pilot in the detachment who had not yet been alienated, and who was still supportive of Fisher, was Crawford. Then again, thought Boyle, Crawford was one of those rare men who found it impossible to stay mad at anyone for long.

Rear Admiral Welch turned back from the wall chart and faced the group of officers he had summoned to the Flag spaces just inboard of the *Concord*'s Combat Information Center. They were there to discuss the latest message from the Pentagon. Another partial bombing halt had been mandated because the North Vietnamese had shown "certain signs that they were now ready to negotiate in good faith." Even before any of them had begun to read his copy of the message, everyone in the room knew that this was State Department bullshit of the highest order.

Welch waited until they had all read the message, a few reading it through twice. When the muttering had ceased and all eyes in the room were on him, Welch asked each man in turn to give his impressions of the contents. They ranged from the usual caviling from the staff's professional weasel, Cmdr. Strickland, to salty disgust from Cmdr. Wilson, one of the A-7 squadron C.O.'s.

The admiral nodded to his chief of staff, Capt. Harry Forrest, who walked to the front of the room. Since several of the officers present had arrived within the past month, Welch had decided that Forrest should give a concise overview of the events which led to the present situation. Furthermore, much of the overview contained information to which only a few of those present had been officially privy because of the mania for secrecy and compartmentalization which had infected the military ever since Johnson took office nine years before. Most of that information was readily available in the press, if one could summon the patience and stifle his anger long enough to wade through the bias and antiadministration adjectives in the papers. The papers, though, were always a week to ten days old by the time they arrived aboard the ship and always came in clumps of five or six and so were rarely read carefully at all.

Forrest was a no-nonsense officer who had been one of the navy's premier test pilots in the early sixties until he had tried just a few seconds too long to save a spinning Phantom during a test flight over the Chesapeake Bay. He had ejected but had been too low for the ejection sequence to work fully. After a long fight with the Bureau of Medicine, he had been allowed to remain on active duty despite his permanently stiffened left leg. His career, now drawing to a close, had been marked by frequent, loud, and universally successful battles with stupid regulations and with stupider officeholders. When he spoke in his deep North Carolina drawl, his listeners were immediately struck by his reason, his subtle force, and his honesty. There was not a man in the room who was not just a little bit in awe of Harry Forrest, and that included Rear

Admiral James Welch, who firmly believed that Forrest was more a statesman in uniform than an ex-fighter pilot.

Using a silver pointer and referring to the wall map, Forrest began with the Communist attack on South Vietnam back in March. "You will recall the 'Easter Offensive' invasion of the south by the NVA back on 30 March. They came out of Cambodia through the Ashau valley here, across the border from Laos here and here, and down through the DMZ here and here. We kind of got taken by surprise: I hear even Secretary of Defense Laird told Congress that it couldn't happen. The ARVNs, the South Vietnamese Army, held fast in spots but ran away in most.

"We had only six or seven thousand combat troops left there after the withdrawal that's been going on for a couple of years. There was no way that we could put the troops back so most of our support was from air power. It was only last month that the ARVN took back Quangtri, here, and regained control of the northern provinces. We believe that the Communists have lost fifty thousand dead and at least that many wounded in the past six months for very little real gain. The way I see it, the NVA is still willing to lose a lot to win. So it's obvious even to the assholes back in Washington that sending messages to the bastards isn't going to cut it.

"The best intelligence estimates say that the NVA purpose was to shoot down the concept of Vietnamization and to grab as much territory as they could before a ceasefire got called. It's working too. I don't believe that the South Vietnamese are willing to pay as much to avoid losing everything they have as the enemy is to get a couple more bargaining chips.

"Anyway, President Nixon ordered Linebacker 1 in May and we began bombing the North almost at will. Back on 9 May, A-6s and A-7s mined Haiphong harbor and over the next few weeks we mined all the rest of them. It appears now that the fuel dump that we blew up during that rescue last July was part of an attempt by the NVA to resupply away from their normal routes. We've flown road recces up the wazoo and they just keep coming. We're finding and destroying as many trucks on the roads during daylight now as we used to find on a good night ten months ago. The Air Force is bombing the hell out of them with the B-52s and everything that will fly out of Thailand. It's working and the North Vietnamese are hurting."

Forrest paused and took a sip of coffee from his cup. He picked up his copy of the message they had all just read. When he continued, he couldn't keep a trace of disgust from showing in his voice.

"Now, comes the problem. Since the gooks are making signs like they want to talk seriously, we've been ordered to ease up on them. I guess as a sign of good faith. There will be no more bombing above the twentieth parallel, which runs across North Vietnam right here. That means no more bombing targets around Hanoi or Haiphong, so once again we give them a chance to resupply and rebuild. Right when we had them by the short and curlies."

Forrest could feel himself getting wound up. I'm getting too old for this shit, he thought. I should be home growing radishes or something. Whatever he said from here on in would only sound bitter. "Any questions?" he asked. When no one spoke up, Forrest nodded at the admiral and took his place at the conference table.

Welch walked to the front of the room. "Thanks, Harry. Okay, here's what I think will happen. Somebody is going to start quibbling at the peace talks and we're going to have to go back and start all over again bombing Hanoi and Haiphong. The gooks have fired about two thousand SAMs at us since we began hitting them hard in May. They are damn near out of them and out of Triple-A too. Even though we have cut most of their supply lines, they will now have time to hand-carry the stuff down the damn roads so when we go back North, it'll be square one all over again.

"What I see happening is that we'll get the word to go back in within two months at the outside. The weather then will be lousy as it always is in December around here so we will not be able to concentrate our efforts as we have in the past. The load will come down on the A-6s with their all weather capability." He held up a hand to forestall Wilson's protest.

"I know that the A-7s can do it, too, Jack, but it's not going to be my call. It's not a dead issue either. Give me a chance."

Welch watched as Wilson sat back in his seat, mollified at least for the present. He began again. "What I am about to say cannot leave this room in any way, shape, or form. If anyone speaks a word the consequences will not be pleasant for him. Or for me either. Do you understand?" There was a chorus of "Yessirs" around the room.

"All right. As far as the American people are concerned, the Vietnam war is over. It is no longer front-page news except when something extraordinary happens. The troops are coming home and those that remain are pretty much out of a combat role. That leaves us on the carriers and the Air Force in Thailand as the only ones we have who can protect what is left in South Vietnam and convince the gooks that we're still serious. Personally, I do not care what happens to South Vietnam anymore. I don't think anybody over here does. What I do care about is our pilots. I include most especially those who are now POWs. We have to hurt the North Vietnamese as often and as badly as we can whenever and wherever we have a chance. The POWs are nothing to the Vietnamese except a bargaining chip. I believe that any peace signed must include their release. We must keep the faith with those men. To do that we must continue to fly and fight as hard and as effectively as we have for the past eight years. Naval Air as a whole has been averaging about four thousand sorties a month against the North since May. We have been losing men and aircraft, too. But we *have* hurt the bastards.

"If, before the president declares the war over, we cease to fly against the enemy aggressively and effectively, only two things will result. Good men will die from someone else's hesitation and we will betray the men who have gone before us. When the next conflict starts, the men we have flying then will recall only that we ended this one by abandoning fellow aviators and wonder why *they* should put it all on the line. Once we cease to be aggressive the first time, there will be nothing to stop us from quitting again. It will be easy."

Welch paused, looking through the complete silence into

the eyes of every man in the room. He continued in a quieter but more forceful tone. "It is your responsibility as the senior officers to set the example. You must lead your men as if the war were just beginning. We cannot back off now. No one wants to be the last man to get killed in a war. But I guaran-goddamn-tee you that the last one will be a guy who is shying away from the job at hand. He's the guy who will make that last mistake. Don't let him be one of *your* guys."

Welch strode from the room. There was a pensive silence for a minute or so, not broken until Forrest stood and cleared his throat. When he had the attention of the others, he began to get down to the nuts and bolts of planning for combat under the new restrictions.

In his stateroom just a few frames aft of the Flag spaces, where the senior officers were now planning the immediate future for the men of the ships on Yankee Station, Lt. Cmdr. Andy Fisher was weeping over his immediate past.

As soon as he had gotten free of Angel 801 and the crew, Fisher had gone below, head down, stepping heavily through the twists and turns of the passageways, neither seeing nor hearing the sailors and officers who stepped aside to make way for him. Once in his stateroom, with the door securely locked and with only his small desk lamp for illumination, he had dropped his flight gear in the middle of the room and sat heavily on the edge of his rack. He hadn't moved in over thirty minutes.

No matter how hard he tried, no matter what he forced his mind to concentrate on, he couldn't get himself away from a continuing replay of the flight into North Vietnam. Everything external to him that he had seen and heard throughout those forty minutes was indistinct now, nearly dreamlike. The only realities of those forty minutes, standing focused and textured and accusing before him, were every nuance of emotion he had experienced on that wild ride. Like an endless tape, they ran through him again and again. He could see his wide-staring eyes, hear his voice quavering, feel again the tremor in his hands. He experienced again the feeling of the certainty of his own impending death. Somewhere as they had approached the ribbon of sand which marked the boundary between the safety of the sea and the land with the hidden guns of the enemy, Fisher had given himself up.

He remembered clearly his rage at Crawford when Crawford had called the A-7 leader and almost volunteered them to go in and try to rescue that pilot. He had hated then how Crawford had looked as they went in, all calm and knowledgeable and fearless. Fisher had in that instant realized how vast was the gulf between himself and the other pilots. None of them were ever afraid and he was always afraid.

Fisher lay back on the rack and stared at the crummy white ceiling with the brighter rectangles where some previous occupant had probably taped foldouts from *Playboy*. He wondered whether his wife had any pictures of him anywhere around the house other than the obligatory one in the parlor. She never had kept his picture out before. She probably still hadn't: they'd only need to be dusted.

Just before he drifted off into the sleep of an emotionally exhausted man, Andy Fisher had the thought that there was absolutely no one on earth who would have mourned him if he had died on that flight. There would have been hundreds at the memorial service but they would be there only because of his wife and father-in-law. One single Kleenex would have wiped away all the genuine tears shed.

With a sob from somewhere within him, some tiny place that Fisher had never before known to exist, he rolled over and faced the wall.

Far forward of Fisher's stateroom, up near the bow of the ship in Wardroom One, Tim Boyle and Mike Santy were playing cribbage, waiting for the evening movie to begin. It was Tuesday, which the pilots of Air Wing 33 had designated audience participation night by acclamation. Every Tuesday, *The Wild Bunch* was shown here in the Dirtyshirt wardroom. The movie had become a cult favorite among the J.O.'s aboard the *Concord*. No one had ever been able to get an accurate count of the Mexicans slaughtered in the last confrontation so they had given up and begun to turn down the sound and shout out all the dialogue, each group of five or so viewers taking a part. Boyle and Santy loved being the Mexican general and, in pathetically bad accents, shouted out a different speech every time it was shown. Soon, the rest of the pilots caught on and began changing the dialogue for their own characters. Rarely could the simplest scene be gotten through without someone breaking up the place with some outrageous line.

The present conversation was concerned with the latest rumor rumbling up from Rumor Central down below in the chiefs' quarters. This one had to do with the new secret restrictions on bombing North Vietnam. There was a big briefing scheduled for the next morning on the ship's closed-circuit television system but since the subject matter was already well known and digested by the pilots and aircrew, many of them expected to sleep through it.

Changing the subject, Santy asked Boyle how he was getting along with Fisher, or "Madam," as Mike had referred to him ever since Boyle had told him about Fisher's admonition to stay away from Santy.

"Actually, not too badly anymore. We sort of leave each other alone. I do my job, say 'yessir' when he tells me that I did it wrong, and go away. He flew over the North for the first time today. I had to down my helo and he and Jack Crawford got stuck with it. Crawford says he did okay. I was kind of surprised since I figured he was going to wait until after the ceasefire before flying a combat mission. Crawford signed him off as a HAC so he gets to go in any old time just like the rest of us. I almost said something cheap about him going in until I suddenly remembered my first one. I was so scared I nearly peed in my pants. I would have too if I hadn't been trying to spot every gook within twenty miles all at the same time. I had my Browning in my hand and was ready to have it out with them with my trusty thirteen-shooter." Boyle looked at Santy. "What's so funny? I spotted half of them, all the ones that nobody else saw."

Santy got himself under control. "No, I was laughing at the

way you said it. I can just see you now ducking behind the instrument panel with your pistol in your hand. My first one, I dropped my whole load on the bad guys. In fact, I was so determined not to miss that I dropped the damned things early, as soon as I rolled in. Somewhere over there are a million toothpicks from the Communist trees I destroyed."

Now Boyle was laughing too. "I guess the only people that got hurt when the Sandman dropped that time were the ones who ruptured themselves laughing. There really is nothing like your first one. All the rest are easier even if some of them are scarier than others."

"Yup. I'm geting better, though. Now I can hit the right country at least fifty percent of the time. Boy, did I feel like an idiot. I came ten thousand miles to attack the enemy's firewood."

With that, the two friends picked up their cards to play another hand. They could finish this game and play one more before the line started to form at the popcorn machine.

Chapter 23

October 9, 1972

Boyle and his copilot, Ted Kruger, took seats in the back of the briefing room in the *Concord*'s Intelligence Center. They were there only to get a general feel for the mission and to make sure that all the frequencies and times that they had been given by their own duty officer were correct. Lately, there had been a series of missions which had been modified at the last minute, and in keeping with the age-old tradition of making sure that there was always somebody who did not get the word, the helo people, who often had to get airborne before everyone else, didn't get the late changes.

Since the rollback of the approved targets to those below the twentieth parallel, the *Concord* had been sending her air wing to strike at any target in the lower part of the country and eastern Laos that was remotely connected with the Vietnamese ability to wage war. There had been some heavy grumbling among the pilots when the rules had changed yet again. They wanted to get on with it, to keep pounding the bastards. Now that the Vietnamese were running short of things to shoot back with the halt was only going to prolong things and make it much worse when, inevitably, the restrictions were again lifted. It was still a source of pride for the *Concord*'s men that there hadn't been any pilots or aircrewmen who had refused to fly this close to the end of the war but stories about some from the other carriers were beginning to circulate. The "heavies"—CAG, the squadron C.O.'s, Capt. Andrews, and the staff—had been watching closely for signs of deteriorating morale but only aggressive grumblings had been seen. These were a *good* sign.

The chances that the airmen took to get the job done were essentially the same as they had been throughout the war; but no one was trying to be John Wayne, which was a better sign. They were all still performing professionally.

Another thing on their side was the fact that all the lessons had been learned and disseminated and all the pilots knew how to stay alive. There were still those whose luck simply ran out or who had a momentary brain fart and got themselves into trouble. They were few in number but, for the rescue people, there was still work to be done.

In the rows ahead of Boyle and Kruger, yawning and sipping coffee from paper cups, were the aircrew who would fly the A-6s, A-7s, and F-4s, sitting in little groups according to squadrons. The weather forecaster was pointing at the large charts he'd brought and pinned up on the forward wall next to the covered charts of the target area. He was describing the pressure gradients around a massive low-pressure system forming in the Indian Ocean. This was nice to know, but since it would be sixteen hours or so before the effects of the associated frontal weather arrived over Laos and North Vietnam, most of the airmen just let the knowledge sift its way into a little storage compartment in the back of their minds. There it would be easily retrievable for comparison with the weather briefing they received prior to their next mission. Their only real concern was how the weather would be for the next three hours or so.

Weather was of much greater concern to the helo crews.

They, after all, always had to fly either below it or in it. The jets, except for the immediate target area, could usually fly above it and not really be concerned until it was time to come down, find the ship, and land. Except for some scattered thunderstorms building later on in the afternoon, nobody was going to have weather problems today. But the A-6s flying the night missions would not have a whole lot of fun, thought Boyle.

Over in the corner of the room, Boyle could see Mike Santy among the pilots from VA-19. Boyle wondered if Mike was as tired as he was. After the movie last night, the two of them had stayed in the wardroom and waited for the stewards to open up the "Mid-rats" line, the midnight snack service where the officers could purchase the infamous "gut bombs." These were double cheeseburgers topped with nearly everything known to man and a few things that science was still attempting to classify. These creations would kill most humans, one would think, but they have absolutely no effect on naval aviators.

The conversation had drifted and the two were surprised when they looked at their watches and found it to be well after 1:00 A.M. Now, it was 0800 and they were paying for it. Being tired before you start a combat mission is not the smartest way to go, thought Boyle.

The weather forecaster asked if there were any questions and when nobody had one, he began to fold up his charts, glad to be done with it and eager to get back down to the weather center and his friends and the hot coffee. Once, early on, he had looked forward to giving these briefings but after he had seen that the pilots were listening to them with only half their minds while the other half was on what might lie in store for them, and then realizing that some of those he briefed on the weather were dead two hours later, he had grown to dread his turn at the podium. Given his choice, he would rather stay down in his little office and never come any closer to the tip of the spear than drawing up the charts.

The next briefer was one of the squadron intelligence officers. He waited for the weather forecaster to leave the room, then pulled out a sliding mapboard from behind the chalkboard, and began with the targets for this launch. It was another bunch of "suspected POL storage areas," places where the Vietnamese had stashed their petroleum, oil, and lubricants, just over the border in Laos along part of the "Ho Chi Minh Trail." There were some Air Force jets due over the same area a few minutes prior to the *Concord*'s aircraft arriving so the Intell. briefer began with some strong words about timing.

Boyle leaned forward to see the chart better. The area surrounding the targets was relatively free of the little red or blue circles denoting Triple-A or SAM sites and there didn't seem to be any significant population centers or defenses on the route in over southern North Vietnam between the coast and the target. Boyle placed his own smaller chart on his kneeboard and compared it with the one in the front of the room; there were no changes from what he had seen yesterday when he had last updated it. He glanced over at Kruger and saw him make a couple of pencil marks on his chart. If somebody went down over Laos, it would mean that the helo would have to fly completely across North Vietnam to get him out, which would be tight on fuel, or let the Air Force "Jolly Greens" from Thailand pick him up.

Boyle listened most carefully to the part of the brief about frequencies and the "safe areas." These were areas of lesser threat to a downed airman, with fewer local villagers or militia around. Most of North Vietnam was woefully backward and a downed airman had a better chance of rescue there than he did around the more built-up areas. Eight years of air attacks had gotten just about everybody in North Vietnam mad at the Americans, so the best possible plan was to avoid everyone.

Still, a man's best chance on the ground was to hide from the enemy, since a six-foot-two white man would not blend in easily with the local population. Even in the most remote areas, there were always more gooks than a man had bullets, so standing and fighting was a loser also. The safe areas were based on a best guess from the intelligence chain. Santy had always believed that these areas were only briefed to give the pilots a warm and fuzzy feeling, much like a St. Christopher's medal or the breastplates of bones the Indians used to face the cavalry's repeating rifles. Boyle remembered the old saying about naval intelligence: We Bet *Your* Life.

When the intelligence officer was finished, Boyle and Kruger eased their way out of the room and headed back to their ready room to begin their own preflight preparation. They didn't need to listen to the rest of it. The flight lead would give everybody their emergency and normal expected approach times and holding altitudes ("EEATS and Angels") and then go over the run-in headings and the famous "Plan B" on what to do if the target was destroyed early or was covered by weather.

Once in the ready room, they sat in the big leather chairs and went over the thick binder which contained all the maintenance forms concerning their aircraft. As Kruger went through the charts figuring up the aircraft's total gross weight and the power available given today's weather conditions, Boyle briefed the two crewmen, Petty Officers Brian Smith and Terry Weaver.

Smith, the first crewman/hoist operator, was an old hand. His first tour had been with the Navy's only helicopter gunship squadron, HAL-3, operating in South Vietnam, supporting the small-boat efforts in the Mekong Delta. He always went flying armed to the teeth, taking along a cut-down M-16 rifle, called the CAR-15, a backpack filled with enough food, ammunition, and assorted other supplies to enable him to survive quite nicely for at least a week. He brought this over and above the gear that the helo normally carried and he kept it close at all times when in the air. Smith had once been shot down in South Vietnam over some territory held by a particularly nasty unit of Vietcong insurgents. The rest of the crew had been killed and all Smith had been able to get out of the Huey before it burned was his pistol, his survival vest, and his own slightly scorched tail. After running and hiding in the boonies for six days, very scared and very lonely, he had been rescued by a patrol of ARVN troops. He had vowed never again to be in that position. Smith could do little about being shot down: that was the pilot's job. But he could avoid being totally defenseless and half-starving after it happened.

Weaver was the junior crewman and the specially trained swimmer. He had been in Vietnam for only two months but already was the favorite of many of the pilots. He followed Smith around like a puppy and was picking up more from the older man than he could have learned in twenty formal Navy schools. He affected the same easy West Virginia accent and even walked like his hero. Boyle believed that Weaver would have jumped into Ho Chi Minh's bathtub if Smith had told him to.

Once all the paperwork was finished and all the weapons and other gear had been inventoried and signed for, the crew headed up to the flight deck. The pile of custody cards that had to be checked and signed was another of the things which aggravated Boyle. Out on North SAR, nobody bothered with that sort of thing and the system had only been reborn back in the *Concord*'s detachment when Fisher got his skivvies in a knot about a missing 35mm camera. The camera had been borrowed by one of the pilots to take tourist photos of Hong Kong but Fisher had done an inventory before the unknown miscreant had been able to get it back in the lockbox. The fact that it had reappeared in the box as mysteriously as it had disappeared was lost on the new OIC. So, the entire system had been revamped, adding an extra five minutes to the briefing time. Boyle did hope that the pictures he had taken of Meghan in Hong Kong with the camera would turn out.

When the briefing in the intelligence center had ended, Santy went down four decks to Ready Room Six with the rest of the VA-19 pilots. Cmdr. Wilson was the flight lead today and Santy was number three, leading the second two-plane section in the four-plane division. Snake Mitchell, as usual, was Santy's wingman and another nugget, Lt. (J.G.) "Banzai" Fujimoto was Wilson's wingie in the number-two slot.

Wilson went over the standard items and each pilot waded through the maintenance binder on his assigned Corsair. Wilson ended with a few words of advice for all his pilots, particularly Fujimoto.

"Okay. If somebody's airplane breaks, his wingman stays with him. No solos over the beach. Keep moving and jinking. When we get to the target, make one pass and get the hell out of there. We'll egress by sections. If somebody goes down, stay with 'em as long as you can and yell for help. If somebody is damaged, escort him out to the water or wherever is closest. Danang is primary divert field and is up Channel 77. If the target is taken out before we get there, we'll break up into sections and do a road recce. You have your sectors. Shoot up anything on the roads and get out. If you don't find anything, don't fuck around pressing the issue. Pick a crossroads and give 'em some new craters to fill in or dump your bombs on some woods and make toothpicks. Once again, one pass. You, Banzai, stick close and do what I do. Got it?"

Wilson looked at each of the young pilots and saw no questions, only determination. They were wearing their warpaint.

Wilson picked up his helmet. "Let's go."

Boyle met the other three members of the crew at the nose of the helicopter. He had climbed down after preflighting the left engine and the left half of the transmission and rotor head. Kruger had done the upper right side. The two enlisted crewmen had looked over the rest of the huge green machine, inside and out. Dividing up the preflight was not exactly according to the book but Boyle figured that they all were in this together and thus could be relied upon to be thorough in their inspections. It also seemed to break down a barrier or two and make the crew more cohesive. This was another of the things Boyle had learned from Bob Watkins.

"My side'll fly," said Kruger.

"Inside looks good," from Smith.

"Bottom and nose are okay," said Weaver.

"Okay. Let's go." Boyle led the way up into the helo.

Down the deck from Boyle's helicopter, just aft of the arresting wires, Mike Santy was completing his preflight inspection. Everything was in good shape, he thought, as he tightened the straps of his torso harness and watched as the plane captain closed up the last of the inspection panels. He looked at the dull green bombs, with the yellow stripes and the ugly fuses and wires, that hung from the racks under his left wing. There was a similar load under the right and he was momentarily glad that he was flying from one of the newer "big deck" carriers instead of the older "27-Charlies." These were carriers designed and built during World War II and later given the modification, called 27C, which gave them an angled deck and the capability to operate newer jet aircraft. The A-7s flying from the 27-Charlies, with their small size and relatively weak catapults, could often get airborne only with about half the bomb load that Santy was carrying today. He believed that if he had to go attack something, it was better that he be able to drop the largest load the airframe could carry.

Once his harness was snug, he walked over to the small boarding ladder which extended from the lower side of the A-7 below the cockpit. It was not really a walk, more of a bowlegged waddle caused by the straps which wrapped around his legs at the hip joints. As he climbed up and swung his leg over the edge into the cockpit, the Air Boss up in the Tower began his "Start Speech" over the 5MC, the flight-deck loudspeaker system. Santy thought that this speech or something very like it had been heard by every naval aviator who had ever flown from the deck of a ship. It was one of the tiny threads of extratemporal tradition which made up the tapestry of naval aviation. It was also one of the tendrils that linked Santy with his father. The speech was probably said on the flight deck as his father started his engine that last time.

"On the flight deck, it's time for the ten o'clock go. Check your helmets on and buckled, goggles down. Check your vests on and fastened, sleeves rolled down. Check chocks and tie-downs. Check for loose gear about the deck. Check intakes and exhausts clear. Start the go aircraft. Start the Angel. Start 'em up.''

Instantly, the rising howls of turbine engines broke the relative silence of the flight deck. Santy was sure that he heard the whine of an H-3 engine from Boyle's aircraft start up first. Tim must have had his thumb on the start switch, just waiting for the boss's speech, Santy thought.

He fastened the last Koch fitting on his harness to the ejection seat's straps, and pulled on his helmet. Thoughts of anything else were shoved aside as he began his own start-up procedure.

One of the things that helo crews hate most is the last five or so minutes before takeoff. Their distaste for it has nothing to do with the dangers of the missions or any particular eagerness to get on with it. It has to do with jet exhaust.

The helicopter is usually positioned on the angled deck about one hundred feet from the forward end of the deck. Ahead and to the right is the bow section of the flight deck where Catapults 1 and 2 are. Before the launch begins, several aircraft are lined up behind these cats awaiting their turn. The geometry of the flight deck mandates that at least one of those jets is waiting with its exhaust pointed directly at the helicopter.

Jet pilots practice something ashore called "tailpipe discipline" where they ensure that their exhaust does not point at their wingman or anyone else because the heat and exhaust gases can cause a marked decrease in the efficiency of the engine in the airplane behind and it can quit simply from choking.

On a carrier, there is very limited space and it isn't possible always to avoid the exhaust from somebody else's airplane. The heat, the unburned fuel, and the carbon monoxide are brutal as they blast through the helicopter's cockpit, and there is not a damned thing you can do about it. The temperature can suddenly reach 125 degrees, affecting the performance of the small engines and the rotor blades of the helo and also causing the crew trapped in it acute discomfort. You instantly become soaked in sweat, which attracts the fuel molecules so that the smell never seems to go away. You try breathing through your mouth but that only makes you taste the fuel for hours to come. The acrid gases make your eyes water as if you were swimming in onion juice. There is no effective countermeasure except dedicated cursing and fantasizing about strangling the pilot of the jet, as if it were his fault or, better yet, the goddamn Air Boss, who doesn't give a shit about you helo pukes in the first place. There can be few experiences in life more intensely miserable than those few minutes.

When the LSE finally gave them the signal to take off, Boyle and Kruger were more than ready to go. Boyle hit the last few switches on the takeoff checklist as Kruger yanked the helo into a higher-than-normal hover just to get out of the jet exhaust.

Boyle scanned the instrument panel as best he could through his streaming eyes. "I think the gauges are good. Get us the fuck out of here."

"Right." Kruger dipped the nose and increased the collective. The helicopter moved slowly up and away from the ship. As soon as they were clear of the deck, Boyle raised the landing gear and Kruger banked left and headed the helo westward toward the coast of North Vietnam, keeping a slight yaw in an attempt to get some extra airflow through the cockpit and cabin to clear the last of the jet exhaust out of Angel 801.

"Goddamn, that sucks. You never have to go through that shit on a cruiser. It may not smell any better but at least you can see."

Kruger wiped his wrist across his face and scrunched up his eyes trying to get the last of the tears out. "Yeah. And it's even worse at night. At least now we don't have to try to fly on instruments half-blind," he said.

Boyle pulled out his chart and put it under the briefing card on his kneeboard. "Okay. Course is 265 for about 40 miles to our point." He glanced at the mileage indicator on the TACAN gauge. It was still spinning, which meant that it hadn't yet locked on to the signal from the ship's antenna. "No DME yet but we're about five miles from the ship. I'll check us out with the Boss."

He keyed the radio. "Tower, Angel 801 is five out. Switching Red Crown."

There was no reply; they were probably still busy with the launch back there. He switched frequencies to Red Crown.

"Red Crown, Angel 801 is with you. Outbound to station." He rechecked the code on the IFF, the radio which sent a signal to radars telling them exactly who the helo was. "Squawking mode three, 3624."

"Roger, Angel 801. Good morning. Radar contact. Steer 263 for 36 for your station."

Boyle rogered Red Crown, leaned back in his seat, and pulled out a cigarette. As he lit it, he keyed the intercom. "Gonna be a real nice day out here." He looked around at the sparkling blue sea and the cloudless sky. "I sure hope all we have to do today is fly around and burn up gas."

Santy taxied onto Catapult 4 on the waist. It seemed that he always went off Cat 4 lately. Just once, he thought, I'd like to go from 1 or 2 on the bow. That way he'd get to practice right clearing turns instead of always turning left as he had to from the waist cats. Oh, well.

He lowered the launch bar into the catapult shuttle on direction from the cat crew. When he was in tension, he went to full power, gave one last check of the engine instruments, ran the stick around the cockpit, and shoved the rudder pedals in both directions, ensuring that he had full control throw in all three axes. He saluted the cat officer to his right and placed his hand back on the stick and his helmet up against the headrest on the back of the seat.

It seemed like a minute but it was only about seven seconds until he felt the catapult release its grip on his Corsair at the end of the stroke. He slapped the gear handle up and banked slightly left. As he was passing six miles from the ship with the flaps coming up, he saw Tim's helo ahead and below him chugging along, heading out too. Behind his mask, he grinned a little and turned his attention to joining up with his flight high overhead the ship.

Chapter 24

October 9, 1972

Cmdr. Wilson, in Condor 301, leveled his wings and eased his throttle forward to get the flight up to speed. Now that the other three were joined in formation, he could maneuver them all as one aircraft. To the left, Fujimoto, in 303, hung in space following every move that Wilson made. To the right, across a gap the size of an A-7, Santy's visored helmet was facing the lead in relaxed concentration. Just beyond Santy's Condor 306, was Mitchell, in 300, keeping a nice tight parade position on Santy. The movements of the individual aircraft were small, perceptible only to the other planes in the flight. To an observer any distance away, it would look like the jets were welded together. It was Wilson's job to fly as if he were alone high in the deep blue sky. The other three ignored the normal visual cues of flight and concentrated on the leader's Corsair, maintaining their positions. If they were doing their job properly, it wouldn't matter what Wilson did. They would all remain fixed in a moving block of space.

Formation flying is one of the true thrills of military aviation. There is a tremendous but subtle pride that accrues to blazing along through the air within just a few feet of another aircraft, matching perfectly every move that the leader makes. Any turn, any climb or descent, any loop, any roll: your whole being is concentrated on the guy in front. If everyone does it right, the wingman's first clue that the lead has begun an overhead maneuver will be that the clouds are now down and the earth is up. There is a peace and silence in a jet in formation that's unbroken by the deep roar of a propeller or the whine and clatter of a rotor system or rarely even a voice on the radio telling you what you are about. It is a beautiful experience once you learn to relax and *think* the control movements that keep you locked in tight on the leader's wing.

As with any such experience, the gods will allow you to do it only in relatively small pieces. You are limited by fuel in the tanks. You are also limited by the job at hand, which is really the only reason you get paid to fly your aircraft. Formation flying is a little reward for taking the risks and doing what your people send you to do.

However, although nice parade formations look good, they will get you killed in Indian Country. Even though the route to the target area in Laos was selected because there was a minimal chance of finding SAMs screaming up at the Condor flight, it was never wise to accept everything you were told on mere faith. The intelligence people were back on the ship reading summaries and putting pins and pencil marks on charts. They were not up here strapped to a jet which was somebody else's target.

One of the more ridiculous rules in the air war was that aircraft were not allowed to violate North Vietnamese airspace unless their mission was in North Vietnam. To bomb the Trail, the airplanes from Yankee Station were supposed first to fly southwest then cross South Vietnam below Quang Tri and into Laos, then fly north until they got to their target area. The trouble you could get into for breaking this or other equally stupid Rules of Engagement was considered by many to be worse than being shot at.

Wilson saw the coastline appear on the horizon. From

22,000 feet, it was first a brown haze creeping into the clear blue, growing steadily higher until the sharp edge of the beach underlay the haze. He signaled his flight to spread out and glanced at them as they moved to a separation of several hundred feet horizontally and vertically. The separation gave them the room to "jink," to move around up and down, left and right. The rule was never to stay straight and level for long and give the enemy a chance to hit you. If you moved at a rate of about two-thirds of your altitude in seconds, for example every ten seconds if you were flying at 15,000 feet, you had a good chance of avoiding aimed Triple-A. Barrage fire was a different matter: then you had to grit your teeth and fly through it. Even though there was no truly heavy Triple-A on the route to the Trail, it wasn't smart to get complacent.

Just before the beach passed under his nose, Wilson called the radar controller aboard the cruiser steaming on station out in the Gulf of Tonkin.

"Red Crown, Condor 301. Flight of four, feet dry at this time."

"Roger, 301, Contact Hillsborough on 256.6 for transit." Hillsborough was the call sign of the series of Air Force Command and Control aircraft constantly orbiting and keeping track of who was where and needed what and controlling aircraft flying in and out of South Vietnam.

"301, roger." Wilson changed to the new frequency and waited a second or two.

"Condors," he said.

"Two."

"Three."

"Four."

"Hillsborough, Condor 301 checking in."

"Roger, 301. We have no enemy air activity today. Contact Nail 17 on frequency 332.7 for control. I understand he's got some targets for you."

"Roger that. Nail 17 on three-thirty-two-dot-seven. Condors switch."

When everybody was on the new frequency, Wilson glanced

down to see that he was still headed to the area where the targets were supposed to be before he called the Nail.

The Nails were a special group. They were Forward Air Controllers, or FACs, flying around low and slow in OV-10 Broncos, twin-engine turboprop aircraft. Much like the scouts that preceded the cavalry in the Old West, they would find the enemy, often by exposing themselves to enemy ground fire, and then mark the targets for the fighters and attack aircraft to bomb. It was not a mission that would ever show up on a recruiting brochure but they were by and large some of the bravest men who ever flew in Southeast Asia. Among the various groups of FACs, the Nails, who operated out of Nakhon Phanom, Thailand, with responsibilities mostly in Southern Laos, were one of the best.

"Nail 17. This is Condor 301, flight of four Corsairs. We're about thirty miles south of you at angels nineteen. Up for your control."

"301, Nail 17. Roger. I've got a flight of Fox-fours working the area now. They should be off in about five. Stand by, I'll call you in."

Wilson clicked his mike switch twice in acknowledgment. Somebody's F-4s were hitting the area now. The smoke from their attacks should make finding the target pretty simple. He called his flight. "Condors, arm 'em up."

Forty miles northeast of the Condor flight, Tim Boyle heard only Wilson's half of the conversation. He had heard the other flights from the *Concord* check in and out with Red Crown. Despite the plan given back aboard the carrier, the other flights had been given different areas from the one briefed. This sort of thing was not unusual anymore because there was not much of North Vietnam left which had not been visited time and time again by Navy, Marine, and Air Force jets. Bombing a society like North Vietnam's was often like hunting ants with a revolver. It hurt some of them, to be sure, but there were always more ants to fill the gaps in the procession to move the men and supplies. The only remaining targets of any lasting value were around Hanoi and Haiphong and even they were becoming less and less valuable. Only occasionally now were the big strikes mustered and then only for large troop concentrations or the supply dumps which somebody tripped over.

Boyle had chosen to follow the progress of the VA-19 aircraft on the secondary radio only because Santy was flying one of them. The other small groups of aircraft were on other frequencies as they worked with separate controllers. If anyone needed him, Red Crown would get him or he would hear the calls on the emergency guard channel.

He sat back in his seat and lit up another Marlboro, almost mesmerized by the sunlight sparkling on the water passing below. To his right, Kruger was flying the aircraft in a long lazy orbit, only using the smallest possible part of his mind to fly.

"Condors, Nail. You're cleared in now. The Phantoms are clearing southwest. Target is a POL storage area. It's easy to find. It's under all the smoke."

"Roger. We're about three out now."

Santy turned inside Wilson to maintain the same relative position, spread out about seven hundred feet from the lead. From what the Nail had just said, there really was a target up ahead instead of the usual "suspected" ones they had been bombing of late. Santy rechecked his switches to make sure they were all set properly. When he looked out ahead again, he could see a blossom of smoke rising into the sky, a cottony black against the high cirrus clouds that were just beginning to appear over the western horizon, preceding the distant weather front.

Below them the land looked crumpled as if it were a sheet of dark green construction paper that some child had attempted to smooth out after wadding it up. The hills were sharp-edged and the valleys steep and twisted. There were many areas and road junctions interspersed throughout the valleys that were scarred with dozens, sometimes hundreds of bomb craters, left by the years of interdiction campaign waged to choke off the supplies moving south to the war.

Most places, fresh fill dirt took the roads back over the same places they had been cut a day or two before and where they would again be cut today or tomorrow.

"Nail 17, Condor 301 has you in sight."

Santy looked down and spotted the white wings of the small propeller-driven aircraft as it flew around erratically a couple of miles southeast of the fires in the jungle.

"Roger, Condor. Nail has you also. The target is the POL site burning up north of my position. The Fox-fours started it burning and it seemed like everything they dropped got a secondary. I don't know how big this area is but if you put your loads around the area and across the road we should do something. The Fox-fours reported only light stuff coming up at them, nothing bigger than 37s. They worked it for quite a while so they should have gotten the bigger stuff if any was there."

"301, roger."

Wilson banked around and lined up for a run across the valley, over the burning fuel dump. Fujimoto turned to follow but was too close and would be in danger of flying through the large pattern of fragments that flew away from the explosions of Wilson's five hundred-pound bombs. Santy saw it and called him.

"Banzai, drop back some."

Wilson, nearly ready to begin his first run, had a momentary thought that Santy was coming into his own. He was getting good at this and his awareness of everything around him and his flight was growing rapidly.

Fujimoto did a couple of little jinks and spaced himself properly then followed Wilson over and down. Pointing his nose at the target, he concentrated on getting the symbology right on his HUD and didn't even notice small white cotton balls and the little red necklaces of the tracers from the weak and mostly ineffective antiaircraft fire coming up from the jungle. Santy, following next from a slightly different angle, saw it but it was falling far behind Fujimoto and was well ahead of his own A-7 so unless the gunners did something drastic, it wouldn't hurt anybody on this pass. There was not enough of it to bother suppressing so he decided to just ignore it.

Wilson, followed by Fujimoto, pulled up and left after their first drop. Santy dropped his pair of bombs and climbed away to the right. Before he reached the altitude from which he'd started his first run, he rolled hard the other way and looked for the other jets. He spotted them just in time to see several dark gray puffs of smoke appear below and behind Fujimoto's Corsair. Before he could key his radio, he heard Mitchell's call, warning the front pair.

"Heads up, Skipper. They just opened up on you with some bigger stuff. Looks like 57s."

"Did you see where it's coming from?"

"Negative. Nothin' but jungle."

Santy looked down and saw that their first run hadn't caused any increase in the size of the fires nor any secondary explosions so they had merely blown up some trees. He called Wilson and suggested that he pick another spot for their next run.

"Roger, that. We'll try the weeds across the road. That okay with you, Nail?"

"Nail concurs. We may have gotten everything there is here. Give it a try about two hundred meters north across the road."

"Condor, roger. Lead's in."

One after the other the Corsairs followed Wilson's lead dropping pairs of five hundred-pound bombs around the area, trying to find any other targets. It seemed that the F-4s who had gotten there first had taken care of everything of value down in the valley.

This reminded Wilson of an earlier time in the war after the first bombing campaign against the North, dubbed "Rolling Thunder," had been halted. The Navy, Marine and Air Force jets had then been used to bomb the Trail for months at a stretch. It had almost been a gentlemen's war for a while. There had been no opposition like there always was Up North. Going back to bombing the Trail after the past few months of attacking into the brutal defenses of the North seemed almost like practice by comparison.

Perhaps it was Wilson's feeling of near-comfort or maybe it was the natural desire to admire one's handiwork. For whatever reason, after Mitchell had made his last pass, Wilson told the others to hold high and went down himself to get the BDA, or bomb damage assessment. This was normally done by the FAC or by a reconnaissance aircraft after the attacking jets departed.

Santy watched as Wilson rolled in on a long, fairly straight run over the burning area of the jungle. Against the lush green background, he saw the strings of tracer drift up almost lazily and the bursts of the larger-caliber guns widely dot the air behind and around Wilson's Corsair. He was just about to warn the skipper that he was taking fire when Wilson abruptly pulled up and away, aborting his run well short of the large column of smoke. There was a few seconds of silence and then he heard Wilson's matter-of-fact voice call the FAC.

"Nail 17, 301. We're complete. Thirty-two Mk-82s total. No secondaries. Request BDA. And be careful, they've got some heavier stuff in there. I took a hit but nothing seems wrong. We're departing east."

The FAC paused only slightly as he watched the flak bursts follow Wilson for a couple of seconds and then stop, probably training around to be ready for the next attack which they would assume was coming. "Roger that, Condor. Thanks for your help. Nice work. I'll give 'em a little while to cool off in there before I check it out. I'll pass your BDA through Red Crown. You're cleared outbound to the east. Switch at your discretion. Nail 17 out."

Wilson told the other A-7s to switch up Red Crown's frequency and waited until they had all checked in before he told them what had happened, in an oblique sort of way.

"Banzai, I took a hit on that last pass. Look me over. It felt like it was on the right side but I can't see anything and nothing is showing up on the gauges. We'll take the short route home."

Santy wondered for a moment about that decision but Wilson was the C.O. He watched as Fujimoto closed in and joined up tightly on Wilson's left wing. He moved under and across to the right side and hung there for a few seconds before he dropped back and spread out again.

"Okay, Skipper. It looks like you have two holes under your wing root, three right behind the leading edge and a couple more larger ones just forward of the landing-gear doors. The belly and the left side are okay. I don't see anything coming out. How's it flying?"

"It's okay. 306, you have the lead."

"Roger, I have the lead." Santy now was responsible for the flight, giving Wilson that much less to deal with as he flew his damaged jet home. Even though there was probably nothing seriously wrong, something bad could always happen and it was better to have minimized early the decision-making requirements.

Santy keyed the radio. "Red Crown, Condor 306. We're complete with the Nail and outbound, estimating feet wet in about ten."

"Roger, 306, Red Crown. Radar contact. Copy ten minutes to feet wet. Your tail is clear."

Wilson looked at his instruments for about the sixtieth time in the last five minutes. None of them was showing anything wrong with his Corsair but one never knew when an insidious little bit of damage could get to be a huge problem. The area of his aircraft which had taken the hits was full of all sorts of wires and was mostly the air duct which led to the compressor section much farther aft. So far, it seemed that he had avoided the "Golden BB," the one lucky round that would bring him down. Below him was the border between Laos and North Vietnam and ahead about fifty miles was the Gulf of Tonkin.

One of the unique things about the A-7 is the turbofan engine. The TF-41 engine, like all jet engines, has a huge series of fans, called the compressor, in the front. This takes in massive quantities of air to be mixed with the fuel and burned in the combuster section directly behind it. The suction of the compressor is so great that even at low power settings it will pick up a man or, for that matter, anything else loose and lying around too close to the intake, and draw him suddenly and fatally down the duct and into the spinning blades. This has the effect of a giant grinder on the object being sucked in but it also will cause fatal damage to the engine.

When something hits them, the compressor blades can deform and begin to disintegrate. Since the compressor is spinning at such a speed that the rate is measured and indicated in percent of maximum rather than in rpm, the destruction of the engine is sudden and usually complete. The blades will break off and damage further stages of the compressor. The turbine wheel itself can come apart and send pieces of metal flying out in a large circle at amazing speeds, shredding everything in their path. What goes down the engine need not be especially large to do the job either. A nickel or a small stone have been known to destroy an engine.

What got Wilson's engine was a small piece of the antiaircraft shell that had burst to his right on that last pass over the fuel dump. All the other pieces of shrapnel had just chewed up some metal or stuck in something without causing any damage beyond the cosmetic. The largest piece, about twice the size of a man's thumb, had penetrated the aircraft's skin well in front of the engine itself. It had stuck partially through the wall of the engine intake duct and stayed there. When Wilson jammed on his throttle to climb up and away after taking the hit, the increased suction had pulled the chunk farther into the duct, making the hole slightly larger in the damaged metal skin. There began a small vibration which caused the chunk to rotate a little. When the chunk had rotated enough, it fit through the hole completely and went instantly back into the spinning compressor blades.

Nobody in the Corsair flight could have known exactly what did it. All the three others could know was that there were suddenly a whole lot of sparks and little flaming things coming out of Wilson's tailpipe as the engine began to eat itself.

Wilson, on the other hand, heard the engine begin to grumble in a strange sort of way and felt a sudden deceleration as the power delivered dropped off drastically. He reduced the throttle and watched the gauges decrease with the throttle movement. As his right hand nosed the Corsair over to keep his airspeed up, he watched the indications decrease far below what the throttle was set for. They continued down below the levels he would have expected for idle power.

"306, 301. The engine just died. I'm trying to relight now." Wilson played with the throttle and pressed the Air Ignite button on the throttle that was supposed to give him a relight if the engine was capable of it. It wasn't.

He reached down and pulled the handle which deployed the EPP, or emergency power package, which used the airflow to produce electrical and hydraulic power in circumstances like this. He glanced down to check that his airspeed was at the optimum 250 knots.

Santy saw the EPP pop out of the right side of Wilson's jet. "Skipper, 301. You had a bunch of junk come out of your tailpipe. It looks like it's fodded." FOD was the acronym for "foreign object damage" which meant that something external had gone through and damaged the engine.

"Yeah. It won't relight." Wilson looked out ahead at the distant horizon. "I don't think I can make the water either."

"Roger. Red Crown, this is Condor 306. 301 is going down about thirty miles inland. Request SAR and RESCAP. Snake, take Banzai out and find the helo."

"Red Crown copies. 306, can you stay with him until the RESCAPs get here?"

"That's affirm. I've got plenty of gas."

The two other jets broke away and accelerated ahead. Santy watched them go and looked back at Wilson. He was glad that Wilson hadn't decided to turn and try to make it to "neutral" Laos. There were far too many bad guys around there. His best bet was straight ahead. Santy looked out and saw mostly uninhabited country. At least, it didn't have any large concentrations of people until they got closer to the coast.

Wilson looked out and saw the same thing. "Mike, I'm

gonna stay with it for a while yet. At least try to get closer to the coast. I'll get out at three thousand."

"Roger. Don't forget to clean up the cockpit." Even though Wilson would probably not forget, the caution served both men. It gave Santy the illusion that he could actually do something to help and it gave Wilson the illusion that he was not really all alone with his problems.

Wilson unsnapped his kneeboard and stuffed it down into the map case in the side console under his right arm. He pulled it back out and removed his chart of the area from the kneeboard and stuffed that down into the lower leg pocket of his "G-suit." He lowered and locked his helmet visor, tightened the chin strap and the clips on his oxygen mask. He rechecked that his harness was locked and gave an extra tug on the shoulder straps. That's about it, he thought.

Santy again looked out ahead as they were passing eight thousand feet. He spotted a confluence of several roads in the distance directly in their path. He checked his vertical speed indicator and saw that they had about a three-thousand-foot-per-minute rate of descent going. About a minute and a half, he thought, about eight more miles over the ground before Wilson has to go.

"Skipper, there's some civilization on the nose. You might want to ease a little right to avoid it."

Wilson banked slightly and leveled his wings as his sink rate increased with the bank. He had steered the Corsair about twenty degrees to the right. It should be enough.

The two pilots were silent as their descent made the terrain become rapidly more sharp and distinct. As they approached five thousand feet, Santy dropped back so as to be able to keep an eye on Wilson after he ejected. Over the years, several pilots had been lost after their wingman lost sight of them. Santy didn't want to have to live with that.

As Condor 301 passed four thousand feet, Wilson looked out at the beautiful blue of the Gulf of Tonkin. It, and safety, were only about twenty-five miles away but the Gulf might as well be on the moon for all the good it would do him now.

Wilson told Santy that he was punching out and placed

himself in the optimum position for ejection. He pulled the nose up to slow the Corsair a little bit, grasped the black-and-yellow handle between his legs with his right hand and grasped his right wrist with his left hand. He drew a deep breath and pulled up on the handle.

Chapter 25

October 9, 1972

Down in his office directly below the flight deck of the *Concord*, RADM. Welch heard the silver bitch box next to his left elbow suddenly come alive. Since the ship was steaming downwind between launch and recovery cycles, there had been little communication other than the normal clipped warnings about routine course changes and other housekeeping matters. Welch could filter these out as he sat at his desk going through the pile of paperwork that seemed never to shrink no matter how many problems were "solved" or how much of the load his staff dealt with. This career of his was becoming less and less fun and exciting with every new assignment. After this one, he expected to go to Washington and spend the next few years dealing with oceans of chickenshit on a global scale as opposed to the smaller runnels he had to wade through now. The prospect was growing less appealing as the time grew nearer.

The metallic voice from the Combat Information Center on the intercom box at his elbow got all of his attention.

"Bridge, Combat."

"Bridge, aye," answered the young voice of the bridge talker.

"Red Crown advises that we've got an A-7 down in Indian Country. They've requested RESCAP and a helo."

Welch recognized Sam Andrews's voice when the bridge answered again.

"Combat, this is the captain. Launch the RESCAPs. Get some more ready. Any word on the pilot?"

"It was Condor 301, pilot Commander Wilson. Red Crown advises that he had a good chute and got down safely. There's no word on whether he's talking to his wingman."

"Bridge, aye."

Welch watched the coffee begin to slide up one side of his cup and felt the deck tilt slightly as the ship began her turn into the wind. Above his head, the sound of jet engines winding up penetrated the eight inches of steel of the flight deck and the soundproofing panels of his office ceiling. He gratefully dropped the draft report he was editing, removed his reading glasses, and stuffed them and his pen in a shirt pocket. He strode out the door and headed for the ladder to Flag Bridge, leaving his marine sentry to hustle to catch up. The young man was surprised that Welch didn't allow him to lead the way through the passageways as was customary nor did he even nod to people as he passed.

Capt. Harry Forrest, the chief of staff, glanced up at the "Attention on Deck" announcement shouted out when Welch walked through the hatch into Flag Bridge. He didn't straighten up, anticipating the admiral's automatic "Carry on" that followed. It took far too much for Forrest to spring painfully to rigid attention, but mostly it didn't occur to him to interrupt plotting the information on the chart which Welch now was approaching.

"Okay, what's the deal, Harry?"

Forrest began pointing at the various marks he had made on the chart with his pen. He had long ago done away with the acetate covering for the chart and the washable grease pencils in favor of permanent ink on the paper chart so that everything could be saved and reconstructed later. More than one pissing contest with higher authority could have been avoided had the chart of an action been saved rather than wiped clean of notations after the fact.

"Well, the A-7 took a hit bombing the Trail here. Rather than follow the same route across South Vietnam that they used going in, they took a shortcut across the neck of the North about here."

Forrest answered Welch's questioning look with a shrug.

"I have no idea why they decided to go out that way but they're in it now. Wilson had some sort of engine failure and wound up ejecting about here. The ejection was apparently successful; he was observed to get out of his chute and head for the weeds with it at the top of this ridge. His wingman is still overhead and reports no unfriendlies in the immediate area. The nearest village or road is about seven miles away, here, so unless we're real unlucky we have some time to get him out. The only problem so far is that Wilson has not come up on his radio yet. There was a brief beeper signal but it stopped shortly after he ducked into the brush."

Welch nodded and glanced at the clock on the forward bulkhead of the compartment: it was just past 11:45 so there were several hours of daylight left. He accepted a cup of coffee from one of the staff and sipped it before speaking.

"Where's the helo?"

"Angel 801, right here, Admiral, and they've got about two and a half hours' fuel left. We've moved them south some, waiting on the RESCAPs. There are two of Wilson's flight overhead the helo but it would probably be better to use the A-7s we're launching now."

Welch walked over to the windows and looked down at two A-7s being hooked up to the catapults on the angled deck with two more waiting behind them for their turn. He looked forward and watched as the carrier's bow slowed and then stopped its ponderous swing to port. The bow was now headed directly into the small white streaks left by the freshening breeze out of the west. Before he could look back at the A-7s, the first entered his peripheral vision as it crossed the deck edge at the end of its catapult stroke. Welch followed it as it turned slightly left and its wheels came up. Immediately, a second Corsair followed, flying the same course. Welch watched as the jets shrank to invisibility in the distance, marked only by twin brown smoke trails that gently climbed up into the clear blue sky before they, too, disappeared into the west.

He heard the third and fourth Corsairs roar down the cat and into the air as he walked back over to the chart and stared down at it for a few seconds. Glancing again at the clock, he ran several ideas through his experience store.

"Looks like they've got it pretty well covered, Harry, but maybe they ought to think about a backup helo, too."

"Already being briefed, sir."

Welch smiled and shook his head gently. "Ah, Harry. When will I ever learn?" He looked around the room.

"Master Chief Hayes," he called.

Hayes stepped forward from his usual inconspicuous corner. He seemed to have a sixth sense about when Welch was going to call for him. He never had to be sent for: he was just there.

"Right here, Admiral."

"I left a pile of papers on my desk. If you would, please retrieve them and everything else that's in my in-basket. I'll go through it up here."

Hayes turned and headed for the hatch leading below.

Welch picked up his coffee cup and moved over to his tall leather ready-room chair mounted in the forward corner of the Flag Bridge.

Boyle glanced up at the two A-7s, with Mitchell and Fujimoto, orbiting his helo. He was keeping the H-3 at a steady 70 knots and gently flying a large oval pattern as he waited for Santy to locate Wilson on the ground thirty miles to the west.

When Boyle had heard the Condor flight check off target

in Laos, he had been relieved. He could get only snatches of the radio chatter over the target but what he had heard had been reasonably calm and unruffled. He realized that he could drive himself crazy listening and worrying about Mike, but he felt that he'd rather hear the mission as it happened than wait for a radio call telling him that something was wrong.

This time, his eavesdropping had served to provide rare early warning, early enough to get some of the internal planning accomplished and to speed up the process when the help was called in, as Boyle was certain it would be.

To Boyle's right, Kruger was sticking his chart under the clip on his kneeboard, after folding it so that the immediate route in and the area where Wilson was down were handy. Kruger had calculated the power required for hovering at the altitude of the position that Santy had passed along for Wilson's location. Whether or not there was enough power available from the engines would make the difference between success or failure in the rescue. The power required depended upon factors from the weight of the aircraft to the density of the air over the rescue site to the winds to the height of the trees. Given the winds that were blowing through the area, there would be enough.

Smith, standing in the door immediately behind Boyle's seat, was carefully making sure, for the third time, that the ammunition belts which would feed his M-60 door gun were lying in the box untwisted and ready to go. He had already moved his CAR-15 and his personal pack of essential survival gear to the deck near his right foot so they would be handy if the helo went down suddenly.

In the rear of the passenger cabin, back by the cargo door, Weaver had gotten himself and his station ready exactly as Smith had done. He was very glad that this rescue was not at night over water. His youthful and unassailable optimism made him count whatever blessings were available in every situation.

Boyle glanced down at the instruments, noting that the oil pressure was just a tad lower on number-one engine than on number two. It was still well within normal limits but Boyle made a small mental note to keep an eye on it during his normal scan. Boyle looked again at the brown haze overlying the land to the west. Now we wait, he thought. I hate this part.

Cmdr. Wilson screwed the top back onto the empty baby bottle that represented one third of his water supply. The water was almost cool and even though he was still thirsty, he fought the temptation to drink another bottle.

Pilots had long ago learned that baby bottles were the best way to carry water along on a flight. They seemed to fit absolutely anywhere and carried enough to take care of the normal thirst built up during combat. Many, like Wilson, kept them in a freezer and stuffed them in their survival vest or G-suit pockets just before they manned up their aircraft. That way, they'd keep some of their coolness longer. Wilson always carried three of them and now, in the post-terror portion of his ejection sequence, the water seemed to have had a calming effect on him.

He put the bottle back in the pocket of his G-suit and picked up his radio. It seemed broken but he couldn't see any damage. He put it with his parachute under the brush and pulled his spare out of his vest. Wilson had had one fail a few years before and never really trusted the damned things so he always carried a spare and two extra batteries.

He had seen no one around during his descent and had heard no one in the five minutes or so he had been sitting here in the brush. He felt fortunate indeed that both he and his parachute had come all the way to the ground and not been hung up in the trees which reached thirty feet or so everywhere around except the spot he had landed in. If he or the chute had been hung up in the trees, his chances for a successful rescue or for evasion would have been greatly diminished.

He pulled the little earphone out of its pouch, stuck it in his ear, and pushed the end of the cord into the jack in the top of the radio. Checking to see that the selector was on the guard frequency, he held the radio close to his mouth and spoke softly into the built-in microphone.

"Condor 306, 301. How do you read?"

Santy had been jinking around the area, being as careful as he could not to revisit the place where Wilson had come down and thus give away his position to anyone on the ground. He was also being careful to avoid avoiding the place too much and thus give it away by implication.

None of his radio calls to Wilson had been answered so far and he was beginning to wonder how the hell he was going to find and identify him without a radio when he heard the voice in his helmet.

"Condor 306, 301. How do you read?"

"Loud and clear. Say your posit and condition."

"I'm okay. I'm in some brush about fifty yards from where I came down, uhh, I think fifty yards west."

"Roger, I saw you come down. Be advised I've seen no unfriendlies in the area but lay low anyway. We've got the helo ready to come in. The RESCAPs should be checking in shortly."

Santy checked his fuel gauge and saw that he was not going to be able to stay overhead Wilson a whole lot longer, maybe thirty minutes if he didn't have to do a lot of yanking and banking around the area. He called Mitchell.

"300, 306. Say your state."

Mitchell looked at his fuel totalizer and noted that he had about thirty minutes' flying time before he'd have to head for the *Concord.* He looked across at Fujimoto who signaled that he had 3,200 pounds, about the same.

"306, 300. We've both got about three point two."

"Roger, 3.2. Break. Red Crown, Condor 306. Are there any tankers around?"

"306, Red Crown. That's affirm. We've got Gypsy 512 headed inbound now."

Those guys aboard Red Crown were like the assistant everybody dreams about. They were always one step ahead of the requirements. Santy thought that if the RESCAPs didn't arrive in the next few minutes, he'd send Mitchell and Fujimoto up to refuel from the Gypsy KA-6D tanker and then they could relieve him over Wilson. The most important thing was to keep somebody handy to cover the skipper. Maybe it would be better to get that out of the way now.

"300, 306. Suggest you coordinate with Red Crown and hit the tanker. Then you can relieve me on top."

"300, roger."

Mitchell asked Red Crown for the tanker's position and frequency. When they passed it to him, he only had about twenty-five miles to go so he broke off his orbit and led Fujimoto eastward, climbing to reach the tanker's altitude.

Down in Angel 801, Tim Boyle heard the conversation and automatically checked his own fuel. They had reduced their rate of flow by about 20 percent by slowing their orbit so they should still have more than enough to complete the mission as long as they didn't have to do a protracted search. The best way to avoid that was to keep somebody overhead Wilson at all times so that they didn't have to blunder around trying to find him after a gap in coverage. If that happened and Wilson was lost to the enemy because of it, it wouldn't be the first time.

From the rough position Kruger had marked on the chart, it looked like they were going to have only about thirty or so miles to fly overland. If Wilson was ready and there was no serious opposition, they could be in and out in about a half hour. If they stayed as low as possible and flew as fast as possible, they should give any enemy troops on the ground only minimum time to see them and open fire. If they stayed low to the trees and avoided open areas, that time would be reduced even further since the foliage would serve to diffuse the sound of their approach and passage. The only tactic that enemy troops could use that would be remotely effective would be to lie on their backs and shoot straight up, hoping that the helo would fly through the concentration of small-arms fire and thus be prey to a lucky shot. Boyle only hoped that they wouldn't have to hover high above the trees at the top of a hill where they would be visible, motionless, for however long it took for Wilson to get himself on the forest penetrator, hook the strap around himself, and be reeled in.

The hover was the part that scared Boyle most. In the cockpit in the front end of a helicopter, you were sitting in what was essentially a glass enclosure: the only metal around you seemed to be designed to support more glass. You had to stand still and be a target, hoping fervently that the bad guys were lousy shots and unlucky to boot. In spite of the speeches from the chaplains, Boyle had long suspected that God really didn't take sides in wars and was therefore not about to take time out to make sure that only the good guys could shoot straight.

Despite his lack of faith in the Divinity's support for his, or any, side, Boyle was not above saying a quick prayer on the off chance that God had temporarily run out of things to do this morning and might remember something good in Boyle's file that he might have done at some earlier point in his life, like maybe giving his school milk money to the missions or visiting the old people in the nursing home with the rest of his Cub Scout pack.

Mitchell watched as Fujimoto backed the refueling probe of his A-7 carefully away from the basket trailing below and behind the A-6 tanker. Once he was clear, he hit the switch that sent the probe back into its stowed position and moved over and rejoined in formation on Mitchell's wing.

Mitchell waved his thanks at the tanker crew and turned away, headed back to the west. On his signal, Fujimoto again spread out into a free cruise position and the two jets lowered their noses as they descended toward 5,000 feet. Mitchell signaled Fujimoto and they both switched their radios back to the rescue frequency.

"Condor 306, 300's back with you. Tanking complete. State 5.0."

Santy rogered them and told them to head inbound and relieve him overhead Wilson. He was down to about ten minutes left before he'd have to leave. He called Red Crown, told them he'd be heading out to the tanker when he was relieved, and received their concurrence.

As soon as the beach passed under his nose, Mitchell called "feet dry" and glanced at Fujimoto to see that he had spread out even farther. It would only be a couple of minutes before they were over Wilson's position, so he rechecked that his armament switches were set properly and he had selected the slower rate of fire on his 20mm cannon. He had forgotten to remind Fujimoto about it before they passed into North Vietnam and momentarily debated telling him now. No sense taking it for granted, Snake, my boy, he thought.

"Banzai, guns," was all he said, receiving two clicks from his wingman.

Up ahead, Mitchell caught a momentary flash of white against the green land from Santy's wing as it rose when Mike banked into a turn. "306, 300. Tally. I'm at your right two o'clock. Slightly high."

Santy looked up and to the right. Just off his nose, he saw the faint smoke trails of his two squadronmates. He couldn't quite make out the airplanes themselves but, nose on, that was to be expected.

The two fell in well behind him so he shifted his course a little to the right and aimed for where he thought Wilson was. "I'll mark the skipper for you."

He lowered his nose and flew straight for a few seconds, calling out, "Marking on top, now . . . now . . . *now*." He pulled sharply up and right, heading east for the water.

Mitchell noted where 306 had been on the third now and stared hard at the spot and the immediate area, fixing it in his memory.

"306, 300. I got it. I am on-scene commander. You are cleared to depart."

Santy answered with two clicks and shoved his throttle forward as he put the coast on his nose.

On the ground, Wilson heard Santy's Corsair pass nearly overhead and then listened to his young pilots. He felt a flash of pride in them. Even though he was now alternating between the shakes from his ejection and hearing all sorts of phantom footsteps in the brush around him, the matter-of-fact voices from the jets above him had a calming effect. He was not alone. Putting his radio close to his lips, he called Mitchell.

"300, this is 301. That last mark was real close. I'm about one hundred yards west of the mark."

"Roger that, Skipper. The RESCAPs are checking in now. We oughta have you out of there real quick. Hang in."

Wilson picked up his pencil flare and smoke marker. He looked up and found a hole in the jungle canopy that he could shoot the flare through to signal the helo when it got close. He was as ready as he could get.

Chapter 26

October 9, 1972

Red Crown, Condor 306 is feet wet." Santy watched the beach pass under his Corsair. He had about nine minutes of fuel left before he had to head back to the *Concord*.

"Roger, 306. The Gypsy is 050 at thirty miles, angels twenty."

"306 is out of five thousand for twenty. 050 for thirty."

Santy shoved his throttle forward and began a climbing turn to a course of 050 and an altitude a little below twenty thousand feet. Within two minutes he was close enough to the A-6's holding pattern to pick it out on the first look. If he could get about three thousand pounds of fuel, he would be able to get back and see this through. Mitchell and Fujimoto had gotten about that much so the tanker should have at least that much left for him. About two and a half minutes to get the fuel, he thought. Counting the approach and breakaway, maybe six for the whole thing.

He cut across the circle and joined in a loose wing position on the inside of the tanker's turn with his refueling probe extended. The pilot looked back at him, nodded, and the drogue began to reel itself out from the belly of the A-6. Santy watched the yellow-banded hose and the metal basket at its end reach the limit of travel and stabilize behind and below the A-6. He gave the pilot a thumbs-up and eased the Corsair back and down behind the drogue. He added just a touch of power and the Corsair moved gently forward until his probe entered the metal basket. He watched as the hose was pushed back into the A-6, marked by a couple of the yellow stripes reentering the belly of the tanker. It had been a near-perfect "plug."

Santy looked for the green light which would show that the system was operating properly but the amber standby light remained steady. He backed out of the basket and came forward again, shoving the hose in a little more forcefully this time. The amber light stayed on, telling him that he was still not getting any gas. He looked down at his fuel gauge and realized that he had maybe two more tries before he had to head back to the *Concord*. As it stood now, considering the fuel he was burning in an attempt to get more, he'd land with a bit less fuel than was required by the squadron and air wing SOP, the standard operating procedures.

Santy backed out of the basket one more time. He drew a long breath and moved back in. This time the hose did not give at all. When his probe contacted the basket, it sent a "sine wave" back up the hose much like the wave in a long telephone cord being moved sharply up and down. The wave traveled up the hose with amazing speed and when it reached the end at the A-6, it came back at Santy's aircraft just as quickly.

Santy saw the wave begin its rush back at his Corsair and backed his probe out just as the basket snapped like the tip of a whip. He waited a few seconds for it to stabilize and tried once more. This time, he managed to get back out a little sooner but the overall result was the same: no fuel.

Fuck, he thought, that's the ball game. The tanker's refueling system was broken. He moved over and up to a position slightly forward of the normal parade formation and waved at the tanker pilot, giving him the thumbs-down. In all of this there had not yet been a single word spoken on the radio. One of the points of professional pride in any air wing is that the radio is used only when absolutely required. Everything is done by hand signals and by being where you were expected to be when you were expected to be there. As with most of the evolutions the jets flew outside of actual combat, In-flight refueling had been choreographed and practiced so that it normally did not require any talking. But things were no longer normal.

"Gypsy, your store didn't take up. I'm about out of time. I'm minimum fuel now so I'm RTB."

The tanker pilot nodded and gave him a thumbs-up and then watched as Santy moved back and away, heading for the ship. The Gypsy pilot had his own problems now with a drogue that might not retract for landing.

"Condor 300 and Red Crown, 306. I'm RTB."

Mitchell heard Santy's transmission and rogered it. He knew that something had gone wrong with Santy's aircraft or the tanker. It was the only reason he'd leave in the middle like this. He thought about the situation.

One of the rules was that you absolutely never flew over the beach alone in combat. There was no sense sending Fujimoto out to bring in the helo because that would leave both of them vulnerable. Both had enough fuel to stay a while yet, at least until the RESCAPs showed up. Even at low altitude like this they had enough.

He knew how Santy felt about now. There are few things in naval aviation more disappointing or more frustrating than being forced to leave your mission in the middle. This is especially so when somebody else's life is on the line.

Boyle also heard Santy and wondered a little. He was also kind of glad that he sounded okay and was headed out. His thoughts were quickly interrupted by Red Crown.

"Angel 801, Red Crown. The RESCAPs are coming on top of you now. Contact Cobra 408, this button."

"Roger, Red Crown. Break. Cobra 408, Angel 801."

"Roger, Angel. Cobras are overhead this time, angels five."

Kruger looked up through the upper window and spotted the four A-7s entering an opposing orbit five thousand feet above the helicopter.

"Tally, Cobras."

High above, the flight leader, Lt. Cmdr. Gary Curtis, waggled his wings and led his wingman away to the west to relieve Mitchell and Fujimoto over Wilson's position. The other two Cobras stayed in the orbit to escort the helo in as soon as things got established.

Curtis was one of those no-nonsense men who believed that quick, positive action was always preferable to hesitation. He flew his missions with as little emotion as possible. He forced himself to stay cold because he felt that getting all fired up and acting from the guts was stupid. He knew well that there were lots of things one didn't do and stay alive so when he decided to retreat he moved as quickly as he did attacking. Get in, do the job right the first time, and get the hell out. He sought no glory, never added a colorful adjective to an account of his success or failure, and couldn't care less if he pissed anyone off. When this cruise ended, he was going to go with the airlines; he'd held up his end for eight years and three combat cruises and soon it was going to be somebody else's turn.

The vector that Red Crown gave him was right on. He spotted Mitchell's and Fujimoto's A-7s flying around in the general area.

"Condor lead, this is Cobra 408. Have you in sight. Give me the posit."

"Roger. He's in some deep brush on the west side of the ridge on my nose. . . . *now*."

"Okay. I have the ridge. 301, do you read?"

Wilson answered instantly, "301."

"Roger, request you fire a pen flare."

Wilson aimed at the hole in the trees, turned his face away, and moved the firing knob inward with his thumb. With a small popping sound, the small red flare arched up, narrowly missed a tree branch, and reached its apex about one hundred feet over the trees.

Curtis saw the flare emerge from the green canopy and memorized the position. The top of the ridge was clear enough of high trees for the helo to maintain a low hover, thus reducing the power required and giving them an advantage by making them less vulnerable to ground fire.

"Roger, 301. Stay put. The helo's inbound. Break. Cobra 403, bring in the Angel. Condors, you're relieved." Mitchell clicked his radio twice and led Fujimoto away to the east and back to the ship, as the Cobra escort answered his lead.

"Roj. 801, Cobra 403. Your initial steer is 265."

Boyle rogered as Kruger banked the helo and descended right down to the deck. He accelerated the helo to the red line and backed it down ten knots to allow for the turbulence caused by the land. Boyle yanked down on his shoulder straps, tightening their grip on his upper body. Almost unconsciously, he adjusted his holstered pistol lying on the seat between his legs. He looked out at the fast-approaching coastline of North Vietnam. In many ways, it reminded him of Pensacola Beach and the Gulf Coast of Florida. Be a nice place to build a bar, he thought, if nobody was shooting at you.

As the beach grew closer, all of these irrelevancies went away and he concentrated on following the instructions of 403 and his wingman whose job it was to guide him in, using their better vantage from five thousand or so feet above, and to protect him as much as possible from the enemy on the ground.

"Red Crown, 801 is feet dry." There was no reply from the radar ship, nor was one expected. An extraneous transmission was never helpful.

Above, the two escorting jets were in their wagonwheel orbit around the Angel's course. They constantly looked for anything on the ground which could be a threat to the vulnerable helicopter; if it was at all possible to go around habitation, the jets would give small course changes to the helo pilots, who were doing their best to stay low and use the terrain to hide behind. At five thousand feet above the ground, the Corsairs, for their part, were well below the SAM envelope and well above any threat from small arms. Only larger Triple-A guns were a hazard but the apparently erratic course they advised the helo to fly minimized the danger for everybody. So far, nobody had opened fire on the helo or at least they hadn't been hit. You can't see rifle and small-machine-gun rounds unless there are tracer rounds interspersed with them.

"Come right ten, Angel. There's a small village on your nose." Kruger banked slightly and steadied up exactly on the new heading, ten degrees to the right. "You've got about fifteen miles to go. It's a straight shot from here on in."

"Click-click."

Boyle looked ahead at the gently rising terrain. The sharp edges of the limestone karst rose abruptly from the trees six or seven miles in front of them. Most of the small valleys were opening toward him so that they would not be forced to climb away from the ground too soon to clear a ridge. On the other hand, it was a real bad idea to fly for long in a valley where the enemy had a chance of shooting down at you. Room to maneuver was necessarily limited by the walls of a valley and to climb out of one meant that you had to slow down some, making your position worse.

Kruger watched the rising terrain come at them and picked a course which would fly close to one of the ridges bordering a valley that seemed to lead in the right direction. He eased the helo slightly to the right and hugged the trees near the top. He glanced at the altimeter and, even though he was still only about fifteen feet over the trees, he noted that it was increasing rapidly toward the four-thousand-foot level where Wilson had come down.

"408, 403. Angel's about five miles out now."

Curtis looked to the east and spotted the disk of the helicopter's rotor system before he could make out the dark green machine hanging below it. The helo was dead on course.

Curtis called Wilson. "301, 408. The helo is five out. Move to the clear area and pop smoke."

Wilson had already moved to the edge of the deep cover he had been hiding in. He pulled the ring on his day/night signal marker and when the orange smoke began to billow from it, he tossed it out into the shorter bushes. As he did, he heard the roar of Curtis's A-7 pass directly overhead.

"Angel, 408. Good smoke on your nose for three miles."

Just as they reached the top of the ridge, both Boyle and Kruger saw the orange cloud rising from a small flat spot across a small shallow valley ahead. Before Boyle could point it out, Kruger transmitted, "Got your orange," and altered course slightly to the left to line up with the wind that Wilson's smoke marker was indicating. He didn't begin to slow down until they were about two hundred yards out and then put in a large nose-up movement to stop in a low hover directly over the flat spot.

Weaver, at the rear cargo door, threw out the forest penetrator and hit the switch which lowered it rapidly the rest of the way to the ground. Before it touched the ground, he saw Wilson break from cover and run over to the penetrator. He had almost grabbed it when he drew his hand back and let it hit the ground, discharging the static electricity. In his eagerness, Wilson had only remembered at the last instant that the charge the helo built up would knock him flat on his ass.

"Steady hover, pilot. Steady. Survivor's climbing on the seat now. Taking up the slack, stand by for weight on the aircraft . . . now. Survivor's coming up. He's halfway up." Weaver guided the cable with his right hand as he operated the switch with his left. Smith was squatting close by to help pull Wilson in.

"Survivor's approaching the cargo door. He's at the door." Weaver grabbed the top of the penetrator as Smith grabbed Wilson, spun him around to face outboard, and pulled him in as Weaver let the hoist down a couple of feet.

"Survivor's in the aircraft. You're cleared for forward flight." As Smith pulled Wilson forward away from the door,

Weaver unhooked the penetrator and shoved it under the seat, raising the hoist to the stowed position as he did.

Wilson sat on the deck where Smith indicated and watched as the two crewmen manned their guns. It was now up to the pilots. He felt the nose dip and heard the whine of the engines increase in pitch as Kruger dipped the nose and hauled in the collective.

Approaching the hover, Boyle had split his concentration between scanning the gauges and looking outside for any sign of the enemy because the helo was then in the most vulnerable part of the entire mission. His right hand was on the throttles, ready to slam them both forward to full power at the first hint of failure in either of the engines. Beside him, Kruger sat hunched forward slightly in the old pose that helicopter pilots learn is the most comfortable and effective in making the small gentle inputs which keep the helo under control. If you fly with rigid hands and arms, instead of with just your wrists and fingers, you overcontrol and make the job twice as difficult as it ought to be. It's an easy thing to just cruise around and stay relaxed but when you are close to the ground or in danger of getting shot, keeping smooth control of your aircraft and yourself is an art.

During the early part of the hover, on one of the many times he scanned the engine performance gauges, Boyle thought he caught another wobble in the oil pressure gauge for number-one engine but when he looked at it carefully, it remained rock steady. He continued moving his eyes: in at the gauges, out at the brush surrounding the area, and then down at the ground below to check that Kruger's hover was motionless. In, out, and down. In, out, and down. Each repetition took only about three seconds but it seemed as if time were moving at no speed at all. Everything his eyes took in registered consciously, every sound that the helo made, and every word Weaver spoke was as clear and distinct as if they were happening separately. There were no distinct thoughts that Boyle would remember, just a mass of sensory inputs all blending into a whole but retaining their individuality, like the instruments of an orchestra.

Kruger waited until Weaver had given him the go-ahead, and then hauled in the collective, increasing the pitch of the rotor blades and their bite of the humid air over the top of the ridge. As the helo began to move upward with the increased lift, he shoved the nose down and stomped right rudder, causing the aircraft to accelerate, turn right, and dive down the side of the ridge all at the same time. He watched the valley floor come at him ever quicker and waited for the helo to get up to speed, easing the nose up and shallowing the dive as they reached 140 knots. He eased in another right turn to get clear of the area by a slightly different route from their approach. Once Kruger had everything stable, he exhaled, realizing that once again he had been holding his breath throughout a difficult takeoff.

Next to him, Boyle listened to Weaver's curt report on Wilson's apparent condition and keyed his radio. "Cobra 408, 801. We've got him and he's in good shape."

Above, Curtis and his number two joined the wagonwheel orbit over the helo. Now, with four escorts instead of two, the helo would have 20mm cannons pointed in four directions at once, halving the time required to get some rounds on anyone firing at the helo.

Neither helo pilot was about to relax with the job only half complete, so they flew generally in silence, cutting all communication to only that which was related to survival. The helicopter bounced and jostled through the currents in the air, dodging and weaving over and across the rugged limestone edges of the country, heading east for the water. Across the ridges, down in the trees, around the biggest ones. Kruger flew precisely, his mind and body always well out ahead of where the helo was now, instinctively planning his moves and keeping the huge aircraft right on the ragged edge of safety.

In every Navy helicopter NATOPS manual, way in the back among the performance charts, there is something called a "height-velocity diagram." It is a graphic display of the relationship between speed, altitude, and probability of survival. There are three areas which are colored differently, indicating the bottom line of the information the engineers and aerodynamicists and test pilots had come up with long before.

A large white area of the chart is unlabeled. If your altitude and airspeed are in this area you should be okay should something bad happen to one or both of your engines. You will have enough time, altitude, and stored energy in your aircraft to do what is required to either safely land or to continue flying at a slower speed. Another area, colored yellow, is labeled "Cautionary Operating Area"; here the probabilities for successfully dealing with a problem are less good but you still have a fair chance.

The third area is colored red and labeled, simply, "Avoid." Here, your chances are not good at all. If you are relatively high and very slow, say 200 feet and 10 knots, or very low and very fast, 50 feet and 130 knots, and something happens to an engine, and thus your helo's ability to produce lift, you are essentially in very deep shit. You have run out of altitude, airspeed, and ideas and there is almost nothing you can do to avoid hitting the ground very hard. It is a fact of life that, in combat, much of what needs to be done in flying a helicopter over land puts it squarely in the red area on the graph.

Boyle and Kruger were about 25 feet over the trees at 130 knots and climbing the last ridge which lay between them and the coastal plain when something broke within the number-one engine, causing an immediate and drastic loss of power. The massive helo yawed abruptly to the left and settled toward the ground.

There was time only to register surprise and utter a curse before Angel 801 settled just enough and smashed into the trees fifteen feet below the crest of the ridge with a slight nose up angle at about 217 feet per second.

Lt. Cmdr. Curtis was on the side of the wagonwheel facing away from the helo's flight path when he heard a garbled transmission on the radio which stopped suddenly, as if cut by a knife. Immediately, he heard one of the other Corsair pilots in his flight.

"Jesus Christ! He hit the fucking trees!"

Curtis whipped into a steep turn and craned his neck to see what had happened. He saw only a large misshapen green thing coming to rest upside down in a small clearing at the very crest of the ridge. Branches and bits of metal were settling back to earth in a horizontal cone-shaped area beyond the point of impact. Several long pieces tumbled back farther away in different directions, apparently sections of the rotor blades hurled away by centrifugal force after they snapped off on impact with the trees.

He keyed his radio. "Red Crown, Cobra 403. The Angel is down. The Angel is down. Stand by."

Curtis set up for a pass over the wreck, slowing up much more than he would normally have done over enemy territory. He lined up to put the wreck at his left front and, as he approached it, banked left to look straight down. When he was about two hundred yards short of the spot, a huge orange-and-black fireball burst from the clearing where the helo lay. As he passed over, he looked down and saw the helo, lying upside down, wrapped in flames which spread ten feet on either side. The nose of the wreck was pointing generally back the way it had come. He couldn't see any evidence of the crew which wasn't surprising considering how badly smashed the aircraft looked.

Setting up for another pass, lower this time, he realized that he hadn't heard a beeper yet but it had only been a minute or so since the helo had crashed. The violence of the impact, even at a relatively shallow angle, could easily be seen from the wide dispersion of pieces, despite the heavy foliage. On his second pass, he looked more carefully around the helo and still saw nothing indicating that anyone had gotten out.

"Red Crown, Cobra 403. The helo hit the ground at the top of a ridge. It's on its back and burning. I don't see any signs of life and I don't think anyone got out. We'll keep looking."

"Roger, 403. We'll pass it on. Be careful in there." The

voice from Red Crown sounded very tired, and very soft, as if he had a friend aboard the helo.

"403, roger." Curtis looked out to the east at the safety of the Gulf of Tonkin. Only eight more miles and everybody would have been home free, he thought, another four fucking minutes.

Chapter 27

October 9, 1972

Santy kept the A-7 at twenty thousand, headed slightly south of east. His fuel gauge was creeping ever lower so he was probably going to have to make it on the first pass. Even descending with the engine at idle power, he would cross the ramp with only about nine hundred pounds.

His first thought on realizing that there was no way to get more fuel was that he could divert to Danang, which would have given him a simpler problem, a long, wide, unmoving runway as opposed to the deck of a ship. Red Crown had given him the news that Danang was well below weather minimums, and driving around in the rain trying to find the runway was less attractive than trying to find the ship in clear weather. As he had turned out toward the *Concord,* he had looked back to the west and noticed how large the cloud bank on the horizon had grown in the past hour. To the southwest, the clouds were even higher and more menacing. Danang was under the leading edge of it all.

Santy called the *Concord* and requested a ready deck for landing. The ship told him to expect a straight-in approach for landing and a ready deck. He rogered and told the ship that he would be off the frequency for a minute but would monitor the guard frequency. He selected the rescue channel and switched back to monitor the progress of the rescue, listening to guard on his auxiliary receiver in case somebody needed to call him.

He listened as Boyle and the RESCAPs arrived over Wilson, and followed the progress of the pickup. He was reaching for the channel selector knob when he heard the Cobra call out that the helo had hit the ground. The news took his breath away like a kick in the chest.

Santy reefed the Corsair around toward the beach instinctively, reversing course and jamming the throttle forward, but rational thought returned just as quickly. He couldn't go back without running out of fuel and compounding the problem for himself and everybody concerned. His experience and training were telling him one thing and his heart and soul were telling him the opposite. Cursing with all the force that was in him, he turned the aircraft back toward the ship and switched off the frequency. It was the hardest thing he had ever had to do.

He looked at his fuel gauge and found that his momentary deviation had put him in a position where he had enough for one pass and a half maybe. If he didn't make it, he was going to have to eject. He kept having to will himself to forget about Boyle and Wilson for just a few more minutes so he could concentrate on flying smoothly and using the absolute minimum of his dwindling fuel supply.

At thirty miles, he pulled the throttle back and began his descent, letting gravity help provide the speed and reducing the required engine power and thus fuel flow. Once he reached the proper altitude, he raised the nose and added power again to maintain the altitude until he could pick up the ball and begin his final approach. One more hopeful glance at his fuel gauge told him that his earlier estimate was still correct: he would have one try. He rechecked that the Corsair was configured for landing: gear, flaps, and hook down.

At three quarters of a mile, Santy saw the yellow ball and called the LSO.

"306, Corsair, ball, point eight." This last told the LSO that he was down to eight hundred pounds.

"Roger, ball. Corsair. Foul deck. Can you give me a 360?" The LSO's voice, deliberately calm as it was, chilled Santy. The deck wasn't clear yet and he had to do one orbit before he headed toward the ship again.

All right, he thought, one turn and if the deck's not clear I eject. No sense flaming out on short final. He raised his gear and flaps.

"Paddles, 306. I can do one turn. If you're not ready for me, I'm getting out."

"Paddles, roger."

When the call came up from below that 306 was coming back low on fuel and needed a ready deck, the Air Boss passed up his usual reaction—to curse the lineage of every pilot in the air wing—and began bellowing over the 1MC, "On the flight deck, we have a low state A-7 inbound at fifty miles. Pull forward. Pull forward. Tractors to the fantail. *Now,* goddamnit."

All over the flight deck, sailors in shirts of all colors piled out of their spaces below and began running aft to get the aircraft which were spotted for the next launch pulled clear of the landing area. Red-shirted ordnancemen, brown-shirted plane captains, green shirts and yellow shirts, all surrounded the aircraft and stood by until a tractor was available to hook up to the towbar attached to the nose wheel.

To anyone who was not familiar with the flight deck and just happened to be watching, this would look like a Chinese fire drill without the choreography. What would not be obvious was that every move was in synchronization with every other. There were men who directed where each aircraft would be towed and stashed out of the way. There were others who were running across the deck, dodging the tractors and aircraft as they did a fast inspection of the arresting wires.

Out on the port side, aft of the wires, several men in white shirts prepared the LSO platform.

From the tower, it looked to the Air Boss as if somebody had just dropped a basket of twenty-dollar bills as the men ran aft to the aircraft. Then there was a steady flow as the aircraft moved forward and clear of the landing area. Today things went smoothly except for one aircraft, an F-4, which was the last one left back there.

There were several men clustered around its left mainmount watching three sweating sailors try to get the wheel back on. Somebody had authorized them to change a worn tire before the next flight. Now, Santy was only ten miles from the ship as the sailors finally were getting the wheel on and enough nuts to hold it for towing. As soon as the wheel looked approximately right, several other sailors, on command, began lowering the jack.

Santy was almost through his one orbit with his gear and flaps coming back down when the tractor began to tow the Phantom forward. The LSO watched the Phantom moving up the deck and then looked back aft to the dot of Santy's approaching Corsair and wondered whether this was going to happen. He mentally picked the last possible safe point in Santy's approach path and told himself that if the green "Clear Deck" light had not come on by the time Santy hit that spot, he would have to wave him off. He was well aware that if Santy went farther there could be a disaster that would make losing one jet look like a good day and that a wave-off certainly meant an ejection.

Santy looked out and picked up the yellow ball centered between the green lines of the datum lights. "306, Corsair, ball, point six." He could almost feel the black and yellow ejection handle between his legs.

"Roger, ball, Corsair. Foul deck. Keep it coming."

Santy eased off some power, setting the nose attitude so that the amber doughnut on his angle-of-attack indexer glowed. He held what he had with only minor corrections, little dips of the wings for lineup and slight moves of the throttle and the nose to maintain attitude and speed. He resisted the temptation to "spot the deck," to try to look at the ship for his corrections as opposed to the lens and the AOA indexer.

The LSO watched him approach, glancing once up the deck to see where the F-4 was: it was just beginning to turn out of the landing area. He turned back and flicked his eyes from the red "Foul Deck" light in front of him to Santy's Corsair.

Up the deck, the flight-deck chief was watching the tractor pull the Phantom across the foul line. As the nosewheel passed over the line with most of the big fighter yet to go, the chief looked aft and made a judgment based on years of experience. He raised his arm and waved at the arresting gear crew back aft that the Phantom was clear. The arresting gear officer hesitated a second when he saw that there was still a bit of Phantom to the left of the foul line. He looked again at the chief's waving arm and turned the deck status light from red to green.

The LSO was raising his hand to wave Santy off when the light changed. He resisted the temptation to shout "clear deck" on the radio and simply lowered his hand.

The tail of the Phantom cleared the line at exactly the same time as the Corsair crossed the ramp and slammed down, catching the number-two wire. When the jet came to a halt, Santy reduced power and raised his tail hook, following the director's signals to a parking spot back down the deck. Watching the Corsair taxi past, the chief unfastened the chin-strap from his helmet and switched his plug of tobacco to the other cheek. He turned and headed for flight deck control. I wonder if there's any coffee left, he thought.

As the engine wound down, Santy removed his helmet, stuffed his kneeboard in it, and handed it and his small green canvas bag which contained his charts and checklists to the squadron maintenance chief. He climbed down the short boarding ladder and stood facing the chief, loosening his harness as he told him that there were no gripes with the Corsair. The chief listened, and then spoke in his usual deep monotone.

"Skipper's down, Mr. Santy."

"Yeah, I know, Chief. I was in there until the fucking tanker broke and I had to head back. I had to switch off the freq. Any word on the crew and the skipper?"

"No, sir, nothing official but rumor says there's no survivors. I just heard it in Flight Deck Control."

Wordlessly, Santy turned and walked to the deck edge, looking west as if somehow he could see what had happened there, far over the horizon. Only once in his life had he had this feeling before, when he was fourteen, the day he came home from school in Jacksonville to find an official Navy staff car parked in his driveway and his mother being comforted by some of the wives from the squadron and the neighborhood. He had felt the same disbelief and cold numbness in his heart as the chaplain knelt before him and told him gently of his father's loss far to the south off the coast of Cuba. Then it was as if the chaplain and his home disappeared and all he could see or hear was his father's face and voice on the day he led his squadron out to join his carrier. That morning, three months before, his father had seemed a tall god in a flight suit as he smiled down and ruffled young Mike's hair, telling him to take care of his mother while he was gone.

Now all he could see was Boyle's face and his laughing eyes this morning at breakfast, only four hours ago. Laughing at another of Santy's incessant attempts to get him to eat a balanced meal before he went flying, Boyle, as always, had maintained that half a pound of bacon, two slices of toast, and five cups of coffee *was* a balanced breakfast. Santy wished with all his heart that Boyle could be standing next to him right now so he could call his best friend a dumb ass just one more time.

Suddenly, Santy became aware of another feeling, one he had never felt before. He would never be certain whether it was his natural psychological defenses kicking in or something else, something deep within the gray mists that shrouded the unknown corners of his mind. He realized that he didn't *feel* that Boyle was gone, but that Tim was still out there somewhere in the weeds, alive. Injured or captured perhaps, but alive. Santy realized just as abruptly that over time he and Boyle had become part of each other, that somehow, over the months and years, gradually, silently, and perhaps inevitably, they had become closer than twins.

Fifteen minutes later, Santy sat in the ready room waiting for the RESCAPs to land. Fujimoto and Mitchell had come back and were sitting silently across the room from him. The feeling that Tim was somehow still alive out there had glided gently and silently back into the mists when confronted by the harsh light and colors of the ready room. It was still in there somewhere just inside the gray, not exactly here but not gone either.

Santy watched on the PLAT, or Pilot's Landing Aid Television, the RESCAP A-7s come back aboard the *Concord*. He was sitting about three rows behind the squadron X.O., Commander Faber. Most of the seats had gradually filled as the individual pilots had learned of the crash of the rescue helicopter. The X.O.'s seat was in the front row one place away from the aisle. The one on the aisle, the empty one, belonged to the C.O., Wilson.

The room was mostly silent; only the SDO was speaking and then only in hushed tones whenever he had to answer the phone. Even the ringer on the phone was on the low setting so as not to intrude on the thoughts and fears of the squadron members sitting around the room sipping suddenly tasteless coffee or fiddling with the pulls on the zippers at the top of their flight suits or smoking cigarettes one after another.

Commander Faber was fidgeting in his seat. He was now suddenly in command of the squadron and really had no idea what to do about it. As the X.O., all he had had to do was to follow Wilson's lead and enforce his policies. He was completely unprepared for the task of setting policy but his biggest problem was that he didn't know it.

When the fourth and last of the RESCAPs had landed, Faber stood and headed for the door, gesturing for Santy to follow. The X.O. wanted Santy, as the next senior man in the original flight, to be there to answer the questions that were certain to arise during the debrief of the RESCAPs and the necessary postmortem of the entire mission. Santy followed silently, wondering how well Faber would do in taking over for Wilson. He hoped fervently that Faber would have half the balls and a tenth the leadership talents that Wilson had had.

Lt. Cmdr. Curtis climbed down from Cobra 408. He loosened his torso harness as he waited for the other three pilots in his flight to shut down their jets and get out. He motioned to the flight-deck chief from his squadron, VA-187, and, over the noise from the still-turning engines, yelled at the chief's helmet earcup.

"We gotta get below and debrief. I got no gripes on this one so it's up and ready for the next go. I'll sign the sheet when I get down to the ready room."

The chief nodded and moved away to meet the pilot of the next Corsair to shut down. Even though the pilots had signaled "Up, up, and up" to the chief as they taxied clear of the landing area, indicating that there were no major discrepancies precluding any of the jets' being readied for the next launch, he needed to know if there were any minor acceptable or "up" gripes that should be fixed, if there were enough time before the next group of pilots manned up in about an hour.

When all four of the pilots were standing at the foot of one of the boarding steps, Curtis asked which of them had actually seen Angel 801 hit the ground. The voice had been unidentifiable in its stridency. The pilot of number three in the flight, Lt. (J.G.) Terry Borden, acknowledged making the transmission. Before he could begin telling the story, Curtis held up a hand and told the other two to head on down to the ready room. He turned and walked toward the hatch in the island structure, gesturing for Borden to follow him.

One level below, Curtis held the door for Borden and

stepped into the intelligence briefing room to a sudden hush. All eyes were on the two pilots, still in their sweaty flight gear. Curtis approached the front of the room where a large chart of the area surrounding the crash site was pinned on a cork bulletin board on the wall. There were four members of Wilson's squadron, including Santy and Faber; Fisher, the OIC of the helo detachment, with his ops officer, Lt. Crawford; CAG, Cmdr. Greenwood; Captain Forrest, the admiral's chief of staff; Cmdr. Finney, Curtis's squadron C.O.; and several other interested but extraneous officers.

Before the questions could begin flying, Curtis spoke up, gesturing at Borden. "Bear, here, saw the helo go down. I didn't see anything until after it was almost over."

All the faces turned to Borden. He pointed at a spot on the chart and began a little hesitantly but quickly picked up volume. "The helo was climbing up over this last high ridge, right here, when it just flew into the trees. I didn't see any ground fire coming up and the vegetation is really pretty dense on the slope but the crest is a little clearing. The helo hit kinda flat and flipped over, mostly onto the crest. It started burning after about ten seconds. They didn't say anything except 'Aw, shit,' on the radio before they hit so whatever happened was real sudden. That's it. We hung around as long as we could but I didn't see any movement or hear a beeper."

Curtis added, "The fire was pretty intense but there were no explosions so the fuel tanks apparently all ruptured on impact. The fire was not widespread, maybe ten yards around the wreck and only a few trees caught but they didn't burn long, no more than five minutes. The fire was still burning when we left but only right around the wreck, and it looked like it was burning itself out. We also didn't see any gomers coming toward it but somebody could have been hidden by the weeds."

Crawford glanced at his boss, Fisher, and looked at Borden. "Did you see anything the aircraft did just before it hit, like yaw a bunch?"

Borden thought for a few seconds. "I was looking at it right as it happened and it seems to me that the nose was yawing some just when they said, 'Aw, shit.' They had been going along real smooth up until then. You know, no jerky moves or sudden large banks or anything. They were right down on the tops of the trees but it didn't look like they hit anything before the crash. I don't know. Does that help?"

Crawford nodded slowly. "Maybe. Those two pilots were both pretty good so screwing the pooch and just flying into the ground is possible but not likely. The yaw could indicate a sudden power loss like an engine failure or something." He stopped and folded his arms, staring at the chart.

Faber, from Santy's squadron, said, "Well, whatever happened, the point is that they've lost us a damn good attack pilot and C.O."

Santy was stunned. Crawford whirled and faced the X.O. but before he could say a word, Forrest's firm grip on his arm stopped him.

In a voice that would freeze an oil fire, Forrest addressed Faber. "Your skipper was only one of five men aboard that aircraft, Commander, only one of five. The helicopter crewmen were risking their lives to pull his chestnuts out. Had they not been there, he would have had no chance at all. Kindly remember that next time you wish to sound foolish."

The X.O. flushed crimson and apologized. Through his anger, Crawford could feel a trembling in Forrest's hand on his arm. He just nodded at the apology.

CAG Greenwood was very glad that it had been Faber who got slammed and not him. He had had the same petty thought as the X.O. had but fortunately had not expressed it. Tapping one finger on his chin, he looked from the chart to Curtis.

"What do you think the odds are for survivors?"

Curtis sighed. "I don't know, CAG. It's possible that somebody might have gotten out but it caught fire pretty quick and the impact itself must have been damn hard. Those helos aren't really designed to take a hit like that. It stayed mostly intact but I couldn't see how much it had been crushed when it landed upside down."

Greenwood looked again at the chart. After a few seconds,

he spoke over his shoulder. "The area looks fairly remote and tough to get at from the ground. What do you think about sending a helo in there to make sure about survivors?"

Forrest had been thinking the same thing, though it was not routine to send aircraft back into North Vietnam to check over a crash site when there was no indication of survivors but he was pleased that they were responding this way. He turned to Curtis. "Did you see any sign of enemy personnel in the area?"

"Not exactly, sir. There is a village up this valley a ways and another on the east side of the ridge but nothing military-looking around." He pointed at the chart. "The ridge has really steep sides and there are wide areas of rocks where they'd have to cross before they got back into the trees. I didn't see anybody and I took no fire from the ground." He looked at Borden. "Did you, Bear?"

"No, sir. Nothing. I didn't even notice the village in that valley."

Forrest looked at CAG, both realizing that in view of the directives passed down from Pearl Harbor, they could be letting themselves in for a bunch of trouble. Before he could speak, Lt. Thompson, the admiral's aide, piped up from the rear of the group. He had come in unnoticed and had heard most of the discussion.

"Captain Forrest, if you are going to need somebody to search the area real quick, I'd like to volunteer. I have, um, some experience in that sort of thing."

Fisher stepped forward. "We can have a helo and crew ready in about an hour, sir. We'd like to know, too." Now that he'd volunteered one of his helos, Fisher was surprised at himself. He had spoken on impulse and he wasn't sure suddenly why he had volunteered his detachment without his customary caveats. He had made a positive commitment and left himself no fallback if things didn't work out.

With a small flutter in his bowels, he realized that it would now be expected that he be the pilot of the helo. He swallowed hard. He disliked Boyle, knew Kruger and Wilson hardly at all, and the enlisted crewmembers were normally beneath his notice. He had no personal stake in this but it was too late to take his words back. He felt his brow beginning to moisten and heat begin to crawl up the back of his neck despite the air conditioning. He turned to Crawford, told him to have a helo readied for the mission, and, saying it quickly before he chickened out, added that he would be the pilot. He was glad to see that Crawford showed no surprise at that.

Cmdr. Faber turned to one of his squadron pilots and told him to get down to the ready room and have the operations officer get a flight of four ready with full RESCAP loads.

Forrest nodded his gray head at Faber and Fisher and gestured Thompson forward with his finger. He waited until the young SEAL was standing next to him.

"Okay, Kevin, who are you thinking about taking with you? You couldn't possibly be dumb enough to think the admiral would let you go it alone, could you?"

Thompson hadn't really considered taking anyone. He hadn't thought the whole idea through but now that Forrest had brought it up, the Lone Ranger bit was a tad foolish.

"Well, there's a couple of guys in the Marine Detachment who used to be in Force Recon. They'd be stupid enough to go. I have to go down there to get the gear anyway."

"Okay, Kevin. Get on down and get what you need. I still have to square this with the admiral so I guess 'stand by' will be the operative command for a little while."

As the young officer hustled out, Forrest turned to those remaining in the room. "Are there any objections to this?" There were none.

"Okay, get the planning done and get the people briefed. I doubt this will have a happy ending but I do think we ought to try."

Forrest looked at each man. Their silence showed that they agreed. On the other hand, the silence might show that they weren't enthusiastic but had no better plan to offer. He nodded and headed for the door.

* * *

Admiral Welch was standing by the chart table when Forrest walked into Flag Plot, the room below the flight deck just forward of the ship's CIC. Forrest joined him and gave him a full description of what had just transpired.

"Harry, what do you think? Should we do this?"

"Me? I don't know, I'm only a staff puke. But if I were the admiral, I'd be pissed if they hadn't suggested it."

"Did everyone agree?"

Forrest lit a cigarette before answering. "Nobody disagreed."

"That's a bullshit answer. What's on your mind?"

"I think they want to try this because they feel they should, not because it makes a whole lot of military sense. I think they realize that it is a mighty shaky limb to be out on." He chuckled. "Even Fisher volunteered to go and I wonder what Glover would say about that."

Welch was mildly surprised at that news. Fisher hadn't shown himself to be anything more than a caretaker, a careerist who wanted only to get his ticket punched and not screw up. One of the best ways for a man like that to screw up was to volunteer. Maybe there's hope for the sonofabitch after all, Welch thought.

"That's good, Fisher volunteering. Doesn't sound much like him, but then again why not, it's one of his crews that's down."

Forrest, looking at the chart, merely grunted.

"All right, Harry. What else is on your mind?"

"Well, Admiral, everybody knows that we've been directed not to try something like this but they want to go anyway. But they also know it won't be their political ass if it goes wrong and Glover comes down on you."

Welch nodded slowly. "Let me guess. They're giving me a chance to say no. That about right?"

"Yes, sir. That's the way I see it."

"Well, I appreciate their concern. I truly do. But every pilot needs to know that he won't be written off if and when he goes down. Send 'em in."

Forrest went to the phone and dialed. He spoke quickly and carefully to the planners at the other end. He hung up and walked back to Welch.

"Thanks, Admiral."

Welch stretched his back, trying to remove one of the ever more frequent kinks. "Harry, did you ask why Wilson chose to go out through North Vietnam instead of the required route? Did he give any indication that he thought his plane was badly hurt?"

"Nope. I didn't ask why and we'll never know what Wilson was thinking." He continued before Welch could follow up. "We know that he probably shouldn't have been there but I don't think that his route choice had any effect at all on what happened. We can be sure that it'll come up later if and when the trogs back at Pearl put down their coffee cups long enough to get curious. For now, I think we ought to ignore those questions and wait to see if anybody raises a flag. Besides, the guys from that squadron have just lost their C.O. and don't need any bullshit coming down on them for a while. It's rough enough doing their jobs without answering the fucking mail in triplicate."

Welch smiled at the disparaging tone in Forrest's voice when he mentioned the "trogs."

"Fair enough, Harry. But make sure all the squadrons reinforce the rules at the next briefings. Okay?"

Forrest nodded as Welch went on.

"And tell CAG to make sure this mission goes with absolutely no farting around in there. If they're all dead and can't be retrieved real easy, leave them. Okay?"

Forrest nodded. That made sense. It was cold but wise.

Welch continued. "One more thing. I am not happy at all about Thompson going out there."

"I figured that, Admiral. But Kevin is. If you'll excuse me, I have to get rid of some of this coffee I've been drinking. Happens more often now that I'm getting old." Forrest winked and walked away, leaving Welch wondering wryly just exactly who was in command of whom around here.

* * *

Thompson descended the ladder into the Marine Detachment spaces. He was a familiar face down here and was greeted gaily by the young marines after the obligatory "Attention-on-deck/Carry-on" exchange when the duty marine noticed that an officer had entered. The Marine detachment aboard a carrier provides security for special parts of the ship and an escort for the captain and whatever admiral is stationed aboard. As with many of the things that are done in the military, the marines were there partly because of a tradition dating back to the days of sailing ships when they would take up firing positions in the main tops to shoot down onto the decks of enemy vessels, picking off gunners and key figures. However, many a sailor has learned painfully not to get in their way when they are hurrying to one of the parts of the ship for which they are responsible and which has just had its security alarms go off. Nor is it a particularly wise move to attempt to intrude upon the captain or admiral without an invitation. The first refusal of the intrusion is polite, the second less so. The third firm and clear. There is never a fourth.

Thompson walked over to the duty desk and asked whether Gunnery Sergeant Gorton was around. The young private reached for the phone and passed the word that "that SEAL lieutenant is here to see you, Gunny."

Less than a minute later, Gorton was pouring a cup of coffee for Thompson and listening with an increasingly eager smile to the idea for going into North Vietnam. He had just the guy to be the third man on the mission. He called over to the desk and had the private send somebody to find Corporal Rivers.

While they waited, they began to sketch out what they needed in the line of personal equipment. Thompson knew that Gorton looked upon this as a brief parole from the tedium of his duties aboard ship.

Thompson reviewed what he knew about the Gunny. A very large farm boy from Wisconsin, he had been a marine for over five years. He had done a tour in South Vietnam in the Marines' Force Recon units. These were specially trained men, much like the SEALs or the Army's Green Berets. Like all who had survived a combat tour in-country with these units, Gorton was tough, smart, and completely devoid of the John Wayne fantasies that afflicted most others who had never been there.

Rivers arrived shortly and was introduced. He had been standing sentry for the captain and thus was wearing a real uniform as opposed to the fatigues that the rest of the marines were wearing. He appeared to be even bigger than Gorton's six-two. Thompson, at five feet nine inches, was not a small man but he felt dwarfed by the two marines, especially after his hand had nearly disappeared into Rivers's huge black paw when they shook hands. The ribbons on Rivers's chest showed that his actions, too, had been large during his tour in-country. There was a Silver Star at the top followed by two Bronze Stars and two Purple Hearts; that was just the top row. Thompson was impressed.

Gorton didn't seem to even consider that Rivers might not volunteer. Then again, thought Thompson, it never occurred to me that Gorton might refuse.

The three spent a few minutes going over the plan and then went aft to find the Marine detachment Officer in Charge. They felt that it might be a good idea to let him know that two of his senior noncoms were about to go off to war for a little while. Fortunately, Captain Forrest and CAG had both called down and informed him of what was going on and that Captain Andrews had agreed to it. Since the marines actually belonged to the ship's captain, he had been the last obstacle. The OIC authorized the weapons and equipment to be issued to the three, even going so far as to offer Thompson his own sidearm for the mission, and smilingly threatening the SEAL with immediate dismemberment if it were not returned unscratched.

An hour and fifteen minutes later, Fisher, sitting in the right seat of his helicopter, Angel 803, watched in his rearview mirror as Thompson and the two marines loaded their gear into the back of the helicopter. Angel 803 had been the standby aircraft for the morning and so needed minimum preparation. Fisher had watched as the four Corsairs flying RESCAP had been loaded with weapons and fuel and then been towed aft and positioned behind the catapults on the waist. He hadn't spent much time watching what went on on the flight deck between launches and recoveries and discovered that it really was like a massive dance, everything done in order and carefully but with scant attention paid to what was happening twenty feet away. It all seemed to come out right at the correct time. There should be a giant "Ta-daah" when it was all finished, he thought.

The briefing and preflight had all gone without a hitch except for Boyle's friend Santy, who had stood in the catwalk and watched every step of the flight-deck preparations carefully. He hadn't said a word throughout the entire evolution, standing as far out of the way as he could. Once, when their eyes met, it had seemed as if Santy had looked right through Fisher. There had been no sign of recognition in the dark eyes, just a sad interest in the goings on. Fisher had felt more than a little uncomfortable with Santy's expressionless scrutiny but did nothing about it.

There had been a small scene just before the briefing began when Santy had shown up in the room with all his flight gear and tried to bump one of the A-7 pilots from the mission. CAG Greenwood had stepped forward and gently placed his hand on the young pilot's shoulder, guiding him to the back of the room and speaking softly and earnestly. At the door, Fisher watched as Santy's shoulders slumped and he nodded sharply, once, as Greenwood spoke. Greenwood then gently eased him out the door, returned to the front of the room, and began the brief.

Now, standing there in the catwalk forward of the nose of the helo, Santy looked for all the world like a lost child at a fair.

Fisher's attention was drawn to the side of his aircraft below his open window by a couple of loud thumps. He looked down and saw the flight-deck officer holding up one finger at him signifying one minute to engine start. Fisher nodded and told his copilot, Lt. (J.G.) Randy Yates, to get out the checklist. When he looked back at the catwalk, Santy was gone.

Chapter 28

October 9, 1972

The first thing he became aware of was blinding pain in the side of his head. The next was a numbness in his left arm, and third was the distinct smell of the dirt and leaves into which his face was pressed. He tried to roll onto his back but something heavy was holding him down.

Maybe if I opened my eyes I could figure this out, he thought. When they wouldn't open on command, he ran his right hand across them and felt a gooey mass covering the upper part of his face. He ran his fingers around the side of his head and traced the origin of the goo to the spot where the pain was and then briefly wondered where his helmet was.

Boyle wiped as much of the stuff from his eyes as he could and tried again. This time they opened but everything was a blur; all he could make out was that there was some light out there. With his right hand, he felt around his waist until he contacted the buckle which held the harness together. He pulled the handle and felt the pressure on his waist ease and this time when he tried to roll over, the seat fell away and he made it all the way until he was looking up at a hazy green. He sat up and wiped his flight-suit sleeve across his eyes and tried again. Now there was more definition to things and he could make out that he was sitting in some kind of woods next to a large tree, facing downhill. His left arm, no longer pinned under the metal edge of the seat, rapidly began to tingle and burn as the circulation was restored. The sudden pain of it made him groan and the sound of his voice brought with it two more sensations: an irregular flat snapping sound like extremely loud popcorn and the smell of kerosene mixed with wood smoke.

A sudden coldness erupted on the back of his neck and rushed through his body as he remembered what had happened: Kruger's warning, the sound of the tree branches hitting the front and underside of the aircraft, the huge *"Whaaam"* as the helo hit the ground, the feeling of being thrown forward, and his helmet hitting the windshield. After that, there was nothing.

Boyle went back further. He recalled the trees flashing by just under the belly as they climbed toward the top of the ridge, the sudden change in the whine from the number-one engine over his head, the nose coming up abruptly and the immediate yaw as Kruger tried to do the impossible, and finally hitting the trees.

He got to his knees and then, slowly, to his feet, putting his hand on the tree to steady himself. When the world settled down, he tried the sleeve across his eyes again and discovered that he was getting his vision back. He wiggled the fingers of his left hand and raised his arm. It was painful as hell but everything seemed still connected and he didn't think anything was broken. He took a deep breath and collapsed to his knees, doubled over. He remembered this pain from once in college, when he had broken two ribs. Boyle again got to his feet and began to move slowly back up the shallow incline of the ridge toward the smoke. After several minutes, he made it into the small grassy clearing at the top and immediately saw what was left of Angel 801 on the far side of the clearing.

There were pieces large and small scattered around, even stuck up in the trees. There was a large blackened area in the grass surrounding the main wreckage where the fire had burned itself out. There was smoke coming from small spots both in and around the body of the helo where stubborn bits still smoldered; the popping sound had apparently been ammunition cooking off. The fuselage lay inverted, leaning slightly on its left side. The entire upper part, beginning with the deck, was crushed and buried in the softer soil. The smell of kerosene from the spilled and burned jet fuel was much stronger here and there was a sharp, nauseating smell that came and went on the soft breeze. The smell of burned flesh.

Boyle moved slowly toward the wreckage, forcing himself with each step to resist the strong desire to run away as far and as fast as he could. His foot kicked something hard and when he looked down, he saw part of Smith's survival pack. It was torn but there were still some things left inside. Boyle stepped over it and moved closer to the helo. The silence, aside from the crackling of little fires and Boyle's short breaths, was deafening. He completed a circuit around the wreck and spotted no signs of life. Just chunks of what used to be an expensive flying machine with five lives aboard.

Boyle went back to Smith's pack and picked it up. As he moved farther away, back toward the trees, he noticed Smith's CAR-15 protruding from a bush and painfully bent and picked that up too. He looked carefully at the rifle. Aside from several deep scratches and some bits of earth clinging to the muzzle, it seemed that it would still work. At least the barrel was straight.

Being careful not to leave any tracks, Boyle moved into the trees and back down to where his seat still lay. He was suddenly very thirsty but when he reached down he found that although that side, the left, of his survival vest was still intact, one of his baby bottles of water had ruptured, blowing the screw top off. He took out one of the two others and began to drink greedily, stopping abruptly when he realized that this was half of his remaining supply. It was half gone but he decided to drink the rest and save the other bottle for later.

Sitting on a fallen tree trunk Boyle looked idly at his seat. It was still attached to the rails which had run along the deck of the cockpit. The entire assembly had apparently torn loose on impact and thrown him clear. Boyle had heard of this happening before but only in the bar back in San Diego. It was known as the "Sikorsky Ejection Seat," the entire thing breaking loose and, with the pilot strapped to it, hurtling forward through the windshield. It was a failure which had saved his life, throwing him across the clearing and down the eastern slope.

The thoughts of his good fortune did nothing to shrink the terrible realization that four other men, all within twenty feet of him, had died suddenly and violently in an aircraft for which he was responsible. He had been entrusted with their lives and they were now dead. There comes with that knowledge an immediate numbness which protects the mind until time and perspective can help deal with it.

Many minutes later, that numbness, combined with the fear that he now felt at his aloneness, down in enemy country with no help at hand, got him off his tree and moving slowly and painfully downhill, away from the wreck and the enemy who was certain to come up here and investigate. He had to move far enough away to hide and take stock and plan something, anything which would keep him out of the hands of the North Vietnamese. Step one in the evasion book is to get the hell away from the wreck because Step one in the enemy's book is to go to it and start the search for the crew.

Boyle had been moving along, slowly and carefully at first, but increasingly quickly as the fear of what might lie ahead slowly gave way to the desire to escape what lay behind. He struck a small trail which seemed to lead downhill at an angle to the slope of the ridge and debated whether to follow it. The going would be easier but there was a greater chance that he might run into Vietnamese from the village toward the coast coming the other way, up to investigate the crash. He decided to follow the trail but off to one side where he would have a lesser chance of blundering into the enemy.

He had nearly reached the bottom of the slope and was stopping to rest just off the side of the trail when he heard something like a dull thud ahead on the trail. He dropped into a squatting position behind a bush and then eased himself down flat. The thud was followed by a laugh and the singsong of Vietnamese voices. He watched through the branches as three sets of legs moved past him on the trail headed uphill. Moving as little of himself as possible, Boyle watched the legs move away and eased himself around on his belly to keep the bushes between him and the Vietnamese. As they moved farther away, Boyle raised his head to see the enemy better.

They were climbing the slope easily, talking normally. None of them was wearing a uniform but each had a rifle slung over his shoulder. Boyle couldn't see well enough to tell how modern the weapons were but they were certainly not the famed AK-47s, so these men were likely not regulars but rather only local militia. On one hand they would not be anywhere near as disciplined as were regulars but on the other hand the locals would know their territory better than anyone else and would be able to track him easier and better than regulars.

Boyle waited a few minutes to make sure that there were no more enemy following the first and climbed to his feet. He remained motionless for a few more moments and then carefully moved forward to the edge of the trail. He waited as long as his patience would hold, trying to hear anything other than his own breathing. He stared across the trail, summoning his courage, then stood, and in three giant steps, crossed the trail and dove into the bush on the downhill side. He lay immobile, trying to become one with the ground, ignoring the pain from his ribs, every fiber of his being concentrated on listening for any human sounds.

When he was certain that the three Vietnamese were the only ones around, he moved on, much more carefully now, parallel to the trail. When he reached the bottom of the slope, he cast about and found a large clump of brush. He looked carefully for an entrance which could be covered easily and when he found it, he crawled in and lay back, trying to get his muscles and nerves under control.

Forty-five minutes after the three Vietnamese had passed by Boyle, Thompson dropped to the ground, followed immediately by the two marines. Behind him the helo stood at the opposite edge of the clearing from the wreckage while overhead the four Corsairs flew erratic patterns, close enough to provide nearly instantaneous cover but far enough away so as not to provide a point for enemy ground parties to aim for.

The flight had been completely without incident and had almost seemed anticlimactic after the preparation and briefings. No one had seen any ground fire nor had any concentrations of people or equipment been found. All that remained now was to check the area and get the hell out.

Fisher had forced himself to concentrate on the job at hand, flying the helo, and stuff his feelings into a locked corner of his mind. He had been aware of all the sensory inputs and had flown almost without thinking, just reacting to whatever came up. He had maintained a determined silence on the intercom, keeping speculation and extraneous chatter out of the situation. His copilot, Yates, was experienced enough that he didn't ask a lot of questions; he merely did his job and spoke only when required.

Fisher watched as Thompson and the marines moved rapidly but cautiously over to the wreckage and tried to peer inside. The fires were all out now and the three inspected as much as they could, lifting a part here and a lump there, occasionally teaming up to move a larger piece to look deeper into the blackened pile of aluminum and severed and charred wire bundles. Once they were satisfied that there was nothing more to be done there, they spread out, rifles at the ready, and moved around the periphery of the clearing seeking any indication of life. When they had covered the entire perimeter and met at the farthest point, the two marines looked at Thompson, who pointed to a track in a patch of clear earth near where the ground began to fall away downhill to the east. The clearing itself was covered mostly with grass except where the fire had burned it away around the wreckage.

Inspecting the area further, Thompson saw another partial track a few feet deeper into the brush. He felt a nudge on his arm and looked to see the corporal pointing to a broken branch on a bush about a foot off the ground. Thompson nodded and looked back downhill just in time to see a figure move from behind a tree and dash to a shrub about five feet away. The figure was not wearing a dark-green flight suit.

Thompson put his hand on the corporal's shoulder and shook his head at the corporal, who was raising his rifle to fire at the figure. He stood and led his two marines in a jog back toward the helo. As the three ran bent over under the spinning rotor blades, the lead A-7 overhead called Fisher.

"Angel 803, Condor 305. I just saw a couple of people in the trees about a hundred yards down the ridge from you. Looks like they might be headed your way. Are you about through down there?"

Fisher glanced over his shoulder at the first of the three piling in the cargo door. "We'll be ready in fifteen seconds. No luck, I'm afraid."

"Roger, understand. I'm not sure who those guys are but I can probably put some ordnance on 'em."

"Negative, 305. We're set. Give me a steer out of here to stay clear."

"Roger. Make it about 150 for a couple of miles and then left to 090."

"150. We're lifting now."

Fisher pulled up on the collective and, as the helo accelerated through fifty knots, banked to the right and headed down the east side of the ridge and toward the safety of the sea.

At the foot of the ridge, Boyle heard the sounds of the jets diminish to the south and threw down his signal mirror in frustration. When he'd first heard the helo approach, he pulled out his survival radio and found that it had been completely smashed by the same impact which cost him one-third of his water. He unzipped the other side of the vest and found that his spare radio was missing, fallen through a large hole torn in the fabric. All that was left was the frayed end of the green cord which had tied it to his vest.

He had been unable to attract attention from the jets as they flew overhead and he couldn't break cover and go dashing through the woods toward the sound of the helo because of the three Vietnamese who were now between him and the wreckage. The clouds from the approaching weather front mostly hid the sun and only a few shafts of bright sunlight had passed over him, so his opportunity to get the Corsairs' attention with the mirror had been limited at best.

It took him quite a while to get himself under control in his little leafy cave. He had had to force himself to get off his ass and start surviving. He had gotten to his knees and pulled off his survival vest. Housekeeping chores like taking inventory of his gear would force him to settle himself down further and try to think.

He took out the small packet of Charms candy and popped one in his mouth for the energy the sugar would give. There was nothing else he needed immediately, so he stuffed everything back in the pockets of the vest, unsnapped the bulky flotation bladders to save some weight and shoved them deep into the brush, and pulled toward him Smith's damaged pack. Inside, he found two sealed cans of emergency water, one part of a C-ration box with a couple of cans left in it, and two extra twenty-round magazines for the CAR-15 taped together.

He picked up the CAR-15 and cleaned off the dirt and grass which had stuck to it. He took his Browning from the holster and looked it over too. He pulled back the slide to chamber a round and checked that the safety was on. Once he had replaced it in the holster, he looked at the rest of his meager pile of gear. Not a whole lot of help to get himself out of this mess. He'd trade it all for one operable radio.

He unscrewed the top from the last full baby bottle, drank half of it slowly and then poured a little in his right hand and used it to wash some of the blood from his face. He tried to use the mirror to see how badly damaged his head was but couldn't tell much with all the coagulated blood. He decided to leave it alone for now rather than risk exposing it to infection by cleaning off the blood. He put the top back on the baby bottle and lay back on the ground. He'd rest a while and then try to think his way out of this mess. There is no sense making decisions when you are still all hyped up, he thought. He remembered what they had taught at survival school. Hole up and think first, then move.

The thinking part was a problem, though. Nowhere in all the schools or lectures or bull sessions had anyone mentioned how to deal with losing your crew. You expected all the emotions that come upon you when you are suddenly torn from the familiar womb of your cockpit and thrown into enemy territory. Yet even though you were aware of them and awaited their onset, you were never prepared for the sheer bigness of them. Nor were you ready for the roller coaster ride they took you on for the first few hours.

In his initial flight from the top of the ridge, Boyle had stuffed down the horror of seeing his helo smashed against the ground, pieces everywhere. It had been much easier then, only two hours ago, to allow the demands of movement to supersede the emotions. The near-meeting with the Vietnamese had drawn out the animal in him, forcing him to be concerned only with stealth and self-preservation. Now, with nothing but the sounds of the jungle to distract him, Boyle's thoughts kept returning to his aircraft and crew.

There was irony in the fact that Wilson had been saved only to be killed minutes later along with his saviors. No matter which way he turned it, the crash looked the same. On the conscious level, he knew that there was nothing he could have done—it had happened too fast. But the other, deeper, level, the one he could not control, told him that he had let his crew and Wilson down, that somehow he *should* have been able to prevent it. He had been entrusted with the aircraft and everything in it and had failed to bring it home. There is not logic enough in any man to overcome those thoughts, especially when he is alone in the woods with the enemy all around and no one to share them with but the accusing spirit within.

Slowly, almost grudgingly, the adrenaline which had been keeping him going for the past two hours left him. Despite his fear of capture, his body could no longer sustain him. He struggled to keep his eyes open for a minute or two and then he was asleep.

Fisher brought Angel 803 up the portside of the deck and eased it to the right to its spot on the angled deck. He and Yates went through the shutdown checklists and climbed out in relative silence, speaking only when necessary. As Fisher reached the flight deck, he told Yates to take care of the paperwork, then turned and followed Thompson below to the Intell Center.

Once inside, Fisher looked around and saw the same cast of characters as had been there before, except that Admiral Welch was sitting to one side being as obvious as possible in making sure everyone knew that he was only there to listen.

Before Fisher could take a seat, Captain Forrest walked over and stuck out his hand, looking Fisher straight in the eye. "Nice job, Andy. You and your crew really did well. Commander Faber and the other A-7 pilots spoke highly of you." He released Fisher's hand and grasped Thompson's. "You too, Kevin. That took some balls." Forrest turned and walked to the front of the room.

Once there, standing tall and regal in front of the wall chart, Forrest began the debrief. There was small chance that anything new would be brought out but it was always best to get everyone's perspective on a mission. If nothing else, much could sometimes be learned from an absence of new information.

"Okay, let's take it from the top. Commander Faber?"

Faber stood and walked to the front. "The area looked pretty undeveloped. There were a couple of gomers moving up the hill but I couldn't see them well enough to tell who or what they were. I didn't see any structures in the immediate area except for the small village to the east I mentioned earlier in the brief." He turned to the other three Corsair pilots. "How 'bout you guys?"

He was answered by three negative shakes of the head. "That's it, except I asked whether the helo wanted any ordnance laid down on the people in the trees. They said no which, looking back on it, was a good call since we don't know who it was in the trees, civilians or military. I also saw a flash of light down there but it wasn't steady or repetitive enough to be a signal," he said, pointing to the spot on the chart. "But I couldn't spot it again on the way out. The area was kind of in and out with the clouds building. There was also nothing on the radio." He sat down again.

Forrest looked at Fisher. "Andy?"

"I've nothing to add, sir. We got in and out with no problem. The Condors gave us great steers and cover. When we got to the area, we found the wreck all right, and Kevin and his marines took a good look around." Fisher took his seat and Thompson stood.

"We did spot those guys moving through the trees. I didn't see any weapons and they didn't fire at us. I think they were just locals out to see what all the noise and smoke were about. The clearing was covered in pretty thick grass but we had found a couple of partial footprints in the dirt at the edge of the clearing. I couldn't get a good enough look at them to tell when they were made or by whom. The ground wasn't soft enough to tell whose boot it was. There were only two tracks but the gomers were coming so we had to get out of there. As to the wreckage, I don't see how anyone could have survived. All the pieces, except for the rotor blades, were pretty much concentrated in the immediate vicinity of the helo, so it looked like the impact was pretty much vertical after it plowed through the trees. I couldn't see that any of the doors or hatches were big enough for a man to get through. What I mean is, everything was pretty much crushed. The fire had gotten to everything too. I don't think there is any chance of survivors." Thompson sat down, suddenly pale as he remembered the mess that had been a helicopter and five men only five hours before.

Forrest scratched his chin as he stared at the map. "Kevin, could those prints have come from a survivor?"

Thompson sighed. "It would be a miracle up there with the loaves and fishes, Captain. Like I said, the ground wasn't good enough to show a clear tread pattern so there's no way I could tell if it was an American boot."

The debriefing continued for a few more minutes and then broke with a final bit of praise from Forrest. As everyone stood and headed for the door, the admiral called softly for Fisher, who turned and walked back to where Welch, and now Forrest, sat.

"Sit down, Andy." When Fisher had done so, Welch began. "First of all, I'm truly sorry about your crew. I knew Boyle somewhat and I liked him. He was a good man. Second, I'd like to add my own 'well done' to Captain Forrest's. You've been here only a short while but you showed me a lot today by volunteering for the mission. You could have sent a more experienced crew but you chose to lead from the front. I like that. I would like to say, finally, that I underestimated you. For that, I apologize."

Fisher could only muster a weak "Yes, sir. Thank you."

Welch stood abruptly, followed hastily by Forrest and Fisher. He looked again at Fisher. "For now, your crew will be listed as Missing in Action. But when you write to their next of kin, please let me include something from me, personally." He nodded a dismissal at Fisher and watched him leave the room. When the door closed behind him, Welch walked to the front of the room and began looking idly at the chart. He spoke over his shoulder to Forrest.

"You know, Harry, those goddamn helo guys are amazing. They go into places and do things I wouldn't even think of. Did you know that the two most highly decorated squadrons in the whole Navy from this war are two helo squadrons? Our rescue squadron and that gunship outfit down south, HAL-3? That's incredible. And all they've got going for them, basically, is sheer courage. All they get from the jet jocks is a ration of shit and a superior attitude until their ass is in a sling and then they get to be believers real quick." He paused, turning to face Forrest.

"What do you think of Fisher now?"

Forrest scratched an ear. "I misjudged him too. I figured we were in for a bunch of trouble after that little show in the club in Hong Kong but he's beginning to act like a real naval aviator. Maybe being away from Glover's influence is helping him but God help us if Glover finds out it was Fisher who flew that one today."

Welch nodded and then grinned. "What can he do to us? Take away our birthdays and send us to Vietnam? Come on, let's get some coffee."

When Fisher returned to the ready room, Santy was sitting in the rear waiting for him. As he stepped through the door, Santy stood and called quietly, "Commander, excuse me. Do you have a minute?"

Fisher couldn't read the younger man's expression. The two hadn't spoken since that night in Hong Kong, so Fisher was a bit wary as Santy approached.

Santy looked at him for a long moment from red-rimmed eyes and then began to speak softly. "Mr. Fisher, um, thanks for trying to find Tim. I know you did everything you could and I appreciate it. And, um, well, I'm sorry I was so rough on you back in Hong Kong."

Before Fisher could speak, Santy turned and stepped out of the room, leaving Fisher staring at the closed door.

Fisher walked to the front of the room, pulling his mail from the little box on the wall as he passed. He sat wearily in his seat next to the duty desk and asked the duty officer to summon the detachment's yeoman from the Admin office. While he waited, he riffled through his mail, separating it into official and personal mail. The stack of personal mail was very small, two advertising catalogs from some outfitter in Maine and a letter from his father-in-law. That once again he had received nothing from his wife was no longer a surprise but that his father-in-law had written was. He stuffed the letter in his flight-suit pocket for later and began to open the official mail. He paid little attention to it, really, for his mind was on the letters he was going to have to write to the families of the four men he had lost today.

For Fisher, war had suddenly become bigger than his own personal part in it. He hadn't figured on just how shitty it could be.

Chapter 29

October 9, 1972

When the rain awoke Boyle by dripping through the brush into his face, he tried to sit up. The pain, seemingly from every part of his entire body, wiped away any last vestige of disorientation and brought him instantly back to where he was, sitting in the dark in a goddamn jungle. More slowly this time, Boyle pushed himself up until he was leaning his back against one of the thicker bushes. He glanced at the luminous hands on his watch and saw that it was just after eight in the evening; he had been sound asleep for about four hours. Between sleep and the sound of this rain, they could have driven an entire division of tanks past here and I wouldn't have heard a thing, he thought.

Boyle pulled out the baby bottles he had emptied earlier and held them under the streams of rainwater running off the leaves of the brush above him. When one was filled, he drank it greedily and watched it fill again. When he had finally taken care of his thirst, he used the water to clean as much of his face as he could in the darkness. He unzipped his flight suit, pulled his T-shirt over his head, and rinsed it as best he could.

Tearing off the lower couple of inches, he fashioned a head-band of sorts and wound it around his head to cover the cut he had received from the crash. He put the remaining upper half of the T-shirt back on to protect his shoulders from the rough Nomex fabric and then pulled the flight suit back on. He used his red-lensed flashlight to find a couple of foil-wrapped aspirin tablets among the items packed in his vest and swallowed them with water from his baby bottle.

Boyle waited for the aspirin to begin easing the throbbing pain in his head and his ribs and thought over the plan he had come up with. The options he had before him were grim at best. He could surrender; but the stories he had heard for months about what happened to helicopter crewmen who were unlucky enough to be captured were more frightening than was simply dying of starvation in the jungle. He was eight miles from the coast and at least fifty from the DMZ to the south. North and west led deeper into enemy territory. East to the coast it would be.

The eight miles he would have to cover would be as rough as any terrain he had ever seen. The ground would be marshy and the jungle thick. He hoped to be able to steal a boat when he got to the coast and get out into the gulf. He knew that just getting to the sea would be a miracle but at least he had a goal. He would worry about the boat when he got there. For now, it was time to get moving.

The three men he had seen earlier would have easily found the wreckage of his helo. He had no idea whether they would assume that everyone aboard had been killed, but if they searched the area at all they'd find his seat and probably assume that there was at least one survivor. The grass of the clearing would have hidden his footprints but he had to assume they'd found his seat. They were certain to inform their higher-ups that they'd found it and organize a search.

The rain would be on his side, washing away any tracks he would leave and making the enemy's progress that much slower; the faster he moved, the more the rain would help. The way it was coming down, his tracks would last only about a half hour. He figured that if the enemy went up the ridge on the path near his little cave they'd probably come down the same way. If they'd passed his hiding place while he slept, the search might already be under way.

Boyle remembered one of his survival instructors telling him to assume that the gomers would search for him as if he had raped Ho Chi Minh's mother. That way he would not be surprised.

Shielding the red light as best he could, he shone it on the small compass from his vest and found east. Gathering the rest of his gear, Boyle crawled out of his little hidey hole and headed carefully and painfully downhill, toward the east and the sea.

Fisher walked into his stateroom and dropped the pile of mail on his desk. He ran some cold water from the tap into the small white sink and splashed it on his face. As he reached for a towel, he considered his reflection in the small mirror. The face stared back calmly, appraisingly, with no trace of the pallor or widened eyes he had seen the last time he had had to fly into North Vietnam. Fisher held his left hand out, palm down and waited for any sign of trembling. There was none. With one more glance at his dripping face, he dried it and sat down in his desk chair.

He held out both hands again, still surprised at the lack of trembling. Fear had lurked close to the surface throughout the entire trip into North Vietnam and back out again but it was now only a memory, like a dentist's drill two hours after it was over. The first time he had returned from an overland mission, his fear had hung in his room for hours, a palpable being in the darkness, standing over him, jabbing at his insides, whispering its presence and its determination to retain its grip on his heart.

He knew it was still there but it was imprisoned somewhere within him, held back by . . . what? Was it courage? He didn't believe that he had suddenly come upon a trove of heroism. Will? No, he had had no spiritual confrontation with himself in the past six hours. A greater fear, maybe? Had he been more afraid of not going than he had of going? He didn't think so. His volunteering had been spontaneous, in response to an immediate situation, giving no thought to consequence either way. It had just been the thing to do.

Fisher shook his head. He was getting nowhere doing this to himself. Why couldn't he simply accept it as it was, mystery and all. All his life he had thought things through carefully before he acted, always with an eye to the next step and more recently with the prodding of his wife and father-in-law. This time, he had simply stepped forward, alone, and then gone on and done it.

He picked up his father-in-law's letter. As he ripped it open, he wondered wryly what the old bastard would think about what he'd done today. He'd probably suggest I see a shrink, he thought.

Fisher was not in the least surprised to find that this first communication since his arrival in the combat zone was written in a neat accountant's hand under an official letterhead. Christ, he can't even forget his position when he's writing to family, Fisher thought. After the obligatory news of the family, including a surprise bit about Fisher's wife devoting some of her time to charity work, Glover got to the heart of it:

As you may have heard, the negotiations in Paris have reached the point where it becomes apparent that the war will shortly be over. You are indeed fortunate that you will be able to make your mark before it ends with minimal risk to yourself. The Navy will in the future seek men who have proven themselves as combat leaders and you will have that achievement to which to point.

One of the most significant ways to demonstrate the ability to effectively lead is to ensure that your unit suffers no unnecessary losses, by avoiding scenarios where undue risk is apparent. You must be careful to see that your men do not act like cowboys, rushing about in a quixotic attempt to do the impossible. It may seem heartless to say, but most of the men who are lost over North Vietnam and survive will be repatriated shortly when the peace accords are finally signed.

I have cautioned your task-force commander about this very point. He has consistently demonstrated an inability to act in these situations without emotion. He has repeatedly risked additional assets and people in often hopeless and dangerous attempts to rescue downed aircrews. He is most clever and I have not as yet been able to prove a flagrant disregard for my directives but now that you are the Officer in Charge of his rescue assets, I know that you will provide me, in strictest confidence of course, with any information on his continued resistance to my policies.

To other matters: I have obtained for you an assignment to the Pentagon as an aide to a senior admiral in the Office of the Secretary of the Navy when your tour there ends. I will see to it that you are transferred as soon as hostilities cease so that you will be able to take advantage of your experience without waiting for your normal rotation date.

The rest of the letter was more of the same and ended with the usual and unemotional pleasantries. Fisher found himself becoming angry with Glover as he reread the significant passages. He suddenly resented the fact that Glover apparently couldn't conceive of Fisher's disagreeing in the slightest with what he wanted. The sonofabitch didn't even do me the courtesy of hinting at what he wants. In a sudden burst of anger, Fisher crumpled the letter and threw it across the room.

Unbidden, the scene in the Intell Center came to Fisher's mind. He had been praised by the other pilots for his performance and thanked personally by Welch for the mission, a mission which had been planned and executed with the admiral's concurrence, not by his direction. That concurrence seemed to Fisher to be more of an act of loyalty toward his men than a disregard for authority. As such it would not be an emotional decision but an act of true leadership and thus far removed from Glover's assessment of Welch's motives.

As Fisher stared at the ball of paper which had come to rest on the deck next to the far wall, it became startlingly clear to him both why he had volunteered to go today and why Glover was wrong about Welch: loyalty.

Fisher had been carried along by the same feeling of loyalty felt by the aviators at the meeting for those who had gone down in Angel 801. Welch pursued rescue missions simply because his men trusted in him to do whatever was necessary to get them out. Fisher had overcome his fear and flown into North Vietnam because others would have done the same for him if the positions were reversed.

All his life, Fisher had never truly been a part of anything: he had been in but never a part. Ever since he had come under Glover's sway, he had allowed himself to be carried along with Glover's plans for his daughter's happiness. Even as his son-in-law, Fisher was nothing more than something to be used.

Fisher walked over and retrieved the crumpled letter. Smoothing it out, he sat down at his desk, pulled out a piece of writing paper and a pen, and began to carefully compose a letter.

He had written it three times before he had said what he'd felt when he'd read Glover's letter. He wrote:

> I know that you wish only the best for your daughter and me, and that this opportunity in the Pentagon is a wonderful step in my career. I do not feel that I have learned as much here as I can. If I am to command someday, as opposed to being an Officer in Charge as I am now, it would be best to have as much actual experience in positions such as this as possible, as opposed to the appearance of experience, as it would be if I were to leave early. I appreciate your efforts on my behalf but I feel that I will learn more and grow much more as an officer if I remain here in HC-17.

Satisfied, he added a few pleasantries and innocuous bits of news about the war and signed and sealed the letter. He took it down to the Flag Admin Office and asked the duty yeoman if it could be sent out with the special courier mail to Pearl Harbor the next morning. Assured that it would be and thus would be in his father-in-law's hands within twenty-four hours, he went up to the wardroom and got a glass of "bug juice" before he returned to his room.

As he undressed for bed, Fisher felt strangely light and free, as if he knew all would soon be well.

Commander Greenwood sat at his desk in CAG office and wearily ran his eyes over the sheet of paper he had taken from his in-basket. He had tried for the past ten minutes to concentrate on his paperwork but it was not working. His mind's eye kept returning to the faces of the pilots in the debriefing after the rescue attempt. There was a sadness and disappointment in the room heavier than he had ever seen there before. Losing Wilson had been a blow from which he was not sure that VA-19 could recover, especially with the X.O., Commander Faber, at the helm. Greenwood doubted that Faber had the talent and drive to pull the squadron back together. He might be competent but that was about all he was. He was not even forceful enough for the rest of the squadron to get mad at. X.O.'s are supposed to make everybody mad and, by doing so, make the C.O. look good.

Faber was an excellent pilot but as a leader he was going to bear watching so that he didn't put the pilots in the position of becoming either too careless or too conservative.

Another problem was going to be young Lt. Santy. He was completely devastated by the loss of both Wilson and, to a far greater extent, the helo pilot, Boyle. Greenwood had sent the flight surgeon to Santy's stateroom with some medicinal bourbon and orders to get him to talk it out. The flight surgeon had reported back two hours later that Santy was now sound asleep and would be okay. The doc also recommended that Santy not be left off the schedule and that he be assigned to one of the first missions into North Vietnam tomorrow. Unfortunately, the weather front which had been approaching all day now covered the land far enough back to the west that the next mission would be at least thirty-six hours away.

The tinny sounds of the 1MC, the ship's PA system, broke

into his thoughts. It was the chaplain with the evening prayer. Greenwood glanced at the clock on the wall, surprised that he had been sitting in his office for nearly an hour and had yet to accomplish a damn thing. He came back in time to hear the closing of the prayer, ". . . with strong faith in Your divine justice and wisdom, O Lord, we place the fate of our five shipmates in your hands. Amen."

Amen, thought Greenwood as he switched off his desk lamp and left the office for his cabin.

Chapter 30

October 10–11, 1972

The rain that kept the aircraft chained to the decks of the carriers on Yankee Station all that night and all the next day also gave cover to Boyle as he made his way eastward. He had found an overgrown trail and followed it through the first night. It had run generally eastward down from the highlands. When daylight reluctantly worked its way through the rain and vegetation, Boyle had crawled into another thicket and tried to rest until darkness came again. He took out a corn-flake bar from Smith's pack and tried to eat some of it.

Boyle had had one of them before, in survival school, and was convinced that the only reason they had been created and packed in military rations was that they gave a man something to do. They tasted like corn flakes, which was remarkable in itself, but had been compressed under about forty tons of pressure until they had the hardness of diamonds. Boyle just sat there and gnawed at the corn-flake bar, repacking it and taking it out again between attempts at sleep.

When darkness again began to fall, Boyle made sure that

he left no sign of his presence, and crept back to the trail. He followed it again into the night until it came to an open area. The ground under his feet was now the consistency of syrup. The roar of the rain beating down on the jungle canopy had had a mesmerizing effect and the change in sound was what had first alerted him to the fact that he was no longer in the jungle. He stopped, puzzled for a moment or two by the difference.

Willing himself to remain calm, Boyle looked about in the deep blackness, turning his body this way and that until he realized that he had hopelessly lost his sense of direction. With no clue about which way was east and not daring to use his light to check his compass, he put out his arms ahead of him and moved forward in the last direction he'd faced when he stopped turning. His hands finally contacted some brush and he moved into it as far as he thought safe, sitting down next to a tree on the side which seemed to be the lee. He pulled the collar of his flight suit as far up as it would go and sat hunched, once again feeling the fear and loneliness which movement had masked for a while. He tried to see what time it was but the hands on his watch glowed only brightly enough to show that they were still there.

Sometime later, Boyle was startled to hear the sound of a truck engine quite close by. He must have slept deeply, for the dim lights of the truck were only about thirty feet away as it struggled down the road which was the open area he had walked into. The engine was laboring in a low gear and, as Boyle rolled onto his stomach to peer back at the road, he heard the gears clash as if a clutch had not been included in the system. The engine surged several times and settled into a higher-pitched roar as it crept past. The two dim beams of light from the shielded headlights waved crazily as the vehicle lurched through the deep ruts in the mud. The engine sound diminished as the truck passed but before Boyle could get his heart rate back within normal limits, he heard the sound of another truck approaching from the same direction as the first.

Boyle thought he remembered this road as a wavy brown line running roughly north-south on the chart as he and his crew had flown over on their way to get Wilson. At least, he only remembered one road on the chart between the coast and the higher elevation where Wilson had come down. If this was the same road, he was about four miles from the coast, almost halfway there. If he was anywhere within the area he hoped he was, there would be a good deal of cover for him to use all the way to the coast. The only village he could recall seeing on the way in was the one the three gomers who passed him on the ridge had probably come from. It was on the west side of the road so he was now at least past it. If so, whatever searchers there were should be behind him also. Boyle was able to take only a few seconds of comfort in these thoughts before he realized that they certainly had radios and telephones and had had plenty of time to alert the whole countryside. His morale took another dip when he remembered that he had no idea which side of the road he was on.

He laid his head on his arms and prayed with everything that was in him for one stroke of luck, that he had blundered to the east side of the road.

When Boyle awoke sometime later, it was almost totally quiet. The rain had ceased and there were no more sounds of engines. All he could hear was drops hitting the leaves as the trees shed the last of the rain. He decided to risk using his flashlight but thought better of it: he could wait for daylight. He fumbled around and found his corn-flake bar and had another try at eating it. The end had gotten wet so he had a quarter inch of easy going until he ran into more of the hard part.

Boyle had gotten through about an inch of the damn thing when he first noticed that he could almost see it. He waited until he could begin to make out a lightening in the darkness above through the leaves and held his wristwatch up toward the sky. It was just past 6:00 A.M. He took out his compass and placed it on the ground, scarcely breathing until the needle stopped wobbling and pointed north. He closed his eyes and nearly wept with relief: he was on the east side of the road and would not have to cross and risk leaving tracks of any sort in the mud.

He sat back against the tree and forced himself to breathe slowly and deeply until he had calmed himself sufficiently to think of his next move.

Boyle picked up the CAR-15 and looked it over carefully. He absently brushed off bits of leaves and flecks of mud from it. Opening the action, he put his eye to the muzzle, holding the open breech to the light. There was nothing obstructing the barrel so he closed the action slowly, chambering a round noiselessly. He flicked on the safety and placed the carbine aside, pulling his Browning 9mm pistol from the holster on his hip.

A good deal of mud had gotten into the weapon from his lying on the ground so he disassembled it quickly and wiped it clean, using the front of his T-shirt. He emptied the magazine, wiped off each round, and replaced them in the magazine and the magazine in the Browning. The terrain was flatter here so he could move faster but there was going to be a much greater chance of discovery now that the rain had ceased.

All things considered, Boyle thought as he collected his meager store of gear, I'm in a deep shit situation.

One hour after Boyle left his thicket by the side of the road, Mike Santy walked into the briefing room and took a seat among the other pilots from his squadron. He was assigned the second mission of the day, which was to be a road recce just inland from the coast of North Vietnam. The *Concord* and her air wing had the first twelve-hour series of missions, running from midnight to noon. The other carrier, the *Independence,* would pick up the load at noon and operate until midnight when *Concord* would take over again.

The past thirty-six hours had been awful for Santy. He had awakened yesterday with a low-grade hangover from the flight surgeon's ministrations and had been informed that he was the squadron duty officer for the day. Since the weather was lousy, there would be no escape in flying so he was forced to sit in the ready room and deal with all the bullshit problems which cropped up. The only bright spot was that the duty left him little time to brood about Boyle. He also had to sit through an AOM, or All Officers' Meeting, called by the X.O., now C.O., to set out the course Faber expected the squadron to take now that Wilson was gone.

The AOM had gone badly. Faber should have simply gotten them together and reviewed the status of the squadron, immersing everyone in a reaffirmation of routine, giving them the feeling that life would go on as before. Instead, he'd explained his planned reorganization to give them something new to think about and move them away from the past. What he had accomplished was to remove them from what was comfortable and stable, thus eroding psychological underpinnings, leaving them drifting without an anchor.

Santy listened to it all and realized that he couldn't care less at this point. He just wanted to get on with it and go home. He'd already lost his anchor. He didn't even care to read the latest letter from Barbara Gibson, the stew from Hong Kong.

Now, in the Intell Center, Santy was thinking of how drastically things had changed the three weeks since Hong Kong, when CAG strode to the front of the room and began the briefing.

Greenwood took a pointer from the ledge under the map board and jabbed it at the map of southern North Vietnam. "Okay. You all know that the gloves are back on. We still can't hit these people where it hurts because of the negotiations in Paree."

He raised his hand to try to hush the chorus of catcalls and groans from the pilots. They were still displeased at the latest changes from Washington. "Yeah. I don't like it either but we've still got a job to do. Anyway, we have no major targets assigned for today but we do have clearance for interdiction

missions—road recces—throughout this part of North Vietnam and over here in the Laotian panhandle. The first launch
was assigned to hit the Trail, in Laos, here, and your cycle
will do the road recce in North Vietnam. The sectors are on
the board. Be suspicious of anything you see on the roads.
You're cleared to take out anything of a military nature in
your sectors but do not spend a lot of time tooling around in
there. If there is nothing to hit, get the hell out and don't
fuck around trying to polish a turd. The gomers have been
deploying a lot of those SA-7 one-man SAMs lately and
they've been kicking the shit out of the low flyers down south
with them. So don't set yourselves up. Keep moving and watch
each other's ass. Remember, they leave a kind of a corkscrew
smoke trail when they're launched. Any questions?"

Greenwood looked around. He expected no questions and
when there were none, he continued.

"Okay. As you all know, we lost two aircraft and five men
a couple of days ago. While it may not have affected anything,
the lead Corsair was violating the rules by egressing across
the North instead of following the prescribed route out. You
are reminded that you are to follow the routes indicated with
no deviations unless absolutely necessary. Clear?" Greenwood looked at each face in the seats. "That's it. I believe
the weather guesser is next."

Santy looked at the square sector, ten miles on a side, he
was assigned. It was just to the south of the one which contained the area where Boyle had gone down. On an impulse,
he leaned forward and tapped the pilot who was assigned that
sector on the shoulder, quietly asking if they could switch.
The other pilot nodded; to him, one sector was exactly like
another.

Ninety minutes later, Santy and Mitchell crossed the coast
into the southern part of their sector and began searching for
any worthwhile targets. The heavy rains of the past two days
had not drained away yet and the land looked as if it had
been inlaid with thousands of mirrors, as the pools and pud-

dles reflected the bright sun and cloudless sky. Santy had briefed Mitchell to take the eastern part of the sector, leaving him to take the western area where the wreck of Boyle's helicopter was. No mention was made of the reasoning behind the selection and Mitchell let the decision pass, resolving to keep an eye on Santy to make sure he remained focused on their true purpose: to find and destroy anything of military value to the enemy and get the hell out.

Santy, jinking over the land, looked down as he crossed the north/south road which bisected the area and swept his eyes out ahead toward the ridge which began the gradual uplift of the land toward the Annamite mountains to the west. There were no towns or villages below except for an isolated one at the northern edge of the sector which had never been associated with any military activity. In fact, there was not even a real road leading to it, just a narrow track, leading from the main road, like the shortcut leading to the schoolyard in the small towns back home.

He banked his Corsair to the right when he came to the ridge and flew northward until he crossed over the blackened oval where Angel 801 had crashed. He banked around and descended, passing over the spot more slowly and much lower, rolling the plane to get a better look. The helo lay in the sunlight like a monument on the side of a long bypassed road. Aside from the one little village to the east, there was no other sign of humanity within miles and the jungle would soon hide all trace of what had happened there, as if it had never been. Santy was turning to the left to make another pass when he heard Mitchell's gentle voice on the radio.

"You know better than that, Mike," he said. "Let it go."

Not trusting himself to speak, Santy clicked his transmitter twice and shoved his throttle forward, climbing away from the ridge and back to the task at hand. He looked back one more time at the black scar on the land. I'm sorry, Timmy, he thought.

Mitchell watched Santy's Corsair begin its climb and returned his attention to the road below. There were many tire tracks in the still wet mud where it hadn't dried enough to assume a uniform color. He followed them to the south for a couple of miles to where they abruptly ended near a huge grove of trees. The road continued into the distance but the tracks did not. They looked like a fan as they turned into the trees on either side of the road.

Mitchell continued his course to the south so as not to let anyone down there know he had noticed anything. When he reached the southern part of the sector, he turned left toward the coast and called Santy.

"Condor 310, 303. I think we've got a truck park down here. There are lots of tracks that stop suddenly."

"303, roger. I'm about five north of you."

Mitchell glanced out and spotted Santy coming south down the road, moving up and down, left and right, as he jinked, but keeping the road in plain sight.

Santy passed over the spot and banked out to join Mitchell. He had taken a long look at the grove of trees as he passed. It was a couple of acres of trees taller than the rest of the lower forest which covered the entire landscape, all the way to the coast, four miles to the east. Unless one really looked carefully, it did not stand out much from the rest of the landscape, but once noticed, it was the largest land feature around. The rest of the area through which the road ran was not capable of hiding a large concentration of vehicles. Troops could be placed anywhere and hidden easily, but trucks were a different matter. If they had to be hidden, this was the place.

"82s first," Santy transmitted. He selected his Mk-82 "iron bombs," which would penetrate the tree canopy and detonate below, shooting out fragments in all directions and adding to the damage in the immediate area of the blast. Once they were all expended, the CBUs, which were less effective over jungle, could be dropped, sending their bomblets down through the new holes in the canopy and scattering more destruction throughout the grove.

"Lead's in." Keeping the grove to the left of his nose, Santy accelerated, bouncing in his seat as the A-7 slammed through the rising thermal air currents over the land. When he was close enough to the grove, he hauled back on the stick and shoved it to the left, simultaneously popping the jet up and lining it up on the target. Now, in a relatively steep dive, he centered the target in his HUD and hit the bomb release. Once they were gone, he banked hard to the right, transmitting, "Lead's off."

As he continued away, turning slightly to see where he had hit the grove, he saw the white spheres of his bombs' twin shock waves rush out from the grove through the humid air.

"Two's in." Mitchell followed a different course toward the target but the result was more spectacular. There were two huge secondary explosions in the grove followed by a massive ball of black smoke with a red-orange center. Mitchell had hit something containing a large store of fuel. Santy lined up on the grove again from the opposite direction but as he dove toward it he saw a flash and a trail of grayish smoke erupt from the edge of the trees on the west side of the road.

"Snake, they've fired a Grail at you! Break left!" Somebody below had fired an SA-7 shoulder-fired heat-seeking SAM at Mitchell. The Grail, as it was known, gave off no electronic signal as did the radar-guided SA-2s which had been making life miserable for American fliers for years over North Vietnam. The Grail had only recently made its appearance in the war and was rapidly changing the balance. Aside from its complete lack of a telltale electronic signal, its second great advantage was its portability. It could be transported and fired from anywhere a man could walk. Unless you saw it fired and picked up the corkscrew smoke trail, you were screwed. Fortunately for Mitchell, Santy had seen it launched. Unfortunately for Santy, there was no one watching his tail.

At the edge of the grove stood a thirty-eight year old Vietnamese army lieutenant named Nguyen Tho Dinh. He had not always been an old lieutenant. Once, he had been a promising young major leading a reinforced company of NVA infantry against the ancient capital city of Hue in South Vietnam during the legendary Tet Offensive in early 1968. His company had fought eagerly and well at first, but food and ammunition had quickly run low and the weight of the American forces had begun to push them inexorably back. Against his orders, the survivors of the company had fought their way out of the morass that was the battle of Hue. Harried from the air by the American and South Vietnamese fighters and bombers, they had retreated slowly westward toward the relative safety of the highlands. When he had shot one of his noncoms for cowardice in an attempt to stop the retreat, he had been shot and wounded by his troops and left unconscious by the trail. He'd later followed his troops along the trail until he finally caught up with them, now a field of napalm-blackened and bomb-shredded corpses at the edge of the forest. His subsequent people's trial had given him the benefit of the doubt, reduced him in rank, and graciously allowed him to continue serving by shepherding convoys of men and matériel to the forces posted in the Demilitarized Zone between the two Vietnams.

Dinh had watched the two American jets fly down the road and believed that they had not noticed the grove where he had hidden his ten-truck convoy. Santy's first two bombs had blown him nearly naked but mostly undamaged into a thicket just to the outside of the grove. He struggled free of the branches and staggered back into the trees. His men lay about: some still, some writhing on the ground, a few firing their weapons straight up in an effort to strike back at the Americans who had turned their daytime rest stop into a small corner of hell. Dinh picked up a Grail missile launcher from the dead hand of a designated missileer and inspected it as another of his men stepped into the road and calmly fired an SA-7 at Mitchell's retreating Corsair. Stepping into the road himself, heedless of the screams of the wounded around him, Dinh rested the missile launcher on his shoulder and waited for the other jet which was sure to return to kill more of his men and destroy what was left of his small command.

Mitchell heard Santy's warning and instantly broke down and to the left, waiting for a few beats before he reversed the turn the other way, pulling hard and grunting against the

G-forces. The missile followed his first move but was too close to make the corrections to follow the second. It wavered off across Mitchell's turn and, with no more heat to chase, sailed away toward the mountains.

Santy saw Mitchell expertly evade the missile. Santy had continued his run but shallowed out his dive as he watched the missile miss. When he turned his attention back to the target, he saw that he had overshot his drop point and turned up and to the right to get set for another run. In so doing, he momentarily flew directly away from Dinh, who fired his Grail at the black hole of Santy's tailpipe. The missile sensed the heat and flew perfectly, correcting itself slightly to compensate for the climbing turn.

Dinh watched, holding his breath, as the tiny missile went directly into the A-7's tailpipe and detonated, leaving a large ball of black smoke in the sky to mark the point. The jet flew on eastward, out of sight behind the trees, before it began to come apart. When it hit the ground, the dull explosion was huge, followed by a silence broken only by the crackling flames and the screams of the wounded in the truck park. In his exultation, Dinh heard only the silence.

Santy heard and felt the explosion inside the aircraft behind him. For a few moments, it seemed as if he still had control of the Corsair and would be able to fly it out. All at the same time, warning lights came on, seemingly all over the panel, and the stricken jet pitched up with no response at all to the full forward stick that Santy instantly put in. He felt the complete deadness in the stick and reached down and pulled the lower ejection handle, blasting himself clear of the aircraft just before it lazily rolled to the right and dove almost straight into the ground.

Santy felt the pulling and tugging as the ejection sequence took place and then a huge jerk on his body as the parachute opened. He completed a full swing under it before he became fully aware of what was happening and when he looked down, he saw that he was descending into some short trees. He crossed his legs to prevent straddling a limb and felt himself crash through the thin upper limbs, then a blow and a blinding pain in his right shoulder. His feet caught on a branch momentarily then slipped free but before they could swing down below him again, he hit the ground flat on his back and everything went suddenly black.

Chapter 31

October 11, 1972

Before the sound could travel the two miles eastward from the grove to where Boyle was struggling through the elephant grass, the detonations of the Mk-82 bombs shook the ground under his feet. He had heard the jets fly over and frantically tried to signal them with his mirror but the pilots' attention was concentrated on their target and they didn't notice his one tiny flash of light among the reflections of the pools and puddles. One flew directly over him relatively low and fast on the run-in for its attack so close he could hear the characteristic roar-silence-roar of a jet's high-speed passage. He had watched the A-7 pop up and roll into its dive but lost it behind the trees before he could see the bombs come off. The jet came back into view as it pulled up, climbing and banking with white vapor trails streaming from the wing tips. The ground shook when the bombs detonated and he squinted to see the second Corsair begin its dive.

Boyle figured that whoever was on the receiving end would be busy for a while, as would any other enemy troops in the area, so he increased his pace as much as the sharp edges of the grass would allow. Only with difficulty did he turn his back on the attack and head east. He had gotten almost to the far edge of an open area and was about to move into the concealment of another treeline when he glanced back once more. He could see a huge ball of smoke climbing above the treeline behind him. Much closer, an A-7, streaming flames from everything aft of the wings, suddenly pitched up and rolled just as a dark thing erupted from the cockpit trailed by a brief flash of fire. The aircraft continued rolling and the nose fell through until it went behind the trees, inverted, almost straight down.

Boyle turned his attention to the pilot whose parachute finally filled only a hundred or so feet above the ground. As the pilot swung below it, Boyle lost sight of him but watched the parachute come down and suddenly deflate as the pilot hit the ground. Boyle knew that there would soon be enemy troops combing the area for the pilot and had a momentary desire to run in the other direction. But running away had never been Tim Boyle's style.

He took off in a shambling half-run, bent forward slightly as the increased effort and deeper breathing sent knives into his chest from his injured ribs. Alternately cursing and grunting, he struggled through the elephant grass and into the low trees where the pilot had come down. Through a break in the scrub, he saw the white of the parachute hung up in the branches of one tree and headed straight for it. He tripped once over an exposed tree root and landed hard on his side. The impact and the pain from his ribs stunned him for a moment but he staggered to his feet and retrieved his rifle and the torn pack. He moved on more carefully until he came upon the pilot lying unmoving, flat on his back, with the shroudlines still connected to the parachute above.

Boyle knelt at the pilot's side and glanced at the helmet which, with the dark visor down and the oxygen mask still in place, completely obscured his face. He unfastened the Koch fittings which attached the parachute to his torso harness and then turned the helmeted head toward him. As he reached to unsnap the fasteners which held the mask in place, he froze.

347

Across the visor cover, bisected by the blue knob which lowered and raised the visor, was the pilot's name: "Sandman." Boyle began to tremble and his hands fumbled with the unfamiliar fittings until he had the mask off and the visor up. Now that he was free of the suffocating mask, Santy's chest heaved, ending the longest two seconds of Boyle's life.

Boyle forced himself to check Santy's body for injury before trying to arouse him. He quickly ran his hands over Santy's limbs and found nothing broken but when he moved Mike's right arm, Santy groaned and his eyelids fluttered. Boyle ran his hands more gently over the arm and finally up to the shoulder. There was a strange lump in the front of it just like the other dislocations Boyle had seen on his teammates back at Boston College. He felt around further and found nothing broken so he released the seat pan containing the majority of Santy's survival equipment and put it aside. He was getting to his feet to try to pull down the parachute which now was like a signpost pointing to them when he heard Santy speak.

"You asshole."

Boyle whirled and looked down at his friend with suddenly brimming eyes. "Me asshole! I'm not the one flat on his ass in the mud." He knelt. "How do you feel? I mean, aside from your shoulder. I think it's dislocated, Mike."

"Yeah, it feels like it. It comes out easy. I did it a couple of times in football. If you put your foot on the joint and jerk my arm up, it will probably go back in." He tried to move but fell back. "Damn, that hurts."

Boyle moved closer to his arm. "You mean now?"

"Yeah. Just press down with your foot some and yank the arm."

Boyle stood and put his foot on the shoulder, grabbing Mike's wrist. "Okay. One . . . two . . ."

"No. Christ, don't count. That only makes it worse. Just do it quick and don't be gentle about it, either."

Taking a breath and gritting his teeth, Boyle jerked up sharply. He heard a sickening pop and felt the lump under his foot move as the shoulder went back in. Santy cried out and rolled away, grabbing the shoulder with his free hand.

Boyle felt his stomach turn over but controlled it with deep breaths. He left Santy panting on the ground and returned to the parachute, tugging it to get it down. It was draped over the top of the tree and try as he might he could not pull it free. There was no way that either he or Santy would be able to climb up and get it, so their only chance was to get the hell out of there before the gomers came searching for the American they had just shot down. He went back and knelt by Santy.

"Okay, Mike. I can't do anything about your chute. We'll have to get away from it. The only direction we can go is to the east, toward the water. Do you think you can move?"

Santy sat up, holding his arm. "Yeah. If we can make a sling or something, that'll help. I . . ." He suddenly stared at his friend and started to tremble.

"They said you were dead, Timmy. I didn't know what to do. I couldn't even write Meg. I tried not to believe it. I . . ." Santy stopped and let his head hang on his heaving chest.

Boyle put his hand on Santy's good shoulder. "It's okay, Mike. I got thrown clear and except for a couple of busted ribs, I'm fine. Now stop this crap so we can get home." He chuckled softly. "Wait'll you see the letter I write Meg about you, you dumbass."

Boyle stood and cut away several shroudlines from the parachute. He knelt again and fashioned a crude sling for Santy's arm, supporting the wrist and sticking the hand inside Mike's flight suit.

"That ought to hold you awhile. Here, take these. I'm fresh out of morphine so aspirin will have to do." He handed Santy two pills and one of his baby bottles of water.

"Thanks. Well, what's the plan?"

"I don't know but there's a bunch of bad guys around here, especially the ones you just shot up. I think that there might also be some after me from the village near the crash. We can use your raft when we get to the water." Boyle reached over and pulled Santy's seat pan closer.

As he turned back to Santy, he ducked involuntarily as

Mitchell's Corsair flashed overhead. Santy was struggling to get his survival radio out of his vest. Boyle knelt and removed it from the vest, handing it to Santy, knowing that it would be his voice the wingman expected to hear, not some stray helo driver.

Mitchell had not seen Santy get hit or go down. As he completed his evasive maneuver, he swung back and picked out the grove again. Suddenly, he saw the fireball erupt from the trees a couple of miles east of the grove. He lined up and dropped two more bombs onto the target as he passed by and headed straight for the spot where the A-7 had crashed.

He switched his radio to the guard channel, expecting to hear the wailing tone of Santy's emergency beeper from his seat pan but there was only silence. That could mean that Santy hadn't gotten out or that it had not worked properly. He hoped it was a failure as he headed east for the water, climbing as he did and keying his transmitter.

"Mayday! Mayday! Aircraft down. This is Condor 303. Condor 310 is down on, um . . ." He consulted his TACAN and gave the position.

"Roger, 303. This is Red Crown. Ident."

Mitchell pushed the switch on his IFF radio, which sent an electronic flash to the radar screen on board Red Crown, identifying his little blip among all the others.

"Roger, 303. Radar contact. Did the pilot get out?"

"I don't know. I have no beeper and I didn't see him eject. I'm going to go look. Stand by."

"Negative, 303. I'll have the two A-7s from the next sector down come up to help. Don't go back in solo. Contact me on 326.3."

Mitchell switched and called Red Crown, who acknowledged immediately, telling him that the other two aircraft, both from Mitchell's squadron, were due in about three minutes. When they arrived, Mitchell warned them about the possibility of SA-7s, made sure that they had him in sight, and headed in to fly over the crash site. Since he was pretty sure that Santy had been downed by an SA-7, he was keyed to watch for another as he headed toward the smoke pillar in the trees. A flash of white against the green terrain scared him for a second until he saw that it was immobile. He banked into a wide circle and flew directly over it from another direction.

"Red Crown, 303. I've got what looks like a parachute hung up in the trees. I didn't see the pilot but at least he got out." He was about to make another pass when Santy's voice came up on the guard channel.

"Condor 303, 310. How do you hear, over?"

Mitchell switched to guard and answered. "310. I have you weak but clear. Say your posit."

"Roger, we're down under the parachute. Is there a helo inbound yet?"

"Negative, 310. We weren't sure you made it. Say your condition."

"I'm pretty beat up. I dislocated my shoulder and my back is killing me. I haven't tried to walk yet. Be advised, there are two of us here. The other is a helo type who went down a couple of days ago. Name's Boyle, that's Bravo-Oscar-Yankee-Lima-Echo. He's hurt too, but he can move."

"Roger. Understand Boyle is with you." Mitchell was amazed. Boyle crashes miles away and he turns up here. From what I heard, I can't see how anybody got out of that helo, he thought. No shit, he's hurt.

"Red Crown, 303. There are two survivors on the ground. The second is Boyle Bravo-Oscar-Yankee-Lima-Echo, from the Angel that went down two days ago."

"303, Red Crown. Understand two survivors. We have Angel 804 and RESCAPs inbound, ETA 30 minutes for the RESCAPs and 55 for the helo."

Mitchell glanced at his fuel gauge. He could easily stay until the RESCAPs relieved him. "Red Crown, 303 copies. Break. 310, 303. The helo is about an hour out. Can you move to the east? I'm worried about bad guys coming from that truck park."

"How close are we to it?"

"About two miles. You're gonna have to get away from

that parachute. Head east and we'll try the penetrator when the helo gets here."

On the ground, Santy looked at Boyle, who nodded. Santy put the radio back near his mouth, pressing the transmit button. "Roger that, Snake. We're moving east now."

Lieutenant Dinh dropped the empty launcher and dove for the ground when he heard the approach of Mitchell's airplane. The bombs went long and exploded beyond the grove and Dinh watched Mitchell head away in the same direction that the one he had hit with the missile had gone. Jumping to his feet, he screamed for his sergeant. One of his younger soldiers ran up to him and saluted, informing him that the sergeant was dead, as were most of the other senior soldiers.

Dinh composed himself and told the soldier to gather as many men with their weapons as he could and to report back to him. He walked carefully through the grove, shielding his face from the heat of the fires that had been his truck convoy only twenty minutes ago. There was a rage in him unlike any he had ever felt before, far deeper than that he felt when his company had given up years before. When his foot contacted something on the ground, he looked down and saw he had kicked a still-smoldering corpse, lying on its back with its hands charred into claws reaching for the sky as if pleading for the mercy which the American flyers never showed. Dinh begged the God he didn't believe in to spare the American pilot from death in the plane he had just shot down. He wanted to hunt the butcher down and kill him slowly. If he were already dead, Dinh would send his corpse to Hanoi anyway.

The soldier ran up leading a group of fourteen survivors of the fifty-three men Dinh had had only a little while ago. The fourteen were all armed and mostly unwounded. Several other men moved about the grove ministering to the wounded as best they could. Dinh was tempted to include them in his small search force but knew that the others would balk at leaving the seriously wounded unattended.

They were young, poorly trained, and still shocked by what

had happened to their pleasant morning's rest. Dinh addressed them in a voice as cold as the grave. "Are these all the weapons we have left? No more of the small missiles?" A few of the soldiers shook their heads. Whether they really knew or were just answering to give an answer, really did not matter. Speed was now the most important thing.

Dinh accepted the answer. "It is not important. We will search and we will find the creature who did this to us. We must hurry if we are to capture him before the Americans can send a machine to steal him from us. When we find him, do not kill him. If you must use your weapons, aim to hit his legs, so that he will live and be able to provide information to the men in Hanoi. Our survival is unimportant compared to his capture." Dinh nodded to one of the older men, a corporal, who seemed to be the most composed. "You are now sergeant. The airplane came down in that direction. Lead us in the search."

The sergeant led off and, after a few paces, he began an easy double-time jog. The others looked at each other doubtfully for a moment but when they saw the expression on their officer's face they wasted no more time in heading off to follow.

Aboard the *Concord,* the rotor blades began to turn on the alert helicopter. Since today's missions were not concentrated on a specific target and would go on throughout the day, the helicopter had not been kept airborne but aboard the carrier in an Alert 15 status, which meant that it had been turned and checked out earlier in the morning and then shut down and parked out of the way back behind the island. The crew had been allowed to spend their four hours on alert in the ready room until they were relieved by the next alert crew, who would spend their four hours of boredom reading or catching up on their paperwork. The only hard-and-fast requirement was that they had to be airborne within fifteen minutes of the launch order.

When the launch order did come in, Lt. Cmdr. Fisher was dozing in a seat in the back of the ready room. He and his crew had assumed the alert about thirty minutes earlier from Crawford's crew, who had had the most boring period of all, the 4:00 to 8:00 A.M. shift. Fisher had been up late the night before talking to his chief petty officers about how to keep the five remaining helicopters of the detachment meeting their commitments now that 801 had been lost. The change to more time on alert and less airborne had been recommended and accepted the day before and last night's discussion had been concerned with fine-tuning the maintenance effort.

Now, as the rotor blades reached the proper speed and Fisher switched the number-one engine into the flight position, he saw that it had been twelve minutes since the order had come down and he was only about thirty seconds away from being ready. He was beginning to enjoy the professional performance of his men, and beating the allotted time was a quiet pleasure, especially since it appeared he'd be ready before the RESCAP A-7s who had been on the same Alert 15 status.

As the huge bow of the carrier began to swing into the wind, a sailor ran up from the ready room and shoved several sheets of paper through the window to him and then ran back to the catwalk. Fisher looked at the top sheet, which listed the position of the downed pilot and the frequencies and call signs he would need if he was to get the guy out. He wrote the information down on his kneeboard and handed the top sheet to his copilot, Yates. When he looked at the second sheet, he stared and read it again then pounded his hand on his knee. Yates caught the gesture out of the corner of his eye and looked to see what was wrong. Fisher, grinning like a three-year-old with a new puppy, wordlessly handed him the second sheet. The words were written hastily in grease pencil, "There are *two* for rescue. The second one is *Boyle!!* He's okay!"

Yates grinned like an idiot too and called the crewmen forward and handed them the paper. Even without the intercom, the pilots could hear their exclamations. Fisher took a breath and keyed his intercom switch. "Okay, guys. Let's stay cool and not get carried away. We still have to get him out. Get strapped in. We're about ready to go."

Two minutes later, after they had taken off, Fisher figured that he could probably be excused if he allowed the airspeed to exceed the red line just a little as he headed Angel 804 for the coast.

CAG Greenwood stepped into Flag Bridge and approached the admiral's chair. Welch dropped the clipboard full of messages that he was forcing himself to pay attention to. "Fill me in, CAG."

"Well, sir. There are no habitations within miles of the guys down but there was a truck park about two miles away. Santy and Mitchell hit it pretty hard and we have to assume that the gomers know that they got one of the jets and will take out after him. Santy and Boyle are moving east toward the beach but it's slow going because they're pretty well beat up. It's all low scrubby forest and the ground is marshy from the rains. The helo can't be there for another thirty-five minutes so it's going to be tight."

Welch nodded and stood. He began to pace, thinking about what lay in store for the two young pilots if they were caught by men who had just been bombed. He felt a shudder run through him and turned to Greenwood. "Do we know exactly where they are?"

"No, Admiral. We had a good mark on where Santy came down but nobody can see down into the weeds well enough to keep track of their progress. All we can do is get estimates of their progress from them on their survival radio. We don't want to keep marking their position because that might tip off the enemy and make his job easier. The other bit of bad news is that we can't spot anybody chasing them, either. We're going to have to be real lucky, because if the gomers do catch up to our boys, we won't be able to do much about it. All we can do is wait until the helo gets there and hope we get to 'em first. But, as I said, the big problem is knowing where they are."

"All right, CAG. I want you to do whatever it takes. Don't

waste time consulting anybody up here. Just do what you think best but get them the hell out of there." Welch realized that he was again violating both the spirit and letter of the directive he had received from Glover two months ago. "Keep somebody near the phone so I can get updates but don't waste time answering questions yourself. Go."

As Greenwood hustled out, the *Concord*'s captain, Sam Andrews, who had been standing to one side, approached with a cup of coffee. He looked at Welch with a small grin on his face, wordlessly acknowledging the limb the admiral had placed himself on. Again.

Welch recognized the look in his old friend's eyes. "I will not allow one of my men to spend one second in the hands of those bastards if there is anything I can do to prevent it. They risk their lives every day. My taking a chance on pissing off Pearl somehow doesn't seem like that big a deal."

Santy and Boyle were pushing through the low forest as quickly as they could, which was about the pace of a fast walk. They had covered a little more than five hundred yards toward the beach and the pain they were both experiencing had driven them to the point where they wanted only to sink to the ground and curl up in a ball. Each knew full well that if he gave up, the other would stop also and thus be captured too by the enemy who was certainly behind them somewhere. So each did his best to ignore his pain and keep moving.

Boyle had cut the strap from the pack he had salvaged and used it to make a sling for Santy's seat pan. Boyle was regretting his decision to throw away his own flotation gear back on the ridge because now the only way he would be able to get out into the water was to use the one-man raft contained in the seat pan. In a pinch it would keep the two of them up for a while. He had slung it and the CAR-15 over his left shoulder and was using his right arm to support Santy. Boyle had gotten rid of as much extra gear as he could, keeping only the water and weapons. Santy's .38 revolver had kept falling out of his shoulder holster, so Boyle had stuffed it into his own survival vest on the left side.

The two managed another five hundred yards until Boyle tripped over a clump of grass and fell, taking Santy down with him. Both cried out with the added pain the impact caused. When they had gotten themselves under control again, they lay gasping on the ground.

Santy struggled to a sitting position. He watched Boyle do the same. "Got any idea where we are, Hiawatha?"

Boyle shook his head.

"Okay, then. Let's see how Snake and the helo're doing." Santy pulled out his radio.

"303, 310. How's it going up there?"

Mitchell answered immediately. "Just ducky, Mike. How are you? Can you give me your posit?"

"We've about had it and I'm not exactly sure where we are. I think we've moved about a half mile or so. We're gonna try to stay here until the helo arrives."

"303, roger."

Boyle looked up through the trees. "How about we shoot up a pencil flare so the Snake can tell us where we are? At least we'll have some idea when this shit is gonna end."

Boyle reached into his vest and pulled out his pencil flares. He fumbled around but couldn't find his launcher. "Shit. I lost the damn launcher. Gimme yours."

When Santy couldn't get it because of his immobile arm, Boyle crawled over and pulled it out of the vest. "Okay, call your boy up there and tell him to keep an eye out."

Santy keyed his radio. "Condor 303, 310. We're gonna shoot a flare so you can tell us where we are. Call when ready."

Mitchell had been orbiting over the water so as not to draw any more attention to the two on the ground. The RESCAPs were just checking in with Red Crown and ought to be there in a couple of minutes. It would be better if they could see the flare, too, so as to eliminate any possible confusion on the turnover.

"Mike, can you hold off for a couple of minutes so the RESCAPs can mark it?"

Santy saw Boyle nod. "That's affirm. Give us the word."

He put down the radio. "As soon as they mark our position, we can find somewhere to hide. You ready?"

Boyle dragged himself to his feet. "Hell, no, I'm not ready." He walked over to Santy and helped him up. "Do you remember back in Pensacola when we bitched about running the two miles and they told us it was for when we were down in enemy territory and had to get away from the bad guys?"

"Yeah, and you wanted to know if we could hide from the instructors instead of running."

"Well, if I ever see that sonofabitch instructor again, I'm gonna give him an hour to draw a crowd and then I'm gonna kiss his ass."

Santy laughed but cut it short when it sent a dagger through his shoulder. "I get the other cheek."

Boyle grinned and then looked at his friend seriously. "What do you think, Mike? Are we going to make it?"

"I don't know. But I'm glad in a way it's the two of us." Both men were silent for a few moments, looking deep into the other's eyes. Santy broke the silence. "We'll make it. I just hope it doesn't come down to a gunfight. You know what a lousy shot I am."

Mitchell's tinny voice on the radio fortunately broke the mood. "310, 303. The RESCAPs are aboard. 311 is the lead. Shoot your flare on my call. About thirty seconds."

"310, roger, thirty seconds."

Santy watched as Boyle moved about looking for a suitable hole up through the trees. He soon found one and stood poised, looking back at Santy, waiting for the signal.

"Okay, Mike. Fire away." Mitchell stared at the green carpet ahead, straining to see the tiny red streak climb from the ground. After what seemed like a week, he saw it dead on his nose. "All right, Mike. I have your flare. It looks like you're about a mile or a little more from the beach. Go due east."

As Santy acknowledged, Mitchell flew directly over the spot and onward for a couple of seconds. He was just about to turn out again when he saw a yellow flash on the ground among the trees and heard two thumps under his seat.

He yelled into his radio. "Mike! There's a ground party about five hundred yards west of you! They just shot at me. Get moving now! I'm going to put some rounds on them. 311, do you copy?"

Chapter 32

October 11, 1972

Lieutenant Dinh struck the man in the ribs with the butt of his AK-47. The young soldier had fired at the American aircraft and, unless they had been most fortunate, had given them away. He began to shout to his men to move forward, for he knew that the American would be back quickly to blast the area with bombs and bullets. Years before, he had been amazed at how wasteful the Americans were in dropping explosives on anything that even looked like it might be a target. Now he knew that that profligate attitude would cause him ruin in his quest to capture the Americans.

Earlier, he had easily found the wreckage of the aircraft and had immediately sent his men out in a circular pattern to find any trace of the pilot. If he were still in the smoking hole left by the crash, there would be no trace of him but if he'd successfully ejected, he would be found. Dinh didn't really care if his men simply found the American's trail or stumbled onto him and were shot for their trouble. Either way, Dinh would have his prize. He had more men than the American could kill with his silly little revolver.

A shout from his new sergeant had brought Dinh and the rest running to the spot where the parachute still was entangled in the tree. The men fanned out in another circle, more carefully this time, and began looking for any tracks that would indicate which way the pilot went. There was no danger that the tracks his own men's rubber sandals were making in the soft earth would be mistaken for the heavy bootprints of the American, but Dinh himself wore boots, so he stood near the center of the area and waited for what seemed an eternity.

The sergeant hurried up to him and led him to some softer ground where there were two sets of bootprints leading eastward toward the sea. Dinh had thought that the aircraft he had hit contained only one man but he put that question out of his mind. Two captured or killed Americans would only raise his status that much higher in the eyes of his superiors. He called his men in and had them move out in a rapid but careful pace on either side of the trail so as to miss nothing in the pursuit.

Now, a little more than thirty minutes later, he could feel the nearness of his quarry. He could have surprised them, making the capture that much easier, but the young idiot who fired his weapon at the aircraft had probably ruined that for him. No matter, he thought, I'll have them by nightfall.

He had gone about seventy-five yards, hurrying his tiring men, when the first bombs detonated above the trees behind him.

The other two Corsairs which had hurried up from the south to help Mitchell provide cover for Santy had expended everything but their cannon rounds in their original sector and so were simply escorting Mitchell. Mitchell still had his CBUs so he told the RESCAP leader, Commander Faber, that, before he left to return to the ship, he could make a couple of runs over the spot where he had seen the flash from the ground fire. Faber suggested that he not do it for fear of hitting the two pilots but Mitchell persisted, telling him that he could deliver the bombs so as not to hazard Santy and Boyle. He rolled in twice, dropping his weapons in pairs from a lower altitude than normal so that they detonated just about fifty feet or so from the tops of the trees and concentrated their bomblets in the immediate area.

That momentary discussion about whether to drop them at all gave Lieutenant Dinh just enough time to get his men away from the deadly hail of shrapnel. The trees absorbed most of the flying metal and the men were unharmed but terrified as the specter of the earlier horror in the truck park rose before them. It took Dinh fully ten minutes after the sound of the jet had diminished into sporadic background noise to rally his shaken men and get them moving forward again. The eagerness which they had shown, despite their labored movements through the forest, was now gone, replaced by a resignation which was only one small push from collapse.

Dinh cared not at all. Now that he was close, his eyes shone with a light that had not been there for the almost five long years of his spiritual coma. He picked up a small tree limb and began to strike his men on their backs, urging them along toward his salvation.

Santy and Boyle had moved out and picked up the pace as best they could when Mitchell called out his warning about the men behind them. The ripping blasts of Mitchell's bombs sounded loudly flat in the jungle behind them, speeding them on their way. They had found a small game trail which made the going a little easier with fewer entangling branches. Still, the effort was wearing them down quickly. Each breath seemed to sear their lungs; with each step, their legs felt more wooden; each tree and branch took longer and longer to pass. When one stumbled, the other would tug and pull him to his feet and hold on until the next fall which was only thirty feet away. The radio in Santy's vest squawked repeatedly with calls from the aircraft above but they ignored it, hardly even hearing as they came closer and closer to the end of their strength.

Both men moved with their heads down as if they feared to look up and find that the forest was truly infinite. Boyle, only a few feet ahead on the game trail, was tempted to throw away what little he still carried in order to lighten the load but a mental image of the clean and impartial sea ahead somewhere with the two of them floating free and safe in the little raft helped him fight the temptation. Santy, groaning with the pain from his shoulder, kept his eyes on the middle of Boyle's back as if he could block out all else by concentrating on the undulating fabric.

Without warning, the trail broke sharply right then left. In his daze, Boyle missed the turn and plowed into the brush, his inertia carrying him several feet into it. He turned his head to avoid the branches hitting his face and eyes. His forward motion had almost stopped when he felt himself abruptly free and falling headlong. He tumbled down the side of a high, steep, ridgelike slope of sand which separated the forest from the beach and lay gasping unaware for a few seconds where he was. He heard a curse and a thump next to him and looked over to see Santy lying there with blood streaming down from one eyebrow where a branch had gashed him. They would never be able to tell accurately how long they lay there staring at each other, neither daring to look up and see where they were, both certain that there was not enough left in them to face more running.

Santy blinked as the blood entered his eye, and rolling over to get at it with the sleeve of his good arm, saw the small waves washing the shore fifty yards away. He rolled to a sitting position and simply pointed. Boyle pushed himself up and looked.

The beach stretched off into the distance on either side, completely empty as far as he could see. Above, there was the sound of jet engines and on the horizon was a dark spot which was moving lazily parallel to the shore.

Santy pulled out his radio but had to wait for a few moments until he had his breathing somewhat under control before he could talk. Then he couldn't remember what the proper call sign for the RESCAP was. Screw it, he thought.

"RESCAP Lead, this is 310. We've made it to the beach.

No idea how close behind us the gomers are. Is the helo handy?"

Commander Faber, in Condor 311, had been wondering whether to call off the operation when he heard Santy's weak call on the frequency. He had been trying for the past forty minutes to raise the two on the ground but had heard only silence. He figured that if they were about to be caught they would have come up and said something so the silence had been comforting and disquieting at the same time. The helo had checked in about ten minutes ago and was now flying a long orbit off the coast, out of small-arms range, waiting like all the other aircraft, for something, anything, that would get things moving.

Earlier, after Mitchell had tried to hit the pursuing Vietnamese, Faber had been about to bring his RESCAPs in to hit the area but held off when Mitchell told him that it would probably be a waste of ammunition, like shooting at sounds in the dark. After Mitchell and the other two original aircraft had departed, Faber and his flight had been reduced to impotently standing by.

Startled by Santy's sudden call, it took Faber a couple of seconds to realize that it was in fact a voice and not a wish that he had heard. "310, Condor 311. I have you weak but clear. Say your posit, over."

Santy had no idea where he was in relation to anything except the Gulf of Tonkin, fifty yards away. He looked around for a reference and followed Boyle's pointing finger to the spot on the horizon. It was moving left to right.

"311, 310. If you have a helo orbiting out there, we are at his four o'clock on the beach at the edge of the weeds." He paused. "You can't miss us. We're the ones lying in a heap." He looked at Boyle who was grinning weakly.

Faber swung his Corsair around and located the helicopter. Using that as a reference, he followed a line from the right rear of the helo to the beach. Fixing the spot in his mind, he banked and began a descent. "Roger, 310. I'm making a pass south to north. Condors stay high."

Santy stared down the beach, waiting for the first sight of the approaching A-7. He didn't see it until it was about a half-mile away. He knelt and began waving his arm over his head, turning his body to follow as the jet streaked by and pulled up and right.

"Okay, 310. I saw you. Break. Angel 804, come right to about 325 and head inbound."

"804, roger."

Fisher hauled the helo around to the inbound course and accelerated as Yates went over the gauges one more time and pressed the intercom switch. "Gauges're good. Power's up. Gear coming down." He pushed the landing-gear handle down and waited for the two little wheels to show in the indicator window.

"Gear's down and locked. I have a visual."

Fisher glanced outside and down behind at the wheel on his side, which was now extended. "I have a visual. Here we go. Heads up, everybody." All he had to do now was think and fly. Everything else was Yates's job.

Lieutenant Dinh kept up his steady pace, ignoring the three of his soldiers who fell out of the column from the exertion. He still had a dozen effectives who, although they were slowing noticeably, were keeping up a distance-eating jog. Dinh was surprised at how loud the jet engine was as it crossed their path somewhere up ahead. The forest diffused the sound so he couldn't be sure of the distance but he knew that the Americans couldn't be more than a hundred meters or so ahead. He slowed his pace and moved ahead in a fast walk, crouched over, his AK-47 loosely aimed to the front. Next to him, his sergeant shouted for the others to spread out into a sort of a skirmish line. Dinh backhanded him across the face, dropping him to his knees.

"Quiet, you fool. They are near."

He turned his back on the sergeant, missing the look of feral hatred that flickered across the man's face.

Boyle heard the sergeant's voice and spun around. He crawled quickly back up to the top of the slope, pointing his

CAR-15 into the brush. The pain of lying on his damaged ribs shot through him briefly but the fear of capture when he was so close to rescue gripped him tighter, driving away all other concerns. Santy dropped next to him and stared into the brush, keying his radio.

"311, we've got bad guys real close here! They're back in the brush. No idea how many."

Faber, already headed down for another pass, followed by the others in his flight, armed his bombs. "Are they too close for me to drop on?"

"That's affirm."

Boyle drew the strap of the seat pan over his head and handed it to Santy. "Get down to the water and inflate the raft. If we can get off the beach, your guys can pound 'em."

"No chance. You come too! I'm not leaving you here."

"I can shoot. You can't. All I'm going to do is keep their heads down. Now go, goddammit!"

Santy rolled down and began to hurry to the water, hunched over and trying to keep below the level of the top of the slope. Boyle turned back to the brush and began to crawl under it. When he could see back down the little game trail, he stopped, extended the wire stock of the rifle and flicked off the safety, trying to control his pounding heart and rapid breathing as he peered into the poorer light of the forest. Within a minute, he saw his first movement and brought his rifle up, wincing at the pain the stretched aiming position caused. He waited until he could make out most of the shape of a man, aimed at the center of it and squeezed the trigger. The rifle bucked and Boyle began to spray the area with single shots. When the magazine was empty, he pulled it out and turned it over, inserting the one taped to the first. When that was empty, he pulled it out and reached into the pouch in his vest for the other two, finding only Santy's .38 revolver. No way am I going to shoot it out with that or my Browning either, he thought, and crawled backward through the brush to the sand.

He got to his feet and began to run toward the water. Santy was standing thigh deep in the small waves, fumbling with the seat pan. Beyond him was the squarish shape of the helicopter heading in. Boyle saw the raft begin to inflate as he reached the wet sand at the water's edge. Something heavy struck him in the lower left side and spun him around to land flat on his back in the shallow water.

Dinh had been creeping down the trail as quickly as he dared. He saw the bend to the right and stepped to the side to peer around it. Boyle's first round went past him and struck the next man in the chest, knocking him flat, unmoving. Dinh dove to his left into the brush and hugged the ground as Boyle's rounds flew throughout the small area. Rifle fire was a surprise to him. He had expected the Americans to have only pistols. He waited until the fusillade ended and began to crawl at an oblique angle, trying to flank what he believed was a single firing position, but carefully in case the two enemy had separated for mutual defense.

He didn't look behind to see whether his men followed, it was *his* enemy up there. He would find them and take them. Or kill them if necessary. When the rifle began firing again, Dinh had moved far enough to the side so that no rounds came near. He crawled faster.

Behind Dinh, the sergeant waved to the three men he could see to move ahead and began to crawl forward and to the left himself. He did not notice that the men remained flat, hiding from the gunfire. Several looked at the body stretched out in the middle of the trail and decided that they wouldn't be the next man to go down.

Dinh reached the sand just as Boyle crawled out of the brush thirty yards to his right and began running for the water. He aimed his AK-47 and pulled the trigger. Nothing happened until, raging at himself, he released the safety. Dinh pulled the trigger again, firing a short burst and was pleased to see that the American went down. He aimed at the other American, who was reaching to help the one he had shot.

He flinched as the roar of a jet passed over him and his burst went wide. One American was now kneeling, supporting the wounded one. There was no need to shoot him now. Dinh knew he could make a capture and the Americans could do nothing to prevent it. He looked up and saw another jet coming at him and buried his face in the sand. If he survived this attack, he could do it.

The jet's cannon shells tore through the trees behind him and then it was past, banking and climbing for another run. Dinh stood and began to sprint across the sand, knowing that each step moved him closer both to his goal and to safety. He tripped once but rolled over and stumbled the last few feet until he was standing over the Americans with his rifle pointed between them. He had won.

Faber had made his first pass just to make noise and keep the enemy's heads down. As he flew down the beach as low as he dared, he saw one American standing in the water and the other just beginning to run from the brush toward the waves. He called the next Corsair, his wingman, Fujimoto. "Two, put some twenty on the treeline now!"

Behind Faber, Fujimoto squeezed his trigger, sending a long stream of twenty-millimeter rounds into the brush. The third A-7 followed, adding his fire to the area but, as he flew over, he saw a figure run out onto the beach and stumble, get up again, and run to the two figures in the water. He couldn't adjust his aim to hit the man in time, so he pulled off, transmitting as he banked over the scene. "Lead, somebody just got to our guys. Take a look, four."

The fourth RESCAP followed, no longer concerned with shooting up the forest. He banked over the top and saw that the third man was holding a weapon on the other two. "You're right. They've got them." He was looking down at every pilot's worst nightmare: capture by the North Vietnamese.

Faber was furious with himself. He felt that he was responsible somehow for this. In a rage, he banked and dove, flying at the trio in the water. Powerless, really, but flying at them because that was all he had left to do. Behind him, Fujimoto followed with no idea what Faber was doing.

Santy had the raft just beginning to inflate when he looked up to see Boyle spin and fall into the water. He let the raft go and reached for Boyle, holding his head out of the waves, wondering dumbly at the pink stain spreading through the white foam of the small waves. As he knelt at Boyle's side, he looked up to see the rifle and the wild eyes of a Vietnamese soldier. He was only dimly aware of what that meant as he looked back at Boyle's unconscious face, lolling in his arms. Momentarily forgetting the pain, he reached around Tim's back with his right arm, supporting him as the fourth Corsair flashed overhead. As the jet flew on, powerless, he watched the Vietnamese look up and laugh.

The gook gestured with his rifle for Santy to drag himself and Boyle toward the sand. As he shifted the inert form of his friend, Santy's left hand brushed against the open pocket of Boyle's vest and the butt of the .38. He kept his hand there and staggered a little, falling back down into the water. The rifle pointed directly at his face as the gook gestured again, more impatiently this time. Santy groaned as his right arm took on more of Boyle's dead weight. The groan brought a widening of the maniacal grin on the Vietnamese's face.

Without warning, all other sound was blotted out by the roar of Faber's Corsair passing only feet overhead. Dinh whirled reflexively and swung his weapon around to face the noise. Santy, hoping with all his being that it would work, pulled out the .38, aimed it at the Vietnamese soldier's head, and pulled the trigger.

Dinh realized that the jet was only making noise and turned back to the Americans. His eyes were just beginning to widen in surprise when Santy's bullet smashed into his face.

Chapter 33

October 11, 1972

Fujimoto, following Faber, although much slower and slightly higher, saw it as if in slow motion. He saw one of the Americans point at the Vietnamese and then the man's arms fly up as his body arched backward and fell into the surf. As Fujimoto passed overhead, he saw Santy—it was clearly he—dragging the other toward deeper water.

"Lead, they're free. Looks like one of 'em shot the gook. Get the helo in here!"

The other Corsairs began putting as much fire down on the treeline as they could, as quickly as they could, each rolling and checking the progress of the men in the water as he passed.

Out in Angel 804, Fisher had slammed his fist onto his kneeboard, knocking the cards and papers loose, when he had heard that the two had been captured. He had been less than a quarter mile from the two in the surf when he had had to turn away. Knowing that his emotions were making his flying dangerous, he gave the controls to Yates and told him to take up a low orbit in case something happened. He was cursing his bruised hand and everything else that came to mind, when Fujimoto's excited voice came over the radio. Fisher grabbed the controls back and bent the helo around, bringing his rotor blades dangerously close to the water through the turn, transmitting, "Angel's heading in," as he did so.

Ahead, only a couple of hundred yards now, he could see the smoke and flying debris as the RESCAPs did their best to destroy everything near the beach. "Okay, crew. We'll probably have to land in the water. Get ready to go in after these guys. It sounds like they're hurting."

Fisher raised the nose, allowing the helo to balloon up a little, gaining a better view of the surface of the water. He spotted the pair struggling in the water slightly to his right just as a series of splashes erupted immediately to seaward of them. Fisher adjusted his flight path and skidded into a low hover between Santy and Boyle and the shoreline. He lowered the collective and put the belly of the helicopter in the water just as several rounds came through the windshield. Fisher felt something hit him hard under his left arm and let out a grunt, but there was no pain.

Yates, in the other seat, heard the grunt as the shock wave from one of the Corsairs' bombs detonating deep in the churned earth of the forest shook the helo. He looked over and asked if Fisher was all right.

"Yeah. I'm all right. Just back me up on the controls."

Up the beach, the sergeant threw down his empty AK-47 and dove for a small depression in the sand next to a tree. Behind him another piece of the forest disintegrated from one of the American bombs. The sergeant had just done his best on behalf of the revolution by expending the last of his ammunition on the helicopter. Now it was time for him to do his best for himself and try to survive.

The sergeant had reached the edge of the sand in time to see the lieutenant rush forward and capture the Americans. The picture of the three in the surf was like a painting, none moving for a few seconds until the airplane flew past, shattering the image and making him jam his face down again. The sergeant picked his head up and saw the lieutenant's head explode and watched him collapse as the Americans moved toward deeper water. He felt no regret at all at the death of the maniacal little officer.

The sergeant began firing at the Americans and watched his bullets splash into the water well beyond. To get his bullets closer he would have had to raise himself but that would surely attract the attention of the jets above, so he blazed away knowing full well that he was accomplishing nothing.

The helicopter gave him a target he could hit without exposing himself, so he waited until it had slowed to a hover and fired his last magazine. He wasn't certain if he had hit it but at least he had fought to the last bullet. Now, curling up in the sand beside the tree, he would let fate take its course without any more help from him.

Yates looked over his shoulder into the rear of the helicopter as first one and then the other of the pilots was pulled in. When the second one was in, he slapped Fisher on the shoulder and yelled, "They're in. Go!" Turning his attention to the instruments, he felt the helicopter lift free of the water and ease forward. The nose was swinging erratically left and right but the instruments showed nothing wrong. He glanced at Fisher in alarm.

Fisher's chin was almost on his chest and he was struggling to see forward as his head slowly lowered. He was deathly pale.

Yates grabbed the controls from him and Fisher let his hands drop. Yates watched him try to turn toward him but Fisher's head fell to his breast and stayed there, rolling with the motion of the helo. Yates called for one of the crew to get up there and then keyed the radio.

"311, we've got them both aboard. Don't know their condition yet. My pilot is wounded too. He's unconscious. Get me a steer to mother and have 'em get the medics ready."

The first crewman came forward and lifted Fisher's head,

putting two fingers on the artery in his neck. After a few moments, he gently lowered the head and, looking into Yates's eyes, shook his head slowly. He placed both of Fisher's hands in his lap, made sure that his shoulder harness was tight enough to hold him off the controls, and walked back aft. When he plugged his helmet back into the crew intercom station, he called Yates. "Pilot, After Station. Mr. Fisher's dead, sir. Both of the survivors back here are alive but one has a bullet wound in his back. I don't know how bad, sir, but his pulse and respiration are strong. The other one has a bad shoulder but that's about all. Do you want us to move Mr. Fisher out of his seat?"

Yates looked at Fisher. For the first time, he noticed the pool of blood under his seat. The grunt must have been when he was hit. Yates looked at the gauges and around the cockpit. "No. It's all right up here. Just take care of the two you have. We should be on deck in about forty minutes."

The chief aboard Red Crown watched the slashes on his radar scope fly their slightly oval orbit as they escorted Angel 804 back toward their carrier. He couldn't see the helo because it was well below his radar horizon, but it was there nevertheless, chugging along at its ridiculously slow top speed. A few minutes ago they had all passed out of his area of responsibility and been cleared to switch frequencies. After they switched, the chief changed his own radio to follow, reluctant to let it go. He had been more of a spectator today than a participant but he had found himself standing at his scope rather than sitting as he listened to the rescue.

This had been his last watch in Vietnam. His relief had taken over and the chief would catch a helo flight to Danang early tomorrow and then he'd be home, sitting in his house, helping his kids with their homework and doing all of the other things that a husband and father should. For him, the war would soon be far away, at the other end of the TV camera, but it would always be there right next to him, too.

He knew he'd probably never meet the men in the airplanes

he was looking at on his scope, even though he knew them all from their voices and call signs. He knew their strengths and weaknesses, their fears and their humor, their sadness and their elation. They knew him, too. They knew that they could depend on him to give them everything in his power and a few things that weren't supposed to be. They respected him as a sort of associate member of their fraternity.

Packed away below in his trunk were several brass plaques, sent over from different squadrons in gratitude for helping a pilot in trouble. The chief had exactly the right spot in his home picked out to hang them. It would be many years before he told anyone what those plaques meant to him and then only in a soft tone with a faraway look in his eyes.

Shaking his head, the chief brought himself back to the present. He took off his headset and began to place it on the hook next to the console. He changed his mind and shoved it into the pocket of his jacket. With a smile, he turned and walked through the light curtain behind the seat.

Boyle came awake slowly as if swimming up through molasses. He saw something shiny and silver before his eyes and tried to focus on it but the effort was too much and he allowed himself to drift back into the fog. He saw tiny bits of startlingly clear scenes mixed with almost shapeless impressions that were just blots of movement behind a veil. He tried to concentrate on the clear ones as they passed him but they stayed just out of his reach. After a time which could have been minutes or hours, two pictures began to repeat themselves over and over among the jumble of the others.

The first was from the cockpit of his helo as the nose came up and the sun reflected from something large before him. After the flash of light came a series of sounds, a curse, and then blackness. The other picture was of a beach. He was running toward the waves, his breathing loud in his ears mixing with the sounds of his boots hitting the sand and the hollow rushing hiss of the breaking waves. He could see Mike bent over the green seat pan as he fumbled to get the top open.

He could feel his shin dig into the first wave just as something heavy struck him in the lower back. As blackness came again, he could see the sea and sky whirl crazily before his eyes.

He had nearly given up trying to freeze one of these frames when he heard a low voice unrelated to the sounds in his mind. He moved his head toward the voice and focused all his attention on it. It was answered by another voice in the same low tones and suddenly both became familiar. He opened his eyes and saw a blurred figure with its back to him bent over another lying in a bed next to his.

The voices became progressively more intelligible until he was sure that one belonged to Mike Santy, though he couldn't put a face or a name on the other. He tried to speak but found that his voice wouldn't work. He tried swallowing but there was no moisture in his mouth at all. After three tries, he managed a grunt.

The blurred figure turned and looked down.

"Well, welcome back to the land of the living. How do you feel?"

Boyle tried manfully to say, "Like shit," but all that came out was another grunt.

The figure, which was beginning to look a lot like Bob Watkins, picked up a cup with a straw sticking out of the top and placed the straw between Boyle's lips. Boyle sucked in some water and swallowed. It tasted so good he continued until the cup was empty. When Watkins removed the straw, Boyle's voice almost sounded human.

"I feel terrible. Where are we?"

"Aboard *Concord*. You're in Ward I in sick bay and it's a little after 2300. You've been out of surgery for about two hours and you're going to be fine."

"Surgery? What happened?" Boyle now became aware of a dull throbbing pain in his left side.

"It seems you got yourself shot in the back running on a beach. That's very bad for the image, by the way."

The memory of the beach scene he had been replaying in his mind came back and with it all the others of the past three days fell into place, including the other one about the crash.

Beyond Watkins, Santy sat up in his bed and filled him in with the rest of the details of the rescue, skipping over the part about shooting the Vietnamese.

"Okay, but what are you doing here, Bob?"

Watkins had been hoping to avoid this part for a while. "Tim, Andy Fisher was killed rescuing you and Mike. Crawford is the next in line and I came back to be the number two."

Boyle looked across the room. He saw absently that the silver thing he'd been trying to focus on was a bedpan. "What happened to him?"

"He got hit on the approach to you and kept at it until you were aboard. Yates took it and flew out of there but Fisher was already gone. The docs say that they're surprised he held on as long as he did. They'll know more later but it really doesn't matter much."

"Damn." It came out sounding not quite like a curse.

Santy spoke up. "I thought he was a dick too, Tim, until he went in looking for you and your crew. I guess we misjudged him."

Watkins shook his head. "No. You didn't misjudge him. What happened was he changed after he got here. I think he found out that he was just like everybody else. No better and no worse. He had a job to do and he did it as well as he could have. Not everybody makes it through something like this. Just be glad you did and remember the ones who didn't."

Neither Boyle nor Santy had anything to say to that and Watkins made his excuses and left the ward, promising to drop in before the two were flown to the hospital in Danang the next day.

After he was gone, Santy refilled Boyle's water cup and handed it to him.

"You had me pretty worried for a while, Tim, but the doc says that the bullet didn't hit anything vital, just tore up some muscle and flab. You're lucky, says he."

"Flab? What flab?"

"He actually said 'fatty tissue' but I think 'flab' sounds

376

better. At least it will when I tell Meg all about this little episode, especially since I'll be home before you."

"What do you mean?"

"We're both going home, but you get to spend a couple of weeks in a hospital over here before you get home. I, on the other hand, will be in San Diego and back among the ladies in a week. I can't wait to tell everybody how I got to save the rescue pilot. I'll be famous."

"Mike, what happened on the beach?"

"Tell you what. I'm kinda tired. I'll tell you all about it in the morning."

Santy lay back on his bed and turned out the light. "G'night, Boiler. Thanks for getting me out of the weeds."

Boyle smiled at his friend's profile. "Good night, Mike. I believe we're even."

At seven o'clock the next morning, Admiral Welch was resting his chin on his folded arms and was looking out the window in Flag Bridge. He was watching the flight-deck crew tow an H-3 helicopter out onto the angled deck. In a little while, it would take off for Danang carrying three passengers. Two would be Tim Boyle and Mike Santy. The other passenger, Andy Fisher, would be in a coffin draped with an American flag. Another pilot who was going home.

Welch turned as Master Chief Hayes circumspectly cleared his throat to get the admiral's attention. Hayes stood holding a folder in one hand and a coffee cup in the other.

"Which do you want first, Admiral?"

"The coffee, of course." He accepted it and sat in his elevated chair. Placing his cup on the windowsill next to the chair, he reached for the folder.

Hayes handed it to him. "It's Admiral Glover's reply to the notification we sent last night. As you requested, we also appended a digest of the copilot's report so he'd have a better picture of what happened."

Welch opened the folder and read the single sheet of paper. After the standard formatted opening, it acknowledged receipt of the notification. The last paragraph was brief:

377

Please accept my sincere gratitude for your handling of the notification process. Although I was not the listed next of kin, I appreciate your concern in allowing me to deal with the notification of Lt. Cmdr. Fisher's wife, my daughter. When the demands of your command permit, I would request as much further detail in the events leading to his death in action as you can provide.

Frank C. Glover

Welch reread the message and looked up at Hayes. "That's not exactly what I expected."

"No, sir. He even used his full name on the signature line. I've never seen him do that before. Doesn't sound much like he's getting ready to hammer you."

"No, I guess not, Master Chief."

Hayes stepped over to the pot and filled his own cup with coffee. He came back to stand next to Welch's chair, looking down at the men working on the flight deck.

"We've sure seen a lot of this, haven't we, Admiral? I mean we've been going to sea on and off for what, twenty-seven years, you and I?"

"Just about. And yes, you're right. We have seen this before. There doesn't seem to be much rhyme or reason to some of it either. Here's Fisher with a career full of promise ahead of him getting killed by a single bullet on a bright sunny afternoon and then there's the other guys who bring airplanes back with more holes than aluminum. I've never been able to figure it out."

"Yeah, I know. You guys pin on your wings, learn all you can, and go to it. Us troops fix your planes when you break them and then launch you off again. There's been good times and bad ones but on the whole I wouldn't trade a minute of it."

He took a sip of coffee. "To tell you the truth, Admiral, there's times when I wish I could start it all over again."

Welch smiled a little. "Me too, Rick, me too. It's been one hell of an adventure."

"Yes, sir. Well. I've gotta go. My cranky old boss will not

be pleased if the papers don't all get shuffled. And I have a small fire to put out with your boy, Commander Strickland. Excuse me."

"Hold it, Master Chief. What is he doing now? And he's not my boy."

"Well, sir, it must be time for fitness reports again because he's starting up another of his EVPs, you know, Emergency Visibility Projects. This time he's decided that my yeomen will refile all the goddamn files."

Welch thought about Strickland. He had been a complete pain in the ass ever since Welch had come aboard. EVPs were a weak officer's tactic to get himself noticed right before the annual fitness report time came around in the hope that it would enhance his rating. The two key points about EVPs are that they are more style than substance and go away seemingly within seconds of the fitness reports being mailed out, and that they rarely cause the originator to actually do any work. That all falls on the unfortunate subordinates, like Hayes's yeomen. Welch knew from the look in Hayes's eye that the project was going to disappear within the next few minutes and that those minutes were not going to be happy ones for Strickland.

He chuckled. "Okay. Just don't make it too hard on him. The guy's really pretty harmless."

"So's gunpowder until you put a match to it." Hayes put down his cup and left, headed down to his office.

Thirty minutes later, Welch was wading through the morning's paperwork when Sam Andrews walked in and stood next to his chair, first helping himself to a cup of coffee. Andrews gave Welch a quick summary of the overnight message traffic and an overview of the day's operations. For the *Concord*, today would be spent refueling and rearming from ships steaming alongside. The air wing would get a day to fix the aircraft and rest the pilots.

Andrews was silent for a few seconds and then spoke without looking at Welch. "Listen, Admiral. There's, um, something I've been requested to ask you."

"What's on your mind, Sam? I get suspicious when you get respectful."

"Well, the men of the helo detachment would like to hold a small memorial service for Commander Fisher on the flight deck." Andrews paused.

"Of course. When is it?"

"In half an hour. But what I need to ask is whether you'd officiate. The helo guys wanted you to. So do all the others. Me and CAG included."

"What about the other men we lost on the helo?" Welch paused. "I didn't mean that the way it sounded. It's just that we usually hold big formal memorials."

"Yes, sir. But the others are still listed as missing in action. There will be a big funeral stateside for Fisher but the troops wanted their own."

Andrews spoke again. "I know what you're thinking, Jim, that somebody who was closer to Fisher, like CAG, ought to do it. But the men feel close to you. They feel that you know them and care about them. Their word was that they'd be 'proud' if you would do it."

Welch was silent for a moment, not really trusting himself to speak, and Andrews looked away. The admiral cleared his throat. "I'd be honored to, Sam. I truly would."

Andrews smiled. "I figured you would so I've set it all up already. I'll send a messenger for you. The uniform is whatever you have on. See you in a while. Oh, we almost had a riot in sick bay. Seems the doc told Boyle that he couldn't go to the service. Santy and a couple of the helo guys swore that they'd haul him up there by themselves. The doc gave in, saying something about it being a cold day in hell before he gave Boyle another painkiller."

Welch chuckled as he watched Andrews leave, and turned back to the window. He wondered what he would say at the service. There was a book of generic eulogies that the chaplains used and he thought of asking for that since he really hadn't known Fisher at all and the Navy had long provided guidance for just this sort of situation. Fisher, who had come aboard as just another Navy pilot, had given his life to save others, had paid a price that actually only an ever shrinking percentage were called upon to pay. His funeral back home would be attended by hundreds of people, who would carry greater or lesser amounts of true grief with them when they came. But those who would carry the real meaning of who and what Fisher had been were those now gathering in ranks between the helicopter and the island. Welch spent twenty more minutes thinking about it.

He saw Andrews, on the flight deck, speak to a sailor who hurried toward the ladder to summon him for the ceremony. As he reached for his hat with all the gold trim on the bill, Welch remembered an old admiral and something he had told Welch years before at the end of World War II. Welch was smiling as he met the messenger at the door.

The wind blew gently across the flightdeck, lifting the flag which covered the aluminum coffin. The coffin rested on chocks, which kept it about a foot off the deck itself. In ranks behind it stood several hundred men in khakis, flight suits, jerseys of all the colors used on the ship and a very few, like the chaplain, in their dress blues. Off to one side, Santy, his right arm in a sling, stood next to the stretcher holding Tim Boyle, who was obviously in some pain but glaring triumphantly at the doctor. The doctor, standing on the other side of Boyle, was doing his best to ignore the look.

As the chaplain spoke the words that sailors had heard for hundreds of years on all the oceans of the world, Welch looked at the men gathered for the service for a man few of them had even met. There were faces deeply lined and surrounded by gray hair, like those of Harry Forrest and Master Chief Hayes over there, and there were faces which had hardly felt the scrape of a razor. But all the faces carried the same expression of respectful pride as they heard the prayer, even the faces of the Marine honor guard, standing to the side.

When the chaplain was finished, he stood aside as Welch stepped to the small portable podium. Welch looked at the coffin and then at Sam Andrews as he began.

"A long time ago, an admiral told me that heroes disappear

when wars are finished. I wish he were here today so I could tell him he was wrong. I wish he could stand here in ranks with us as we sadly send a hero home. I do not say 'in glory' because there is no glory here. Glory is for the poets and the historians and the movie directors. Glory is a lie that only those who have not been where we have been can believe. Glory is in the paintings of great battles that hang in museums. It is not in the men who are in the paintings.

"I believe we send Lieutenant Commander Fisher home, rather, in honor. He gave his life for two other men whom he had never known until he came aboard this ship. He risked his life knowingly and willingly so that they could live.

"Any man who lives honorably is a hero. It takes courage to do that, a courage that must be summoned every hour of every day. It cannot be dragged out and dusted off only in special circumstances. It must always be there, close at hand. Lieutenant Commander Fisher had that courage and he summoned it into the last moment of his life. All most of us will remember about this man is what he did yesterday, one day out of his thirty-six years. But that is enough.

"I will remember what you have done throughout my time as your commander. I have seen you day in and day out for weeks on end under conditions that those back home cannot imagine. I have never seen you fail, I have never seen you take the easy way, I have never seen you quit. If that is not living in honor, then I don't know what is. Living in honor makes you heroes, too.

"I doubt if any of your names will be in history books. But many who will read those books will benefit from your sacrifice. When peace comes again, you will continue to do your jobs as best you can and then you will go home. But others will come out here and take your place.

"When you are relieved and you pass the watch to another generation, you will know that you have served well and honorably. You will have made a difference.

"I wish that admiral could be standing here among you now. Maybe he'd understand that he was wrong."

Welch stepped away from the podium, and the chaplain

stood to lead the men in the "Navy Hymn." When they came to the verse that begins, "Lord, guard and guide the men who fly," Welch clenched his jaws in an attempt to maintain his composure. In all his years as a naval aviator, he had never been able to get through that verse without choking up, evoking as it did all the memories of all the times he had heard it sung.

After the Marines fired the three volleys and the bugler had sounded "Taps," the chaplain said the benediction. Fisher's coffin was gently carried to the helicopter, followed by Boyle in his stretcher with Santy walking alongside, his hand on Boyle's shoulder. Welch stood to one side, holding his hat in his hand, and watched the rotors begin to spin up. He turned his back on the downwash as the huge green helicopter lifted off and flew away.

"Nice speech, Jim. Thank you."

Welch turned and saw Andrews standing behind him. He smiled and walked away toward the bow, gently touching the noses of the aircraft as he passed.

Andrews watched him until the admiral stopped at the bow, shoulders square, standing in the sun and staring out across the wide blue sea with the wind from the ship's passage flapping his pant legs and ruffling his gray hair.

Carroll's Glossary

(Stuff you probably lay awake nights wondering about but couldn't find anyone to ask, or, if you did get lucky and find someone to ask, it was a guy in a flight suit and sunglasses who gave you a ridiculously patronizing answer and made you feel like an idiot for wasting his time by asking anything so dumb.)

Perpetrator's Note: *The explanations contained in this Glossary are not precise because if normal naval terminology were used, we would need a glossary to explain the Glossary. I'd also rather not make this my life's work so the terms will be explained in real honest-to-God American English.*

Official Antilawsuit Disclaimer: *None of the explanations listed herein are originally those of the author. They have been meticulously transcribed from dozens of beer-soaked napkins collected in officers' clubs all over the world. Many of the contributors are no longer with us, so be respectful as you read.*

AIO This is the squadron Air Intelligence Officer whose job is to keep the squadron's flight crews up to speed on whatever the "Threat" is. They keep all sorts of classified stuff in their safes and spend most of their time ashore making sure that they haven't lost any of it. At sea, they hang out in the carrier's intelligence center (CVIC) with the other AIOs and figure out all the things about the enemy that pilots never get around to caring about until five minutes before launch time. They keep millions of classified slides of everybody else's ships and aircraft that they show during singularly boring periodic training sessions in the ready room while the audience snores quietly in their seats.

When they brief the crews, they tell them everything they have about the mission and the bad guys in the area including rumor, supposition, guesswork, and what they have plagiarized from *Time*, *Newsweek*, *Penthouse*, and *Motor Trend*. They then cheerfully raise their coffee cups in salute as the flight crews go out and do the job. Their motto is, We Bet *Your* Life.

Aircraft Carrier An extremely large boat used for carrying lots (seventy or more of them) of aircraft around. There is no way to convey the sheer size of a carrier to someone who hasn't seen one. They serve twenty thousand meals a day, carry more than three million gallons of fuel for themselves and their aircraft, and have around five thousand men aboard. The littles ones have a displacement (don't ask) of about eighty thousand tons. They are over fourteen stories tall and the length of 3½ football fields. Try to imagine the Empire State Building steaming along on its side. The only problems with them are no girls and no beer allowed at sea, and the fact that when you are trying to find them at 3:00 A.M. in the rain when your jet is running out of fuel, they suddenly become the size of a matchbook.

Air Wing The flying complement of a carrier, comprised of two squadrons of fighters, two of light attack, one heavy attack, and four or five "others" for specialized missions. Used to be called an Air Group but that made it sound too unorganized for the management types. They searched long and hard for something topical to change it to but "Air Committee" couldn't be made into a suitable acronym. Finally, they came up with "Wing," which is really sort of middle-of-the-road. My suggestions, "Air Horde" and "Air Gaggle," were carefully ignored.

A-4 Skyhawk This little jet doesn't figure in the story at all but I flew them a bit and feel that I ought to mention the progenitor of all effective jet attack aircraft. If any aircraft kept the Navy in the Vietnam war it was the "Scooter." It was quick, nimble, and could carry a decent bombload. They could suffer major battle damage and still make it home. When you got in one of these babies, you were in a real man's airplane, not one of today's electronic wonders, where you have to have your computers vote on whether what the pilot does is okay. In the A-4, if you screwed up you had no one to blame but yourself, but if you did it right, you knew that it was your skill, unaided by an electronic crutch, that did it. If I had ever found one that could cook, I'd have married it.

A-7E Corsair II Usually referred to as the "SLUF" for "Short Little Ugly, um, Fellow" (Yeah, that's it, *Fellow.*). A small single-seat attack jet made by LTV for the Navy (The Air Force flies the "D" model.). This was the workhorse of the Navy until replaced by the F/A-18 Hornet, which is chock full of all sorts of zippy-do video marvels to make the pilot's job easier. The A-7 was an awesome aircraft to fly and incredibly effective. It is still one of the best in the world at blowing up things. The F/A-18 "Plastic Bug" is designed both as an attack aircraft and as a fighter so it can "fight its way in and fight its way out." Great concept, but if I were in an aircraft that could suddenly turn into a fighter, my bombs would be gone in a heartbeat when the MiGs showed up.

One more thing. Hornet pilots do not like to be referred to by the abbreviation for their job, *F*ighter *A*ttack *G*uys. They get real testy about it and have been known to zap people with their Nintendo controllers.

A-6E Intruder This is an extremely unpretty, all-weather, heavy attack aircraft built by Grumman. It can carry up to fourteen tons of bombs and can hit targets virtually anywhere at any time. The two-man crew is comprised of a pilot and a bombardier-navigator (B/N), who is uncharitably referred to as "self-loading baggage" by some in the aviation business. However, the B/N is there for a reason—pilots spend an awful lot of their time looking in the rearview mirror, not to spot enemy aircraft sneaking up from behind but to see how their manly crow's-feet are coming along. So much time, in fact, that they need someone along who can tell them where they are, hence, the B/N. The A-6 guys have a saying which may sound a trifle self-aggrandizing but does make a neato bumper sticker: "Fighter pilots make movies but attack pilots make history."

"Ball" or **"Lens"**   The nickname given to the Visual Landing Aid System on a carrier. This is a system of lights and lenses which indicate the proper glideslope to the pilot when he's on final approach or "in the groove." There is a horizontal row of green datum lights and a yellow light in the center. When the yellow light is lined up with the green, everything is looking good: keep it up and you should catch the optimum number-three arresting wire. If the ball is above the green, you're above the glide path; if it's low, so are you. Being *real* low shows you a red ball which is approximately the color of the inside of the fireball you're going to create when you hit the back of the ship unless you do something quickly to correct your approach.

Briefing   This is one of those terms which are a one-word lie. There is never anything brief about a briefing. There are all sorts of these before every flight wherein the pilots and crews go over everything that has to do with the flight. There is a big one in the Intell Center during which everybody receives "THE PLAN." Then there is the smaller one in which the members of a flight receive "THE PLAN." After that one, if one is in a multiplace aircraft, the individual crew members get their piece of "The Plan."

Even if your crew has been briefed for the same mission twice a day for ten years running, you have to brief *everything* the same way *every* time you go. If you don't and something bad happens, like maybe aliens steal your canopy after takeoff or your box lunch catches fire, the Mishap Investigating Board will spare no effort in proving the conclusion that it was the lack of an adequate brief that caused the hard-boiled egg to ignite the orange juice.

The amazing thing is that one briefing covers all. For example, if you brief a plane guard mission and then, right before takeoff, it gets switched to something completely different like looking for the admiral's missing wildebeest in the Serengeti, that's okay. You don't have to be rebriefed. Just don't screw up and try to claim that you weren't adequately briefed. The Board will hammer you anyway. They take courses in it.

CAG Commander of the Air Group. This term has stuck since the early days of naval aviation. Today he is properly titled "Commander, Carrier Air Wing." This is abbreviated "COMCVW" and pronounced "CAG." Makes sense, huh? Now we are just leaving the era of the "Super CAG." This was a position dreamed up to let CAG have equal status with the captain of the carrier, who was still required by naval regulation to be the HMWIC (Head Man What's in Charge). The purpose as it was disseminated from the bean counters in the Naval Military Personnel Command was to give a greater number of deserving officers a better shot at making admiral. Which is, of course, the standard "perfect" solution to all military problems, make some more chiefs for the Indians to answer to. In writing, in triplicate. It was due yesterday.

Call Signs These are of two types. The first is the type used for units and subunits. Originally, these were employed to make things easier for pilots and to confuse and confound the enemy but once pilots found out how cool they sounded to outsiders, particularly the ladies, there was no way of restricting them for use only in the air. After people got bored with the basic drabness of the original ones like "Blue Leader" and "Red Two," they soon quit buying drinks for the pilots. So, in a move slick enough to be worthy of Congressmen seeking a pay raise, the pilots came up with more colorful ones like "Pukin' Dog Six" and "Diamondback One," and my personal favorite, "Slug 602." The girls were back, as were the free drinks. The patrol plane types tried to get in on the fun but because of an odd psychological reaction to the inherent safety of their aircraft, all they could come up with were ones like "Pterodactyl," "Flamingo," and "Pillowcase."

The second type is the personal call sign. This actually has a valid purpose in combat. When things get all exciting and sweaty, it is very simple to forget the side number of the aircraft you're flying that day. But you rarely forget your name; when you get a lookout call with your name on it, you *move*. The personal call sign is usually a cute and original play on one's name, like "Dusty" for a guy named Rhodes, or it can be given because of a personal characteristic like "Gasser" for a guy with a flatulence problem, or "Exxon" for a guy who is relatively clumsy. The best kind are the ones given for a personal peccadillo, preferably something outrageous, done while on liberty, like "Duke," given for starting a fistfight with five large locals in a bar and losing big, or like "Ralphie" for throwing up on an admiral's shoes. The first two kinds are sort of average in that nothing is done to *earn* the title but the third kind raises one from the mundane obscurity of squadron tribal lore to the highest sacrarium of naval aviation mythology. One final note: scatological or sexual words and terms are basically taboo as call signs and are used only as nouns of address. For example, "Hey, asshole!" does not indicate a call sign, merely a state of being.

Duty Officer Every military unit has at least one duty officer, twenty-four hours a day, 365 days a year. In larger units, such as carriers or naval air stations, there are a whole bunch of spear-carrier duty officers who report to a sort of Big Duty Officer. On a carrier, for example, there are somewhere in the neighborhood of thirty-eight thousand duty officer jobs every day, which is not bad considering that there are only about five hundred officers aboard. Each junior officer gets to stand these watches according to a rigidly haphazard rotation policy. This policy is in place to keep the noise from the J.O.'s' whining down to bearable levels, about where a Rolling Stones concert would be if your head were in a speaker.

The watches themselves are not particularly taxing. There is one called the Integrity Watch Officer which is comprised of the junior officer, a college graduate and recipient of over a million dollars' worth of flight training, sitting around for four hours in Flight Deck Control waiting for the quarter-hourly reports from each of the equally bored enlisted patrol that all the aircraft on the flight and hangar decks are still sitting where they were chained down fifteen minutes ago and that no one has made off with any of the sixty thousand-pound fighters. Another swell duty is that of Boat Officer. In this one the J.O. gets to ride in the liberty boat all night between the ship and shore taking in the liberty party and bringing them back when both their money and livers have given out. What you have is a pilot, whose entire knowledge of small boats consists of being able to differentiate one from a Bengal tiger, standing out on the deck in the rain while the three professional sailors drive the boat back and forth. His main job is to prepare an impassioned speech in his own defense for use at his court-martial should the boat sink or run over a smuggler's dinghy or something equally probable.

E-2 Hawkeye Called the "Hummer" from the distinctive sound of its engines. These are the radar surveillance planes carried as part of the air wing aboard a carrier. They are as capable as the famed USAF AWACS aircraft but do the job with 25 percent of the crew without the kitchenette or bunkroom. They keep the overall radar picture of what happens around the carrier and guide all the other aircraft to and from their destinations. On countless occasions, they have kept the other pilots in the air wing from doing something either dumb, embarrassing, or merely fatal (never me, you understand, only those other guys). Suffice it to say that the taxpayers have gotten about seventy-five times their money's worth for every one they've bought.

F-4 Phantom This was the main U.S. Navy fighter aircraft during the latter stages of the Vietnam War and for nearly twenty years overall. It was also adopted by the Air Force and the Marine Corps in a rare flash of interservice common sense. It was used as an interceptor, as an air superiority fighter, for ground attack, reconnaissance, flak suppression, Wild Weasel Anti-SAM missions, and whatever else somebody could dream up. While it may not have been the best there was in each of these roles, it was the only jet aircraft ever built which could perform them all well. The aircraft was not pretty on first look but it rapidly grew on you until it became almost beautiful in a forbidding sort of way. It was big, tough, mean, fast, and reliable as hell: it was the Dick Butkus of military aircraft. I have never met a Phantom Phlyer who didn't swear by them and the many times I got to fly in them were quite a thrill. There is an odd sociological footnote that goes along with these monsters: virtually every wild, rowdy, and certifiably crazy friend that I have flew the F-4 at some time in his career. There is certainly a hefty research grant in there somewhere.

Flag Bridge This is a special room in the island structure of a carrier where the admirals get to sit in chairs and watch what is going on on the flight deck. They can also walk around and look at what all the other ships in the force are doing. There are lots of shiny buttons and nifty telephones and big radar repeater screens that the admirals can look at and say "Hmmm" mysteriously whenever the mood strikes them. There are also a lot of other officers, called "The Staff," around to keep the admiral from hurting himself with the scissors or eating the mucilage. In the real world, this would be called an "Adult Day Care Center."

H-3 Sea King This is a 19,500- to 21,000-pound helicopter built for the Navy by Sikorsky. It has been said that the H-3 doesn't really fly, it just vibrates so badly that the earth rejects it. But it is without doubt the most effective all-around maritime helicopter ever built. It has successfully operated in every climate, on every ocean, performing every mission the Navy has dreamed up. As a submarine hunter, it had no equal. It is large, slow, heavy, and less-than-sleek, but it is one magnificent flying machine in the hands of a decent pilot. It is also referred to as the "War Winnebago" and the "Whistling Shitcan" but, oddly enough, never by those thousands of people whose lives have been saved by one. They brought me home every time, for seventeen years, and that's good enough for me.

Intelligence Services Each branch of the armed forces compiles information from as many sources as possible so as to provide as clear a picture of a situation as possible. Deep in the bowels of a windowless building somewhere, analysts put everything together and put out a highly classified summary which no one who actually needs to read it is permitted to see since the need for secrecy far outweighs the individual's need to survive. What the concerned person or unit does get to see is a digest of the summary, thus giving rise to the firm belief that the Intell guys are the ones who pulled the legs off a grasshopper and told it to jump. When it just lay there glaring at them, they realized that they had made a historic discovery: if you pull the legs from a grasshopper, it becomes deaf.

There are several distinct intelligence services in the military. They're evaluated below:

1. Naval Intelligence, nearly oxymoronic.
2. Air Force Intelligence, the same as 1 without the "nearly."
3. Army Intelligence, the same as 2 without the "oxy-."
4. Marine Corps Intelligence—nah, that'd be too easy.

"Liberty" The term has nothing to do with the concept as used in the Declaration of Independence. To a sailor, it means a period of relatively free time spent ashore and away from the demands of service on a warship. Liberty is granted in port for sailors after the completion of the "Normal Working Hours" and for everyone who is not on watch or in the duty section. In the old days, the days of the Real Navy, sailors would go ashore and partake of the local traditions and culture. This activity could vary from burning down the Texas Bar in Naples over drink prices to starting a small riot in Barbarella's in Malaga over a bimbo, to drag-racing taxicabs through the streets of Istanbul. It used to be a lot of fun and a good way to relax and help the local economies. Nowadays, with the advent of the Corporate Navy, the fun is somewhat more mundane. Visits to cathedrals and art museums are on the rise, as is taking pictures of the antipasto in Ciro's with the ubiquitous 35mm camera so that Mom will know what a good boy she raised.

The best place on the planet for liberty is St. John's, Newfoundland. In the winter (the *slow* season), there are seven women for every guy. I once had two women discussing which one would buy me a drink and I hadn't met either one. The best things about St. John's are that there is neither a cathedral nor an antipasto within thirty miles and the taxis are really fast.

LSO   The Landing Signals Officer. Known as "Paddles" from the early days of carrier aviation when he stood to the left of the landing area and used two orange flags to show the pilot what corrections to make so as to land with the least amount of damage to himself and his aircraft. At night, he wore a suit with little lights on it which made him look like a matador after a lightning strike. When the Optical Landing system came along, LSOs were almost out of a job but, dreading the loss of power and fearing their return to the ranks with the rest of the pilots, the LSO Protective Union (AFL/CIO) convinced the Navy that they could still be of use if they could just stay out there and be "advisers" with radios. So they are there still, out in the wind and the cold rain, ever ready to help the pilot land. Heroes all. It makes you want to weep.

Naval Rank Structure   Naval ranks have deliberately been kept the same for hundreds of years. The other services have never been able to figure out the ranks or the system of striping on the sleeves of naval uniforms. This gives us a distinct advantage because people in the other services will usually believe that a Navy Lieutenant Commander outranks a Colonel from the other service; thus we can get better rooms in the BOQ. Here are the junior officer ranks and their official other service equivalents from the bottom up:

Ensign = 2nd Lt.	The lowest rank. Considered barely able to go to the head (toilet) alone.
Lt. (J.G.) = 1st Lt.	The perfect rank. Too senior to take the crap that an Ensign does but too junior to get any real responsibility.
Lt. = Capt.	The backbone of the services. Lts. do all the work and catch the blame for disaster, but watch the credit for success go to more senior officers.
Lt. Cmdr. = Major	The beginning of the ranks of real responsibility. Beyond this point, there is a drastic and progressive reduction in the fun of being a naval officer and naval aviator. This is caused in large part by the natural tendency to take one's position and oneself seriously.

Author's Note. The Royal Navy has a rank called "Subleftenant." Since I've never been able to figure out even approximately where that falls in the structure, I alternated between saluting them and ignoring them. I was never called on it either way so I still don't have a clue.

Navy Chow   This is another word for food. Actually, it is not exactly food but rather some stuff that you put on a plate and eat with a fork, and that will probably not kill you. Most chow is made from two sources, UMS and OFS. UMS, or Universal Meat Substitute, is pumped aboard and kept in huge tanks below the waterline. For each meal, UMS is piped under pressure to the ship's galleys (kitchens) and run through molds like Play-doh. It comes out looking and tasting almost but not exactly like nothing you've ever eaten before.

OFS, or Other Food Substitute, is piped to different molds and comes out either like rice with double starch added or green beans which are actually sort of brown. The only genuine vegetable served at sea is broccoli, which is grown in patches of cultivated sludge among the tanks containing UMS and OFS.

Several menu items have earned nicknames over time:

Sliders are hamburgers, *Rollers* are hot dogs, and *Chicken Curry* is nauseating.

Dog is allegedly soft ice cream. It got its name from the original compound, which was a brown semisolid stuff which you were careful not to get on your shoes. Later, several other types were developed and served, none of which tasted like anything in human experience, so they were simply named by color: Pink Dog, White Dog, and Yellow Dog.

RAG   This stands for "Fleet Replacement Squadron," formerly "Replacement Air Group." These are special squadrons in which naval aviators are trained in the specific type and model of aircraft they will fly in the fleet. They are staffed by fleet-experienced pilots and are billed as the place where the best are sent to train the new guys. However, no matter how hard they try they still can't get anybody to use "FRS" when speaking. Additionally, they can't stop anybody from telling the new guys: "Forget all that crap they told you in the RAG, sonny, this here's the Fleet."

Rules of Engagement (ROE)   These are a set of rules which govern warfare. They specify when and how force may or may not be used in confrontation with the enemy or with someone who may be an enemy real soon. The rules were originally designed to minimize damage and injury to passersby from the use of military power at war. Unfortunately, like Frankenstein's monster, they quickly took on a life of their own. During the McNamara era, there were times when DoD would not allow targets to be struck solely because of the perception that to do so would violate the ROE. The irony in the fact that those who pointed to the rules as the determining factor were often the very ones who had arbitrarily created the rules in the first place seems to have eluded them. Another major problem with ROE is that often only one side will adhere to them. We Americans with our mania for fair play create them but an enemy will often use our restraint to his advantage. However, by and large, it is better to be on the side which is honorable enough to try to bring some moral and legal order to the chaos of battle.

Not all the rules made sense nor were they all easy to follow. For example, there were times in my experience when, after getting the hell shot out of my Huey, I was not permitted to shoot back at the bad guys without permission. You can be sure that I held my fire until the guy up the chain put down his gin and tonic and gave me the green light. Yessir, I really did play by the rules. Far be it for me to do anything as heinous as to break an intelligent rule like that one. "Honest, Skipper, sir, those rockets must have fired by themselves. It was an electrical malfunction."

"Tower" Pronounced "Tahr." Also known officially as "Primary Flight Control" or more simply, "Primary." This is the lair of the "Air Boss," who is responsible for safe and efficient flight operations within five miles of the carrier. It's a wonderful job for a semilucid borderline psychotic type who has a major self-image problem and a large store of pent-up aggression to get out. The organization is pyramidal. There is a "Mini-Boss" who is in training to take over when the Air Boss's tour is up, sort of a "red-shirt" Ayatollah. Under them are several dozen sailors who quietly wager on the chances for success of the individual pilots in the landing pattern. The sailors also talk on the radios and adjust the bells and whistles so that everything runs smoothly enough not to interfere in any way with the semihourly tantrums thrown by the Boss.

Off to one side are the representatives from each of the squadrons on the ship. They are there allegedly to "Gain Experience and Fuller Knowledge" by observing flight operations from this lofty perch. The real reason they are there is that squadron commanders long ago learned that they can use the young observer as a layer of insulation between them and the screaming and yelling. The C.O. can tell instantly by the shade of the observer's pallor when he returns to the ready room how much trouble the squadron is in. There is also an official card with various graduated shades of white that the C.O. can use to compare with the observer's face in case the kid can only babble and weep about his experiences up there. Ever at the forefront of social development, even before the great civil-rights movement of the sixties, the Navy had come up with an interracial card to preclude the Air Boss from taking advantage of the slight shading differences and sandbagging the squadron C.O.